# Seasons Of Forgetting

## *Seasons Of Forgetting*

When the music stopped, Joanna reached across the bed, snapped off the phonograph and the lamp next to it. Going to the window and raising it slightly, she rested her head on her arms and gazed outside across the campus, inhaling the crisp night air. It was so quiet she could hear the acorns drop through the branches of the oaks near her window, landing with tiny snaps on the piles of leaves below.

She'd quickly fallen in love with this little college after her first visit. From her window she could see almost every one of the stately old buildings, nothing having changed much since Manning's founding in the mid-eighteen-hundreds. It had become home, more home in many ways than her real one where as an only child she often felt the absence of someone to talk to, to share with. Here she'd found roommates, friends, Doris, and finally this tiny room she called her own. Yet none of it was enough. She felt herself yearning for something more.

Where was her life going? Sometimes she felt the winds of fate simply picked her up and carried her wherever they were blowing. Here she was, a year away from graduating as a teacher, and she wasn't even sure that's what she wanted.

Worst of all, there was no one special in her life. Many of her friends, Beth included, were engaged and planning weddings after graduation. What was wrong? Why couldn't she make a plan and stick to it? Set some goals, make more of an effort to meet new people, accept some of the offers instead of turning them down without giving the men a chance ... what, or who, was she waiting for?

# What they are saying about
# *Seasons Of Forgetting*

"It's not your average predictable romance novel. A compelling book that creates characters so realistic you will share in their happiness, pain, frustrations and love. So emotional that you'll have to keep reminding yourself that it's only a book. Jeanne Howard is an inspirational writer who tells a story with passion and conviction."

—Joy Snyder
*Women on Writing Spotlight Editor*

"*Seasons of Forgetting* shows Jeanne Howard to have a genuine gift for entertaining and involved storytelling."

—*Midwest Book Review*

"I will not soon forget this poignant and intelligent novel. Joanna and Jared's doomed love affair has left an indelible impression on this reviewer. I just wish I could shake off the yearning for a second chance at a happy ending, for a season that isn't colored by the awful pain of remembrance."

—Cheryl Jeffries
*Heartstrings*

# Seasons Of Forgetting

**Jeanne Howard**

**A Wings ePress, Inc.**

**Contemporary Romance Novel**

# *Wings ePress, Inc.*

Edited by: Jeanne Smith
Copy Edited by: Jeanne Smith
Cover Artist: Trisha Fitzgerald-Jung

Excerpts from *This is My Beloved* by Walter Benton
used with permission of the estate of Walter Benton.

*All rights reserved*



Wings ePress Books
http://www.wingsepress.com

Copyright © 2006 by Jeanne Howard
ISBN 978- 1-59705-977-0

Published In the United States Of America

Wings ePress Inc.
3000 N Rock Road
Newton, KS  67114

# Dedication

"There are only two lasting bequests
we can hope to give our children.
One is roots; the other ... wings."

—Hodding Carter

To my parents...
my mother who was my anchor
and my father
who encouraged me to fly.

# *Prologue*



*August 15, 2001*

Brian was finally asleep. Joanna sank gratefully into the cushions of the sofa, every aching bone reminding her that today she'd turned sixty. Keeping up with her almost six-year-old grandson took far more energy than she had anticipated.

The house creaked and moaned every now and then as gusts of wind off the ocean assaulted the walls. It had been an oppressively humid day, the kind that inevitably ended with a thunderstorm. She could feel and smell it in the night air as she made the rounds closing windows, listening to the thunder rumbling to announce the storm's imminent arrival.

The only light in the den came from the computer on the desk in the corner. *If I walk out of the room right now, I can pat myself on the back for finally being strong. But I know I won't.*

Like every other day for the past two years, Joanna sat at the desk, gently touched the keys and watched the service provider's home page spring to light.

Her fingers moved almost automatically, all the while her conscience chided her for giving in yet one more time. *You'll never get over him this way, Joanna. Forget him, Joanna; he's forgotten you.*

Her fingers moved anyway, entering the password, clicking on the e-mail icon.

Habit took over. Joanna closed her eyes, remembering, and wished. *Please, please let him be there.*

# One



*1961*

*"Who's the plainest one of all?"*

A chill autumn rain whipped across the quad, soaking Joanna's shoes and lashing her umbrella. She tried belatedly to miss a large puddle, but landed in the middle of it anyway.

"Oh, damn!" she muttered. "Why now, when I'm already late and I know Doris is waiting?"

Joanna and Doris Wayne, the college's counseling psychologist, had been working for three months on a research project Doris had designed. Joanna's task involved long hours of painstakingly transcribing tapes of interviews, but there was a definite upside to the tedium. The two women always managed to find plenty of time for conversation, and Joanna was learning a lot about human behavior. After some initial reluctance, she had also begun to delve into the years of her own troubled childhood to face some of the trauma and hurt that lurked there.

They had met when Joanna was a freshman, and their friendship deepened during the ensuing years. It never struck Joanna as odd that her best friend was old enough to be her mother. Doris's warmth and accepting attitude made their ages irrelevant.

Glancing inside as she walked along the patio, she spotted Doris, who wasn't alone.

"Oh, damn, damn, damn!" she swore again, this time louder. Sitting across from Doris was Jared Fowler. Joanna had never met him, but she'd heard enough from her drama major friends to know the girls had crushes on their handsome professor. She paused only long enough to look with dismay at her reflection. Her hair was soaked and plastered limply to her face, so she took a quick detour to the ladies' room down the hall.

"Oh, no, now what do I do?" she asked the bedraggled image in the mirror. It was worse than she expected, but all she could do was take a hair band from her purse and scoop the long, wet hair into a scraggly ponytail. *Oh, well,* she thought, *Doris has certainly seen me looking worse than this.*

"Mirror, mirror on the wall, who's the plainest one of all?" she murmured at her reflection. She could hear her grandmother's response to her childish wish to be as pretty as some of the other girls. *"You're never going to be beautiful, Joanna. You're plain, but you're smart and that's better than beauty."* The teenage Joanna believed otherwise: being a brain was certainly no substitute for being pretty. Grimacing at the mirror, she turned away.

The snack bar was jammed and noisy as usual, with music blaring above the babble of voices as Joanna threaded her way among the tables.

"Sorry I'm late," she said to Doris as she stood the soggy umbrella against the wall.

"Don't apologize. This nasty weather is slowing everyone down." Doris gestured to the man across from her. "Joanna, I understand you've never met Dr. Fowler. Say hi. I was about to explain our project."

Joanna held out her hand. "Hello, Dr. Fowler, I'm Joanna Ransome, Doris's sometimes capable sidekick."

"Jared Fowler," he said, half rising, his voice startling her with its rumbling depth and rich resonance. He took her extended hand and held it firmly, his eyes fixed on hers. "It's nice to meet you."

Settling in her chair, Joanna had trouble taking her eyes off the man across from her. She forced herself not to stare.

"I'm really curious about the work you're doing," Jared said. "It sounds complicated, but Doris says she can put the research in a nutshell for me."

"Watch me," Doris said, grinning. "What do you know about Carl Rogers?"

"A little. I took several courses in psychology at the graduate level and I've read some of his work."

"Well then, all I need to do is refresh your memory," she said. Sitting back in her chair, Doris neatly summarized Rogers' basic ideas about human behavior.

He believed people form a "self-concept" in early childhood, a kind of storing house for feedback they got from everyone around them. This feedback helped a child paint a picture of himself based on how others see him. Once that self-concept was formed, Rogers said, people behave in ways that must be consistent with it. They are unconsciously driven to keep that perception of "self" in sync. They accept experiences that fit the self-concept, but they distort those that don't, or else they deny them completely. So far, no one had ever done a study to prove Rogers' theory.

Doris had administered two psychological tests to one hundred students to measure their level of mental health, and then had them stand in front of a full-length mirror wearing pairs of special glasses. Some of the lenses were pane glass; others distorted images in degrees from slight to drastic. As they reported how they looked, their responses were written down. Eventually Doris would compare their test results to the visual reports to see if, and how much, neurosis made a difference in how people saw themselves.

Joanna knew Rogers' theory inside and out, so as Doris talked, she took advantage of the chance to scrutinize Jared Fowler.

He *was* striking … tall, lean, trim and not overly muscular. But it was his voice that was absolutely compelling. Every word vibrated with richness, turning a simple sentence into something either very dramatic or very sensuous.

"…into the picture?" Joanna heard him say, as she pulled herself back into the conversation.

"I'm sorry, I missed the question," she said, flustered at being caught not paying attention. She felt he'd been reading her thoughts.

"I asked how you fit into the picture," Jared repeated, his brown eyes dancing.

Joanna laughed self-consciously. "I'm the drone, better known as a research assistant. I listen to the test tapes and transcribe them. I also charted the visual reports in the glasses phase of the experiment."

"It certainly sounds like an interesting project. Is this your last year, Joanna?"

"No, one more to go, including student teaching, before I get my degree."

"In psychology?"

"No, I'm an English major."

"I would have thought you'd be following in Doris's footsteps," he said, his right eyebrow arching expressively.

"I haven't ruled it out. I think I'd like the counseling part, but I still have a year to decide whether to go on to graduate school for another degree. It would be fun being a perpetual student, but not very practical."

"From what I hear, you'd make a very good counselor or anything else you decided to do," Jared said, his intent gaze making her blush.

He stood and pushed back his chair, running his hands through his fine hair, then trying to restore the neat part he'd mussed. "I've got to get on to my next class," he said, looking out the window with a frown. "I hate the thought of venturing out, but there's no putting it off. There are students waiting for a quiz, so I'm on my way. Doris, your experiment is fascinating. Keep me posted on your results. Joanna, it was good to meet you."

"Ah sure will," Doris said, her Southern accent pronounced. "Y'all take care, Jared."

Joanna tilted her head to look up at him. "Glad to have met you, Dr. Fowler. I won't be in any of your classes, but maybe we'll run into one another again anyway."

"No doubt. It's a small campus," he said as he put on his raincoat and picked up an umbrella and a well-worn briefcase, "and I spend a lot of time here. See you both later."

Joanna watched him walk away, his head held high as he strode toward the door.

"I'm kind of surprised you've never met Jared," Doris said. "I thought everyone knew him."

"I knew *of* him and I've seen him around, but never this up-close and personal. He's gorgeous. That five o'clock shadow makes him look so sexy. Is he a new love interest, Doris? What a find! I love that hypnotic voice. How long have you known him? Have you been holding out on me?"

Doris put down her cup. "Slow down! Don't be silly. I've known Jared since I first joined the staff. Our paths have crossed a few times when he's referred some of his students to me for counseling. But there's nothing else there. Sexy? I don't see it. He's not my type, whatever *that* is. You can also stop drooling—he's married, though rumor has it not very happily. Didn't you know?"

Joanna was still hearing his voice in her head.

"Yeah, I suppose I heard somewhere but I didn't remember it. Why are the fantastic ones always taken? I can't imagine anyone being unhappily married to *him*."

"I've only seen his wife once, at a faculty party a couple of years ago," Doris said. "They seemed mismatched, all right. She was quiet, almost withdrawn. Someone even remarked to me afterward she had as much personality as a piece of cardboard. Unkind, perhaps, but pretty accurate. There's no accounting for how people choose mates, is there?"

As they talked, the rain stopped and hazy sunshine cast an eerie orange glow on the trees.

"Well, I've got to get back to the dorm to study," Joanna said. "I'll be over later to tackle those tapes."

"I'm due at the office," Doris lamented. "It's been a long day and I'm ready for it to be over. See you around seven."

~ * ~

The sun had set and darkness was draping itself over the campus as Joanna briskly made her way across the quad and let herself into Doris's apartment with a spare key.

"Yoo-hoo," she called. "It's me. Ready to roll." She walked into the combination living room/office and was greeted by the familiar sight of the tape recorder and typewriter sitting side by side on a battered old card table. Doris came out of her tiny bedroom putting the last roller in her hair, wearing a pair of pajamas with a matching robe.

"I told you I couldn't wait for this day to be over. Sorry about the p.j.'s, but I had to get more comfortable."

"I envy you." Joanna sighed and sat in front of the typewriter. "You look very relaxed."

"Sure am. Take off your shoes and get comfy yourself. I've got some reading to do while you decipher the dialogue. Sometimes I wonder how you can understand my Southern drawl."

~ * ~

At nine-thirty, Joanna reached for the "Off" button and listened to the tape recorder wind down. It was time to get back to the dorm. In tomorrow's early class, Dr. Sonja Hendricksen was giving her interpretation of the symbolism in the Faulkner novel they were studying. That material would be on the mid-term exam, and Joanna knew she'd better be able to regurgitate Hendricksen's ideas, whether or not she agreed with them.

"'Night, Doris," she called toward the bedroom, illuminated only by the light of the reading lamp above the bed. "I'm leaving. See you tomorrow?"

"Don't think so." Doris came out rubbing her eyes, glasses dangling from her hand. "I have clients all morning and I'm leaving straight from the office for New York. Angela and I have plans for dinner in the city and a show on Saturday."

"I'm glad you're going," Joanna said with an affectionate hug. "You can use a break. It's nice you and Angela have kept up your friendship. I don't know how much time I'll have for the project this weekend, but I'll try to finish before you get back."

~ * ~

The tiny sliver of moon didn't do anything to light her path or her spirits as she hurried back to the dorm. Here it was Thursday, and she was facing another dateless weekend. She didn't know how to change that, since none of the guys on campus interested her even a little bit. Sure, she had plenty of friends, but sometimes as she watched the couples walking hand in hand, she wondered if she'd ever find someone who fit the list of "must-haves" she'd created in her mind. Sometimes she worried she was too particular, her romantic ideal too unattainable.

She'd been lost in thought as she walked and before she knew it, Bentley House was dead ahead.

The front hall was unusually quiet as Joanna added her name to the sign-in sheet. Taking the worn concrete stairs to the third floor, she heard muffled music from someone's radio and, as she passed the large group bathroom, the sounds of running showers.

"Oh, hi, Joanna. Working with Dr. Wayne again?"

Joanna turned with her key still in the lock to see Beth Armbruster, her next-door neighbor and former roommate, wrapped in a towel, padding across the hall.

"Yep, another fun night of transcribing. I'm almost finished, though. Frankly, I don't know what I'll do with my spare time when it's over. What have you been up to?"

Beth followed her and stood in the doorway of Joanna's cozy room. "My passion now is acting. I hope you can find time to come see my debut on the college stage next month."

"Oh, I'd almost forgotten about that, but I wouldn't miss it for the world. You've been rehearsing a lot, haven't you?"

"With Fowler as the director? Rehearse is his middle name. He's a very good director, besides being quite an actor himself. But he's a real perfectionist, so there's never a time that isn't right for rehearsal."

"I met him for the first time today." Sitting on the edge of her bed, Joanna dropped her shoes to the linoleum-covered floor. "He's very charming. Have you had many courses with him?"

"Just two. And you said it—he *is* charming. Might even become the campus's most eligible bachelor. Scuttlebutt has it he and his wife are about ready to split. I don't know details, but they have two kids he seems to adore, so maybe it's all gossip. Anyway, he practically lives on campus in that office in Kenton Hall, and most of us think of him as more of a pal than a professor. He's such a great teacher. Time in his classes flies by, mostly because it's so neat to listen to his voice."

"Two children? What a sad thing for them. It must be very hard for everyone concerned," Joanna murmured.

"Yeah, it sure is a shame, whatever it is," Beth agreed. "Well, goodnight, Jo. We're scheduled for an early rehearsal, so I've gotta get my beauty sleep."

"'Night, Beth. Have fun tomorrow."

Joanna closed the door and turned on her record player, the sounds of Beethoven filling the tiny room. She undressed and dropped a cotton nightshirt over her head, pulled the bedspread down, set her alarm clock for seven a.m. and reached for the book of poetry that usually helped her settle for sleep.

Tonight, though, it was hard to concentrate. Her mind kept drifting to Jared Fowler. She wondered about his troubled marriage, his children. She could hear his exquisite voice and see that expressive eyebrow. She played back every second of their brief encounter, not even wondering why those few insignificant moments should be so unshakeable.

When the music stopped, Joanna reached across the bed, snapped off the phonograph and the lamp next to it. Going to the window and raising it slightly, she rested her head on her arms and gazed outside across the campus, inhaling the crisp night air. It was so quiet she could hear the acorns drop through the branches of the oaks near her window, landing with tiny snaps on the piles of leaves below.

She'd quickly fallen in love with this little college after her first visit. From her window she could see almost every one of the stately old buildings, nothing having changed much since Manning's founding in the 1800's. It had become home, more home in many ways than her real one, where as an only child she often felt the absence of someone to talk to, to share with. Here she'd found roommates, friends, Doris, and finally this tiny room she called her own. Yet none of it was enough. She felt herself yearning for something more.

Where was her life going? Sometimes she felt the winds of fate simply picked her up and carried her wherever they were blowing. Here she was, a year away from graduating as a teacher, and she wasn't even sure that's what she wanted.

Worst of all, there was no one special in her life. Many of her friends, Beth included, were engaged and planning weddings after graduation. What was wrong? Why couldn't she make a plan and stick to it? Set some goals, make more of an effort to meet new people, accept some of the offers instead of turning them down without giving the men a chance. What, or who, was she waiting for?

Joanna cast a final glance across the lamplit street toward the quad and closed the window and curtain. For some reason she couldn't identify, she felt sleep wasn't going to come easily.

~ * ~

The unnamed thing must have nagged at her most of the night. She woke feeling groggy and out of sorts long before the alarm clock went off. The dorm was quiet and dawn was just streaking the sky when, carrying her towel and fresh underclothes, she went across the hall to the bathroom and stood under a warm shower, hoping to shake the malaise.

Outside, the air smelled like autumn, crisp and fragrant. She crossed the street that faced her dorm, separating it from the student center. The leaves on the ground were still wet with overnight moisture and there was a definite nip in the air. Winter was creeping in.

There was no line at the service counter. Balancing a cup and plate in one hand and her books in the other, she sat at the closest table by the window. There was still more than a half hour before class, so she opened the novel to review the chapters they'd be talking about and was soon absorbed in the story. Minutes later, she felt someone watching her and quickly looked over her shoulder.

# Two



"Good morning, Joanna."

She wouldn't have needed to see him to know Jared Fowler was there. No one else had a voice like his. Her own name had never sounded so beautiful.

"Hello, Dr. Fowler. You're on campus awfully early, aren't you?"

"Yes, I am. We have a read-through at eight for the fall production. I thought I'd catch a cup of coffee before we got started. May I join you?"

"Of course." Joanna waved to the empty chair across the table and closed her book. "I think I've had about all I can take of Faulkner anyway."

He put down his cup, tucked his briefcase under the table and sat, all in one graceful motion that reminded Joanna of an athlete or a dancer.

"I don't know how anyone could stomach Faulkner this early in the morning," he said with a grin.

They sat in comfortable silence. He was a virtual stranger, yet she felt an easy companionship that was both surprising and pleasant. He sipped his coffee and gazed out the window.

"I love the campus this early in the morning," he mused. "I like to walk along the path through the woods to my office and relish the solitude. What brings you out so early?"

"I don't really know. I didn't sleep well. I woke up feeling sluggish, so I decided to have breakfast to jumpstart my day. It's unusual, believe me. I rarely show up for anything until at least ten. I'm not what you'd call a morning person, and I hate eight o'clock classes."

His smile made Joanna catch her breath. She had never met anyone so attractive.

"Ditto. I get up in the morning because I have to. There are classes to teach and rehearsals to direct and that's what pays the bills, so I'm up, whether I like it or not."

"Do you live close by?"

"In Yardley. We're renting a house for now until I know whether we're going to stay in the area. I've applied for a fellowship to do some post-doctoral work in the Midwest, and if it comes through, we'll be moving."

"How exciting for you, Dr. Fowler. I hope you get it if that's what you really want."

"Jared. Please call me Jared. I hate being treated like some creaking old academic. I don't see myself that way at all."

"Okay, Jared it is. Creaking is hardly the way I would describe you anyway."

"I guess that's a compliment, so I'll accept it gratefully. The old part certainly might fit, though. Sometimes I think thirty-seven is a bit late to be contemplating the life of a student again, don't you?"

"No. You should do whatever you think is best. I assume the other post-doctoral students would be close to your age anyway, wouldn't they? Besides, if that is your dream, what difference does age make?"

"Well said, and also very wise for a what—twenty, twenty-one-year-old? But what about you? Why did you decide to become a teacher and why English?"

"Twenty, twenty-one next August, and I guess English because I love words—poetry, prose, fiction, non-fiction, about anything written. I get lost in books and I want everyone to feel the same way about them. Teaching seems to be a way to accomplish that."

"Admirable." Jared drew a wallet out of his pocket and flipped it open to a small folder of pictures. Turning it toward her, he pointed to a beautiful child with pale curls and bright blue eyes. "This is Marina. She'll be eight in May. This week, she wants to be a dancer when she grows up; next week it might be an airline stewardess." Turning up the photo, he pointed to the other beneath it. "And here's Michael. He's five and a very serious little man. They're special people."

"They're beautiful!" Joanna exclaimed. "Where does Marina get the blonde hair and blue eyes? Michael looks like you, but definitely not Marina. Does she resemble your wife?"

"No, she doesn't. Victoria has very dark hair. The fairness must be a throwback to some distant relative with very strong genes."

"Do you have a picture of your wife?"

"No," Jared replied quietly, closing the wallet and putting it back in his pocket. He looked up at Joanna and she saw a flicker of sadness—was it mixed with anger?—in his eyes.

"So tell me, Joanna Ransome, what big plans do you have for the weekend?" he asked smoothly, changing the subject adroitly. It totally escaped Joanna's notice that he had remembered her last name after only one hearing.

"None, really. I'll be spending some time tomorrow at Doris's working on the final pieces of transcription that need to be done before she can do the comparisons. Otherwise, it's studying and more studying."

"Sounds as though you'll be awfully busy. I'm housesitting for a good friend who's away until September. Dan has a little place in the country that needs occasional attention. I'll be going there to tend to the plants, rake some more leaves—Lord, they seem endless!—the usual fall chores. The children come along sometimes and help in their fashion."

Joanna glanced at her watch. "Look at the time. I've got to get going. Sorry to run like this, but I'll be late for class if I don't get moving."

He stood and picked up his briefcase. "I'll walk with you as far as my office. That's if you don't mind the company."

"Not at all."

The early morning chill had given way to sunshine. It was going to be a warm day for early October. They went across the street to pick up the winding brick path that led through the woods toward the library where her class met. Colorful gold and red leaves fell around them. To the left of the path was a tiny fir tree that barely came up to Joanna's waist. It was perfectly formed and fragrant with the aroma of Christmas.

Jared stopped and looked down. "Hello, tree."

"Do you always talk to trees?"

"Only this one. He was just a baby when I arrived here four years ago, and I'm kind of watching over him. I always say hello when I pass by."

Joanna reached down and gently touched a branch, feeling the softness of the pine needles against her hand. "Hello," she said. "You're really very beautiful."

Jared grinned. "He says he likes you. He's very particular about his friends."

They walked the rest of the way in silence. At Kenton Hall, the theater and music center, he turned to go up the sidewalk leading to the steps of the pillared Georgian building.

"Thanks for the breakfast conversation, Joanna. It was nice talking with you. I hope we can do it again."

"Me, too. Have a good weekend."

She continued along the sidewalk toward the library. As she turned to go up the steps, she glanced back. Jared was still standing on the portico watching her. Seeing her look his way, he waved and went inside.

~ * ~

After class, instead of going back to her dorm, she went down the walk to the lake and across the parking lot to Doris's apartment to put in a couple of hours on the project before lunch.

She worked steadily, stopping only to get a Coke from the refrigerator. It was very quiet in the apartment. The only sound besides the clacking of typewriter keys was the echo in Joanna's mind—Jared Fowler's voice. It took rigid discipline to focus on what she was doing when his face and voice kept cutting into her concentration.

At noon, she turned off the tape recorder, went into the kitchen, fixed a sandwich and got another Coke. Outside, the lake shimmered in the sunshine, tempting and warm.

Carefully carrying her lunch while she maneuvered out the front door, Joanna walked down the lawn to a bench on the water's edge. She was watching the ducks swimming in lazy circles, her eyes half closed against the midday sun, when the quiet was shattered by the sound of a car horn. Turning, she saw a station wagon, blue and white, stopped at the edge of the lake. Jared Fowler leaned over and waved out the passenger side window. Joanna thought he might stop and get out of the car, but he drove slowly off with another wave, heading away from the campus.

Joanna returned the greeting, lowered her hand and watched the car as it reached the main highway and turned south.

~ * ~

There was a social hour in the dorm Sunday night to welcome a new foreign exchange student, but after introducing herself and saying hello, Joanna retreated to her room to study.

She propped the book up on the windowsill, as always quickly becoming engrossed in her reading. After what seemed like hours, she looked up, rubbed her tired eyes and looked out across the campus. The trees in front of her window were about bare, their leaves piled in soggy heaps on the ground.

Beneath the street lamp outside the student center, something blue caught her eye. She looked a little harder and realized the shape was a car, parked in the small lot at the side of the building. Not just a car, a station wagon. Blue and white. Jared Fowler. She wondered what he was doing on campus on a Sunday night.

The temptation to put on a jacket and go across the street to the snack bar pulled at her. She could easily find an excuse for showing up, and it would be fun to talk with him again. But the exam was coming in the morning and a chat with Jared Fowler wouldn't earn her an "A" so she tossed aside the urge and buried her head in the textbook instead.

~ * ~

"Well, hello, Miss Ransome, how are you?" Dr. Gunther Hirsch, one of her favorite professors, held the door for her as she went into the snack bar at midday on Monday and stopped to talk. In mid-sentence, he suddenly paused and exclaimed, "Jared! I haven't seen you around campus for ages. They must be keeping you very busy over there in the theater. How have you been, my friend?"

Joanna turned to look over her shoulder.

"Very well, thank you, Gunther, and yes, I'm swamped as always, though I sometimes think I create my own chaos. Hello, Joanna," he said. "It's nice to see you again."

"Thank you. Dr. Hirsch was reassuring me I have nothing to worry about with tomorrow's psych exam." She looked at the older man. "I've never had a moment's problem with your lectures, Dr. Hirsch, so I'm sure I'll be able to do well. It's kind of you to care."

"My pleasure. You're an outstanding student and I enjoy having you in class. Jared," he said, turning toward the faculty dining room, "I'm glad I bumped into you. Don't be such a stranger."

Jared turned to Joanna. "Are you stopping in for lunch?"

"Uh-huh, but not in the cafeteria. It's early in the year but I'm already tired of their famous shepherd's pie."

"May I join you? I'd rather be in the snack bar than with the faculty types in there." He gestured toward the doorway through which Dr. Hirsch had disappeared.

"Of course. Anyone who dislikes dining hall food as much as I do is always welcome."

Jared led the way from the counter to a table for two by the window, arranged his meal, put their empty trays on a table nearby and settled facing her.

"Where do you live, Joanna?"

"On campus I'm over there," she said, gesturing out the window and across the street, "in Bentley House. Atlantic City is my hometown. I've lived there most of my life. Went to grade school and high school there, the usual small town stuff."

"I don't know if I would call Atlantic City a small town," Jared commented. "It has a reputation as a world-class resort, doesn't it? I've never been there, though, so I only know what I've read and heard. It's on my list of places to visit one of these days."

"I'm probably too close to it to see all that, but I suppose you could look at it that way. The ocean sets it apart from most small towns and in the summertime, it *is* a different place, hardly boring at all. It's got kind of a split personality. I've worked in a small family hotel for a couple of summers and I have to admit, the streets and beaches are jammed from Memorial Day through mid-September. The tourists certainly don't see the same town I live in the rest of the year."

Jared lit a cigarette and sat back in his chair. "Why did you pick Manning State?"

"That's a good question. I know my folks and friends were surprised. I'd been accepted at other colleges, all better known, but there was something about Manning that grabbed me the first time I visited. I like the smallness, the intimacy and the friendliness. I'm sure I wouldn't be having lunch with a professor at any of those other schools."

"It is a nice place," Jared agreed. "Funny you should say that ... 'having lunch with a professor.' I don't see myself as so much different from my students, or from you. We all have common interests and we're all just people, regardless of age or title. I hope you won't let the academic degree thing get in your way of getting to know me."

~ * ~

It was Thursday before Joanna ran into Jared again—literally, and this time on his turf.

Kenton Hall's lobby was nearly dark except for the huge lamp that hung on a long brass chain from the uppermost eaves of the portico. Lights were on in some of the second and third floor rooms as evening classes began.

Joanna made her way down the deserted hall toward the auditorium, her footsteps echoing off the polished tile floor. As she rounded the corner toward the backstage classrooms, she collided with him. Her purse fell off her shoulder; his papers scattered across the floor as he reached out to keep her from falling.

"Oh, Jared, I'm so sorry!" Joanna bent down for her purse and began to gather the papers together. "I guess they need a traffic light at this intersection."

"It was my fault," Jared replied, squatting down to help. "I was too engrossed in my own thoughts and wasn't watching where I was going."

Joanna handed him the stack she'd recovered. "Is rehearsal over? I'm meeting Beth Armbruster for a late dinner."

"Yes, we quit about ten minutes ago, in fact. I think she's probably down in wardrobe." He took a few steps toward his office at the end of the hall. "It was very nice seeing you, Joanna." Then, shifting the stack of papers from one hand to another, he put two fingers to his eyebrow in a light salute. "Enjoy your dinner." He turned and walked slowly down the hall.

Joanna stood for a moment where he'd left her. It was Old Spice. That was the fragrance she had smelled when they collided. Old Spice. It had always been one of her favorite scents. She found its muskiness comforting, like a warm, woolen blanket in front of a fragrant fire.

More and more about Jared Fowler was intriguing her, though she told herself sternly this was one intrigue she dared not pursue.

# *Three*



Doris Wayne was jubilant. Abandoning her usual reserve, she flew into the snack bar, rushed over to the table where Joanna sat reading and held both hands, thumbs up, high in the air.

"We did it! We did it!"

"Did you finish the comparisons?"

Dropping into the waiting chair, Doris nodded. "I did, and I found exactly what I expected. Now I can present some real evidence that Rogers was on target."

"Oh, Doris, that's great. Tell me about it."

"Tell *us*, Doris."

Without even turning around, Joanna knew Jared was there.

It had been a captivating two weeks. They had met almost every day for coffee, Coke and long conversations, talking about any and everything and discovering common interests, one of which was writing poetry. Often, they would arrive at about the same time, sit and slide typewritten pieces of paper across the table to one another, reading in silence and then talking about what the poems revealed.

Jared's poems were sensitive and expressive, exposing a personal warmth and depth to which Joanna responded by writing about feelings she'd shared with few others. She looked forward to seeing him, so she arranged her schedule to include their moments together, knowing he was doing the same. Increasingly, time spent with Jared was turning into the focal point of her days.

"Is your project finished? What did you find?" His hand brushed Joanna's arm as he slid into the chair next to hers.

"It's just the way we thought it would be," Doris said, gesturing in Joanna's direction. Joanna was flattered by Doris's use of the plural; she really had been an important part of the research then.

"The students whose tests showed the most neurosis also saw themselves most unrealistically through the lenses," Doris explained. "Some looked through pane glass and reported themselves grossly out of proportion while some looked through lenses that *did* distort and reported seeing no difference. The more severely disturbed saw no change in their images no matter *what* glasses they put on. That's strong evidence that people deny and distort what they perceive in order to make what they see conform to their self-concepts."

Almost without pausing for breath, Doris went on. "And, like Rogers, I believe this explains our behavior in everyday situations. We all see the world from inside our own phenomenal fields, subconsciously colored by our past experiences. And we use whatever defenses we need to reinforce those perceptions."

Jared exhaled loudly. "Wow! That's pretty heavy stuff, but it makes a lot of sense. What's next?"

"The annual conference of the American Psychological Association in July. I've got plenty of time to get a paper ready to present, and with Joanna's help, that's my next step."

"Well, I'm delighted for both of you," Jared replied. Turning his gaze toward Joanna, his voice softened.

"Now that your research is over, there'll be a big hole in your schedule. Next semester, why not be part of the spring musical? You know we're doing *Oklahoma!* in April and auditions start after the Christmas break. There are plenty of parts, including a chorus. Besides, I'll need a lot of help behind the scenes."

Joanna had considered being a part of the musical even before she had met Jared. Beth's enthusiasm for the theater had rubbed off a bit and she figured it might be fun to be in the cast. Now, though, she was having second thoughts.

Working in the musical would mean constantly seeing Jared. They rehearsed intensely and Jared practically lived on campus, Beth had said. How long, Joanna wondered, would she be able to control her feelings for him if they were together so much? Wasn't it dangerous to be with him more often? Already, he was on her mind a lot and she caught herself thinking of him in ways that definitely weren't healthy.

"I don't know." Joanna looked at Jared thoughtfully. "It might be too much. I'm not sure it would be wise."

"I think I get the message," he said, returning an equally serious look. "But I would still love working with you. And with that, I'm off to class." He turned to Doris, who was watching them with a therapist's scrutiny. "And congratulations again, Doris. You can be very proud of what you accomplished."

Joanna watched him leave, unable to take her eyes from his retreating figure, his stride confident, his head held high.

Doris followed Joanna's eyes. "You look like you would like to go with him wherever he took you."

"Is it that obvious?" Joanna frowned, looking down at the table. "I *would* like to, but it's such a stupid pipedream. It's so uncharacteristic of me. How could I be thinking about him that way? Face it, I'm not sure what I'm thinking. I'm not sure of anything these days."

"Come over tonight and let's talk, if you think it will help," Doris said. For once, Joanna couldn't read the expression on her friend's face. She didn't know if that was a good thing.

~ * ~

The walk across campus took longer than usual. Joanna was in no hurry to put her feelings for Jared Fowler under Doris's microscope.

The light in the apartment window was soft and inviting, its glow spreading over the lawn. Headlights from passing cars reflected in the lake.

Doris was standing in the living room when Joanna let herself in. She was still dressed in her business suit, looking like she might be welcoming a client.

"Hi, honey." Doris greeted her with a hug that seemed to last a little longer than usual. "I'm glad you're here. Come sit and have some hot chocolate." She gestured to the sofa across from the window and the cup on the table in front of it.

For the first time since they'd met, Joanna didn't know where to start. Doris sat and waited.

"I've never felt like this," Joanna blurted out, standing to pace the small room. "It's so fast and so strong, I'm overwhelmed. I don't know what's happening or what to do about it."

"You're developing feelings for Jared that are pretty powerful and you're afraid of where they'll take you," Doris said, holding up a virtual mirror in which Joanna could view her own emotions.

"Oh, yes. I think of him constantly. I hear his voice when I'm trying to concentrate in class or fall asleep at night. I didn't think anything could feel like this. And a relationship with him is totally out of the question, so what do I do?"

"You're facing a real dilemma."

Joanna sat. "Part of me wants to just take one day at a time and see what happens. The other, more rational part of me, wants to stop everything where it is now. The problem with that is I'll still see him. Unless I change colleges, I'll keep running into him. I don't even dare try out for the spring musical because Jared's the director."

"You're in a difficult position," Doris said. "You *have* been seeing an awful lot of him. You seem to be developing a real closeness. That won't make avoiding deeper involvement any easier. What do *you* want to do? What do *you* see happening?"

Joanna didn't answer while she swallowed a sip of her drink.

Doris sat back in her chair, crossed her long legs and waited, her hands forming a steeple beneath her chin, her sympathetic blue eyes on Joanna's face.

"I'm sorry, Doris. I'm having a bad time and I can't even put words to what I'm feeling. I can't believe I'm thinking like this—me, of all people. He's married, for heaven's sake! But Jared's the kind of man I've always dreamed of. He's witty, intelligent and handsome. I love being with him. He's not afraid to let his emotions show and he's very compassionate. I've only known him a couple of weeks, but already I'm looking forward to spending time with him." Her voice dropped. "I know he can never be the answer to those dreams, and the smart side of me has been whispering a warning ever since that first day. But I must not be paying attention. Otherwise, why not just shrug him off, go on with my life as it was before he came along and stop spending time with him?"

Staring down at her fingertips, Doris seemed deep in thought. Finally, she looked up, her eyes soft and caring. "I'm sorry, Joanna, but I see this as something that will end badly for you. Attractions can be very powerful and sometimes irresistible, but this one—this one will end with your being hurt, I'm afraid, if Jared shares your feelings. He's a complicated man. At the risk of sounding like a psychologist, I think he shows a lot of narcissistic tendencies. Remember the glasses and mirrors? A narcissist needs to be loved and his subconscious directs him in ways that fill the need. My guess is he's being pulled toward you as strongly as you are to him. I would hate to see that happen; you mean too much to me."

She reached across the sofa and took Joanna's hand. "I can't tell you what to do or how to deal with this, you know. The only thing I *am* sure of is I'll be here. There will be many times when you'll need to talk, and I can be a sounding board. But I can't make decisions for you, honey. As hard as that will be, only you can make them."

"You haven't solved my dilemma," Joanna said wistfully. "But it's helped being able to talk about it, to put my doubts and fears into words. Frankly, I don't know what's going to happen. I could be dead wrong and be only imagining he feels something more than friendship for me. I have to talk with Jared first. I find it impossible to believe he could, but if he does, we'll have to agree to keep our relationship casual, not let it go any further. I'm sure he'll see that."

"Don't bet on it. He's a lonely, unhappy man. His life is this campus, his work and his children. I think he's the kind of person who needs more; he needs to *be* with someone. It wouldn't take much to make that someone be you. And why not? You're a lovely, caring and warm person, Joanna. Being just a friend might be something he'll try for a while to keep on seeing you, but I don't think it'll work for very long."

Joanna stood and picked up her cup. "Well, it has to." She went into the kitchen, rinsed the cup and put it in the dish rack. "Thanks for helping me try to sort this all out. I know what I have to do."

She hugged Doris and turned toward the door, looking back over her shoulder. "I'm so happy for you about the project, but I'll miss my time here." She reached into her purse, took out a key and handed it to Doris.

"I'm returning this. I won't be letting myself in anymore now that our work is done."

Doris waved it away. "Keep it. I'll still need your help with the paper, and I want you to have a key anyway. You might need this as a safe haven to run to when you need quiet time to think or a shoulder to unload on. Besides," she said, grinning, "it'll be good for me to leave a key with you for the next time I lock myself out of my own apartment."

The evening breeze was chilly as Joanna began the trek back to her dorm. She hurried up the walk toward the quad, glancing ahead toward Kenton Hall. Jared's office light was on. Not tonight. They would have to talk eventually, but not tonight. Besides, she didn't even know what she wanted to say.

# *Four*

*"Wanting is not having."*

Joanna kept herself very busy for the next several days working on the finishing touches to a paper for Dr. Hirsch. She'd made up her mind to avoid the snack bar, but every trip to the library took her past the little pine tree by the path. Each time, she heard Jared's voice. *Hello, tree.*

She was on her way to the library for a three o'clock class when she saw him coming down the path.

"Hi," she said, hoping she sounded calmer than she felt. "How are you?"

"Doing fine. Working hard. Midterms are fast upon us. Then there's the prep for the auditions. Have you given any more thought to trying out?"

"I've thought about it, but my course load next semester will be pretty heavy and I don't think I'll have the time."

She had decided on the spot. Her heart had skipped a beat when she saw him; she felt the heat in her face and knew there could be nothing but trouble by working with Jared in the musical. She thought she saw disappointment in his eyes.

"Maybe that's best. I'm quite a demanding taskmaster, as I'm sure Beth has told you, and we have a lot of rehearsals. I'm sorry, though. We would have had fun working together. I hope you'll reconsider."

Joanna moved past him toward the library. "It's been good seeing you," she said, her voice sounding tinny in her ears. "I've got to get to class."

"I'll be in the snack bar for a while before I head home. Maybe you'll stop by?"

Joanna didn't answer, just gave him a weak smile, turned toward the library and walked on.

After class, as she walked out with her friends, someone said, "Anyone for a Coke?" and the group swept out toward the student center. Joanna didn't know how to break away and felt a twinge of resentment at feeling she should even want to ignore her friends.

Jared sat at the table for two. Cigarette in hand, he was reading a book, glancing every now and then out the window. Joanna knew he had seen her and the others as they crossed the campus and that he was waiting for them to come in, for her to sit with him. Nodding slightly in his direction, she pretended to be involved in a discussion with her friends and sat with her back to Jared. She felt him watching her, knowing he was waiting for her, but she stubbornly faced front and joined in the conversation, feeling very childish but not knowing how else to handle her discomfort. If she were serious about keeping her relationship with Jared on a casual basis, she needed to start now, let him know he didn't always come first, that she had a life that didn't include him. She needed to convince herself as well. After a while, she got up, picked up her books, said her farewells to the others and turned toward the door. Jared was gone.

She was about to cross the street in front of her dorm when his car pulled up at the curb. He leaned over to the passenger side and rolled down the window.

"Joanna, I'd like to talk with you if you have a few minutes. Can we take a ride somewhere?"

Now was as good a time as any.

"Sure." She slid into the car. "Drive on, Jeeves," she said with forced lightness.

Taking the road that wound behind the dorms, Jared went out the back gates of the campus. They rode for a few minutes in silence. He smoked his Winston down to the filter, put it out in the ashtray and immediately reached for another.

"You don't smoke, Joanna?"

"I tried it once during a really stressful time last year, but never really got into it."

"They tell me it's not good for me. But I've smoked since my Navy days, sometimes heavier than others. At least now I've switched to a filter. Smoking always seems to relax me and I enjoy it too much to quit."

"When were you in the Navy?"

"I was a kid, eighteen when I enlisted in 1942. We'd just gotten into the war and I'd always wanted to learn to fly. Joining the service was my way of getting away from home, having free flying lessons and being where the action was. I flew fighters in the Pacific, came home with only a minor injury and decided I'd better leave my hero days behind and get serious about the future. College was an option, thanks to the GI Bill. I got my bachelor's and master's degrees in Virginia, and my doctorate in '53 from UC at Santa Barbara. I stayed on and worked there for four years, but this job was a step up, so I made the move."

"Let's see." Joanna rolled her eyes upward. "I was a year old when you enlisted in the Navy and I was in sixth grade when you got your Ph.D. and began teaching. You'd practically lived a whole lifetime before I even got started."

Jared swung the car onto a side street that seemed to go nowhere. In the purple twilight, Joanna could see rows of houses under construction.

"Where are we?" she asked as Jared pulled the car over to the curb and turned off the ignition.

"No place in particular, just a spot where we can talk. You've been avoiding me lately. I miss our snack bar time and I need to know why. Have you stopped wanting to talk with me, or is it because you're feeling the same thing I am, that something's happening between us? We do need to talk, don't we?"

Hearing his earnest tone, Joanna said, "Okay, I *have* been avoiding you. It's not that I haven't wanted to spend time with you; it's more like I'm afraid of spending *too* much time with you. I feel like I'm backing away from the life I've known and being pulled into a place I never dreamed I'd go and it scares me. I'm very confused, but I know we need to talk."

"I'll start," Jared lit another cigarette and inhaled deeply. He leaned back against the door and shifted his legs out from under the steering wheel, resting them crossed at the ankles on the shifter hump. Taking a deep breath, he fixed his gaze steadily on Joanna's face.

"You know I'm married, but you don't know the whole story. Vicki and I have been practically strangers for the past several years. Things were good between us until a few months after Michael was born. But then, she got very depressed and I couldn't get her to talk to anyone about it. She kept insisting she'd get over it. I'd done enough reading to know that post-partum depression didn't usually last that long or go that deep, but try as I might, I couldn't get her to see anyone or even talk to her doctor. Since then, her withdrawal has gotten progressively deeper. I can't seem to reach her, and the worst part is I don't want to try anymore."

Watching the end of his cigarette glowing in the gathering darkness, Joanna listened silently.

"About six months ago, Vicki's younger sister Genna came to live with us so she could take classes at the county college. Genna's pretty much taken over the care of the kids and the house. I don't know what I'd do without her."

He looked over at Joanna. "On the first day of classes this semester, I saw you sitting with Doris in the snack bar. From where I sat, I couldn't tell what you were talking about, but I couldn't stop watching you. You were so expressive, so animated! I found myself envying her. It's been so long since I could talk with someone like that. I thought about coming over and making small talk just to be part of the conversation, but I decided there was nothing to be gained by it. Why would I fool myself into thinking you'd be interested in anything an old man like me had to say? So I gave myself a good talking to. And it might have worked. But once we started to get to know each other, sitting together for those few minutes almost every day, sharing our thoughts and fears, I knew I was being pulled into something I couldn't control. I'm drawn to you, Joanna. It's unlike anything I've ever experienced. It's like a connection I feel whenever I'm near you, even when I'm not. You're on my mind and working your way into my heart. I don't know what to do about it."

They were quiet for a few minutes. What he'd said hung between them, heavy, expectant.

Finally, Joanna let out a long breath. "I know. I can't explain it either, but it happened to me the day I first met you. I felt connected in a way I've never experienced. And the more I got to know you, the stronger the feeling got. Doris has warned me against getting too close to you, as if I hadn't told myself that already, but she can't tell me how to avoid it. Like you, I'm struggling with it."

She looked across the car, searching for his face in the blackness. "I promised myself not to be alone with you, to try to keep my feelings for you in perspective. This friendship is the best we can hope for without falling into something so complicated it would tear both of us apart. We have to be on campus together as the friends we've become. Nothing more. I'm very sorry about your marriage, honestly I am. Sorrier for your children, but for all of you, really. If Vicki goes on like this or gets even worse, what will you do? You can't force her to seek help. Would you take the children and move out?"

"No. Oh, not because I wouldn't want to, but because I couldn't. Vicki's parents would fight me all the way. They live in Florida, and they'd like nothing better than to have Marina and Michael living, if not *with* them, then as close as possible. They're very wealthy, so they'd be able to set Vicki and the kids up in style, try to deal with Vicki's problems and raise my children almost as their own. They could hire the best lawyers. It wouldn't be a fair fight, not on an associate professor's salary and anyway, judges don't take children from their mothers. I know I'd lose the kids."

He reached for her hand and kissed it gently. "Now I find someone else I don't want to lose. I couldn't stand it if you had to go out of your way to avoid me. I would miss seeing you every day. You're right, of course." He let go of her hand and reached for his pack of cigarettes. "We can't let this go any further. You described it as 'complicated.' I'd call it disastrous. If it were just the three of us—me, Vicki and you—we wouldn't be having this conversation at all. I'd be in the process of getting myself free so there'd be no strings attached. But it's not. What I do determines my relationship with my children for the rest of their lives. I'm not willing to be a part-time dad, visiting on holidays or having them for a month in the summer. They deserve better than that. But I'm selfish enough to think I deserve better, too."

His voice had grown husky, even deeper than usual. "I want you in my life. I need someone like you to share with, and I know I can't have you as anything but a friend. If that's the best I can do, I'll settle for friendship. It's better than nothing at all."

Joanna sighed. "Doris has a saying she's always tossing my way when I'm crying on her shoulder about one thing or another. She says 'wanting is not having.' She's definitely put it well. What we might think we want we can't have, and for both of our sakes, it's best left at that."

Jared leaned across the seat to take her in his arms. She rested her head on his shoulder and breathed in the warm, comforting scent of his skin.

Releasing her slowly, he turned the key in the ignition and started to pull away from the curb. His voice was unsteady. "I'll take you back to campus. I'm sure you have a busy day tomorrow."

They rode most of the way in silence. As they neared the college, Jared looked at her. "We'd better assume our best 'professional attitudes.' You never know who might be out walking around that might wonder what we're doing together."

"P.A. assumed, Doctor," Joanna said lightly, trying to break the seriousness of the past hour. She moved as close to the door as she could get and sat up perfectly straight.

Jared pulled into the parking lot by the student center, the car illuminated by the streetlight above. "I'm glad we talked. As complicated as it makes things, I'm glad you feel something as special for me as I do for you."

"I think you're a wonderful man. If things were different—but they're not. And I couldn't stand being here day after day without seeing you and talking to you, so let's do it the only way we can ... as friends."

She opened her door and got out of the car.

"Are you going inside?" he asked.

"No. I need to get some studying done."

"I'll be going then. Sleep well, Joanna. I'll see you ... whenever," he said, looking at her sadly.

She turned and walked toward the dorm, still feeling the press of his warm lips on her hand.

# Five

*"The fear was always there."*

As she went about her routine the next week, Joanna told herself she needed to forget that conversation, the sound of his voice as he talked about his growing feelings for her and especially the kiss on the hand. But as she lay in her quiet room at night, she played it all back over and over like scenes from a favorite film classic.

Each morning brought fresh anticipation of a few minutes with Jared, the excitement she felt when someone merely mentioned his name. Even walking by the blue and white station wagon parked in its place made her smile to herself, knowing she'd sat in it with him, laid her head on his shoulder, felt the touch of his lips. Once in a while, she'd glimpse him walking up the steps of Kenton or see the back of his head as he sat in the faculty dining room and she'd think of what no one else knew, hugging the secret of their deepening relationship to herself, mindless of the way she was nurturing a fantasy of something unattainable and dangerous.

~ * ~

The end of October was approaching; the weather was getting chillier and the campus buzzed with preparations for the big Halloween dance.

The night's weather could have been scripted for a grade-B horror movie: a half-moon shadowed by clouds, overcast, foggy and damp. As she walked across the street, Joanna saw the orange candles flickering on the tables in the snack bar already filling up with costumed partygoers. She intended to have a light snack and spend the evening reading.

The line was long. As she waited, she looked idly around the room. Her eyes stopped at the table for two near the window. Jared was there, looking at her steadily, intently, as if willing her to find him in the crowd. She gave him a little wave.

"Happy Halloween," he said, holding a chair for her. "Where's your costume?"

"I don't do costumes," she replied, looking around the room at the assortment of creatures and characters. "And I might ask you the same thing. Where's yours?"

"Okay, we're even. After trekking from store to store with the kids until they each found that 'perfect' costume, I've pretty much had it with Halloween. Besides, I'm a little too old to be begging for goodies at some stranger's door."

Joanna frowned. "That was the only part of Halloween I even remotely enjoyed. Ever since I was little, I've hated the whole atmosphere around it. Hated the ghosts and goblins, never went into a haunted house. I've never found any fun in being frightened."

"It's all good-natured, isn't it?"

"I wish I could see it that way, but I've never been comfortable with even make-believe scary things."

Jared sat quietly, waiting for her to continue.

"When Halloween comes around each year, I get as far away from it as I can," she went on. "I guess that makes me really strange, doesn't it?"

"No. There must be a reason you feel like you do. Have you ever tried to figure it out?"

"It doesn't take much figuring, but I'm sure you don't want to suffer through the tales of Joanna's demons."

"I want to hear whatever you need to talk about. Clearly there's something disturbing that Halloween conjures up and maybe talking about it will help dispel those demons. Try me."

"I'm almost embarrassed to talk about it. It seems so silly ... it was so long ago. But you asked, so where shall I start?

"My parents were divorced when I was three, so you know why I understand about your children. Anyway, my mother and I went to live with her parents in upstate New York. Then, when I was six, she got a nursing job in Atlantic City and we moved there. We lived with her sister and brother-in-law, and she worked nights at the hospital. Mom always made it a point to remind me we were guests in their house and mustn't offend anyone, so I was always on guard, always afraid of saying or doing something wrong.

"It was the first Halloween we lived there. My mother was working. I was in bed upstairs in the room I shared with her when the hall light went out. Having a light on was terribly important to me; it kept me from feeling afraid. Anyway, I was terrified, lying there imagining what might be lurking in the dark. I called to someone to please turn the light back on. There was no answer except for a low, menacing growl coming up the steps, closer and closer. I'll never forget the fear, Jared; it was cold and choking. I tried to scream but I couldn't. As the growling got louder and I began to cry, I heard my aunt scold my uncle for scaring me and realized who was making that ungodly sound. He laughed all the way down the stairs, but he never did turn the light back on and I laid there terrified until my mother came home," she said, shuddering at the memory.

"She must have been furious with him," Jared said quietly.

"Maybe she was, but she never said anything to him. Not a word. She told me she wished we could live somewhere else, but she couldn't support us on her own, so I'd have to be patient. I didn't want to be patient. I just wanted to be somewhere else, somewhere away from him. Whenever she was at work, he would change into a different person, always mocking and threatening. He seemed to be lurking around every corner, waiting for some way to frighten me, to say something hurtful and cruel. I dreaded being in the house when he was around. That's my first conscious memory of missing my father. I wanted a daddy who could make him leave me alone."

"What a wretched experience for a child so young. How terrible it must have been for you. Did you live there long?"

"Three years, and it's funny but that's the only memory I have ... no happy birthdays, Christmases or anything. A missing childhood. When I was nine, my grandparents bought a house next door and Mom and I moved in with them. They were wonderful people and I should have felt secure, but I never did. The fear was always there. Sometimes I think it still is."

She looked up and smiled ruefully. "I'm sorry. I don't know why I got into this heavy topic tonight. I certainly didn't intend to unload it all on you."

"Don't apologize. I admire you immensely for having gotten through all that and I appreciate your sharing it with me. You're a very strong, very beautiful person."

"No one's ever told me that," she said, looking down at her hands. "I've always wanted to be beautiful to someone. Too many fairy tales about princesses, I guess, but I never think of myself that way. I find it hard to believe anyone else could."

Jared started to reach across the table for her hand, but pulled his hand away quickly and sat back in the chair instead.

"You don't see what I do then. You don't see the depth, the warmth, the tenderness. You don't see the marvelous eyes, the graceful hands and the expressive face that glows or clouds up depending on what you're feeling. Obviously, you don't see yourself as you really are, like the people in Doris's mirrors. That's too bad, but trust me. I see someone beautiful when I look at you."

"Thank you. I'll take your word for it. Do you tell Marina she's pretty?"

"Oh, yes." He leaned over the table with his arms at his sides. "She never tires of hearing it. I tell her she's my beautiful blonde bombshell, even though I know she doesn't understand that old-fogey expression. She knows I think she's the prettiest little girl in the world and I hope she believes it. I want my children to grow up feeling good about themselves, even though it's taking a lot more energy than I thought it would. Kids are pretty perceptive, aren't they? They know when things aren't right but they don't know why. Impressions and feelings kids pick up when they're very little color their whole lives. Isn't that what Doris proved?"

Joanna's voiced dropped. "You don't have to tell *me*. I know my mother was only doing the best she could, but the damage of those early years has gone very deep. I guess I've never felt truly loved, truly *good enough* for anyone."

They sat quietly for a few minutes, oblivious to the partygoers around them, not noticing that most were beginning to leave for the dance in the gym. As the noise subsided, Andy Williams could be heard singing "Willow, Weep for Me."

"I love this song." Jared cocked his head to one side. "Williams has such a mellow style."

"I don't think I've ever heard it," Joanna replied. "It's not one of his hits, is it?"

"No, but I hear it now and then on the radio. I like to close my eyes, enjoy the emotion in the lyrics and think about what it used to be like before."

"I understand and I know what you mean. I think, like many people, I live inside my own head a lot," Joanna said quietly. "Just sitting here listening to that melody, I can drift away and be anywhere or anyone I choose. Do you ever feel that?"

"All the time. Since Vicki's—what do I call it, transformation?—I've been alone a lot. I talk to the kids, sure, but on their level and about things they care about. I haven't had anyone to share with for what seems like so long I guess I've withdrawn a lot, too. I miss sharing."

"Maybe she needs time, Jared. Maybe there's something so painful in her life this is the only way she can handle it. Did you know her long before you were married?"

"We didn't grow up together, if that's what you mean. I met her in Virginia when I was working on my master's. She was studying art. She seemed so strong and vulnerable at the same time, not to mention very pretty, and it went from there. We were married in less than six months, so no I hadn't known her long before we married. That was probably a mistake for both of us."

"You're honest about your feelings, too."

"It helps to face them and try to deal with them. I've tried to find answers to what changed her, and to what I can do about the way we're living." He looked up and smiled wryly. "Don't have any yet, though. I know if it weren't for the children, I'd hate going home at night. And after they're in bed, I often go back out again."

"I saw your car in the center's parking lot one Sunday evening after we first met. I wondered why you were on campus."

"If you'd asked me, I probably wouldn't have been able to tell you. I find myself here a lot. Even before I knew this was where you were. I feel safe here, I guess. Something about this quiet, secluded campus wraps around me like Linus's security blanket, makes me feel like nothing else exists but what's on these few acres. Now I know there was always something pulling at me to be here. I'm finding it even harder to stay away."

He sighed, looking at his watch. "And harder to leave, but I must. It's time I went home to the children. Genna took them trick or treating tonight and they'll be waiting to show me all their loot." He stood and put on his coat. Each movement was deliberate, slow.

"Good night, Jared. Thank you for listening and spending your Halloween with me. It's the nicest one I've ever had, and the company was perfect."

"Good night. I'll wait here until I'm sure you've gotten safely across the street. I'd hate to think of some vampire on the prowl for a lovely neck to bite grabbing you and taking you away."

~ * ~

She felt his eyes on her back as she walked across the street. In her room, she went straight to the window and looked out. His car was backing out of the parking lot. She wondered what he would find when he got home. She could see him playing with the children, talking with them about their adventures going from house to house as they filled their bags with candy and fruit. She could see the three of them huddled together over a table in the kitchen of a house she could only imagine.

She wanted to be there, too. It was getting harder and harder to deny the truth. She wanted to be anywhere Jared was, feeling the way she felt when she was with him.

Standing at her dresser brushing her hair, she thought, *Mirror, mirror on the wall ... maybe I'm not so plain after all.*

# Six



*"They're beginning to wonder, don't you think?"*

"Hey, Joanna! Wait for us!" Beth and a group of her friends hurried to catch up as Joanna walked up the sidewalk to the dorm.

"Let's go to dinner," Beth said. "We'll put our books in our rooms and meet back here, okay?"

As the girls scattered in various directions, Joanna went to check her mail in the slots above the sign-in sheet. There was a postcard from Julia, a high school friend who was visiting her cousin in South America, and a letter in an unfamiliar handwriting. There was no return address and it wasn't stamped so it must have come from a campus office. Ripping it open, she started up the steps and stopped with one foot on the first landing.

> *Dear Joanna,*
> *I went back to my office after the kids went to bed on Halloween to sit and think and to know I was in the same place as you. I wondered what you were doing, if you were thinking of me.*

*I'm trying very hard to do what's right, but I have to face the fact that I don't want to be just a friend. I don't want to keep my distance and wear my professional attitude all the time. I want to hold you, feel you next to me and get lost in the contentment I feel when I'm with you.*

*I've heard about people who've met and been instantly attracted, then stayed together all their lives. Before now, I always doubted it could happen. How, I thought, could people tell, that fast, that they'd found the other half of themselves?*

*Now I know. When I leave you, I feel like half of me goes but half stays behind. I want to hurry back because I don't feel complete without you. Life should be lived with the kind of contentment I feel when we're together. All this certainty after a mere month? Absolutely.*

*Because we must, we'll go on this way, won't we? I wish with all my heart it could be otherwise. I wonder what it would be like to kiss you, to give you the love you've been missing. I think of you constantly, and not as one friend thinks of another.*

*Love,*
*Jared*

She stood on the landing, holding the letter in trembling hands as Beth and two other girls came rushing down. "Let's go, Jo!"

"I just remembered something I have to do." Joanna folded the letter and put it back in the envelope. "I'll have to eat later. You guys go on without me."

"Okay. See you," Beth replied as Joanna took to the stairs.

Once inside her room, she sat on the bed, opened the letter and read it again. Had he known? Could he really read her mind? She'd wanted to kiss those lips ever since he put them so gently on her hand. She wanted to hold him close, make all his trouble disappear for as long as she could. And here he was, telling her the same things, for the first time opening his heart to her. She read the letter over and over again.

Putting it down on her desk, she reached for the box of stationery she kept in the top drawer.

> *Dear Jared,*
>
> *I've just read your letter for the fourth time.*
>
> *Yes, I was thinking about you. You and Marina and Michael sitting at your kitchen table, looking through the goodie bags at all the treats they brought home. I wanted to be there, too; I wanted to share the fun and the laughter. Mostly, I wanted to be with you.*
>
> *I think of you more than you know. I spend far more time than I should waiting for the next conversation, the next time you walk into the snack bar looking for me.*
>
> *It's probably good that Thanksgiving will be coming soon. I'll be spending the holidays at home with my family and you'll be with yours. It will help us regain some perspective and continue on as friends when we get back. I know we have to keep it this way. You've become too important to me to imagine not seeing you or talking with you whenever I can.*
>
> *Love,*
> *Joanna*

She folded the paper and put it in an envelope, addressing it to Jared's office. Pulling on her jacket, Joanna left the dorm, walked slowly across the street and dropped the envelope into the campus-only box in front of the student center, then went into the snack bar for a quick sandwich and a Coke. It wasn't very crowded, so she took the table for two by the window, looking out at the quiet, dark campus.

She felt him come in. When she looked up, there he was, standing at the back door, his eyes sweeping the room. As his gaze rested on her, he smiled a greeting. As she smiled back, Joanna was suddenly aware that many of the people in the room looked from him to her and then back to him again. She wondered what they were thinking.

He made his way to the table, put down his cup and took off his coat.

"Hello, Joanna." It was the same deep voice she heard in her dreams. He looked very tired.

She watched him ease into his chair and run his hands through his hair. "Hello. I just mailed you a letter."

"Did you get mine? Silly, isn't it? I hope you don't think I'm foolish, writing letters when I see you so often." He didn't wait for her to answer. "But there are things I want you to know, things I need to say, that can't be said sitting here."

He looked around the crowded room. "They're beginning to wonder, don't you think? Not that I worry, but we don't have any plausible reason for being together so much; you're not even one of my students. We won't be able to sit and talk like this much longer, you know that as well as I."

"It's occurred to me, too, but I don't know what to do about it. How do we avoid each other? Take turns coming to the snack bar? Look the other way when we meet on campus? This is a very small place. How can we do that?" Joanna almost whispered the words, conscious for the first time of the closeness of the tables and the number of ears possibly attuned to their conversation.

Jared lowered his voice as well. "We probably need to be more realistic than we've been. Lord knows *we* know how hard we're working to keep this on a 'just friends' basis, but imagine what everyone else must be thinking."

"I don't know what to say. If we can't meet here every few days or so and talk..." Her voice trailed off, leaving the sentence and the thought unfinished.

"Let me think about it," Jared said. "I'll be in touch soon, I promise."

He stood, put on his coat and turned toward the door. Several of the students looked up; one or two nodded a greeting. Joanna watched the straight, tall, confident figure stride out the back door and then, finishing her Coke, she picked up her jacket and went out the front, not looking at anyone as she left.

After signing in, she went straight to her floor. Several girls were in the hall, chattering loudly. As she turned the corner, the voices hushed and grew quiet.

"Oh, hi!" one of the girls called. "We missed you at dinner."

"I'll join you another time," Joanna said, letting herself into her room, wondering if even the girls in the dorm were beginning to talk about her and Jared. It appeared the campus cocoon was no longer protecting them. They should have seen it coming, but if they had, they'd ignored their own good sense.

She sat at her desk, opened a book and tried to read. Tomorrow was a big exam in Shakespeare class and she wasn't ready. Time was, she'd have been studying nonstop for days, ready to ace the test, thoroughly prepared. She thought about how things had changed. Meeting Jared had stopped her life in its tracks and sent her spinning off in a totally different direction. She felt like she wasn't the same person. Somehow, he'd changed her. Before, what was important was being a good student, enjoying her college years and going on to a good job, maybe marriage and kids. Now what did she want? The answer was simple. She wanted Jared.

That was the last thing she remembered before she dropped off to sleep. Her dreams were a troubled mixture of emotions that left her exhausted when morning came, feeling like she hadn't slept at all.

There was no sign of Jared the next day or the day after. On Friday, there was another letter.

> *Dear Joanna,*
> *It seems like a long, long time since I've seen you—two whole days in reality, an eternity in my mind. I've spent the*

*time missing you, missing being able to talk with you. This won't work. Meet me at Kenton at seven tonight? I'll take it from there.*

*Love,*
*Jared*

Should she do it? How would meeting him keep the relationship from getting deeper? What sense was there in going to the next level? At least on campus, there was the protection of caution, the safety of limiting their time together to avoid suspicion. Why should they risk anything else? She thought about it all day. She muddled through a pop quiz and walked from class to class still thinking about it, knowing in her heart there was really no question about it—she would go anywhere to be with Jared.

# Seven



*"Will there be a next time?"*

The day seemed to drag. At five, she and Beth and a few other girls went to the cafeteria for dinner. Afterward, someone suggested a movie in town.

"Count me out. I've got to spend some time at Doris's," she said, letting the lie slip out easily. "There's still work to be done on her project and I've been too busy lately to do it. I promised tonight."

Joanna headed back to her room, put on light makeup and dressed casually but fashionably in gray wool slacks and a soft blue blouse. Jared had never seen her dressed like this. She wondered if he'd notice.

She saw his car parked on the side lot in the shadows as she approached Kenton Hall. As she drew closer, he got out and came quickly toward her. "Let's get away from here," he said, going around the car to open her door. "I have a friend I want you to meet."

They drove out of the campus gates toward town. As soon as they were on the open road, Jared looked over and raised his eyebrow.

"Is this what happens when you shed that Manning sweatshirt?" he teased. "You look more beautiful than ever."

Feigning seriousness, she said, "Thank you, kind sir. I wasn't sure you'd recognize me without it. Where are we going?"

"A little surprise. It's a place that's perfect for us to be able to sit and talk. We'll be there soon. And on the way, I've got some great new stories to tell you."

Joanna was soon laughing uncontrollably at the new puns Jared had been saving for her.

"Oh, stop!" she said, wiping the tears from her eyes. "I don't know where you find those corny things."

"They sorta come to me. How could anyone resist such a great play on words like 'transporting young gulls across staid lions for immortal porpoises'?"

Joanna was still laughing when Jared turned off onto a side street by the railroad tracks and pulled into a parking lot next to a small, white building with bright neon lights across the front. As they walked toward the little wooden door, she read "The Downtown Club."

Jared led her into a narrow room dominated by a gleaming wooden bar on the left. On the right were tiny booths for two, while toward back of the room were a few larger tables.

He motioned to a booth about midway into the bar.

"This is a good spot," he said, taking her coat and hanging it on the hook with his. "What will you have? It's self-service here, so tell me your pleasure and I'll be the barmaid."

"What are you going to have?"

"I always drink manhattans. It's my favorite cocktail."

"My stepfather makes a mean one and it's my favorite, too. Make mine the same."

As he approached the bar, Jared stopped to talk to a man sitting at the far end. In a few minutes, the bartender placed the two glasses on napkins and gave them to Jared.

"Here you are," he said, handing her a glass of almond-brown liquid with a big maraschino cherry on the bottom.

He held his glass up between them. "A toast: to Joanna, who brightens all my days."

Joanna blushed and touched her glass to his. They drank in silence for a few minutes until their reverie was broken by the sound of music. Joanna looked over and realized the man to whom Jared had spoken had gone up to the baby grand piano behind the bar. After a few seconds, he began to play "Misty."

"This is my all-time favorite Mathis song," Jared said. "I love the way Jim always plays it for me ... so much expression and emotion! He's got an amazing repertoire and seems to remember everyone's favorites. If we come here again, you'll find he's remembered yours and he'll play them for you."

"How did you arrange this?" She waved toward the empty room. "We're the only souls in this whole place. What did you do? Rent it for the evening?"

"No. I'm good, but not quite that good. We're very early. Usually, the club doesn't come alive until after eight, but I wanted us to get here early enough to be able to enjoy Jim's music and talk without having to shout over the noise."

~ * ~

The club was filling up, getting noisier as groups of people stood three deep at the bar.

Jared leaned across the table. "We certainly don't have the place to ourselves anymore. Would you like another manhattan?"

Joanna nodded and Jared moved through the crowd to the bar. She watched him as he waited for their drinks. Being with him was like something out of a dream. A few weeks ago, who would have thought they would be together like this?

"What do you want Jim to play for you?"

"How about 'Unchained Melody?' It's so haunting and sad. Would he do it?"

"Stay here." He managed once again to get through the crowd to catch the piano player's eye. Jim leaned forward, listened and looked over at Joanna, giving her a thumb up.

"He'll get to it," Jared said. "I asked him to do yours and then play 'Misty' again for me."

They drank in silence, listening to the music.

Jared's eyes searched her face. "Penny for your thoughts. Are you sorry you came?"

"No, I'm not, but I guess I should be. I promised myself no alone time. We talked about how unwise it would be. But am I sorry now? No, I love being with you, talking to you, listening to you. I want to know everything about you. We can't talk like this on campus, so I'm glad we're here."

"I didn't work very hard at helping you keep your promise, did I? Anyway," he said, looking around the room, "we're certainly not alone, now are we?"

"No, we're not."

Just then, conversation seemed to drop to a lower level and Joanna heard "Unchained Melody."

She closed her eyes, listening. When the song was over, she opened them and Jared was looking intently at her.

"Where did you go?"

"Nowhere in particular, wandering into the song, hearing the words as Jim played the music. It's a very plaintive melody, don't you think?"

"I must admit, I really wasn't listening. I was too busy watching your face, wishing I could be wherever you were."

"Well, I warned you," she said lightly. "When I hear music or read a good book, I'm gone. And that song has taken me far away ever since I first heard it."

"If you'd like, I'll find the sheet music in the store and practice it. One of these days, I'll find a way to sing it for you."

"I'd love that." Joanna reached for his hand without thinking, touched his fingers and then, suddenly self-conscious, pulled away. She reached for her glass and took the last sip.

"Another?" Jared asked.

"If I drink any more, I'll have to crawl to the car. No, thank you, I'm finished for the night. It's been a long time since I've had more than one manhattan, so I'll be smart and stop now. Have another one if you'd like."

"No, I don't ever want to drink alone again. It's been much too nice having someone share my favorite cocktail with me. Are you ready to go?"

He helped with her coat as she stood marveling at how warm she felt, whether from the manhattans or Jared's hands on her shoulders.

"I'm a little woozy," she said, grinning. "Guess I can't hold my alcohol. I'd better go easier on the manhattans next time."

Jared held both her arms and looked down at her seriously. "Will there be a next time?"

"I hope so. It's perfect here. We can talk, listen to good music and be away from the campus gossips. I'm glad you brought me."

They acknowledged Jim's farewell wave, left the bar and walked slowly toward the parking lot.

Sliding across the passenger seat, Joanna unlocked the driver's side door and opened it for Jared. She went midway back to the other side and stopped, wanting to stay close.

"So you liked my little hideaway?"

"It was wonderful. Everything about it was perfect."

They finished the ride in silence, Jared smoking, music playing on the radio. As they neared campus, he looked at her and raised his eyebrow.

"Getting close to home, Miss Ransome," he said with mock sternness. "Remember the P.A.!"

"How could I forget?" She slid all the way over to the passenger door.

Jared returned to the parking area behind Kenton Hall, turned off the engine and reached across the seat to touch her shoulder. "Thank you. I loved every minute of tonight."

He opened the door, got out and came around to her. Taking her hand as she stepped out of the car, he drew her to him for the briefest of moments and kissed her on the forehead, his lips lingering.

"I'd love nothing better than to walk you home. But I'll stay here until I'm certain you're safely inside. Sleep well. I'll see you Monday."

# *Eight*



*"I want a fairy tale ending."*

It was like leading a double life. In the public one, Joanna went to classes, spent time with her friends, worked with Doris and faithfully attended the fall play to cheer Beth on, being careful to blend into the audience and not hang around backstage near Jared.

She prudently guarded the other life, the private one, the life that revolved around time spent with him.

Thanksgiving presented a dilemma. Joanna had always looked forward to the holiday, but this year, for the first time, she didn't want to go home, to leave the campus and Jared. The past weeks, so filled with him, made her reluctant to spend time anywhere else.

> *Dear Joanna,*
>
> *You'll be leaving soon for home and a holiday with your family. I'll miss you. Vicki's parents arrive Wednesday. On Friday, everyone's going to drive to northern New Jersey to visit Vicki's aunt. I wasn't invited*

*(and that's okay), so I'll be by myself until they come back on Sunday.*

*For the first time in my life, I'm dreading a holiday. Oh, not because of the possibility that Vicki's moods may spoil things for everyone, although that is a consideration. I'm dreading a stretch of days when I'll know you're farther away than at any time since we met.*

*I'll miss Friday night with you and Jim at the club. I'll miss talking to you, telling you silly stories that make you laugh. I'll be at odds with myself, feeling disconnected and alone. I'll wonder what you're doing and wish I were free to be there with you.*

*Even though I'll see you before you go, we won't be alone, so I want to tell you now how much I'll miss you. Imagine! Five whole days apart and I feel like it's a lifetime. What have you done to me to make me need you so?*

*Love,*
*Jared*

She read the letter as she crossed the campus to her last class before the break. When it was over, instead of going back to the dorm, Joanna turned toward Kenton Hall, mingling with a crowd of students on their way there. She knocked lightly on Jared's door.

"Come in," he called.

She peered around the door. "I hope I'm not disturbing anything."

"Hello! How lovely of you to call," he said with feigned formality. "Welcome to my home. It's not much, but it's where I hang my hat and hide when everything gets to be too heavy."

"It's very quiet and comfortable." Joanna turned slowly to examine the room. She walked over to a large frame that dominated one wall. "What are these?"

"A collection of playbills from productions I've directed. Many of them were projects I particularly enjoyed and I like looking at them to remember what fun they were. Over here is a smaller group of programs from musicals I've been in. I wish there were more, but I never seemed to have enough time."

"Very impressive." Joanna sat on a plush chair in front of his desk. "Being in theater must be very exciting. I can see you love your work."

He sat in the chair next to her and pulled it around so they were face to face. "I do. I've found some very promising talent and redirected a few of the not-so-talented to other pursuits. I guess I've never lost my desire to make it to the big time myself, even though I know that'll never be."

"Don't be so negative. Who knows what might happen? But I *am* surprised you're here, at Manning State, I mean. This little college can't possibly satisfy your ambitions. What attracted you to it?"

"New York. I wanted to get closer to New York. That's where the excitement is, where the best theaters are and the newest playwrights try out their work. I love going over for the off-Broadway stuff, to see what's new. I appreciate the work of the strugglers, the ones who aren't stars and may never be. I'd love to be able to work in an actual theater setting as a director, but it's very hard to get a chance. Perhaps one day.

"To what do I owe the honor of your first visit? I've often hoped I'd get to share my office with you."

"Your letter." She took it out of her notebook and put it on the desk in front of her. "I won't have time to answer it before campus closes down for the holiday, and I wanted to."

He settled back, lit a cigarette and waited, eyebrow raised.

"I'll miss you too," Joanna said frankly, meeting his eyes. "It will be very strange being at home with my mind filled with thoughts of you. I think the hardest part will be not being able to talk about you, particularly to my mother. We've always been very close and I've never felt the need to keep something from her. But this? Can I expect her to understand our friendship? No, I know she'd worry about me, about us, and it would ruin her holiday. So I'll go home, spend time with my folks and wait impatiently until it's time to come back."

Jared made a bemused smile. "Not so long ago, I would have looked forward to the alone time. No stress, no Vicki. Now it's not at all appealing. I would rather stay at work because it would mean you'd be here, too. How are you getting home?"

"Mark Peterson. He's a senior who lives a few miles from the shore. He usually takes me as far as his house and my mother meets me there."

"Well, I hope you relax and enjoy being with your family. I certainly intend to try to do the same, but the idea of being with Vicki's parents for two days is somehow a bit daunting. Fortunately, the children will ease the awkwardness and provide built-in entertainment."

"And then you'll have your solitude."

"So I will. I might go out to the country to spend some time at Dan's. The plants will need watering and I can enjoy the quiet and some good reading for a couple of days. I guess I'll play it by ear and do whatever I feel like."

Joanna stood, put the letter back and picked up her books. "Well, Mark's due to pick me up in a couple of hours and I'm not packed yet, so I'd better be on my way."

They walked slowly to the door. She put her hand on the doorknob and turned to say goodbye. Jared was standing very near. He bent his head, raised her chin with his index finger and grazed her lips with his. It started as a light, casual kiss goodbye, but the moment their lips met, the kiss grew deeper and lingered. Her books dropped to the floor as Joanna clung to him with an intensity she knew had been barely contained. He returned her embrace, one hand entwined in her hair, the other gently brushing her cheek. They drew apart, then came together more slowly, Jared caressing her face as he met her lips lightly again and again, then gently parted them for a long, deep kiss. Finally, she moved back ever so slightly.

"I wish we hadn't done that," she whispered, looking at the floor.

Jared smiled wryly. "No you don't, dear heart. You wanted it as badly as I. We've both been fighting it for weeks, pretending we could keep up the façade. This was inevitable. The question is where it goes from here. We'll have to face that one day, you know."

He bent to retrieve her books. She searched his face as he straightened, seeing the image that was her last conscious thought each night and the first each morning.

"Okay, I confess. I've wanted to kiss you since the first day we met. But I wanted to try to play by the rules, too. Now ... now what have we stepped into?"

Jared started to open the door. "We'll talk about it soon. Call me if you can." Moving swiftly to his desk, he scribbled on a piece of paper and handed it to her. "This is my number. No one will be there after Friday afternoon and I won't go to the country until I hear from you. Can you manage it?"

"I'll find a way."

~ * ~

Joanna hurried to her dorm, wanting to skip with happiness like a little girl, a tangle of thoughts rolling around in her head, jumbled together in a curious mix of joy and fear. Kissing Jared was just as she knew it would be. She'd imagined it so many times she knew exactly how it would feel. And now that they'd lost the battle—*had it ever been a battle or just a brief skirmish?*—she was filled with joy, her heart bursting with excitement. But while she rejoiced, she felt the cold knot of fear and guilt in her stomach. This shouldn't be happening. She knew it shouldn't be happening. So why had she let it? Why didn't she turn away and walk out of his office? Better yet, why had she gone there in the first place?

She closed her suitcase and sat on the edge of the bed to wait for the blast from Mark's horn. She shrugged off the questions and promised herself not to think about it too hard. Let the future take care of itself.

~ * ~

The day after Thanksgiving, relatives back home, house restored to order and good china packed away, Joanna declined a shopping trip with her mother. Being surrounded with family and bombarded with questions about college had been stressful. She needed some time alone.

"Thanks, but I'm really okay. Honest I am," she responded to her mother's concern. "I want to take a walk on the beach. I know it's chilly, but I won't stay out long and it will do me good."

Catherine glanced at her watch and frowned. "Okay, honey. I won't be gone more than a couple of hours."

~ * ~

It was only three blocks to the beach, that incredible stretch of soft gray-white sand and endless mirror of water that crashed in great waves or lapped gracefully on the shore, depending on the winds. Since she had been a child, being on the beach had been one of Joanna's favorite pastimes. She never seemed to tire of it, no matter how old she got.

Today, she needed the serenity of the sea, the time to walk, to think, the time to try to make sense of the events of the past two months.

Despite the sunshine, it was windy and cold as she walked along the boardwalk and down the wooden steps to the beach. There were a few other brave souls out, as intent as she on taking some time with nature, savoring the sounds and smell of the ocean. Walking along the water's edge, listening to the squawking of seagulls overhead, dodging to keep her shoes from getting wet and burying her face in her collar, she thought about Jared. It seemed she was always thinking about Jared. Never too far into the future where it became murky and shadowy, but always of the next time they could be together. It was easier to take her relationship with him one day at a time. This day, she simply wanted to see him, be with him and feel the touch of his lips on hers once again.

It was nearly four o'clock when she got back to the house. Catherine wasn't back yet, so she took the scrap of paper out of her purse and gave the number to the operator.

"Jared Fowler."

"Hi," Joanna said breathlessly. "How was your holiday?"

"Well, hello." His voice seemed even deeper through the telephone line. "It was long and lonely. Actually, it wasn't as bad as I feared as far as the family was concerned. Now, though, it's quiet and I'm missing you all over again. How was yours?"

"Good. It was nice seeing everyone and we all ate too much. I went for a walk on the beach this afternoon and tried to relax, but I couldn't think of anything but you."

"Come back." His voice was low and urgent. "Even if it's only for a few hours."

"You must have been reading my mind. Mom has to be back at the hospital tomorrow. My stepdad's going hunting with his buddies and I can use his car. Where can I meet you?"

"At the Shop Rite supermarket a few miles north of campus. One of us can leave a car in the parking lot for a little while without worrying about it being disturbed. Okay?"

"I'll be there," Joanna promised. "Look for me at about eleven."

~ * ~

When Joanna awoke on Saturday, the house was so quiet she could hear the ticking of the cuckoo clock in the living room. On the kitchen table was a note in her mother's neat handwriting:

*Gone to work. Be home by about five. Enjoy your day.*

*Love, Mom*

Joanna ate a sparse breakfast, showered, dressed quickly and jotted a note to her mother.

*Mom: I've gone north to visit a friend from school. Might be late, so don't wait for me for dinner. I'm still too stuffed from Thursday anyway. See you when I get home.*

*Love, Jo*

It wasn't really a lie, after all. She *was* going to visit someone from school, although the word "friend" no longer adequately described her connection with Jared.

As she drove, she mulled over that connection. It went against everything she believed moral and decent. Hadn't Catherine always bitterly denounced Joanna's father because he had cheated during their marriage? Didn't she hate him because of it? And how had Joanna herself felt as a child when her dad was with his new family, those other children, while she was left alone in constant fear? She'd hated him, too. Was she part of Jared's doing the same to his children? Maybe she was, and if so, why didn't it bother her more? Why not get out of this before she couldn't? It was almost to that point anyway. Even when she wasn't with him, she thought about him all the time. The feeling was powerful and exciting, but intensely confusing and frightening at the same time. Unanswered was the ever-nagging question of where the relationship was headed.

She pulled into the supermarket parking lot in just under two hours, driving slowly while she looked for the familiar wagon in the sea of cars. There it was, at the end of the row. Seeing her, Jared stepped out and waited as she pulled in to the empty space next to him.

"Let's leave mine here," he said. "No one will bother this old heap and I wouldn't know what to do if anything happened to yours."

"Where are we going?" Joanna asked as he slid into the passenger seat next to her.

"I'll direct you. Turn left onto the highway and we'll go from there." He reached across and touched her knee. "I've missed you and I'm so glad you're here."

"How could I not be here? My mind already was, so why not the rest of me?" That was the answer to all her earlier questions, she knew, and she accepted it without further examination.

They left the residential area and drove into farm country. The further they rode, the larger the wooded areas and the fewer the houses. After about ten minutes, Jared pointed ahead of them. "See that milepost there? Just after it, turn left. There … the narrow driveway where the mailbox is. Turn in and then stop while I open the gate. This is the driveway to Dan's cabin," he explained. "I've been wanting to bring you here."

Joanna pulled onto the lane and waited while Jared opened the gate. He closed it behind her and got back in the car. It was a short drive through dense forest before the little house appeared in a clearing in front of them. It was surrounded on three sides by trees, all but the evergreens bare, holding the promise of heavy foliage come spring. The small front yard had turned winter brown.

"How beautiful. How did Dan ever find this place to build a house?"

"I don't know for sure, but it suits his needs to a 't.' No one bothers him; he can enjoy his solitude and he has plenty of wildlife to keep him company. Ever since his wife died, he's needed a place like this. Their house in town held too many reminders."

They walked up the sidewalk while Jared took a ring of keys from his jacket pocket, sorted through them and opened the front door. "After you."

"Oh, my," she said, taking in everything at a glance, her eyes finally resting on the fireplace that covered the entire wall. "This is lovely. That fireplace is exquisite."

"Dan built it himself. It's made of Jersey stone, and when the light hits it just so, it glitters like it's flecked with thousands of diamonds. I've spent many a night with him sitting here while he talked about Stephanie's death. She was only thirty and Dan's had a terrible time dealing with her loss."

"How awful for them. It's not surprising he's sunk so much energy into this house. It's probably helped him cope with his grief."

Jared took off his jacket and reached for hers. "You're very insightful. Keeping busy has been good therapy for Dan, but he still has a long way to go. This winter is part of the process. He's gone with an expedition to Alaska to do research. On what, I'm not exactly sure, but I know it has something to do with polar habitats. Anyway, he asked if I'd keep an eye on the house and use it once in a while if I needed to get away. I've leaned on Dan a lot, too, when I've needed a friend, and he's always been there for me."

He moved closer to Joanna and hugged her tightly with both arms. "This is what I needed," he said, his eyes half-closed and dreamy. "Now I'm whole."

Before Joanna could answer, he bent and met her lips, kissing her deeply. She felt herself falling, falling, clinging, sinking into him as his kisses grew stronger. He stepped back and took her hand, leading her to the large sofa in front of the fireplace.

"Are you hungry?"

"As a matter of fact, I am."

Jared moved toward the kitchen. "Relax for a minute. I'll be back."

~ * ~

After lunch, they cleared the table, washed the dishes and wrapped the leftovers. With wine glasses refilled, they returned to the sofa in the living room.

Joanna raised her glass in Jared's direction. "That was very satisfying. A toast to the chef!"

After a minute, he looked at her seriously. "It's probably none of my business, but I've been wanting to ask."

"Don't ever 'want to ask.' You know there's nothing I'd keep from you. What is it? You sound so serious."

"I'm curious about something. So far, I've learned quite a bit about you, but I'm surprised there was no one in your life when we met. How is it that someone so beautiful isn't involved with anyone? What about it? Has there been someone important? Have you ever been in love?"

"Have I ever been in love? That's quite a question. Have I ever been in love?"

She sat quietly, sipping her wine. Looking up at Jared, she said, "I suppose I thought I was, but how does anyone know? I mean really, truly know. I was in love with the same boy from third grade until we graduated high school, or at least I thought it was love, but then he ended up breaking my heart. That's a story for another time, if ever.

"My first year here at Manning, I thought I was in love with a man I met in Florida when I was there vacationing with Doris. He found someone closer to home. Both times, I was terribly hurt, but looking back I see neither was real love, not in the 'for life' way. Not in the way that will satisfy me. Does that make sense?"

"Yes, it does. I don't know how to define it either. The older I've gotten, the more I wonder. When I met Vicki, I thought I was in love, and maybe I was. But wouldn't true love have made me fight for what we had instead of giving up on it? Wouldn't true love have made Vicki try harder, too? It's very complicated and maybe there isn't any point in defining it. Maybe we should trust our emotions and follow them wherever they take us. I know I love you. I confess it wasn't something I fought very hard. Having said that, though, I realize the crossroads we've reached, and I can't go on without knowing where you stand and what you want to happen next."

"What I want and what I can have are two different things. I'll be totally honest; I want *you.* I want you to be with me, children or no children. I want to spend the years with you, grow old with you. That probably isn't what you want to hear, but you asked."

Jared got up, went to the kitchen and came back with a full glass of wine and the bottle in his hands. Joanna covered her glass. "I've had enough, thanks. It's a long drive home."

He sipped his wine quietly for several minutes. Finally, he put down the glass and leaned toward her. "I suppose I knew that was coming. I know how strongly I'm attracted to you and I'd be lying if I told you I didn't feel the same from you. It's that connection thing we've talked about since day one.

"I don't know what I thought would happen." Jared paused, looking into space. "Did I think we'd simply meet in the snack bar every once in a while and talk? Did I think we'd just go to the Downtown and listen to Jim? Did I think we could keep our relationship from going forward, taking us to a point where it's too late to turn back? I don't know what I thought."

"You probably didn't think at all. Like me. Oh, I told myself I was thinking. I'm still struggling with the immorality of being so attracted to a married man. But all the time, my heart's pushing me to you, closer and closer until I know as certainly as I've ever known anything that there's no turning back.

"As to your other question, what would I like to have happen now? I want a fairy tale ending." She sighed and turned away. "But fairy tales aren't real, are they? Can I picture myself as the other woman, the one you see when you can snatch a few hours from the family? Can I see myself like that for a long period of time? No, I don't think I can. And how about the children? If you leave them for me, can I live with the guilt? It's a terrible dilemma and right now I don't have any answers."

She reached out and gently caressed his cheek. "I've fallen in love with you," she said in a near whisper. "But I don't know if I could stand the person I would have to be if we were to take this relationship any further."

Jared put both hands in his lap and sat staring at her face, concentrating as if he would never see it again, his eyes sad. Then he looked down, his voice breaking.

"I would never have you be anything but the person you are. I could never hurt you by asking you to diminish yourself in your own eyes. Having gallantly said that, I don't know how I could survive if you were to tell me we couldn't see each other again. I'm the one who's not free, so you're the one who calls the shots. Say the word and I'll find a way to be as invisible to you as I was before we met."

When he looked up, tears were streaming down Joanna's face. "Oh, my darling, don't cry ... please don't cry." He took her in his arms and cradled her close. "I don't want to see you unhappy and yet I can't change the situation I'm in. Please don't cry."

He moved her away just far enough that he could wipe the tears from her face. He put his finger beneath her chin and tilted it up to meet his lips. But this kiss was different, more urgent, as he murmured her name between kisses. Joanna responded, pulling him closer. They rested against the cushions, faces only inches apart, coming together again for kiss after kiss.

Suddenly Jared pulled away, stood and turned his face. It was several seconds before he said anything. When he did, his voice was calm, controlled.

"You'd best be heading home. If we stay here any longer, it will only lead us where we know we can't go."

He turned, his hands raised helplessly at his sides.

"I can't deal with this. I want you like I've never wanted anyone, but the cost to both of us would be too high. For once in my life, I'm doing the right thing. Let's get out of here and I'll come back later to clean up."

Without waiting for her to answer, Jared retrieved their jackets, helped her on with hers and opened the front door. They were quiet as they got in the car, circled the driveway and headed out through the woods. She stopped at the gate; Jared got out and opened it. She drove through to the road and waited for him to get in.

"Do you remember the way back?" Jared asked, his voice strained and unnatural.

Joanna gripped the wheel with her eyes fixed on the road. "I think so."

She pulled into the parking lot and eased over to Jared's car. She turned off the engine, but he made no move to get out. He sat, his eyes downcast. Finally, with a deep sigh he looked up and into her eyes.

"I meant what I said. I could never have you be anything but the person you are. It would hurt you too much to be that other woman you talked about and I'm afraid our relationship wouldn't survive the struggle. Doris was right, wasn't she? Wanting is not having. I don't want to accept that, but it seems to be the only path open to us. I'll step back. Rather than lose you entirely, I promise I'll deal with this dilemma as best I can without compromising you or your future."

He turned and opened the door. Looking back, he reached for her hand and held it tightly for a moment before getting out of the car and closing the door.

"Drive carefully." He leaned down to look into the window. "I'll see you when you get back to campus."

~ * ~

Joanna was vaguely aware of driving home, spending time with her family and going through all the motions, but it happened in a blur, a haze composed of doubt and fear. Was her relationship with Jared over before they'd even begun? What would they do with the feelings that were overwhelming them? In spite of everything, the right and the wrong of it, how could she simply let Jared slip out of her life?

# Nine

*"What am I doing to myself?"*

Joanna was back on campus for three days before she heard from Jared. She made more trips to the snack bar than she could explain, hoping to find him. Finally, after her last class on Thursday, there was a letter in her box. She waited until she was alone in her room before she opened it.

> *My darling Joanna,*
> *This is far more difficult than I thought. Why is doing the right thing so painful? It's been hard to sleep, hard to work, hard to do anything. My mind is in chaos, torn between what I know I should do and what my heart is begging me to do.*
> *Last night, I read to the children before I put them to bed. Michael asked me why I was sad. Funny, we grownups think we're so clever at hiding our emotions. We forget that children don't have any filters between their perceptions and reality. They call it the way they see it, no holds barred.*

*I wonder. Am I hurting them by staying tied to this loveless marriage and being the sad daddy? Or am I asking that question so I can rationalize my way into leaving Vicki? I don't know. Undoubtedly my thinking is clouded by my need for you. Anyway, I find myself constantly aware of how beautifully you would fit into my life and wanting to make it so.*

*Tell me again ... tell me again you love me, but that wanting is not having.*

*Love always,*
*Jared*

Joanna put the letter back in its envelope and went down the hall to the phone.

Jared answered on the first ring.

"Hi, it's me."

"Joanna," Jared breathed softly, his deep voice making her name sound like a prayer.

"I need to see you," she said. "Can you get away tomorrow night?"

"Of course. What time?"

"How about seven?"

"I'll see you then."

She fell asleep that night wondering whether she'd done the smart thing by opening a door her conscience told her should have remained tightly closed.

~ * ~

The next day, she didn't care whether it was smart.

At the club, they sat quietly, looking at one another, hands joined across the table.

Finally, Jared broke the silence. "I was so happy to hear your voice. As the days went by, even after I wrote the letter, I was getting more and more afraid I'd lost you. Of course, I couldn't blame you if you did decide to end everything. I know being with me comes at a heavy price. But when you called—how do I describe the feeling? My heart jumped into my throat and I wasn't sure I'd be able to speak. I don't know where we're going, my darling. I'm struggling with what comes next, although I'm not sorry I've found you and love you like I do. But I want you to know that, if you're suffering because of our relationship, it's best we end it now. Don't you agree?"

Her voice was steady, emphasizing each word. "I. Don't. Agree. Every time I think of what my life would be like without you, I know why I can't let us end. I need to be with you, no matter what the cost or the lonely days when we can't be together. We have a lot of time and I want to spend as much of it as I can with you."

The bar was beginning to fill up with noisy people, making it hard even to hear Jim's piano. Jared finished his cigarette and took the last sip of his drink.

"Shall we go?" he asked.

"Isn't it a little early?"

"Yes, but I can hardly hear you anymore and I want very much to hold you. Shall we?"

"Where to?" she asked as they pulled out of the parking lot.

"Let's go to Dan's." He took the ramp to the highway that ran along the river. "It's not far."

It was pitch dark along the country road. There were no streetlights, and Joanna didn't even see the lane to the woods until Jared turned into it.

"Give me the key," she said. "I'll open the gate."

Jared drove through and Joanna relocked the gate. Minutes later, they were inside the warm cabin.

She sank into the sofa, holding her hands out to Jared. "Come sit."

"I was worried we'd never come here again," Jared said, reaching out to caress her cheek, pushing her hair away from her forehead. "I don't know what I would have done if you hadn't called. I don't know what I'm going to do now that you have."

"I couldn't do anything else. You're part of me and I can't ignore that. Don't you see how lucky we are? How many people have a connection like this, even for a minute? How could we turn our backs on it? Even if it ends tomorrow, I want whatever we *can* have."

She wrapped her arms around his neck, her final words muffled as his mouth covered hers, softly at first and then with more urgency.

Joanna's hand slipped under the collar of his open shirt, caressing his smooth chest. With his free hand, he gently unfastened each button on her blouse, slipping it from her shoulders. He buried his face in her neck.

"I love how your skin feels," he murmured. "What would I do without you?"

"Shhh ... you'll never have to worry about that."

He lay back on the cushions with his eyes closed as she unbuttoned his shirt from his throat to his waist, kissing his chest as her fingers moved.

He eased the strap of her bra off her shoulder and kissed her bare breast softly, circling it with his lips, his breath warm as he reached the nipple, erect and waiting for his kiss. Then he stopped. As if he had heard an alarm or a warning bell, he sat straight and looked at Joanna gravely.

"This can't happen, my darling. Not here, not now. God only knows I want you more than I've ever wanted anyone. I want to make love to you and never stop."

He drew away from her so he could see her face. "Am I the first man for you? I need to know."

She nodded.

"I thought as much. There's a wonderful innocence about you as well as the passion of one far more experienced. And that's another reason why not here and not now," he said, gently replacing her bra strap and lifting her blouse back onto her shoulders, fastening the buttons.

"I don't understand," Joanna said. "Making love with you is what I want as much as you do. What does my being a virgin have to do with anything?"

"It means our first time together will be all the more special. I'm honored beyond words to be the first man you've chosen to be your lover, but that's all the more reason why we'll wait. This isn't the time and place. I don't want to make love with you and then take you back to campus at midnight. I want to love you until we're both exhausted and then fall asleep next to you and find you there when I wake up. I want us to have time when it finally happens. Not this way … not for an hour and then nothing more. I want our first time together to be precious, something always to be remembered and treasured."

He leaned over and kissed her gently. "It will be special," he whispered. "I promise."

~ * ~

Monday morning as she showered, her mind drifted as always to Jared. He'd been tied up with the kids all weekend, except for a quick phone call on Sunday afternoon to say hello. She heard the longing in his voice as he apologized for not being able to be with her.

"Just one generic apology," she'd said. "The children come first; we agreed on that from the beginning. This is not the first and it won't be the last time you'll have to tend to their needs before we can be together."

She gathered her books for class and headed for the snack bar for a quick muffin. It had been several days since she'd been there, several days since she'd done anything that had once been very much a part of her routine.

Jared was at the table for two by the window, sitting across from Doris. They stopped talking when they saw her.

"May I butt in?" she asked, teasing. "Or is this conversation private?"

Jared rose. "Not at all. Doris and I were catching up."

He looked at Joanna with love in his eyes, picked up his briefcase and put on a heavy coat and scarf. "I've got to be on my way. It's gotten quite cold, hasn't it?"

"Before we know it, Christmas will be here," Doris said. "It must be an exciting time for the children."

"Always," Jared agreed. "Their lists keep getting longer, so I suppose Santa will be even busier than ever. Marina doesn't believe anymore, but Michael still waits for the hooves on the roof and she plays along. It's a magical time for them." His hand rested briefly on Joanna's shoulder, then he moved away from the table. "Take care, both of you."

Joanna finished her muffin and hot chocolate in silence. Looking up, she met Doris's gaze.

"Later, Doris. I know you probably have a million questions, but I really can't talk about it here."

"Of course you can't. And I don't have a million questions, or any questions, for that matter. You know me better than that. I want to hear what you need to tell me, not to satisfy my curiosity but to help you in any way I can."

"I'm grateful, believe me. I don't even know what to say that you probably haven't already figured out. Everything's changed, gotten more confused and wonderful at the same time. I love him more than I thought I would ever love anyone."

"I can see that. But I'm sorry your life is in such turmoil. Let's get together Wednesday. If you need to, we can talk then."

On Tuesday, there was a letter.

*My darling Joanna,*

*I've spent the days since Friday alternately being angry with myself and wanting to do it all over again.*

*I'm angry because I keep going one step further in this relationship of ours, knowing we're sinking deeper and deeper into the quicksand, already almost up to our necks in something so potentially fraught with pain.*

*I should be the one to step back and call a halt to this. I am far older than you, far more experienced. Although I've never felt the kind of emotion you bring out in me, I know the path we're taking could bring both of us a lot of heartache. I should step back, but I can't.*

*And still I'm longing for the chance to do it all over again. Why? So I won't stop. So we'll let the wave of feeling sweep us off our feet and carry us with the tide, out further and further, until we're no longer in control, lost in the depths of the love we share.*

*I guess what I'm telling you, my darling, is that my need for you is overwhelming my good sense, my honor, my fear of the future. In days to come, our bond will grow stronger, more gripping. Where will it lead? I wish I knew. I do know, though, that each day I look forward to a few precious moments of either being with you, writing to you or thinking of you. My days begin and end with you.*

*Love always,*
*Jared*

~ * ~

"I'm losing myself," Joanna said, meeting Doris's inscrutable gaze. "Before I met Jared, my life had some kind of direction. I studied hard, I had friends, I went home occasionally and I spent a lot of time with you. Look at me now. My grades are still acceptable, but no thanks to any effort on my part. I haven't been home since Thanksgiving, and even then, I couldn't stay very long. And you and I haven't sat and talked for what seems like months. Okay, I'm exaggerating a bit, but you see the change. I've only known Jared for a few weeks, but that's all it's taken for me to drift off into a whole new world."

She raised both arms, palms upward, and shrugged. "I'm giving up everything because of my feelings for Jared. What am I doing to myself?"

"This is the first time in your life you've ever felt anything like this, isn't it? You've fallen hard for Jared and he for you."

"We connect. That's the only word I can think of that describes what happens between us. We can be together for hours without saying anything out loud and still understand what each other feels."

"I'm not going to ask any questions. I only need to know what you want me to. But keep this in mind: Jared has another loyalty that rises above his feelings for you. Oh, he may not care whether his marriage succeeds or fails. But he very much needs the connection with his children, the feeling they look up to him and love him. Make no mistake about it. Jared will weigh any decision he makes about his future on how it will impact that relationship. I'm afraid you'll come out a poor second, no matter what he feels for you."

"I know. Don't think I don't. I see the look in his eyes when he talks about those kids. Granted, he doesn't talk about them much, probably because he thinks it'll upset me. But when he does, like yesterday when he was talking about Christmas, I feel how much he wants to do the right thing for them. Still, I'm grasping for straws, hoping for a change in his situation that will give us a chance to be together without taking him out of his children's lives."

"Does Jared know you're thinking like this?"

"Probably not. He once asked me what I wanted to happen and I told him I wanted Vicki to disappear and for us to grow old together. He didn't respond one way or the other. Every now and then, though, he says something about not knowing where we'll go in the future, so I guess I've taken that to mean he's actually considering we might go *somewhere*. I'm probably hearing what I want to hear, aren't I?"

"I don't know, honey. One of these days soon you need to have a frank talk with him. I know the excitement of being in love has muddied your thoughts and let you overlook the consequences to *your* life, but somewhere along the way you're going to be hit with them. As long as you're nurturing illusions of a happily-ever-after, I'm afraid you're going to be hit harder than you're prepared for."

"You know me very well. I want a happy ending and I don't see one. But I can't imagine life without Jared, so I keep going forward. I'm like your test subjects, denying what's real. I'm lost in Jared and I don't want to find my way back."

~ * ~

It wasn't long before reality came back anyway. Joanna got her junior practicum assignment at the college's laboratory school.

"I'm looking forward to it," she told Doris as they sat in the snack bar that afternoon. "Ever since I came to Manning, I've been heading toward a career in the classroom without really knowing if I belong there. This is my first real sample of teaching honest-to-goodness kids."

"Don't put too much stock in it," Doris cautioned. "Usually, practicum isn't anything like real teaching. The students are hand-picked—you know, only the best and the brightest—and you're sharing the responsibility with the other members of your team. But it will give you a taste. When do you start?"

"When we get back from Christmas break. We're expected to have our first lesson plan handed in by the tenth and then we actually go into the classroom on the fifteenth. Now that it's gotten here, I've got some butterflies. But I guess that's only natural."

"I wish I could be here to cheer you along."

"Oh, yeah, you're going south for Christmas. I would tell you to have a good time, but I know you will anyway. I have very mixed emotions about Christmas this year, like I did with Thanksgiving."

Doris looked over the rim of her coffee cup. "Because?"

"Jared, of course. I can't imagine not seeing him for so many days."

"Well, it will be this way for as long as his loyalties are divided, so you'd better get used to it."

"I know, but it doesn't matter. My feelings keep growing stronger. I belong with him. It's getting harder and harder to accept I can't be."

For the first time since they met, she saw her friend's eyes glitter with anger.

"I was very much afraid of this," Doris said crisply. "Jared should have thought of the consequences to you from the beginning. Your life's upside down and it's his doing. I'm worried about you, that's all."

"Thanks. I know how much you care about me. It's a shame you see Jared as the villain because it's not all his fault. I'm a big girl; I could have walked away. Who knows? Maybe we can make it work. But even if we can't, that doesn't mean it's all gloom and doom. I'm happy, truly I am. Just being with Jared makes me happy."

"Mirrors and glasses, Jo. Remember them. Denial and distortion. No one's immune from using those defenses when they're needed. No one."

# Ten



On Thursday, there was a letter.

*My darling Joanna,*

*News! Vicki talked with her parents tonight and they've invited the family to spend the week after Christmas in Florida. They always have tons of gifts for the kids anyway. Usually, they spend a few of the vacation days with us here, but this year they want everyone there for the week.*

*Of course, I told Vicki I would make the trip. You understand this is something I have to do. But my offer wasn't received well. Vicki said she'd welcome a week without me around. She said she could use the time to think and decide what she wanted to do with her life. She accused me of forcing her to abandon her career to stay at home and be with the kids while I pursued my goals.*

*Is that what's causing her anger? I know she was preparing for a career in the art business, but once we married, she never talked about it. She and Marina were wonderful together and she was such a good mother. When we found out about Michael's coming, she didn't seem unhappy at all. I thought she welcomed another child as much as I did. I wonder now if she saw Michael's arrival as another long delay before she could pursue her dreams. I wonder if she's been stewing over this ever since he was born. I wish she had let a counselor help her deal with whatever it was, but she didn't. Now it's gotten beyond the point where I care if she figures herself out or not.*

*As much as I'll miss the children, I'm looking forward to being with you as much as we can. Maybe we can find a way to spend a few days alone. I have an idea we can talk about on Friday night ... 7:30? I love you.*

*Jared*

Joanna put the letter down in her lap. She realized she'd been holding her breath as she read, still stunned by the news that Vicki didn't want Jared on the trip to Florida. Although he said he was disappointed about not being with the children, she couldn't miss his tone as he talked about being able to spend time with her.

~ * ~

Jim wasn't at the piano when they walked in. Someone else was at their table, so they sat at the bar.

"Now tell me. I can't wait a minute longer," Joanna said, taking a welcome sip of her drink, feeling the liquor warm her as it went down. "What's this idea of yours?"

"Have you ever seen Manhattan at Christmas?"

"Only once I can remember, when I was about twelve. My mother and I and some of her friends went to the show at Radio City Music Hall. It was so long ago I can't remember much about it."

"Why don't we go?" Jared asked. "Why don't we take a few days between Christmas and New Year's and spend them in the city? There must be a way to work it out. I already know where we'd stay. It would be our very special time, the first of many, I hope. Could you get away?"

"Well, I'll have to be home Christmas day. I should stay Tuesday in case some of the relatives stop by. But by Wednesday my parents will be back at work. I could probably come back then and we'd have three days."

"Are you sure you won't raise suspicion or create a worry for your folks?"

"I'm sure. Ever since I've been in college, I've rarely stayed home the entire Christmas break. Usually, I come back as soon as the dorms reopen so I can study for finals, so if I want to do that, there won't be any questions asked."

"Wonderful. When will you know for sure so I can make the arrangements?"

"I'll talk with Mom tomorrow and mention that I'll probably be coming back to campus on the twenty-seventh. One way or the other, I'll call you."

"Good. As soon as I know it's definite, I'll get everything set up. What would you like to do while we're in the city?"

"Oh, everything we can. You said you knew where we'd be staying. Is it a secret or can you tell me?"

"A very good friend of mine who used to be in Los Angeles theater is an executive with Statler hotels. He's often said I should call him if I was ever coming to the city so he could be sure I was well taken care of. The week we're talking about is a very busy tourist time and maybe he can't do anything on such short notice, but I'll give him a call as soon as you tell me you can make the trip."

"The Statler?" Joanna asked incredulously. "That's very expensive, isn't it? Jared, you can't afford that, can you?"

"You don't have to worry. Joel will take good care of us. As I said, we go way back and we've done a lot of favors for each other. Let me be concerned about the cost."

"Thank you," Joanna said, finishing her drink. "This is so exciting! But won't your friend be curious about who's with you? Won't he expect Vicki?"

"Joel's *my* friend. He's never met Vicki. We never brought anyone along when we got together. And he won't ask questions or pry; that's part of what makes our friendship so special."

"He'll be a very good friend if he can pull this off for us," Joanna said. "Manhattan at Christmas! It sounds so beautiful I can hardly wait."

~ * ~

Her mother's voice was upbeat, filled with her plans for the holidays. "Of course, I'd love to have you stay home right through to New Year's, but I understand you have a life to live, too."

Joanna called Jared immediately.

"Well? Shall I call Joel?"

"Yes. I'll be able to come back to campus on Wednesday morning."

~ * ~

On Tuesday, there was a letter.

*My darling Joanna,*

*I can't believe I'm doing this, but here goes. You can back out of this trip if you need to. There, I said it. As much as I want to spend some really alone, just-the-two-of-us time, of course I realize going to Manhattan brings us to another line yet to be crossed, but once crossed never to be retraced.*

*I want the days with you, Joanna. I want to shut out the real world and live in a fantasy with you in the city of lights and magic. I want to believe we'll always be there, just us two.*

*Think about this, my darling. Think about where these days will take us. Bail out if you must. You have my promise I will understand and never question your decision. I am too far gone to be the noble one. The very thought of being with you for even three precious days is enough to make my heart sing and my spirit soar.*

*You can give me your decision tomorrow night. I know you're going home Thursday, so let's take a quick run to the club. Besides, I have something I want to give you.*

*Love,*
*Jared*

Joanna put the letter down, thinking about what he'd said, the part about magic and reality. It was time she faced the truth: she saw only the magic, felt only the excitement. She had blocked out the troubling voice of truth, pretending nothing existed but the world she wanted to see. Jared's letter was like a splash of cold water. He still saw the reality. Oh, he pushed it aside, to be sure, but he still saw it. Which of them was more honest? Which was less likely to be hurt if it ended? More to the point, did she really believe it could ever end? She knew the answers to those questions and wished she didn't.

~ * ~

The clear winter sky was dotted with stars when she crossed the campus on Wednesday night. Far off on the other side of the lake the faint melody of madrigal singers floated through the crystal night as they began their tour of the dorms, stopping at each to carol and enjoy a hot drink before moving on to the next stop. Often they sang until after midnight, their soft harmonies bringing a hush to the candle-lit buildings.

"What will you do when campus closes down tomorrow?" she asked as they settled in the car.

"I'll go out to Dan's for a bit, I guess. Then I'll enjoy the kids for a day or so until Christmas. They'll be leaving Tuesday and you'll be back Wednesday. At least I hope you'll be back then."

"Let's save that until we get to the club," Joanna said. "I don't want to be interrupted."

Jared looked down at her and raised his eyebrow. "I'm not sure how to take that. Is it good or bad?"

84

"It's good, but there are some things I want to make very clear before we go away together, and tonight's the time to do it."

~ * ~

As Jim began "Unchained Melody," Jared raised his eyebrow again. "Well?"

Joanna took a deep breath and looked at him intently.

"This has to be the last time. Swear to me this will be the last time you'll offer me a way out. If you don't know by now I have nowhere to go, that I couldn't leave you no matter what, then maybe we're not as connected as I thought. I belong with you; I belong *to* you. That's all there is and I don't want to have to question our relationship time and time again."

Jared lifted her hands and caressed them with his lips.

"I don't know how you came to me. I don't know what angel guided you into my life. I know that from the moment I saw you, I knew you would always own a piece of my heart and the longer we're together, the bigger that piece becomes. I keep offering you an out because I feel so guilty over what being with me is doing to you. And yet, I'm powerless to step away, give you back your life and go on with the shambles that would be mine."

"That's just it. I wouldn't want a life without you in it. So please, please don't ever bring this up again. We're beyond turning back; we both know that. Let's look ahead and enjoy the future, whatever it holds."

"You're amazing, truly amazing. Okay, I agree to your terms. No more talk of backing out. No more pangs of conscience. Seize the joy. What a beautiful way to begin the holidays. Oh ... I left something for you out in the car. I'll be right back."

He returned carrying a thin package wrapped with holiday paper and a large red bow. "Merry Christmas. I hope you like it. When you've opened it, I want to tell you why I chose it."

Joanna unwrapped a slender book entitled *This Is My Beloved*.

"Who is Walter Benton? I've never heard of him."

"He's a poet who wrote back in the early forties. I first read his work several years ago and was deeply affected by it. I wondered then what it must be like to love someone with such intensity that the emotion evokes such intense phrases, such beautiful images. When I met you, I understood Benton for the first time. He says things I want to say. I wanted you to have this book so you would know that. One day soon, I'll read his poems to you so you can hear the words I wish I had written for you."

He reached across the table and took the book away. "I want it back now. Just for a few days. I want to pack it and take it to Manhattan with me."

"I didn't even get to read any of the poems!" Joanna exclaimed, astonished.

"You're not meant to, my darling. I wanted to show you the book so you'd know I have a gift for you. I want you to listen to the poems before you read them, so when you do read them, it will be *my* voice you'll hear."

# Eleven


*"He's not worth suffering over."*

"So, did Santa bring you everything you wanted?" Joanna's mother asked as they sat at the kitchen table over lunch the day after Christmas.

"As always. You and Dad manage to make the holidays lovely."

Catherine shifted in her chair so she was facing her daughter.

"Jo, I've had a very strong feeling lately there's something important happening in your life you're not sharing with me. Am I wrong?"

Joanna sat staring at her cup.

"I know you, honey. I've watched you go through the broken hearts, the highs and lows, and I can read you like a book. When you were younger, you always ran to me with everything. I know the expressions in your eyes, and I'm puzzled about what I'm seeing now. Is it so bad you can't tell me about it?"

Joanna looked up, seeing the warmth and understanding that were always there when she needed them.

"Yes and no. There *is* something happening in my life. It's not like anything I've ever felt and maybe that's why I'm reluctant to put it into words. I hope you'll understand when I tell you I'm not ready to talk about it yet. I would love to include you, but it's only been a couple of months and I'm not ready to share it."

Catherine looked at her intently. She got up, walked around the table and hugged Joanna, her arms around her shoulders, her head close to her daughter's.

"I hope it's a good thing for you, Jo. I wouldn't want to see you hurt. I assume there's a man involved in all of this. I wish you could tell me about him because it would ease my concern over why you think you can't. I won't pry, but answer me this, honey. Does he make you happy? Do you come first with him?"

Try as she might, Joanna couldn't fight back the tears. She lowered her head and let them fall onto her hands.

Her mother turned her around and pushed away the chair so Joanna could stand and be folded into a comforting hug.

"I was afraid of this. Whoever he is, honey, he's not worth suffering over. Anyone who truly cared for you wouldn't make you cry."

Joanna pulled away and walked hastily into the bathroom. She came back, drying her eyes.

"I'm sorry. I didn't mean to do that. I didn't mean to worry you and now I'm sure I have. This thing is so very complicated, that's why I don't want to talk about it yet. I don't know where it's going, if anywhere. But I can tell you he's worth a few tears and some unhappy moments. I'm okay, just somewhat overwhelmed, but really all right. Please, please don't worry," she said, hugging her mother again.

"Promise me, Jo. Promise you'll talk to me whenever you need someone to lean on. I know you and Doris have a very special relationship and she's always there for you, but don't shut me out, honey. You've always come first with me. I only want your happiness. Promise?"

"I promise. When I can, I promise I'll tell you everything."

~ * ~

As Joanna repacked her bag, she included the sweaters and slacks she'd gotten from her parents. Her aunt's present was especially welcome, though very uncharacteristic. It was a nightgown, not at all like the casual things one would expect for college dorm wear. This was pale blue satin, ankle length, with thin straps at the shoulders. With it was a matching robe of the same pastel shade, the collar and sleeves trimmed in a deep navy. A pair of slippers, furry mules in the same dark blue, completed the ensemble. It was an unusual gift, but very welcome for reasons Joanna couldn't reveal.

~ * ~

Early Wednesday morning, Joanna came out of her room to find Joe in his hunting gear at the door waiting for his friends, a coffee mug in his hand.

"Here, hon, let me put that bag in the car for you. I can do it on my way out."

"Thanks, Dad. I've got to get going, too. Is Mom in the kitchen? I want to be sure to see her before I take off."

"No, honey, I'm here," her mother said, coming out of the bedroom buttoning the sleeves on her uniform. "You know I wouldn't let you leave without saying goodbye."

Joanna gave her mother a hug and kissed her on the cheek. As Catherine began to say something, a truck pulled up in front of the house and tooted the horn.

"That's for me," Joe announced, reaching for his hunting rifle and duffel bag and taking Joanna's suitcase in the other hand. He leaned over and kissed Catherine lightly. "You know where I'll be. Call the camp if you need me. I'll be back on Friday afternoon. Have a good time, Joanna. Be careful with my limousine. I'll see you when you get back."

"I'm going too," Joanna said, putting on her coat. "I'll see you Saturday. And please remember what I said—don't worry. Everything is just fine."

"You'd say that, no matter what," Catherine admonished, "but I trust you'll tell me about it when you're ready."

~ * ~

Joanna's excitement mounted the closer she got to the campus. Could it be possible that in only a few hours she would be in Manhattan with Jared?

When she arrived, she went up to her room, conscious of the utter quiet of the dormitory, none of the other students having returned so early. Carefully assessing the contents of the little suitcase she quickly unpacked, she matched the outfits together and exchanged one sweater for a heavier one. After packing everything into a much larger piece of luggage, Joanna let herself out of the dorm just as Jared pulled up to the curb. It seemed as though they were the only two people at Manning. The parking lots were nearly deserted, with no signs of life on the paths between buildings. Jared put her bag in the back of the wagon and pulled away from the dorm. Sitting close to the window, Joanna fought the urge to kiss him hello. The minute they rounded the corner onto the highway, she slid over to him, put her arm on the back of the seat behind his head and lightly caressed his neck.

"I'm so glad to see you. It was only a few days, but I missed you very much."

He smiled over at her and leaned sideways for a brief kiss, his eyes still on the road.

"You haven't said anything, Jared. Is something wrong?"

"No, my darling, not now. I wish I could say the same for the last few days."

"Why? What happened? Was it the children?"

"No, thank goodness. They're fine. Christmas Day was fine. The children were marvelous as always. They loved their gifts. I guess that was the start of it all, their excitement." He lit a cigarette and continued. "You see, they wanted to show everything to their friends. What I didn't realize was Vicki hadn't told them they'd be leaving for Florida so soon, so they thought they'd be home for a while. We talked about it and they were okay with leaving everything at home ... okay, that is, until they found out I wasn't going with them. Vicki hadn't told them that, either. It's my fault; I left it to her to explain I wasn't going. I should have handled the situation better. Marina was upset, but you should have seen Michael. He's a quiet child, so he didn't cry or throw a tantrum or anything like that. He simply came to me and sat in my lap, his head on my chest, asking why I was staying here and not going with him. How could I explain I wasn't invited? That, in fact, I was told not to go along? So, I made some lame excuse about needing to stay home so I could work, but they begged me to forget about work and go with them. I managed to get Vicki aside in the kitchen and told her I thought she should reconsider for the kids' sakes, but she was adamant. She said their insistence on my going showed they were too attached to me and needed time away as much as she did. There was no reasoning or arguing with her, so I went back in and told the children I was sorry but I couldn't go."

He stopped and looked at her as they paused at a traffic light.

"I hated the looks in their eyes. Marina announced she wasn't going and Michael didn't say anything, just wrapped his arms around my leg until I picked him up and hugged him. I sat with them and talked about how much their grandparents wanted to see them, about the wonderful gifts that would be waiting for them and how I would be home to see all of their new toys when they got back. I talked, Joanna, oh did I talk! Only once did Michael say anything and that was to ask if I'd promise to be there when they came home. Of course I promised. Then I took them up to bed and read to them until they settled down. When I went back downstairs, Vicki was in the spare bedroom she's commandeered as her own refuge with the door closed and the light out. I tried to talk to her, but she didn't answer. This morning, the airport taxi was at the door at nine and they were gone. I can't get over how frightened they were. I know they sense the tension between Vicki and me and they're probably afraid I'm going to leave them."

Joanna searched his face. "I'm so sorry. That must have been devastating. Were the children still upset this morning?"

"No, you know how kids are. They were far from overjoyed, but once again I told them I'd be there when they got home and they went down the porch steps holding onto Genna's hands. Vicki got into the cab without looking at me. Probably just as well. I'm sure my resentment over how this whole thing was handled would have shown on my face."

"Jared, listen to me. I know how this must be eating at you. We don't have to go to Manhattan now. Your heart can't be in this trip after what's happened. We can go to Dan's for a while and talk and make the trip another time."

Jared pulled the car over to the curb and turned to her.

"Forgive me, my darling, but I had considered asking you to postpone the trip. I was afraid my mood might spoil our first time away together. I confess that was my thinking yesterday, when you were at home and I was so involved with the children and so mad at Vicki. Now? Now, they're on their way to Florida where I can't be of any help to the kids or further aggravate Vicki and you're here next to me. Being able to tell you about it has helped tremendously. Thank you for giving me a chance to change our plan, but no thanks. There's nothing to be gained by that except to deprive us of the special memories we'll be making every second we're together. I promise you, being with you will be the best tonic I could ask for. Are you still willing to go?"

Joanna reached out and gently caressed his cheek. "Then let's go. What are we waiting for? There's a magical city out there waiting for us."

For the rest of the trip, Jared talked about the children and their reactions to their gifts. Joanna told him about her holiday, including the conversation with her mother.

"I'm sorry she's so worried. I'm sorry you can't tell her about me, and what we've found together. I hope it didn't spoil your time with her."

"No, nothing could do that. Sure, she's worried; she's my mother and she wouldn't be my mother if she didn't worry. Nothing I can say will stop her, not until she sees I'm doing okay and nothing tragic has happened to me. Some day I'll find a way to tell her about you and she'll simply have to understand."

~ * ~

At noon, Jared pulled the car under the canopied entrance of the hotel where the bellman removed their bags. Leaving the car for the parking attendant, Jared and Joanna went up the steps into the lobby to the front desk.

"Welcome to the Statler, Dr. Fowler," the clerk said. "Mr. Dunbar left this for you with instructions to us to make you comfortable."

Jared opened the envelope bearing the hotel crest and read the brief note, smiling broadly. "Good ol' Joel," he said, taking Joanna's arm. "He came through for us in spades."

When they reached their floor and found the room, Jared paused before inserting the key.

"I feel like I should pick you up and carry you over the threshold," he said, his eyes twinkling. "What would you say to that?"

"I'd say never mind. I'm trying to keep both feet on the ground, thank you very much."

The door swung open on a large room richly furnished in deep burgundy and gray, the plush carpet cushioning each step. Joanna saw the long, large windows and rushed over to part the drapes and look out.

"Oh, come look at this! It's all of Manhattan right outside our window. It's breathtaking."

Jared stood behind her with his arms around her waist, his face close to hers, looking over the skyline. "What's breathtaking is you," he said, kissing her throat. "I can't believe we're really here."

She turned and met his kiss, long and slow, savoring the taste of him, the lingering aroma of his skin.

"Ah, that's what I needed," he said. "Do you know how good it feels to hold you? I wish I knew how to tell you. But that will come later, even if they're not *my* words."

# Twelve

*"Could God understand?"*

Jared came out of the bathroom as Joanna finished putting away her things. "How about some lunch? Hungry?"

"Famished. Seems it's been a long time since breakfast."

They had lunch in one of the hotel cafés, looking out the windows at the crowds of people hurrying by, jostling each other as they passed.

"I never fail to be amazed by the pace of this city," Jared said. "How about we put on our woolies after lunch and take a walk? I'd like us to see a few blocks in daylight before the lights come on so we can really appreciate the effect. Are you game?"

"Sure. I'm ready any time you are."

~ * ~

It was a breathtaking experience. The huge skyscrapers formed a kind of tunnel and the wind raced between the buildings, accentuating the cold. They walked for what seemed like hours, swept along by the tide of people that seemed to travel at breakneck speed on the sidewalks.

Joanna was speechless. She discovered after the first try that talking was almost pointless. The noise of the taxis, the incessant clatter of car horns and the press of people made conversation impossible. Finally, they broke free of the crowd and ducked into a doorway.

"Are you tired, my darling? Shall we go back and rest before dinner?"

Joanna gave him a grateful smile. "If you don't mind. All this walking is really exhausting. I thought I was made of tougher stuff, but I could use a break."

"Say no more." Jared stepped to the curb and hailed a passing cab.

Back at the hotel, they stopped at a piano bar and sank into heavily padded leather chairs. Jared ordered manhattans, lit a cigarette and leaned back, closing his eyes. "It's been a long time since I've walked that much or as fast. After dinner, we'll hop a cab and see the sights without the strain on our feet. When we get somewhere we want to explore, we'll get out, walk a bit and then find another cab. How does that sound?"

Joanna stifled a yawn. "Excuse me," she said, smiling. "It really isn't the company. Your cab idea sounds perfect. I'm not sure how much more my feet could take today. Is there a special restaurant in the hotel you'd like?"

"Joel has taken care of that for us. It was part of his Christmas gift, he said in his note."

"I'm looking forward to meeting him. I want to thank him in person."

"I had hoped to see Joel, too. But he's off this week to be with his parents. They're getting up in years and he tries to see them at the holidays if he can. He sent his regrets but said he would love to meet you one of these days."

When they were back in their room, Jared sat and lit a cigarette.

"I hate to intrude on our time, but would you mind if I called the children to be sure they got to Florida safely and all's well?"

"Of course not. Go ahead and I'll get ready for dinner.

Joanna dressed in a long, black velvet skirt with a white blouse trimmed in lace. When she came out of the bathroom, he was still sitting, his cigarette burned down to the filter in the ashtray.

"Is everything all right?" Joanna asked, moving to him and kneeling at his feet. "You look like it didn't go well."

"No, my darling, it was fine. I spoke to both of them, although Vicki wouldn't come to the phone. Her mother answered and at first didn't want to put the children on the line, but I think their excitement at hearing who it was made her think better of it. Marina was all excited about her gifts from her grandparents and Michael got his usual assortment of trucks, books and games, so he's happy, too. They miss me, they said, but they sounded happy. It's just that this is the first time they've been away for so long and I'm finding it a little strange."

"I understand," Joanna said, resting her head on his knee. "When you aren't with them, you don't know what's being said or done that might influence them. Did they mention their mother?"

"No. Vicki's mother said she was too busy to talk to me, but her tone told me Vicki simply didn't want to. But enough ... let me look at you." She stood and turned slowly for his approval. "You're so beautiful, my darling. The simpler the garment, the lovelier you are in it. Give me five minutes and I'll be ready."

Joanna caught her breath at the sight of him when he came back into the room. He was darkly handsome in his black trousers, white turtleneck and black jacket, looking every bit like the Prince Charming of her dreams. How, she wondered, did someone so incredible choose her?

~ * ~

After dinner, they waited at the hotel's front entrance where a bellman quickly summoned a cab.

"Well, love, how do you like it?" Jared asked an awestruck Joanna as she peered through the passenger window. "Isn't it terrific?"

"Terrific doesn't cover it. It's like a fairyland."

"Let's ride around some and then go to Rockefeller Center. Would you like to do that?"

"You're my guide. Anywhere you say."

"Take us for a long ride," Jared told the driver. "How about up Fifth Avenue to Central Park, across and then back down to Rockefeller Center."

When they arrived, Jared helped Joanna from the cab and they turned to look at the shimmering fantasy in front of them, the huge tree decorated lavishly for the holiday. They went up the walk that encircled the skating rink below, found a niche in the crowd and stood pressed together watching the graceful figures on the ice.

"Are you cold, my darling?" Jared asked, pulling Joanna close. "The wind's died down, but it's still really brisk."

"No, I'm not cold, but it does feel better this way," she said, snuggling into his coat.

"Would you feel up to a short stroll?"

"Of course. Where to?"

"Only across the street. I thought you'd like to see St. Pat's. It's very impressive."

The interior of the Gothic cathedral was hushed and aglow with dancing lights from votive candles in tiered banks along the altar rails of the sanctuaries. Women in lace veils or with tiny handkerchiefs on their heads knelt before statues, deep in prayer. Joanna hastily flipped the velvet hood of her long coat over her hair as they sat in a pew looking at the windows reflecting the lights from inside the church.

As she sat, her Catholic upbringing took over and she remembered her catechism, the hours of instruction in the tenets of the Church. She had been such a deeply religious child, fantasizing about becoming a nun, spending long hours in church, believing that by living a godly life she would wind up in heaven for all eternity. How could that same girl be here? And why wasn't she feeling guilty? Where had her parochial school conscience gone? How could she be sitting in God's house with a married man, knowing very soon she would be sharing his bed? Could God understand? Wouldn't He want her to have this kind of love in her life? Surely, He would want Jared to be happy, too. She glanced at Jared and met his smile. She realized instantly there wasn't enough guilt in the world to make her give up this time with him. They lingered for several more minutes, then made their way to the massive doors.

"Are you ready to go back?" Jared asked. "We have plenty of time to see more, but now I want to be with you, just the two of us in our own room behind our own door. What do you say?"

Joanna looked at his pensive face. "I want to be with you. It's been a full day, and I'm as ready as you are."

~ * ~

The housekeeping staff had seen to everything. One small lamp was lit, the coverlet on the bed was folded down and two soft terry robes with the Statler emblem were laid out.

Still on Jared's arm, Joanna turned and fitted herself to him, molding her body to his from the waist down as she took off his jacket, reached under his shirt and pulled it over his head. His hardness pressed against her as she kissed his neck and shoulders. Suddenly unsure of what she should do next, she stepped back, her hands still on his chest.

Sensing her reticence, Jared leaned forward and kissed her lightly. Slipping her coat off and letting it fall, he unfastened the buttons on her skirt, which followed the coat into a dark velvet heap on the floor. The lacy white blouse took a little longer to shed. Jared slowly undid one button after another, finally pushing the garment off her shoulders, his eyes on her face.

Jared's mouth was on her shoulder as he reached around and deftly undid the hooks on the bra. Cupping her breasts in his hands, he kissed them, pausing to look in her eyes before moving from one to the other. Gently, he guided her onto the bed, leaning over to arrange the pillows behind her head. After he had removed the rest of their clothing, Joanna reached down to touch him tentatively, not knowing how she could bring him pleasure.

He moaned softly as he caressed her. "Ah, God, you are so beautiful," he whispered, kissing her from her neck to her ankles. "I have never seen anyone so beautiful."

As his hands moved on her skin, Joanna drifted into a world of sensation. She let herself surrender to his touch, losing herself in it. She was vaguely aware when he gently parted her thighs, his fingers working magic as they slowly caressed and then found their way inside. Joanna felt a strange new heat spreading over her, her pulse racing faster and faster. When at last he entered, there was no real pain, just an insistent pressure that made her gasp as he filled her, their connection taking on a whole new dimension. He stopped for a moment and then very slowly began to move, leading her in a dance they'd rehearsed for many weeks. Carried on a tide of feeling that ebbed and flowed, time lost all meaning while somewhere far away she heard Jared's muffled voice call her name.

Holding her close, Jared looked down, his eyes dark and deep. He bent and kissed her—her eyes, her forehead, her nose, her chin and finally her mouth, parting her lips with his tongue, gently nipping with little kisses, arousing her. Responding with equal fervor this time, moving in rhythm with his body, she reached far into her soul to give him everything she had, to take everything she could, to become part of him in a way that fused them into one, one heart beating in one chest, nothing separate, nothing distinct, a searing heat that melted them together inexorably, eternally. When it happened, Joanna was aware only of the rising warmth at the core of her being, spreading out like ripples in a pond until she was consumed with feeling and unspeakable pleasure. Then they were still, breathing becoming slower, more relaxed.

Jared's voice was huskier and deeper than ever. "My darling, my darling, I will remember this night for as long as I live."

He moved to her side, one hand holding hers while the other traced the outline of her face as she turned to look at him, the glow of their lovemaking still shining in her eyes.

His eyebrows knit in a slight frown. "Did I hurt you? I would hate it if I caused you any pain."

"No. I don't know how to describe it. All my life I've wondered what it would be like when I finally found the man I'd love. I fantasized like most women, I suppose. I read everything I could get my hands on about making love and I talked with friends who'd already done it. I dreamed it would be wonderful, but there was nothing that would have prepared me for this, for you, for what I feel when you touch me. I love you now more than ever, and I always will."

"You've given me the greatest gift, my darling," he said, rising on an elbow to better see into her eyes. "Now I understand the poets who say life only has meaning when it's shared with one true love, the one person who was destined to make life complete. You are that person for me. I love you more than I ever thought possible."

They lay quietly for a while, eyes closed.

"Can I get you anything, my darling?" he asked finally. "Are you hungry or thirsty?"

"Something to drink would be wonderful!"

Jared swung his legs over the edge of the bed and stood, teetering slightly then regaining his balance. "How about a manhattan or two?"

"Sounds heavenly."

She watched as he turned toward the telephone. She had never seen a man's naked body and was fascinated by his beauty and quiescent power. As she moved on the bed, Joanna felt wetness between her legs. She reached for her robe and stood.

"Jared?"

"What is it?"

"Look here." Joanna pointed to a reddish stain on the sheet where she had been lying. "Aren't you supposed to take that and hang it out the window or something?" she asked with a grin. "Isn't that some kind of trophy that wins you the admiration of all the tribesmen?"

Jared chuckled. "You've got us confused with royalty." His expression turned serious, his eyes bright. "But no, my darling, it's not a trophy. It's part of the gift you gave me tonight, one you'll never give again, so it's all the more precious."

# *Thirteen*

*"My life is forever changed."*

When Joanna awoke, she found Jared propped up on the pillows reading the Benton book. Seeing her open her eyes, he put it down and took her in his arms, kissing her softly then more urgently. Joanna responded with renewed passion, her desire to please him guiding her hands, her mouth and her tongue instinctively in ways that heightened their senses. When they'd reached another jarring climax and rested in each other's arms, Joanna kissed Jared's chest lightly and ran her hand from one nipple to the other.

"I could stay here and love you all day," she said, touching his lips with her finger.

She felt his smile. "Lovely. I wonder which of us would wear out first. But, since you offered..."

~ * ~

"So where are we going?" Joanna asked later after they'd showered together and had a room-service breakfast. She pulled a heavy knit sweater over her head and put on a red wool scarf and heavy jacket.

"How does the top of the world sound? I can't take you to Mount Everest, but the Empire State Building ought to be just as good. Besides, the view is simply unmatched."

As they went through the doors of the hotel, a chill wind hit them with surprising force. Even the doorman was holding his cap as he greeted them.

After a short walk, they entered the revolving doors of the tall skyscraper and took one of the elevators to the eighty-sixth floor.

In front of them was a parapet about four or five feet high topped with a steel fence in a lacy diamond-shaped pattern that allowed them to peer through at the sights below. Grasping the fence, Joanna looked down and gasped.

"Oh Jared, look at this, look at this!" she exclaimed to him over her shoulder.

Holding her close, Jared peered out. "There's Central Park and out there's New Jersey," he said. Pointing out all the things he wanted her to see, he leaned forward to catch her lips as she turned to speak, leaving soft kisses.

"This is a whole new world," he said. "We're seeing *our* world for the first time. I feel that way about everything now, my darling. We've come into a world of our own and nothing will ever be the same again."

Walking from one side of the building to another, they picked out familiar sights on the ground. People came and went unnoticed, as though they were the only ones there.

"I wish we could stay here," Joanna said. "Nothing can touch us. We're safe from the worries and problems, just us two with no one else in our world, our Oz."

"Wouldn't that be wonderful? When we get back to Manning, I want to show you a place that might be almost as good for us. But for now, this is our own Emerald Palace."

"It is, isn't it? If only it were a bit warmer. How long have we been up here? What time is it anyway?"

Jared pushed away his glove to see his watch. "It's after three. I could use a cup of hot coffee and a cigarette, maybe a sandwich. Might not even want to drink the coffee, just hold it to warm my hands. What do you say? Had enough?"

"I think so. I can't feel my nose."

Down on the first floor, they found a coffee shop and gratefully slid into a booth against the wall. When the waitress had taken their order, Jared reached across the table for Joanna's hand.

"I meant what I said when we were up there. The world is different now, isn't it? Do you feel it?"

"Yes, I do. *We're* different. When we came to Manhattan there were two of us. In a few hours, we stepped over an imaginary line that took away our separateness and we emerged one person. I'll never again be the Joanna you met two months ago. How could I be? I suspect it'll be a struggle to go back to that life, to try to function as just another college student. No, I'm a different person, more a part of you than ever. My life is forever changed, for the better, I believe, for having found you to love."

His eyebrow lifted. "For the better? In spite of everything, the uncertainty, the lack of a future to plan, you can still see this change in your life as a good one?"

Joanna waited to reply while their sandwiches were put on the table.

"Uh-huh. As long as I can remember, I've never wanted more out of life than to be loved and to find someone I could love with kindness and respect. Then I met you. At first, though I was enormously attracted to you, I admired your talent and your achievements. Then, as I got to know you better, I found I had a great deal of respect for you. Many men with marriages as unhappy as yours would simply walk out, put themselves first and to heck with the kids. My dad did; he walked away and I know growing up without a father took a heavy toll on me. As hard as it is sometimes to accept your loyalty to the children, I respect you for it. So you see, finding you has made a significant change in my life. And because of who and what you are, that change is for the better. I have what I wondered if I would ever find and, no matter what happens, I'll never lose it."

"My wonderful Joanna. You mention your birth father often, but you haven't talked about him much. Why?"

She paused, choosing her words carefully. "My father wasn't really in my life when I was growing up. Oh, I saw him on the holidays when I would go to visit him and his family, and as I grew older, we went to dinner occasionally and talked on the phone now and then. In spite of the fact she remarried when I was ten, I truly don't think my mother ever got over the hurt of his leaving. That decision of his to abandon us colored our lives in ways we wouldn't have been able to imagine. An angry mother and vengeful grandparents raised me to hate him. As soon as I was old enough, I even changed my name from Craig to Ransome."

Her voice dropped very low. "So how could I live with myself if you did the same thing to your children? As much as I want to be with you for the rest of my life, how could I be the new wife your children resent? I haven't come to terms with that yet. But forgive me if I don't want to think about it now. I want to look in the mirror wearing Doris's funhouse lenses and say there's nothing wrong with what I see. Is that too much to ask?"

"No, my darling, it isn't. Lord knows I've been doing the same thing, trying desperately to make this our reality because I want more than anything to stay with you." Tears welled in his eyes. "No, I can't be the dad who walks away. But a lot of what happens will depend on Vicki as well as me. When she gets back, I'm going to ask again that she see someone, offer to go with her if necessary, just to get her to a counselor. Staying married to her for the sake of the children won't help them if we don't deal with the anger. That isn't what I want for Marina and Michael. Or for me."

He sighed and reached for his coat and gloves. "All that awaits, my love. For now, though, the evening is here, the city lights are bright and cheery and we should go back to our little one-room home where we're warm and I can love you to sleep." He hugged her close as he helped her with her coat.

In the room, they hung up their coats, put away the scarves and gloves and sank down in the chairs. Joanna closed her eyes, not even opening them when she felt her shoes being removed and Jared's hands rubbing her feet. He put one under his arm while he worked on the other until both were pink and warm. She opened her eyes. "Thank you. That felt wonderful."

"Be back," he said. When he returned, he had changed into one of the terry robes. "Now I'm more comfortable, too. Do you want to get out of those heavy clothes?"

"As a matter of fact, I do. I want to put on something special."

Taking a bundle from the drawer, Joanna went into the bathroom and stripped off her clothes. She splashed her face with warm water, brushed her hair swiftly and then dropped the pastel nightgown over her head, adjusting the straps on her shoulders. The matching peignoir went on next, followed by the slippers. Joanna turned out the light and went back into the room.

Jared was asleep on the bed. On the nightstand was the book of poetry he'd bought her for Christmas. Taking a blanket from the closet, Joanna covered him and sat on the edge of the bed watching him. His face was beautiful in repose. He was breathing lightly, looking content and serene. Joanna loved him so much she thought her heart would burst. What would become of them? How could this miracle they had found ever be lost? She sighed, lay back on the pillows and closed her eyes. It was warm and comforting, being there. She knew with Jared she would always feel this safe and loved. Almost immediately she was asleep, her breathing unconsciously matching his.

~ * ~

When they awoke, they were entwined in one another's arms. Jared kissed her gently.

"I love your gown, my darling. Blue is definitely your color."

"Thank you. I hoped you'd like it." Her voice was thin, her eyebrows knit thoughtfully.

"What is it? What's on your mind?"

"I didn't want to talk about this, not now anyway, while we're here together in a place where problems shouldn't exist. But I guess I can't avoid it. I need you to promise me something."

"If I can, you know I will."

"Don't forget me when you're making decisions about the future."

Jared started to say something, but Joanna put her fingers to his lips. "I'm not finished yet. Promise me you'll remember what we have, what we've found here. I don't want you ever to forget this, no matter what. Promise me?"

"Oh, my darling, how could I ever forget? No matter what the decision or when it has to be made, how could I leave you out of it?"

"I don't know, but I'm terribly afraid. I know I'll never stand in your way if you decide to spend the rest of your life with Vicki for the sake of the children. I've been there; I've been Marina and Michael, and I would never want their lives to be as tainted as mine has been. I won't be able to pressure you. But what we've shared is all that will argue my cause when you have to weigh your options."

Jared turned and held her close. "I will never forget you, my darling. Never. No matter what happens. No matter where our lives take us. I will never forget you. I love you, and I always will."

She clung to him as if he were a life preserver in a raging sea, her face buried in his neck. Finally, she pulled away.

"I'll try not to bring this up again. We'll face whatever we have to. But I want you to know you are who I want, you will always be who I want, for as long as I live." She kissed his hands then rested her head on his chest. After a while, she stirred.

"Why don't we lighten up a little and order some dinner?"

~ * ~

They ate mostly in silence, struggling to find a way to erase the somber mood Joanna had unwittingly created.

After dinner, he stood and crossed to her chair, taking her face in his hands. "Do you know how happy you make me? I know I'm running out of ways to tell you." He went to the table by the bed, picked up the book and came back to sit in the chair next to Joanna.

"I thought of this last night, after the last time we made love. Listen...

> "'Your eyes never opened after the last kiss.
> "'We had loved hard—it's all over your throat and hair, it lies on your mouth like a wild red flower; it's on your cheeks and forehead in waning radiance. Your hand half-sleeping finds me...your touch is very dear.'"

"Benton has a way of putting my own feelings into words. Listen," he said, as he read several verses. He put the book down and continued to recite from memory, his voice growing husky and unsteady.

> 'I need love more than ever now...I need your love, I need love more than hope or money, wisdom or a drink.'

His eyes filled with tears. 'And God has made no other eyes like yours.' His voice broke, and he took her into his arms. She felt his tears on her face, but he would not release her far enough for her to look into his eyes. He stood holding her tightly.

"Forgive me, my darling," he said finally. "Give me a minute."

When he came out of the bathroom, he'd regained his composure. He smiled apologetically. "I don't know what came over me. I'm not normally such an emotional person. Something in you brings out the sentimental fool in me, I suppose."

"I don't ever want to make you sad," Joanna said.

"You don't; you always make me very happy." He moved to the phone and called room service to order a pitcher of manhattans.

"I want to freshen up a bit," she said, touching his arm as she walked into the bathroom. She stood for a long time looking in the mirror at an unfamiliar face—older, sadder, with eyes that foresaw impending tragedy, lips swollen from the ferocity of their passion. Who was this woman? Who had she been before? Who would she be when reality intruded as it inevitably would? Joanna knew the answer. She also knew she would always belong to Jared, no matter what the future held.

He had poured the manhattans and added the cherries, lowered the volume on the radio and put out all the lights but one. They sat drinking in silence for a few minutes.

"Tell me more about you, Jared. It seems like I've done all the talking about myself and you've been quiet about your family. Tell me about them."

"There's not a lot to tell. I told you before I joined the Navy to get away from home, but I didn't mean to make it sound so bad. My mother and I were very close; she was a good friend as well as a parent. It was a different story with my father. He didn't seem to be able to express his emotions well. I don't remember ever being kissed by him."

"That must have been a difficult way to grow up. You deserve a lot of credit for turning into the loving, demonstrative person you are. Your children certainly are the beneficiaries of that love."

"I've tried to learn from the shortcomings of my father. It was very hard being both mother and father to the kids after Vicki began to withdraw. I don't know what I would have done without Genna these last months."

"Do you ever talk to her about your troubles with Vicki?"

"No, not really. She sees what's going on. Once in a while I see an expression on her face that tells me she's as puzzled as I about what's happened to Vicki. She seems to want to help me, to make life easier if she can by pitching in with the kids and the house. I don't know what she thinks will happen down the road."

Jared finished his manhattan, laid his head on the back of the chair and closed his eyes. "Mmmm, that was excellent."

Joanna still had half a glass left. Jared's eyes stayed closed, so she picked up the book and read the rest of the poems while she sipped the cocktail. Benton was a sensitive and talented poet. His work was filled with emotion and imagery, truly unlike anything she'd ever read.

Her eyelids heavy with fatigue, Joanna reached over and caressed Jared's forehead until he opened his eyes dreamily.

"Did I do it again? I'm sorry. You leave me feeling deliciously relaxed, so much so it's hard to avoid falling asleep. That doesn't make me very good company."

"You're the only company I want," Joanna said, taking his hand. "For now, though, I think we could both use some sleep. Come to bed."

All Joanna remembered was Jared's warm, wonderful body, the tenderness of their lovemaking, the ferocity and the gentleness of his kisses as she fell asleep, his hand across her chest, resting lightly on her shoulder.

~ * ~

Joanna opened her eyes with a start. Jared was still, his head almost on her shoulder. She lay there and listened to his quiet breathing, watching him.

Today was their last day in Manhattan. Tonight would be their last together for who knew how long. Her throat tightened, and the hot tears filled her eyes. What would life be like when they went back? Nights in a dormitory room, days going through the motions of being a student and an occasional time spent with Jared at the club or in the snack bar? After this? After this, they should be going home together. They should be able to slip into bed each night together, have breakfast together and love as freely as they had these past two days. She was overwhelmed with sadness. Getting up soundlessly, she went into the bathroom, sank to the floor on the soft carpet and sobbed quietly.

Dawn was just bringing the faintest of lights into the room when she returned to bed, no tears left to shed. She stood looking down at Jared's handsome face, her heart heavy. She slid under the covers as close to him as she could get. He stirred slightly and reached out to touch her before sleep pulled him back. One more day.

# Fourteen

*"We do have to go back, don't we?"*

When Joanna awoke, Jared sat in the chair reading. There was a breakfast cart next to the table with deep red carnations in a vase on the tray.

"I didn't have the heart to wake you. You were sleeping so soundly. So I ordered breakfast and let Mr. Benton keep me company while I waited for you. Did you sleep well?"

"Very," Joanna lied. "And you?"

"Slept like the happy man I am. Breakfast?"

"Give me a sec," she replied, sitting up. "I'll be ready in a minute."

The face in the mirror really needed some cosmetic help. Her eyes were swollen from the night's tears and she looked very tired. Joanna applied a cold washcloth to her eyes and sponged her face. After she'd brushed her teeth, she used the washcloth again, hoping it would erase some of the evidence of the kind of night she'd had. She straightened her shoulders and went back into the room. Jared had put out the meal, laying one carnation over her plate. He rose and came to her as she neared. Putting his arms around her, he raised her face to his, his eyes searching.

"What's wrong, my darling Joanna? What's happened?"

He traced her eyelids lightly with his index finger, down her cheeks to her mouth and back, his hand smoothing the hair at her forehead. "Joanna? You've been crying. Tell me."

"I had a hard time sleeping, that's all," Joanna lied again. "I must have had a bad dream that woke me and then I couldn't get back to sleep. I'll be fine after I've had my morning orange juice and some of those fluffy eggs."

She kissed him lightly and sat, taking a long drink.

Jared ate slowly. "I'm concerned about you, my darling. Obviously, you didn't sleep well and I don't believe you're telling me the truth about why. But I won't push you to talk about it unless you want to. What time did you wake up?"

Joanna gave him a grateful look. "I don't honestly know. I didn't see the clock. Anyway, it was very dark and then almost light when I came back to bed, I do know that."

"Then I suggest an easy day. The bellboy said it's supposed to be unseasonably warm, in the lower fifties. Let's take advantage of it and do some sightseeing. Do you like sailing?"

"It's never been one of my favorite things. When I was a child, my stepfather's brother had a boat we'd go out on occasionally. As much as I love the ocean, I was never very comfortable being in such deep water, especially when it was choppy. Why?"

"Well, only if you'd like, of course. I thought we might take a ferry ride. It's a little over an hour altogether, but the views on this particular cruise are phenomenal, especially on a sunny day like this. Even if the water isn't mirror smooth, I don't think you'll feel any strong motion that will make you uncomfortable."

"All right. Where do we go?"

"Across the harbor to Staten Island, one of the most scenic short trips in the world, I would guess. I think you'll love it."

~ * ~

There was hardly a cloud to mar the sky's azure beauty as their cab wove in and out of traffic, the driver's face set and concentrating. He stopped in front of the ferry terminal at the foot of Whitehall Street. All around them were the tall buildings of the city's financial district, tapering down to Battery Park, a tiny patch of greenery and benches on the southernmost tip of the island.

A large, triple-tiered ferry had eased its way into the pier, and crewmen were busy tying her to the moorings. Moments later the gates opened, allowing the incoming passengers to board. When they reached the turnstile, they deposited their tokens and walked up the gangplank onto the main deck. Windows lined both sides as did rows of blue benches, almost like church pews. The ferry filled quickly with people of all colors speaking a variety of languages who milled about jockeying for position near the rail. Jared took Joanna's hand and led her toward the stairwell.

"We'll see a lot more from up on the top deck. Are you game?"

Joanna allowed herself to be guided up the iron steps and onto the open deck where they found places on the rail.

The breeze picked up as the ship slowly pulled away from the shore. They stood very close to each other against the wind, Joanna held close in Jared's arms.

"Aren't the seagulls beautiful?" Joanna asked, watching the graceful white and gray birds circling overhead.

Jared chuckled. "I read a poem a long time ago that said something cute about buoys and gulls, flotsam and jetsam. I can't remember any more of it. Look at them, Joanna. They're so free."

As the wind grew stronger, Joanna snuggled closer to Jared, her head bent into his chest.

Jared looked at his watch. "We should be almost arriving at Staten Island. Let's go downstairs for a few minutes and watch the docking."

They stayed and watched as the shore crew scuttled about preparing to receive the ferry and unload its cargo of people and autos. With a few bumps that made them grab the rail to steady themselves, the ferry eased into its berth and came to a stop.

Jared turned to Joanna and put his arms around her, his breath warm on her cheek.

"I wish we could take over this old tub and sail and sail and never come back," he said fiercely. "We could find a tiny island somewhere warm and sunny, pitch our tent and stay there forever, just the two of us, closing out the rest of the world. How I wish we never had to go back."

Joanna could only nod against his chest. Remembering the cold grip of fear she'd felt in the middle of the night, her tears started and she fought to keep them from spilling over.

"Now it's my turn to be the sentimental fool," she said when she could trust her voice. "Please let's not talk about that now. Let's not bring in anything that will spoil our day."

A crewman called out for everyone to go ashore, so Jared guided Joanna through the now-empty ship and out into the terminal. He reached for her hand, holding it tightly as they found the line for the return trip and took their places at the end of it. Occasionally, he reached out to smooth her hair, his hand resting beneath it to caress the nape of her neck.

*Your touch is very dear,* Joanna remembered from Benton's poem. She wanted to say it, but knew the words would come out more as a sob than anything intelligible, so she swallowed hard and concentrated on the feel of his fingers on her skin.

They didn't have to wait long until the doors opened and they were able to go through the turnstile and back onto the ferry.

"Shall we go up top?" she asked.

They went up the stairway, once again inching through the crowd to the rail.

"Joanna, look!" he said, pointing in front of them.

Ahead of them was the splendor of Manhattan Island, skyscrapers touching the clouds, fading sunlight dancing off gleaming buildings.

"It's our Emerald City, isn't it, my darling?" Jared asked. "Our Oz. Now all that's missing is the wizard himself, ready to grant our wishes. I wish we could find him."

"I wish he existed," Joanna said quietly, staring straight ahead as the island came closer.

Before they knew it, they were swept along in the crowd of people rushing from the ferry into the dimming daylight.

They sat in the taxi, touching. "Where would you like to go for dinner tonight?" Jared asked. "It should be something very special for our last night in the city."

"Let's not go out. I know we haven't seen much of Manhattan, but this is such a special night. I don't want to spoil it by being around a lot of people. Besides," her voice dropped, "we may not get this chance again."

Jared looked at her intently. "We'll do this again, I promise you. I can't promise you much, but I'll make good on this one. We *will* do this again."

~ * ~

Back in their room, Joanna found a red rosebud on the pillow with a dainty red bow and streamers attached to the long stem. Jared picked it up and handed it to her.

"I wracked my brain for quite a while to come up with some way of starting tonight out in a special way, but nothing came to me except flowers. Obviously, a huge bouquet wouldn't do; they'd never survive the trip home and then what would happen to them? But a single red rose, that's different. It will last several days in a vase on your desk."

"When did you have time to do this?" she asked, holding the rose to her nostrils to smell the faint fragrance of the tightly furled flower. "We've been together all day!"

"I have my ways," he said with a mysterious grin. "Never underestimate the power of a man in love. Do you like it? I don't even know if you like roses."

When she looked up at him, her eyes were moist. "I love them. All through those awkward years when young girls yearn for romance, I dreamed one day some handsome man would give me roses. In my daydreams, nothing but red roses would do." She stood on tiptoe and kissed him, loving the way his eyes closed at her touch.

"Thank you, darling."

Jared crossed to the armoire, opened it and turned on the radio. For the first time Joanna could remember, he seemed at a loss for words.

He sank into one of the deep leather chairs and put his head back, looked at the ceiling and sighed.

"What time do you have to be back tomorrow?" he asked, his voice flat.

"I hadn't thought of it," Joanna replied steadily. "I've tried my damnedest not to think of it. I've taken off all the glasses and refused to look into any mirrors. I've tried to concentrate on the reality we've made here." She sat and sighed as heavily as he. "But try as I might, the outside world keeps intruding. We do have to go back, don't we? Our lease on this tiny piece of heaven runs out in a few hours. When do I have to be back? Whenever I get there, I suppose. My parents think I'm coming home sometime late tomorrow afternoon, but they learned a long time ago to be flexible where I'm concerned."

"Well, I have an idea I want to share with you."

"Tell me," Joanna said, putting her arms around his neck.

"Would you spend New Year's Eve with me?"

"How? Oh, I could stay at Manning, that's not the issue. My parents would understand my wanting to stay through the weekend, what with teaching starting and all that preparation to do. They always go out with their crowd on New Year's Eve, so I'd be home alone anyway. They'd rather I stayed at school where I might be having a good time. But where could we ring in the New Year?"

"How's this?" he said thoughtfully. "What could be a better way to usher in our first New Year's Eve together than to sit in front of a roaring fire, watch the colors in the flames and toast with our manhattans?"

"Dan's?"

"Why not? I'd probably stay there anyway. It's been a while since I checked on the place and I'd rather be there than at home. Having you with me would be absolute perfection. What do you say? Shall we?"

Joanna thought about it. Being with Jared for New Year's Eve would be idyllic, but was it merely postponing the inevitable? It would be hard enough to go back to life as usual after these three days; how much harder would two more make it? It didn't matter; she wanted as much time alone with Jared as she could get.

"Let's do it. I'll give my folks a call when we get back to Manning tomorrow and let them know I'm not coming home for a few more days. I will need to go home on Tuesday, though, so my dad can have his car back. When does everyone get home from Florida?"

"I imagine sometime Monday night. Marina has to be in school on Tuesday, although Genna still has the rest of the week before her classes start. I'll call when we get to Dan's to be sure." He fell silent, looking at the floor, his expression thoughtful and somber.

At the sound of the bellboy's knock, he looked up and moved to open the door.

From the delicate cold plum soup to the light mound of chocolate cake, dinner was perfect. They ate slowly, making small talk. Jared poured himself a cup of coffee and lit a cigarette. Joanna folded her napkin and placed it on the table, watching him stare into space.

"Penny for your thoughts," she said.

He raised his eyes slowly to meet hers. They were heavy with sadness.

"They're not worth a penny. I wish I could stop them from intruding on my contentment."

She got up and went over to his chair.

"Don't say any more." She stood behind him and gently massaged his shoulders, leaning down to kiss his ear. "I know what's hanging so heavily over you. Even adding a couple more days, we can see the end of our time together. You have no idea what you'll face when Vicki comes back; I can't imagine being Joanna coed again. Just thinking about it makes me feel incredibly sad and very frightened. What will we do when we're too far apart for this?"

She went around and leaned over to touch Jared's face. She was so close she could see herself reflected in the deep mirrors of his eyes. With a groan, he drew her into his arms, cradling her on his lap like a child, his face buried in her hair.

"I don't know, my darling. I don't want to think about it. I never want to let you go. For many reasons, we probably should never have come here. Not only because of the obvious risks to both of us if anyone found out, but because of the level we've come to. I can't imagine going back home to deal with whatever Vicki has to throw at me, trying desperately to be a good father. I don't want to live in that house when I only want to be where you are. So what did we accomplish by doing this? There are so many things that tell me we shouldn't have come, but I don't care about any of them. I've had you to myself, to love, to laugh with, to climb to the top of the world with, and if I had to do it all again, even knowing the difficulty ahead, I would do it gladly." He kissed her lightly. "What I will regret, possibly for the rest of my life, is that all of this may have caused you pain. Believe me, I never intended you any hurt. I wanted to love you, to be with you. In spite of the fact I can't make any promises about tomorrow, I wanted us to have today. Was I wrong?"

"If you were, so was I. I wanted this little fairy tale of ours as badly as you. I don't have any illusions. I know the tough decisions ahead and I might not come out a winner. Does knowing victory is out of reach stop a marathon runner? He runs for the joy of it, for the feeling of exhilaration he gets in the running. If I knew we would be apart tomorrow, never to meet again, I wouldn't undo what we've done or cut short what little time we have left. That makes two of us, then, who wouldn't take back a single moment."

# *Fifteen*



Jared's light touch woke her. "Good morning," he said, bending down to kiss her eyes open.

"You're up already?" she asked, stretching full length, arms over her head. "What time is it?"

"About eight. I thought we should get a head start so we could have some breakfast after we pack. Would you like to eat in or go downstairs and have brunch before we leave?"

Joanna sensed his effort to be matter-of-fact and she went along. "It's probably better if we shower and pack, get our bags downstairs then grab a bite on the way out. What do you think?"

"Let's go."

~ * ~

After brunch, they waited while the car was brought out and the bags loaded. Giving the hotel a last look, they pulled out from under the canopy and Jared swung the car onto Fifth Avenue, downtown toward the Lincoln tunnel. Joanna switched on the radio; they sat in thoughtful silence or sang along with familiar songs as they sped toward Manning. Soon the territory began to look familiar. They stopped at the supermarket while Jared went in for the things they'd need for their brief stay at the cabin, and then drove the short distance to Dan's.

It had become a familiar pattern. Jared stopped at the gate, Joanna unlocked it, Jared drove through and Joanna closed and locked it behind them. The sun was brilliant on the bare trees, throwing off slanting rays as it shone through the boughs of evergreens lining the little lane.

Jared carried the bags into the bedroom.

"Are you sure Dan wouldn't mind this?" Joanna asked, following him.

Jared put the suitcases on the bed and opened them both. "I'm sure. When he comes back, the house will be as if he never left it. I'll see to it. In the meantime, Dan knows I've stayed here from time to time. When he gets back and meets you, he'll understand why we came. I promise."

Leaving her to unpack the few things she needed, he went into the living room and arranged kindling and logs for a fire. When she came out of the bedroom, he was on his haunches, the poker in his hand, lifting the kindling to let the fire catch more easily.

"Shouldn't you call your folks?" he asked. "They're probably expecting you any time now."

"Oh, my heaven!" Joanna gasped. "I totally forgot." She sat at the desk in the corner and dialed the operator, giving her the number of her parents' home.

Jared went into the kitchen, put on a pot of coffee and some water to heat for Joanna's hot chocolate. When he came out, Joanna was off the phone.

"Is everything all right? Were they upset?"

"No, not at all. I hate lying to them, though. They assumed I'm going with some of the girls to a New Year's Eve party on campus and I didn't say anything to make them think otherwise. I'm sorry, but at midnight tomorrow I'm going to have to call them at their party to wish them Happy New Year. It's a family tradition we've done every year since they were married. I hope you don't mind."

"Of course I don't mind, my darling. You do what will keep your parents' minds at ease and preserve your traditions. That's a very nice one, by the way."

Joanna flopped down on the sofa, tucked her feet beneath her and rubbed her hands together.

"When are you going to call the children? It's been a few days since you spoke with them and they'll be home before you know it."

Jared rolled his eyes. "I guess I should call now. It's just that each thing we do that pulls reality in closer takes a little bit away from our time together." He got up and went to the desk.

Joanna heard him give the number to the operator. She went into the kitchen with their cups and ran the water loudly in the sink so she wouldn't inadvertently overhear the conversation. She walked slowly back into the room when she heard him replace the receiver.

He looked over his shoulder. "They're getting homesick. Michael said he misses me very much and wants to come back. Marina said they had lots of things to show me." He crossed the room and took Joanna by the shoulders. "I thought we'd have all day Monday to ourselves, but it looks like they'll be home earlier than I expected. Vicki asked me to pick them up at the airport. I'm sorry."

"She spoke to you? How did she sound?"

"Distant, very business-like. But she had to speak to me because she needed something. Otherwise, I doubt she'd have gotten on the phone. I'll have to go, of course; the children are so excited about seeing me."

Joanna moved back toward the sofa and sat, her feet on the floor, chin in her hands.

"I wouldn't expect you to do otherwise. This is what we've been talking about all along, isn't it? The children coming first? Well, here's test number one. What time do they come in?"

"Their flight gets in at two. If I'm to be there on time, I should leave here no later than twelve-thirty. That really cuts our day short."

Joanna held her arms out and motioned for him to sit next to her. "Listen, we knew we'd have to come out of our fantasy world sooner or later. Am I happy about losing those last few hours we'd hoped for? Of course not, but look at what we've had. I refuse to let disappointment ruin it and you shouldn't either. Now, dig out that Johnny Mathis album you bought in Manhattan. Let's put it on the record player, sit in front of your fire and shut everything out for as long as we can."

~ * ~

"Happy almost New Year's Eve," Jared said when the music was over. "What a lovely way to celebrate. How about breaking with tradition and going to listen to Jim? He'd certainly be surprised to see us on a Saturday night, but I'd love a nice big manhattan about now, and then maybe a little dinner in a couple of hours. Does that sound good?"

Joanna's eyes were still closed. "Absolutely yummy," she said dreamily. "I can't think of anything I'd rather do now than leave this warm house, get into a cold car and go out into the elements ... all for a manhattan." She laughed. "But the lure of Jim's music and dinner? Now that's worth it."

~ * ~

When they walked into the Downtown, a crowd had already gathered. No familiar faces were among the people at the bar or at the tables and even the bartender was a stranger. The cover was on the piano keys and Jim was not in sight. Jared went up to the bar, ordered their drinks and spoke to the bartender. He came back empty-handed.

"What a disappointment! Jim's off tonight. He'll be back tomorrow night for the New Year's Eve party. Let's go somewhere else."

Jared pulled out of the parking lot and headed north on the highway.

"Where to?" Joanna asked.

"We need to eat. I'm afraid I only picked up a few things so we can't cook at the house. There's a nice little restaurant out in the country not far from Dan's where we can have a leisurely and, I hope, quiet dinner."

It was a large, very old building. The sign read "Ye Olde Spread Eagle Inn." Jared parked in the almost empty lot on the side. A crooked wooden step led to the white front door. Inside, a single candle flickered on each of the tables, which were covered with red and white checkered vinyl tablecloths. A very large bar filled most of the front of the room. The waitress led them to a table in the corner and handed them menus.

After dinner, Jared raised an eyebrow in a silent question and Joanna nodded her reply.

The ritual of the gate completed and the car parked in front of the cabin, Jared helped Joanna from her seat, steadying her as she weaved slightly from the effects of the manhattans.

Inside, they could see their breath. Jared had forgotten to turn the thermostat up before they left, and the fire had died down to nothing. Rubbing his hands together, he hurried to the wall and turned the dial.

"I'm sorry, Joanna. How forgetful! It'll take a few minutes before we're warm."

Joanna sank into the sofa cushions and pulled a colorful afghan over her lap and legs. She flipped open one side of it, patting the place next to her. "Come cuddle with me," she said, looking up and back at Jared. "We'll manage nicely like this."

He headed for the kitchen. "In a minute."

She closed her eyes and snuggled deeper into the woolen blanket. Soon, Jared came back with two cups of steaming liquid.

"Here, sip this," he said, handing her a cup wrapped in a cloth napkin. "It's very hot, but it'll feel good after this cold air."

As they drank, pausing occasionally for light, teasing kisses, Joanna shed first the afghan, then her coat, then her sweater as the room grew more comfortable and the hot chocolate warmed all the way down to her toes.

"Just think," Jared said quietly. "Only one more day left in this year. And what a year it's been. I can't believe I thought it would be more days to be endured, to struggle through, to live alone except for the children, my students and my work. Until that day in October when I met you. Who could have known? Who could have predicted you would come to love me? Who could have known what we would come to mean to each other, the happiness you would bring me, the incredible love we'd make together?"

~ * ~

Morning sun streamed in through the windows of the wood-paneled bedroom. Joanna was in Jared's arms, his half-open eyes watching her with love. "You were wonderful last night," he said. "We keep getting better and better together, don't we?"

"Practice makes perfect. Happy New Year's Eve," Joanna said, turning for a quick kiss. She got up, went into the bathroom and came back a few moments later.

"My turn," Jared announced as Joanna slipped under the covers for warmth.

Joanna concentrated on him as he returned, walking across the room naked. She loved to look at his body, his legs long and perfectly formed, his narrow hips moving gracefully with each step. She saw him rising as he neared the bed and slid in next to her.

"We're going to be a while," he murmured, fitting himself to her. "We have something very important to do."

What seemed like hours later, they were still in bed, the sheets rumpled, pillows on the floor.

"Enough for now, my darling?" Jared asked. "I think we could take a break. There's some place I want to show you. Come to think of it, you probably already know it. Surely sometime in your three years at Manning, you must have either heard of it or actually been there."

"I give up. What are you talking about?"

"Bowman's Tower. Have you ever seen it?"

"No, I don't think so."

"It's part of the Washington Crossing State Park, on the banks of the river. You're in for a treat," Jared said, swinging his legs off the bed.

~ * ~

They drove north along historic little roads, past relics of the revolutionary war and the restored cabins where George Washington's army had struggled to survive that harsh, frigid winter in 1776. Along the river they drove, the roadway climbing to a steeper grade, the evergreens dense. A sign to their left directed them ahead to Bowman's Hill, where they turned onto a dirt road and began the ascent. Almost at the very top, they pulled in to a graveled area lined with picnic benches. In front of them, a bit further up the hill, was an imposing stone tower that rose up to a shuttered window below the parapet on top.

Inside, the darkness was broken by light streaming down from the window. An iron staircase wove in a spiral from the base to as far as they could see.

"We climb up?" Joanna asked.

"Only if you want to. But I guarantee the view from the top is well worth the effort."

"Lead on," she said gaily, motioning for Jared to go ahead of her. As they climbed, she counted. Pausing only occasionally to catch their breath and rest their legs, they finally reached a landing in front of the tiny window carved out of the side of the tower, collapsing into one another's arms.

After a few minutes, they made their way up the final spiral and emerged into the sunlight and sharp wind of the parapet, a rectangular platform that overlooked a panoramic view of the surrounding forests.

"One hundred forty-four steps!" Joanna announced. "I thought we might not make it! Oh, Jared, it's beautiful," Joanna ran from place to place, looking out over the top of the wall. The river was a narrow ribbon far below.

She went back to where he stood, his arms resting on the ledge, chin on his hands, a faraway look in his eyes. She slipped her head under his arm.

"This is almost as good as the Empire State. The view is certainly very different … no city, no skyscrapers, but this is Central Park hundreds of times over," she said, waving her arm to encompass the entire expanse of forest below. "How did you find this place?"

Jared laughed deep in his throat. "Look at it. How hard is it to find? It beckoned me the very first time I saw it sitting high on this hill. I come here often to leave the world behind and think. I try to pretend nothing hurtful or sorrowful exists down there. It's wonderful for that, even though there are often too many people for my liking. This is a very popular tourist spot in warmer weather."

"It must be even more beautiful then," Joanna agreed. "I can't wait to see it next fall when the trees are all different colors."

"We'll come back as often as we can take that climb. I've dreamed of bringing you here to share this place so close to heaven, holding you with only the clouds and the sun to see us."

He looked over his shoulder and they listened, hearing voices far below. Laughter echoed down the tower's spiral as the newcomers neared.

A young couple burst through the tiny doorway holding hands, their faces flushed with the exertion of the climb.

"Looks like we have company," the young man said, smiling at Joanna and Jared. "Hope you don't mind."

"Not at all," Jared replied. "There's plenty of room for everyone. Enjoy!"

He turned back to Joanna as the couple moved around to the other side.

"See what I mean? Even in the dead of winter they come. There's something about being up here, so far from everything, that's irresistible."

Around the corner, they could hear the excited voices of the young couple. Then everything was still.

"How I envy them," Jared said. "So young, their whole lives ahead of them, none of the complications we face. What I wouldn't give to trade places with them, to have a future so bright, so certain."

The cold stab of fear struck Joanna again. She shivered.

"Too cold, my darling?" Jared asked. "Let's go down."

The magic suddenly gone, Joanna nodded.

They called farewells to the young people and slowly descended the stairs, the climb down far less demanding than the one going up the rustic steps.

~ * ~

"Do you want to go back to the club for New Year's Eve?" Jared asked as they drove back to the cabin. "Jim will be back."

"I would rather stay home. We can hear Jim any time, but this is our last chance to be together overnight and I don't want to cut it short. Do you mind?"

"Mind? No, I don't mind. In fact, I hoped you would say that. A big, crackling fire and you in my arms—that's how I'd like to welcome the new year."

~ * ~

They sat before the fireplace, lost in their own thoughts. When she looked at his face, Joanna saw Jared's eyes were heavy and very dark.

"Don't," she said, putting her finger to his lips. "Don't say anything sad. Don't tell me how it's going to be in the morning when we have to go back. I know. Forget about tomorrow ... please."

Jared held her close, his head in her shoulder. "It's almost midnight," he whispered. "Don't forget to call your folks."

Reluctantly, Joanna went to the phone and dialed the operator. Jared left the room to straighten the bed and put her rose back on the pillow.

"They're having a wonderful time," she said, hanging up the phone. "They were glad I called."

"Come, let's go to bed," he said. He pushed the embers around to be certain they would die out, turned off the lamp and followed her into the bedroom. Nestled close together, they surrendered to sleep, no sound breaking the silence of the forest.

~ * ~

Jared reached for his watch, sighed heavily and put it back down on the night table.

"What time is it?"

His voice was wooden. "You don't want to know. Time to get up. Time to get ready to go."

Not trusting herself to look at him, Joanna put on her robe and began stripping the sheets from the bed. Jared took fresh ones from the closet and they remade the bed, putting the wrinkled, well slept in ones on top of the washing machine in the corner of the kitchen.

"I'll come back and do the laundry some time this week," Jared said.

Although they showered together, there was no time to linger. Dressed, they packed their bags. Joanna tidied the living room while Jared swept the ashes into a pan and dumped them out the back door into the bin on the step. They kept busy, trying to stave off the departure. Finally, everything was done. The thermostat was turned down; Jared put their bags in the car and they drove out of the lane.

Holding her rose, Joanna sat close to him as they drove back to Manning. As they neared the campus, habit took over and she slid across the car seat to the passenger door. She stared straight ahead, afraid to let Jared see what was in her eyes. It was finally over. For five and a half days, she had fashioned a reality that fit her dreams. She had learned how exciting love was and pretended their time together wasn't going to end. But it had, and in a few minutes, Joanna knew she would be alone again.

Jared pulled up in front of Bentley, took her bag from the back of the car and carried it to the door.

"This is as far as I can go, my darling," he said, his voice heavy and dull. "I'll call you as soon as I can."

Wanting to touch him but knowing she couldn't, Joanna lowered her head, walked into the dorm and stood at the doorway. Jared got back into the car and waved before he drove away.

The silence was overwhelming. Leaving her suitcase by the door, she went up to her room. She looked around as if she'd never been there. She felt like a visitor who could leave at any moment and return to the cabin, to Jared, the fireplace, the quiet music and the big soft bed. She didn't know what she was doing there or, worst of all, how to go on.

Fighting back tears, Joanna fled the room, locking the door behind her. She ran down the steps and dragged her suitcase out to her car. She put her head back on the seat and sobbed as she hadn't since she was a child. For the longest time she cried, until she was too exhausted to cry any more. Fiercely wiping tears from her face, she started the ignition and drove off campus, heading south toward home.

# *Sixteen*

*"It's just how it is, that's all."*

It was cold and cloudy on Tuesday. Her parents were back at work, so Joanna slept in. She woke barely refreshed and lay in bed wondering how Jared had fared, what he'd found when Vicki returned. She had worried about him, seeing the desolate look on his face as he drove away alone.

Her mother had taken Wednesday off so she could drive Joanna back to Manning, insisting on having her home one more day. Mark could make the return trip alone, she told Joanna. Besides, the ride back would give them more time to talk. But the weather changed everything. When they left at midmorning, the sky was threatening snow, low clouds moving slowly, heavy and gray. Catherine was in a hurry to get to the college and home again before the weather turned ugly. Joanna was grateful for her mother's preoccupation.

Conditions worsened the closer they got to campus. By the time they arrived, it had begun to snow lightly, but the moisture-laden sky looked like it would soon dump a lot more.

Joanna hurriedly kissed her mother goodbye and waved her on her way. She glanced at her mailbox as she went toward the stairs. It was empty. There were no phone messages taped to her door. She could hear laughter from the other end of the hall. Some of the students were drifting back, although classes wouldn't start until Monday. She retreated to her room and closed the door behind her. After unpacking swiftly, Joanna sat at her desk staring out the window, wondering how to get back to what once had been her life.

There was a timid knock on her door.

"Yes?" she called.

"Jo, it's me," came Beth's familiar voice. "I wasn't sure you were in there. Nobody saw you come back. May I come in?"

Joanna straightened her shoulders and opened the door.

"It's good to see you," Beth said, reaching out for a hug. "How was your break? What did you do? Did you have a date for New Year's Eve?"

"Break was fine; I didn't do much of anything and no, I didn't have a date for New Year's Eve. What about you?"

For the next ten minutes, Beth talked about the trip she and Paul had taken with her parents to Bermuda. Joanna barely heard a word, her mind wandering off where she knew Beth could never go.

"...and I guess he'll start auditioning by midweek," Beth was saying. "Fowler is sure to want to get going as soon as we all get back. Are you sure you're not up to a bit part in the chorus? I know he's looking for some good voices."

"Yes, I'm sure. I'll have my hands full with junior teaching."

Beth shook a finger at her. "Likely story. You know you'll do great. You've probably already got all the lesson plans done and in the can waiting for Monday. Everyone else will be scrambling to catch up with you."

As Beth turned to leave, she reached out and picked up the book of poetry sitting on Joanna's desk.

"Who's Walter Benton?"

Before Joanna could stop her, Beth opened the book to the rose pressed in the pages. She looked up at Joanna, her eyes wide.

"What's this? Tell me again, Joanna Ransome, are you sure you didn't do anything special over vacation? No date for New Year's?"

Joanna retrieved the book, closed it and put it back on the dresser.

"Just an old souvenir from a long time ago," she said as casually as she could muster. "Nothing to get excited about."

Beth didn't look convinced, but she went out the door anyway, looking back over her shoulder. "Are you going to eat tonight? The cafeteria's still closed, but the snack bar's open. We could grab a burger later. What do you say?"

"Don't count on me. I'm really pretty tired. I could use a nap. Check with me later, okay?"

Joanna turned the radio on and lay on her narrow bed staring at the ceiling, her eyes heavy from lack of sleep. Two days without Jared.

~ * ~

She slept longer than she'd planned. When she turned on the lamp, she saw a note on the floor near her door.

> *Hey, sleepyhead! It's five o'clock and I've gone to dinner. Come on over if you wake up before six. You do have to eat, you know. Beth*

Joanna looked at her watch. Almost five-thirty. Outside, the wind had picked up and the snow was falling heavily. If she didn't go now, she might not get anything to eat until breakfast. Throwing on her heavy jacket and digging in the closet for her boots, Joanna hurried downstairs and across the street to the Student Center. The table for two by the window was empty.

Joanna picked up her order and joined Beth and a few other girls. She found herself looking over at the door every once in a while, half expecting Jared to come in.

If anyone found her unusually quiet, it wasn't mentioned. Joanna listened to the conversation, feeling very old and removed from the world they talked about. Finally, using work as an excuse, she broke away. Wrapping her scarf securely around her neck, she trudged through the deepening snow.

Resolutely, she opened her notebook, took the cover off the typewriter and tried to begin an outline for the lesson plan. The phone rang. No one picked it up, so after the third ring, Joanna went down the hall.

Her voice was tired and heavy. "Hello. Bentley third floor."

"Joanna," Jared's voice was very soft. "Oh, thank God it's you."

She sank to the floor, the receiver cupped in her hand. "Jared! Oh, Jared, I'm so glad you called. Is everything all right? Are *you* all right?"

"It's a long story, my darling. I have a lot to tell you, but now's not a good time. I only wanted to be sure you were back on campus and you were okay. Are you? Okay, I mean."

"No," Joanna said honestly. "I'm about as far from okay as I can get. But I'm here and I need to see you, to hear what's been happening. When?"

"I'm afraid Friday night will be the earliest I can get away. I'm sorry, but the children don't want me to leave them. And there are other things happening as well I have to deal with."

Joanna clutched the phone until her knuckles were white. "Like what?" she asked in a whisper. "Tell me."

"I can't now. I'll be at Kenton at seven on Friday. We can talk then. I miss you so, Joanna, believe that and please try to be patient with me. I'll see you soon."

Joanna opened her mouth to tell him she loved him, but he had already hung up. She sat on the floor cradling the receiver, hearing the voice she loved, feeling utterly alone and abandoned.

Beth and the others were coming up the stairs. She quickly replaced the receiver and ducked into her room.

~ * ~

Joanna spent most of Thursday in the library, working with the other students on her team getting their lesson plans ready. Friday crawled from hour to hour. Road crews had cleared the snow on the campus streets, and although it was still cloudy and cold, there was no more precipitation in the forecast.

Finally, it was time. She was waiting when Jared pulled into the parking lot. In spite of the darkness, he didn't move to greet her with a kiss. Instead, he backed out and drove quickly off campus, smoking a cigarette, staring at the road. Joanna felt her heart constrict with fear. Not knowing what to say, or even if she should say anything at all, she sat looking at her hands. Soon they were at the lane and inside the cabin.

Jared took her in his arms and held her tightly. He found her mouth and kissed her as though it had been years since he'd last done so. She tried to speak, but he wasn't finished, pulling deep kisses from her mouth, murmuring her name again and again. Finally, he released her enough that she could look at him. His usual smile wasn't there.

She reached up to caress his cheek. "What is it? What's happened? Please, please tell me."

He didn't answer, but looked steadily into her eyes as his own filled with tears.

"What is it? You're frightening me! What's wrong?" she asked, her voice rising with anxiety and a tinge of anger.

"Sit down, Joanna. I'm trying to figure out what to say and how to say it."

Joanna felt a spasm of fear. She sat stiffly, feet on the floor, hands on her knees. He sat next to her and lit a cigarette with a shaking hand.

"I took the children to a movie yesterday afternoon. Vicki was waiting for me when I got home with a letter that had come. I don't know why she opened it; it was addressed to me. But she did.

Anyway, she threw it on the floor in front of me and stormed out of the room."

"What was it? What upset her?"

Jared looked at her and swallowed hard. It seemed like he was trying to force the words out of his throat.

"I've been offered a new job. Remember how I talked about how difficult it is to break into theater? How few chances there are for directors? Well, somehow someone at Roosevelt University in Chicago heard about me. Whatever they heard was good, I guess, and they've offered me the position of assistant director of their theater along with teaching several graduate classes and advising some master's candidates. It's something I never dared hope for. This isn't the post-graduate fellowship I applied for, not even close. This is a chance to work in one of the most prestigious university theaters in the country..." His voice trailed off as he clutched Joanna's hands. "But how can I go? It doesn't matter to me that Vicki might not want to make the move. What matters is that I would be a thousand miles away from you. How can I do that?"

"Chicago." Joanna's voice was flat. "When?"

"They want me to start immediately after Labor Day. Some of the renovations will be finished by then and I could have an office in the theater. They want me to be on the job by the beginning of September."

"I see."

"They want me to go out there as soon as possible to sign a contract and look at two or three houses near the theater they could rent for me. They'll make all the arrangements to pack and move us. They even sent a pamphlet about a nearby school for the children."

He stopped speaking abruptly. "What am I talking about? How can I sit here across from you discussing the kids' school? This can't be happening, not now, not when I've just found you. Please, say something."

"I'm as overwhelmed as you. When do you have to give them your answer?"

"The director assumes I'll accept. Why wouldn't I? Anyone would jump at this chance. How can he know what this offer does to us? I'm sure he thinks I'm already planning the move. At any rate, he's asked me to go out there at the end of the month, so there isn't much time. What *will* this do to us? How could I ever bear to leave you?"

Joanna struggled for something to say amid the awful tension. "You said Vicki was very angry? Will she refuse to go?"

"I don't know. She simply yelled something about my turning her life upside down and closed herself in her room. Genna, the children and I ate dinner, I played some games with them and then I sat in the dark for the longest time after they went to bed trying to organize my thoughts." He closed his eyes. "Oh, God, why this? Why now?"

Joanna sat in stunned silence, her mind blank, her eyes wide. Jared held her hands, searching her face, waiting for her to say something. Finally, she blinked hard, focusing with some difficulty.

"Joanna?" Jared said softly. "Joanna?"

"I'm sorry," she said. "This is such a shock. I remember when we first met, you said something about applying for a post-doctoral fellowship in the Midwest. It barely registered because we were so new and I had no intention of falling in love with you. In fact, until now, I hadn't given it a thought. I guess I assumed that, even if you got the fellowship, you'd turn it down and stay here at Manning with me. That isn't going to happen with this offer, is it?"

When he didn't reply, she went on. "No, I guess it isn't." She was quiet for a moment. "I'm so torn. The selfish part of me is screaming for you to stay, to wait at least until I graduate before you plan a future. The part of me that loves you beyond all reason wants what's best for you ... now, not next year when this chance will surely be gone.

Don't ask me to choose. I can't, not now." She rested her head on his shoulder, feeling the tears coming, giving in to the emotion that was overtaking her. He stroked her hair as she cried.

"Oh God, please, please darling, don't cry," he begged, his voice ragged, his own tears evident in his tone. "I can't bear the thought of leaving you, ever. Look at me, please." He tried to gently push her away from his shoulder, but she clung to him, unable to stop the tears. Finally, she quieted, kissed his neck, his cheek and then found his mouth, her lips salty, the track of her tears running down her face.

"I can't. I can't face being here alone. When you left me on Monday, I couldn't even go into my room and imagine living there again. I didn't fit in at home; I don't belong at school. I'm not the person I was before I loved you. How will I cope if you're so far away? What will I do if you leave me?"

The tears came again. Finally, Jared pulled away and stood. He went into the bathroom and got a box of tissues, handing a few to Joanna as he wiped his eyes.

Sitting back down, he turned to face her.

"I have a lot of thinking to do. This came out of the blue, hitting me as hard as it's hitting you now. I was terrified of your reaction, panicked at the thought of how you would take the news. I guess I knew how devastating it would be and I knew I couldn't do anything to ease the pain."

He looked at her intently, anxiously. "I can't promise you I won't take this job," he said in a low voice. "You're right ... it won't come my way again. Next to this, the post-doctoral fellowship is hollow, nearly meaningless. Being at Roosevelt would open a whole new career to me and give me the chance I've always wanted, to be involved in major theater productions that are seen by the most influential people in the field. On the professional side, there's really no reason for turning it down. But leaving you? How could I begin to think of that?"

Joanna's eyes were heavy and red-rimmed. He reached up and pushed her hair out of her eyes and away from her forehead, stroking her face gently. Leaning over, he kissed her. She clamped her eyes shut tight, fighting back more tears.

"Let's give it a few days' rest. I don't have to call the university this quickly. For all they know, I'm still not back from break and haven't even gotten the letter. Let's take some time to digest this news, figure out how to deal with it."

"Okay. Okay. But keep talking to me. Keep letting me know what you're thinking, what's happening at home. I need to be part of this decision, the planning. It affects me too, please remember."

He leaned over and kissed her again. "How could I forget? Remember what I promised in Manhattan? I will never forget how important you are to any decision I make."

"Tell me about the children. How did they make out in Florida? Have you and Vicki had any chance to talk? Has anything changed? I'm sorry, but I'm trying to find anything but Chicago to talk about."

"Don't apologize, dear heart. You deserve to know everything." He sighed, lit a cigarette and sat back on the sofa. "The kids did fine. Oh, they missed being home with their playmates and they say they missed me. I don't doubt that, but they're treated like royalty when they visit Vicki's parents, so I'm sure the time passed quickly for them. Vicki? Has anything changed? No. She avoided me from the airport all the way home. When we got there, I told her I thought we should talk. She shrugged and went into her room. I haven't tried again. We've been going through the motions. Then the letter came and now I don't know what she's thinking.

"There's too much happening now. The offer, the children, and Vicki, all of them clamoring for my attention. And the person I'm most concerned about, the one I worry about most—you—I'm at a loss to comfort, to make this easier on. I can't even ask you to go with me."

"I could, you know … go with you, that is. I could finish school anywhere in the country. I'm paying my own way with the money my father left me and I could get along easily. But even if you asked me to go to Chicago, I couldn't simply drop everything and move. I have people to consider, too. My parents would be just devastated; they'd never understand how I could pull up stakes and move halfway across the country to be near a man with a wife and two children. I would be putting a stake in my mother's heart. I couldn't subject her to the talk in town, the pity she'd get from her friends ... there's Catherine Ransome, her daughter ran off to be that professor's mistress. I couldn't do that to her," Joanna said emphatically.

"No, of course you couldn't. You're far too caring a person. That's one of the reasons I love you so much." He drew her into his arms. "Oh, I've missed you so. It was so hard to drive away and leave you standing in the doorway. I fought the urge to turn around, put you back in the car and keep driving to God knows where. When I got to the airport, I didn't feel like Marina and Michael's father, or anyone they knew, for that matter. My mind was still on you ... you in your beautiful blue gown, you on the ferry, you falling asleep in my arms. These last days have been empty except for my anticipation of being with you again. Now here you are and I have to make you cry. Will you ever forgive me for what I've done to your life?"

Joanna put her index finger to his lips. "There's nothing to forgive. We'll get through this somehow. We won't let this destroy what we've found. Now let's not waste any more time talking. I have to be back by midnight or I turn into a pumpkin, you know. For now, just hold me and make it all go away."

They made love desperately, as though it might be their last time. When it was over, they clung to one another, each reluctant to be the first to move away.

Finally, Jared said, "I start auditions for the play Monday. Funny, when we broke for vacation, I was so excited about this musical. Now I wish I'd never decided to do it. There'll be long evenings of rehearsals and weekends spent working. Are you sure you won't be a part of it with me? It would give us more time together."

"Let me think about it. After your news, I might change my mind. I'm not clear about much of anything. Okay?"

He leaned over and kissed her eyes and lips. "I'll try to call you over the weekend. Do you have plans? Will you be around?"

Joanna looked at him sadly. "Yes, I will. I don't have plans; I don't have a life that doesn't include you, so when you're not with me, I drift … no plans, no nothing. That's a terrible way to be, isn't it? It's just how it is, that's all."

# *Seventeen*



*"I wish it could be otherwise."*

Jared didn't call. By Monday, Joanna was bewildered, heartsick and hurt. A couple of times she thought about calling his house, taking the chance he'd answer, prepared to hang up if it was Vicki. But she didn't want to add to his worries ... he had enough on his mind.

The first day of team teaching was filled with meetings, lectures and a glimpse of the class they'd teach. Joanna was too distracted to care about any of it.

By four, she was in the snack bar, watching out the window at the path through the woods, seeing the little fir, hearing Jared's voice. *Hello, tree.*

It was late when he finally arrived. His shoulders sagged; his confident stride was reduced to a labored gait. When he got to the table, he looked for a moment like he would simply lean over, take Joanna in his arms and greet her with a long kiss, but he sat down opposite her instead.

"I'm sorry. I couldn't call. The whole weekend was miserable for everyone and I knew my voice would give me away and make you worry more."

"What happened? Do you have time to tell me?"

"Yes. I have a meeting at seven with Art Farms to talk about the play. I've asked him to do some of the auditioning for me."

Joanna looked at his handsome face creased with worry, his brow furrowed, the stubble of his beard a dark shadow on his face.

"Oh, Jared, I hate to think of you going through this … now of all times, with everything that's going on. What happened? Was it the children?"

"Partly, yes. Vicki told them we were going to move; they'd have to leave Genna and their friends, Marina her school. She just blurted it out, almost like she was punishing them for something. I was hoping to move slowly, find ways to bring up the possibility of a move without scaring them or making them think the decision didn't include their wants and needs. Not Vicki. She didn't wait. So most of the weekend I dealt with two very unhappy, frightened and angry children, Marina especially. After church Sunday, I took them to Dan's to try to spend some alone time with them and that was a big mistake, believe me."

"Why?"

"First of all, I had a tough time plowing through the snow on the lane to reach the cabin and then I had to shovel a path to the front porch. But that was the easy part. I hadn't counted on what it would feel like to walk into the house without you. It felt like someone had punched me in the gut. I couldn't wait to get out. It was like I'd brought the children into a place that belonged exclusively to us, to you and me. I had to get out of there. They didn't want to go; they wanted me to build a fire and let them play in the yard, but I couldn't. Once again, the poor bewildered kids got hustled around. None of this is their fault and yet I'm afraid they're feeling really left out."

"And Vicki?"

Jared shrugged helplessly. "As always, Vicki's just being Vicki," he said bitterly. "She barely acknowledges me. She speaks to Genna and the kids almost in single-word sentences and plays the martyr. She would do us all a favor if she'd leave and go live with her parents or go anywhere, as long as it was far away."

Joanna wanted to touch him so badly she ached with the wanting. "I'm so sorry."

"How I wish there were some way to resolve this," he said, his voice plaintive and dejected.

"So do I. For your sake and the kids'. The coming months will be terrible if Vicki goes on this way."

"The coming months," Jared echoed dully. "I don't even want to think about them." He was quiet.

"Have you had anything to eat?"

"No, I forgot all about it. Have you?"

"No, but there's time before your meeting. Would you like to go out for a quick bite?"

"We couldn't go far. There's not a lot of time. Are you willing to risk any of the places near campus?"

"Why not? After all, it's only natural you might want to buy your newest cast member a sandwich to celebrate, isn't it?"

For the first time since he'd come into the room, Jared smiled. "Oh Joanna, I'm so pleased. You've decided to be in the play?"

"Yep. I thought about what you said. It made sense to me that we should grab any chance we have to spend time together, even if we're not alone. So I'm in, if you still have room for me."

"I've only begun auditioning. Even if every spot were filled, I'd create a place just to have you near me."

~ * ~

Gradually, seeing Jared only briefly each day, Manhattan seemed to fade into the background. Reality was campus life ... teaching, which Joanna found not be as much to her liking as she'd hoped, time in the library and at her other classes, slowly slipping back into the way things were before she walked into the Statler on Jared's arm. Soon, Manhattan seemed like something she'd only dreamed. Try as she might, she couldn't conjure up the feeling of waking to Jared's touch, falling asleep after love.

There were only two weeks before Jared was to make the trip to Chicago to either sign a contract or turn down the job. He told Joanna he wanted to give them his decision in person, considering the faith the university had shown by offering him the job sight unseen. He'd booked a flight for the twenty-ninth, canceling play rehearsal until February fifth without explanation, wanting to ward off the questions he'd face if people knew where he was going.

"I haven't told anyone about this," he told Joanna as they sat in the snack bar late one evening. "There'll be time enough for that when I get back."

On Friday night, Joanna put in for a two a.m. sign-in so they could go to Dan's. It wasn't the same as staying all night, but it made their time together less hurried, less fraught with tension about the inevitable parting.

Saturday, there was a letter.

> *My darling Joanna,*
>
> *I'm too much of a coward to do this in person. I can't bear the look in your eyes when I tell you, I guess, even though I believe you already suspect.*
>
> *I can't turn down this opportunity. I can't. Looking at it as objectively as possible, there is nothing for me here. This is a dead-end job and, if I stay now, I'll still be here long after you're gone, becoming angrier and angrier with myself for having missed the chance to move on.*
>
> *I have to go. And for now, I have to include Vicki and the children. For the life of me, I don't know what's going to happen.*
>
> *When we first met, I said I could never be a part-time dad, that come what may I could never leave the kids. That seems like so long ago. I believed it at the time, but now I'm far from certain. I am certain, though, that with everything else that's happening in their little*

*worlds, I don't have the heart to heap the crushing blow of a separation on them.*

*I don't want either of the choices in front of me, my darling. Either I hurt the children or I hurt you. There's no other way. I wish it could be otherwise.*

*We'll talk about everything if I see you again on Monday. I wouldn't blame you if you didn't show up at the first rehearsal, or at any of them if you decided to take what is left of your life and go on without me. God almighty, the very thought you might do that makes me want to scream. But I can't ask anything of you because I can't promise anything in return. I can only tell you again how very much I love you and how dark my life would be without you in it.*

*I love you, my darling, and I always will.*

*Jared*

Joanna read the letter over twice, the second time through a blur of tears. She'd known what his choice would be. How could it be anything else? But seeing it in black and white made it final— cold and certain. In a few months, Jared would be gone.

# Eighteen



When she was called to the phone Sunday afternoon, she raced down the hall, expecting to hear Jared's voice at the other end of the line.

"Hi, sweetie!" Doris. Joanna had forgotten Doris had come back yesterday. Of course, she'd forgotten; there was no room anywhere in her thoughts for anyone but Jared.

"Oh, Doris, it's good to hear your voice," she said, meaning it more than Doris could have known. "How was everything?"

"Wonderful. I saw so many old friends and colleagues, went to so many parties ... I guess I'm ready to get back to work but it won't be easy. And you? How about you? Are you okay?"

Joanna shook her head no.

"Joanna? Are you?"

"No. I'm really not, and I don't know if I can hold it together long enough to talk about it."

"Try," Doris said. "Come on over, or would you like me to pick you up?"

"No, I can walk. Thanks, Doris, I could really use the company. I'll be there in about a half hour."

When they had settled on her sofa, Doris reached for Joanna's hands and held them tightly. "Tell me whatever you want me to know."

At first, words came easily. Joanna told her about Manhattan, the hotel, the Empire State Building, the ferry ride and the beauty of the city in all its Christmas finery. Then she got to the coming home part and her voice faltered.

"It was terrible. I felt so awfully alone. It was like someone had turned off all the lights and my whole world got dark and frightening. I've haven't felt that way since I was a child and I can't fight my way out of it. But that's not the worst."

When she finished telling about Jared's new job, she sat looking at the floor, unable to meet Doris's eyes.

"I'm so sorry," Doris said, holding her close. "You must be terribly lonely and confused."

"I am," Joanna admitted. "And you have every right to say you told me so. I didn't listen; I told you I could handle whatever came along. I honestly believed I could. But I've never loved anyone, not like Jared, and I can't handle it. I feel like I'll simply stop breathing when he leaves, like my life will just end."

"You didn't really believe it would come to this," Doris said, compassion in her eyes.

"No, I didn't. I went along in my fantasy world, thinking somehow I could make it work by wanting it to. But I can't, can I?"

"No, honey, you can't. It was fun while you could pretend. It was just you and the man of your dreams, riding off into the sunset. But it doesn't usually work that way. You need to hang onto your heart and protect it from what might happen down the line. Understand, honey, Jared's going to live his life and pursue his dreams. I wish I knew a way to show you how to do the same for yourself."

~ * ~

Despite Doris's warning, after her first class Monday Joanna went to Jared's office, knocked quietly and walked in.

"Joanna!" Jared stood up quickly and crossed the room to take her in his arms. "Thank God you're here. Can you stay and talk?"

"That's why I'm here; I need to talk. In a few days, you'll be on your way to Chicago. I'm in class and teaching every day and we may not have much time alone. Now might not even be good, but I don't want to wait until we're at the club or at Dan's." She stopped for breath and stepped back, Jared's arms around her waist.

"Oh, my darling, I'm so sorry," he said. "I really don't have a choice. I never want to leave you, but this opportunity is a once-in-a-lifetime thing. I desperately need you to understand."

Joanna freed herself and sat down. "I do understand. Honestly, I do. Understanding has nothing to do with being hurt or disappointed or feeling second best. And I'm feeling all of those things. But I still understand. If this job hadn't come your way, I know you'd be marking time until something else came along that would help you move up. This happened earlier than you planned."

Jared was standing at the arm of her chair. "I told you in my letter I never want to leave you. I meant that as honestly as I've ever meant anything. If there were a way to take you with me, to start out in Chicago with you, I would jump at it. But I can't, Joanna, I just can't. I couldn't bear the looks on the children's faces if I were to tell them I was going away and they couldn't come with me. They would feel totally abandoned. How could I live with myself? More to the point, how could we live together with that image haunting us day after day?"

He sank to his knees at the side of her chair, his head resting on her arm. "I'm so torn, my darling. Seeing the hurt in your eyes is a terrible price to pay for doing what I think I have to do. If only..." His voice broke and he was quiet.

Joanna reached over, ran her fingers through his hair and caressed his forehead as if he were a small child.

"I know you don't want to hurt me. I believe you love me as much as I love you. This is very hard for you, too, I know. In any other circumstances, I'd admire you for caring so much for your children. I still do, even though you're sparing them at my expense. Our expense. I wish I could end this right now. I see so much pain ahead for both of us while you struggle. I'm not a strong person; all I ever wanted was to find someone to love and who would love me. I'm not sure I can take losing you inch by inch in the days ahead. If only I could say good luck, kiss you goodbye and walk out of here. It would take a long, long time, but I think I could eventually have a life of my own that wasn't haunted by you."

She searched his eyes and winced at what she saw. "But I can't. There's a line in one of Benton's poems, one you didn't read to me and now I know why. He says, *'I shall never forget you…nor will your memory be ever free of me. For your arms are my home—and my arms the circle you cannot leave, however far you go.'* That says it for me. Even if I were to walk out of this office now and never see you again, I wouldn't be free. So why punish myself? Why punish us? You'll be with me all my days, if only in my heart, so why shouldn't I want you with me for as long as I can have you?"

She leaned over and kissed his hair, her heart aching with the pain of loving him.

"Do what you have to," she said in a still, steady voice. "I'll take whatever I can get. I promise to be as strong as I can, to cry as little as possible and to make memories out of each second we have together. Maybe one of these days we'll look back on all of this, when we're reminiscing together about the early years, and be able to smile about how silly my fears were. I hope so."

Jared lifted her to her feet, blinking back tears. "I don't deserve you. If I were half the man you think I am, I would be walking away from you … now, before there's any more hurt. But while you're willing to be strong for my sake, I'm not willing to do the same for yours. I'm not strong enough to end what we have. I couldn't stand being without you."

She raised her face to his and kissed him. "Now we know where we stand. For me, there's no turning back, no going to the place I was before I met you. There's only you and what I can steal of the time that's left. I'll worry about putting it all back together again when you're gone."

~ * ~

Joanna didn't take the part in the chorus. Instead, she became the chief production assistant. That way, she could spend time with Jared and be involved in the organization of the play. They worked long hours, staying overtime in his office with no one asking why.

~ * ~

"I'm not enjoying teaching at all," Joanna told Doris over a Coke on Thursday. "I'm sure it's because my heart isn't in anything these days, not so close to Jared's leaving, even if it is for only three days."

Doris sipped her coffee but didn't answer.

"Maybe teaching isn't my thing," Joanna ventured. "It's possible I made a mistake choosing this profession when I really didn't know anything about kids or how I would react to dealing with a bunch of them at one time."

"Junior practicum isn't ideal," Doris said. "You'll know for sure if you've made a mistake when you're actually in a classroom on your own next year. Do you have any idea where you'd like to teach?"

"There's a school not far from here that's supposed to be very good. Claybourne Junior High. I've thought of applying there. I hear it's very competitive, but they take about ten seniors from Manning every year, so I might have a chance."

"I know the principal at Claybourne, Brad Fischer," Doris said. "Shall I put in a good word?"

"Much appreciated. I want to stay close to Manning so I don't have to travel too far. I'll have a car on campus next fall, thanks to my dad. He's buying a new one and donating the old Fairlane to me, but I'd still rather not have to travel too far if I don't have to."

"Consider it done," Doris said, finishing her coffee and reaching for her coat. "How's the play coming along?"

"Okay, I guess. It's too early to tell; we've only had three rehearsals so far and, with Jared gone for a few days, practice is cancelled until he gets back." She sighed as she put on her jacket. "I wish I could go with him."

Again, Doris didn't answer. As they walked toward the door together, Joanna put her hand on Doris's arm.

"I need your friendship and support. Please don't be angry with me or with Jared. It'll make it all the harder for me to talk to you like I've always counted on doing. You've been a rock these past years and if I ever needed you to be here for me, it's now."

~ * ~

After an abbreviated rehearsal on Friday night, Jared and Joanna spent some time at the club, listening to Jim, drinking manhattans, not saying much.

At Dan's, Jared put on the radio and sat next to Joanna. She leaned against his shoulder. "What time do you leave on Monday?"

"My plane goes out at nine in the morning." He looked down at her hands knotted tightly in her lap, reached down and gently uncurled them, stroking her fingers one by one.

"I arrive in Chicago at about eleven their time. I gain an hour, remember."

Joanna lifted his hand and kissed his fingers then pressed them against her cheek. "I'll miss you. Will you call me while you're away?"

"Every day. More than once a day if I can find you. Can you give me your schedule so I know when I can reach you?"

"I'll jot it down before we leave, in case I don't see you before you go."

"Willow Weep for Me" began to play softly, Andy Williams' voice filling the room with richness and feeling. Without another word, they walked to the bedroom, leaving the radio on, letting the strains of the music accompany their lovemaking, but not hearing much of it over the sounds of the music they made on their own.

~ * ~

At about two on Sunday afternoon, Beth knocked on Joanna's door.

"Yes?" Joanna called.

"Phone's for you," Beth said, giving her a strange look.

Joanna opened the door, thanked her and went down the hall to pick up the dangling receiver.

"Hello?"

"Hello, love."

"Where are you?"

Joanna heard the door to Beth's room close softly as she sat on the floor, the phone close to her ear, her head bent.

"I'm at the drugstore down the street from the house. Michael's had the sniffles for a couple of days so I came out to get him some cold medicine and I took advantage of being out of the house to give you a quick call. I wish I could come to campus, my darling, but I don't see how I can do it. The kids want me home tonight since I'm going to be away for the next few days and I can't really tell them no. You're probably getting tired of hearing me ask it, but please try to understand."

"Of course I do. I'm very glad you called."

"When I get back on Wednesday night, it should be early enough for me to spend some time with them and then come to you. Can you get a late sign-in?"

"No, they're only for weekends, but I've already put in for Friday. I'll hate not seeing you, but it'll make Friday all that much more special, won't it?"

"Anytime I can see you is special. I'll be back on campus on Thursday, so maybe we can catch a few minutes alone then. Save me some time?"

"I'll see you in the snack bar on Thursday, first thing in the morning. Be safe, and please don't forget to call."

"I'll miss you terribly. Remember I love you and I always will."

Joanna stood slowly and hung up. She was almost back to her room when Beth's door opened.

"Jo? Can we talk for a sec?"

"Sure, come on in." She held the door for Beth and closed it behind them.

Beth sat at Joanna's desk and turned the chair to face her. Joanna perched on the edge of her bed.

"What's up?"

Beth looked at her straight on. "That was Jared Fowler on the phone, wasn't it?"

"Yes." There was no sense in lying; Beth certainly recognized Jared's voice.

"Jo, I don't think he was calling about the play. I know this is none of my business and you can tell me so and throw me out, but I'm concerned. All of us who know Dr. Fowler have noticed the change in him recently. For weeks, he was happier and more upbeat than at any time since he's been here. Then, since we've been back from winter break, he's been almost morose, depressed like none of us has ever seen him. Do you know why?"

Joanna didn't answer.

"Jo? Someone mentioned to me the other day about how strange it is that you've been out every Friday night since we've been back and you don't get in until almost two. You told me you're not dating anybody and I can't imagine you're staying at Dr. Wayne's every weekend. Is it Dr. Fowler? Are you seeing Jared Fowler?"

Joanna stood and moved toward the door. "I really can't talk about this." She paused by the desk and put her hand on Beth's shoulder. "I'm grateful for your concern and your friendship, really I am, but I can't talk about it. Try to understand."

Beth gave Joanna a piercing look. "No, I really don't understand, but I respect you too much to push. Listen, I know how unhappy Dr. Fowler has been; we all do. I know what a warm and loving person you are; we all know that, too. It wouldn't surprise any of us if he turned to you for some happiness in his life. I can't escape the fear that if anything *is* going on, you'll be the one who gets hurt. This is a small place and people talk. Take care of yourself. Watch out for Joanna. Promise?"

Joanna hugged her friend. "Thanks. I'm doing fine, believe me."

"Remember I'm next door if you need me," Beth said, patting Joanna's arm fondly. "Don't try to carry it all by yourself. And you can be sure whatever you tell me will stay between us. I'm not joining in the campus guessing game, but I did think you should know it's going on."

"Thanks. You've always been a good friend."

~ * ~

Jared called at least twice a day while he was in Chicago. Joanna didn't care who answered the phone, and after the second call, no one was surprised to hear his deep voice. When he called Tuesday afternoon, Joanna heard him trying to restrain his excitement, but she could read him well enough to hear it coming through.

"This place is amazing, my darling. I can hardly wait to tell you about it. It's not at all what I expected and that makes everything all the more difficult. I had hoped to be able to come back and tell you I didn't think I would fit in out here, but it's turning out to be just the opposite. I feel as if I've been heading toward this place my whole career and I've finally come home. If only you could come with me and we could start again."

With each phone call, Jared's excitement mounted and Joanna grew more apprehensive. She wondered how long it would take him to forget what they had, once he was in Chicago, settled in his new "home."

# Nineteen

*"I looked at the calendar this morning."*

Jared made his way through the woods as Joanna crossed the street. She watched him pause next to the tree. Closing her eyes, she heard his voice. *Hello, tree.*

"I have so much to tell you," Jared said when they were seated at their table. "I don't even know where to start. It was a fantastic experience. Everyone was great and very enthusiastic about my joining the staff. It'll be very different from anything I've ever done. I'll have quite a bit of responsibility, from overseeing the work of their first group of master's candidates to teaching two graduate level courses and, of course, working with the stage productions in the Auditorium Theatre."

Joanna watched his face brighten, heard the excitement in his voice. Managing to keep hers level, she said, "It sounds like you'll be there at a very exciting time. It'll be thrilling for you to be on the ground floor of something this dynamic."

Jared smoked the last of his cigarette, musing almost to himself.

"I'll have to let President Reade know I'm planning on leaving. He'll need time to replace me in the department. I don't think a formal resignation will be necessary until later in the semester, but I'll leave that up to him."

Joanna felt irrelevant, almost as if she were an afterthought. This wasn't what she had waited for. Feeling the muscles in her face stiffening, Joanna reached for her coat.

"I have to go. I have class at ten and a lot of work to do before then."

"Oh, please don't go yet. I haven't even asked how you've been, what you've been doing, how junior practice is going."

"I understand. You're the one having the adventure. It sounds like you can hardly wait to leave."

She finished putting on her coat and scarf, drew on her gloves and picked up her books.

"Maybe I'll see you later. Now I really need to go."

"Joanna, come on! This isn't the way I wanted it to be the first time I saw you. It wasn't supposed to be like this ... so impersonal, so matter-of-fact."

"Well, that's how it turned out, didn't it?"

"When can I talk to you?"

"That depends on you, I suppose," she said, her eyes glistening with tears. "Call me later when you know if you can fit me in."

Jared began to rise from his chair, one hand outstretched. "Joanna? Joanna, don't leave it like this. We need to talk more; you know we do."

"Not now. You see, I waited for you to come back, filled my days with thoughts of you and marked the passage of time by phone calls, barely getting through the hours. It wasn't that way for you. Fine. I'm feeling sorry for Joanna right now. I'll stop by your office and we can talk, start all over again. Meeting here wasn't a good idea. I'll see you later." She whirled and almost ran to the door, mindless of the curious stares in her wake.

She didn't go to class. Instead, she went back to her room and sat in front of the window, still wearing her coat, staring across the campus. She saw Jared leave the Student Center, watched him cross to the path through the woods. He continued on until she couldn't see him anymore. This was the way it would be. He would continue on until she couldn't see him anymore, but instead of being mere yards away, it would hundreds of miles.

Beth glanced into Joanna's room as she passed by.

"Jo? Are you on your way out? Jo?" She went into the room and tapped Joanna on the shoulder. "Are you okay?"

Joanna bobbed her head but didn't turn around.

"No, you're not, are you? Oh honey, you're not." She knelt next to Joanna's chair. "What's happened? Will you tell me?"

Joanna turned slowly, tears on her face.

"Nothing's changed. I still can't talk about it. Not because I don't trust you. We've always been closer than that, because I don't trust myself to talk about it. I'm sorry."

"Hey, don't apologize. I'm not prying; I'm very worried about you. If talking about whatever's going on will help you, I'm always ready to listen. I hate seeing you upset like this."

"You don't have to worry about me; I'm okay," Joanna insisted.

"Don't give me that! I'm watching you let your work slide. You don't go home anymore and you don't spend any time with your friends. There's something big happening with you, and it's making you miserable. Of course I'm worried. I care about you. Please, talk to me."

Joanna gave in with a sigh of relief. "It *is* Jared. It's been Jared since the day in October when I first met him. We tried to be just friends, but there was this connection from the beginning that kept getting stronger and stronger and we finally quit fighting it. He's brought me a lot of happiness, and I know I've done the same for him. He means everything to me. I don't know how I'll live when he's gone."

"Gone? Where's he going?"

"You might as well know ... everyone will very soon anyway. He's accepted a new job in Chicago. This will be his last semester at Manning; he starts there in September. That's where he's been since Monday and I guess he'll tell President Reade today."

"Oh, I'm sorry. How awful for you! I won't ask any questions—the details aren't important anyhow. But if there's any way I can help, please talk to me."

"Thanks. I can't imagine how I'm going to make it when he's gone, or, for that matter, until he leaves."

~ * ~

Joanna skipped lunch. Instead, she went to Kenton Hall and knocked quietly on Jared's office door.

He opened it, took her hand and drew her inside.

"Oh, how I prayed you'd come. I've been sitting here listening to the footsteps outside my door, holding my breath when anyone came near, waiting for you, hoping you wouldn't decide to stay away."

"Welcome back, darling," she said.

"How I missed you. So many times when I was out there, I turned to tell you something, to share a thought, show you a sight. You've become so necessary to me, Joanna. How can I tell you?"

"No need. I know how you feel. I'm sorry about this morning..."

Jared put his hand gently over her mouth.

"Don't say it. Let's pretend this morning never happened. I had to prattle on and on about something that could have, no, should have, waited for another time. The way the conversation went this morning, that was my fault. What I really meant to say was 'how are things going for you?'"

"Now, they're fine." She walked with him to a chair, her arm still around his waist.

"No, I mean it. Tell me. What did you do while I was away?"

She looked at him seriously. "I waited for the phone to ring. I dreamed about you at night. I listened to our favorite music and I read Benton. Then I waited for the phone to ring. It was a very long three days. Satisfied?"

"I guess I deserve that. There I was, busy every moment, absorbing so much that's new and exciting, hardly able to stand the wait until I could share it with you, but busy nonetheless. It was different for you, wasn't it? You were still here, trying to carry on as usual. What have I done to you? How will you stay behind—here, surrounded by memories—for another whole year?"

"Frankly, I don't know. It's what I'll have to do, that's all. Anyway, this little preview was more than I wanted. I don't want to think about a whole year of those kinds of days. Please, let's not talk about that now."

"We need some time together," he said. "Can you go home this weekend?"

"Are you serious? Why?"

"You could sign out for home and stay at Dan's instead. I'll be with you every possible moment, I promise. We need time together," he repeated, leaning over to her chair until she could see herself in his eyes. "Please, do this for us."

~ * ~

They skipped the club on Friday night, eager to get to Dan's, to be alone. As the fire rose, they sat on the sofa, nursed their manhattans and talked, Joanna about the loneliness of the days without him, her unhappiness with teaching; Jared about the children, the new job, his anguish at leaving her behind.

"I tried countless times while I was out there to imagine what it will be like to be living there permanently, without being able to see you every day. It didn't seem real; I couldn't envision my life without you in it. I know it was hard for you being here while I was away; it'll be hard for you once I'm gone and you're still here, but despite the challenges of the new job, I'll be as alone as you."

~ * ~

February sped by, time seeming to have grown wings now that Jared's leaving drew nearer. It was the last week of team teaching and Joanna was anxious for it to be over. After every play rehearsal, she ticked off the remaining days on the calendar in her room, knowing her time with Jared would soon end.

The week before dress rehearsal, as she crossed off yet another day, she stopped and hastily flipped the page back to January. With a sinking feeling, she realized she had skipped her period last month and was already nearly two weeks overdue again. Gripping her dresser top with both hands, she stared at her own reflection in the mirror. *Oh, no,* she thought. *Now what?*

> *My darling Joanna,*
>
> *I looked at the calendar this morning and felt a fist close around my heart. Even though we have five months left, look how rapidly the last six have passed. I want to grab time in both hands and hold it fast, refuse to let it slip out of my fingers.*
>
> *When the play is over, let's go to Manhattan again. With the impending move, I can easily find a reason to be in the city for a few days. Actually, there's a new off-Broadway play we could see; it might be something I might want to tackle at Roosevelt, so that alone justifies my being away.*
>
> *I know it means missing some classes, but see what you can do and let me know. We could leave for the city on the morning of the 11th and stay through Saturday.*
>
> *It won't be the Statler this time, my darling. We're on our own and something of lesser luxury will be the order of the day. No matter where we are, though,*

*what's important is we'll be together again in Oz, looking for a wizard to give us more time.*

*I'll wait to hear from you. Remember I love you and I always will.*

*Jared*

Such a beautiful letter with such a tempting offer. He saw something on his calendar that caused him distress; Joanna saw something else when she looked at hers. She was sick with the realization she'd have to tell Jared about her fears. He was so blissfully in the dark, so unaware. Good God, why hadn't they been more careful? That wonderful week at Christmas hadn't caught them by surprise; they'd had plenty of time to prepare properly. She assumed she'd be safe. *Stupid,* she chided herself. *What do you know? You never slept with anyone and you didn't bother to educate yourself beyond the damn romance stories in the magazines? What will Jared do? How will he take this news?*

At first, she debated not telling him at all. Maybe there was someone else she could turn to for help. *Doris won't be a sympathetic ear,* she thought. *And even if she would be, how could I dump this on her? She's the one who warned me about this relationship. And Mom? Oh no, not Mom!* They'd never had a real "talk" about sex. Joanna had learned what she knew through suggestive comments, giggling conversations in school and then later, copy after copy of *True Story* with its accounts of secret trysts and torrid love affairs. There was a certain reticence about the topic that always seemed to give her the feeling her mother looked on sex as something best not discussed. *So, she's out.* And besides, Joanna reasoned, *this isn't anyone else's problem. It's mine and it's Jared's.*

~ * ~

"Joanna? What is it? What brings you here so early? Your class isn't for another hour, is it?"

She walked in, put her books on his desk and turned to face him.

"Yes, I have an hour or so and I needed to talk to you. It's very important and I don't want to wait."

"Oh, I hope you'll say yes to my suggestion that we go to Manhattan after the play. Is that it? Will you go?"

"It's not that. Of course I'll go, but we have something to deal with before we can make any more plans."

She paused for breath long enough for Jared to interject, "Is it your parents? Is something wrong?"

"No, darling, it isn't. But something might be wrong and I need your help. Badly, I'm afraid," she said, her voice quavering. "I think I might be pregnant."

For a second, Jared's face registered dismay, then concern.

"Are you sure?" His voice was quiet and even.

"No. I missed my last period and I'm late this month. There aren't any other symptoms, only that. But I've been as regular as clockwork since I was twelve, so I've got to admit I'm frightened."

Jared frowned, his brows tightly knit.

"Well, we need to know, don't we? We need to get you to a doctor for a test before we go on to the next step and talk about what to do."

"What doctor? I wouldn't dare go to the infirmary," Joanna said. "Confidentiality or no confidentiality, it'd be all over campus in an hour I'd been there for a pregnancy test."

"Of course you can't. Do you know any local doctors? Anyone you would be comfortable with?"

"No. I'm very healthy. I've never consulted with a doctor since I've been here and my family doctor at home takes care of routine things. Do you think I should go to him?"

"Not unless you want to. I was thinking perhaps my doctor would agree to see you. He's a young man and we've been pretty close besides the doctor-patient thing ever since I've been here. What do you think?"

"I'd feel better about seeing someone like that. Can you call him now and set something up?"

~ * ~

At two the following afternoon, while Jared was in class, Joanna took his car and kept her appointment with Joshua Milton. Her hands shook as she opened the door to his office and she answered his questions with a tremulous voice. Despite his efforts at putting her at ease, she was awkward, stiff and very scared as she lay on the table, feet in the stirrups, while he gently examined her. When he'd finished, without comment he handed her a paper cup, instructed her to leave a specimen for lab analysis and said he would see her in the office when she was through.

His chair was empty when she went in. She sat at his desk, hands folded, feeling slightly dizzy and totally terrified.

Drying his hands, he came in the back door of the office and sat.

"If you are pregnant, Miss Ransome, it's too early for a manual exam to show it. We'll have to wait for the test results which should be back in about three days."

His voice softened and Joanna couldn't tell whether he was sympathetic or critical. "I'll call Jared when I know for sure. It'll probably be sometime Monday."

~ * ~

Joanna put the car keys on Jared's desk and was about to leave when he opened the door and closed it behind him.

"So? What did Josh say?"

"Nothing for sure. He said it was too early to tell from an examination and we'd have to wait probably until next Monday for test results. I'm so scared."

He held her close, his face in her hair. "Don't worry, my darling, we'll handle whatever we have to. It's going to be okay."

"But what if I am? What if there's going to be a baby? What would we do?"

"We'll talk it out," he said softly. "We'll explore our options and decide the best course to follow. I think we'd be foolish to make plans for something that may never happen."

~ * ~

The weekend was filled with rehearsals and classes, only a few hours open for a quick run to the club. Joanna knew Jared was struggling with the possibilities just as she was, but neither of them talked about what a positive diagnosis would mean to his plans, his family, or hers.

~ * ~

She went back to her room after class Monday afternoon and found a note taped to her door. Jared had called. She went down the hall and dialed his office.

"Joanna? I've heard from Josh. Can you come over?"

"I'll be right there," she said, hanging up without asking about the test. She wanted to be with Jared when she heard the verdict.

As she crossed the quad toward Kenton Hall, she saw him standing on the top step, waiting for her. He gently took her arm, led her into the building and into his office where he turned her to face him.

"There's no baby, my darling," he said, tears in his eyes. "It must be some kind of irregularity with your cycle, Josh said. He said if you're concerned, he'd be happy to see you again, but the test was definitely negative."

He pulled her close. "In a way, I'm relieved, but in another I'm very sad. I know we would have been in utter chaos had there been a child on the way, but we would have been forced to deal with it and then we would have had a wonderful miracle to share. I'm sorry for the worry and the fear."

*Strange, I'm not sad,* Joanna thought. *I'm so very relieved, not just for Jared, but for me and for what this would have done to my mother. Still, a baby would surely have forced the issue, either kept us together permanently or driven us apart. I wonder which way it would have gone?*

She tightened her arms around Jared. "I think I needed to hear that, one way or the other. Of course, we would have been in terrible trouble. But those few days of imagining what it would be like to have your child, to see your face in that baby's, was a fantasy I found sweet all the same."

~ * ~

There was little time to dwell on the scare they'd experienced. After a hectic two days of frantic last-minute adjustments, the first dress rehearsal on Wednesday went off without a hitch.

On Friday morning, Joanna's mother called. With the unexpected change in the weather, she and Joe had decided to come up for the Sunday matinee.

"Don't worry about entertaining us," she said. "I know you'll be busy with the production and the cast party afterwards. We wanted to see the play and hear the music. Do you mind?"

~ * ~

Joanna sat in the snack bar with her parents, enjoying a light lunch, talking about the unusually warm early April, her teaching experiences and the play.

As always, Joanna felt Jared come into the room before she actually caught sight of him. When she did, she was stunned to see him heading toward her table, holding his children by the hand, one on each side.

"Ah, the real star of our production!" he exclaimed theatrically, gesturing toward Joanna. "I'm sorry to barge in like this, but I wanted very much to meet Joanna's parents and to introduce you all to my children."

Jared leaned over and whispered something to Michael, who promptly went to Joanna and held out his hand.

"How do you do? I'm Michael Fowler," he said, his face sober, eyes fixed on the floor.

"And I'm Marina Fowler," said the pretty little blonde. "I'm almost eight and I'm in the second grade."

Joanna stood and took Marina's hand. "Dr. Jared Fowler, Marina, Michael, I'd like to introduce you to my parents, Catherine and Joe Ransome," she said. "And I'm Joanna. I'm very glad to meet both of you. Can you sit with us for a while?"

Jared shook hands with Joanna's parents and stood with his hands on his children's shoulders.

"We really can't, as much as we'd like to stay and talk a bit. I brought the kids to see the play and they want to go backstage first to see all the sets and props, so I told them we'd make a quick stop here for a soda and get over to Kenton before the cast starts to show up."

Joanna sat back down, still smiling at the children, who stood close by their father. *What would our little one have looked like?* she wondered. When she looked up, she knew Jared was thinking the same thing.

"Of course," she said, meeting his eyes with longing. "Perhaps we'll get a chance to do it another time." Turning her attention to the children, she said, "It was very nice meeting both of you. I hope you enjoy the play and we get to see each other again one of these days."

"We're moving, you know," Michael blurted out. "We're going to live in Chicago, right, Dad?"

Jared patted Michael's shoulder, looking steadily at Joanna, his deep-set eyes begging her understanding.

"Right, son, but not for a while yet. We have plenty of time to enjoy being here and maybe we'll have a chance to see Joanna again."

Saying their farewells, Jared and the children went up to the counter, the perky pink bow on the back of Marina's dress bobbing as they made their way through the tables. As they left, Jared turned and waved to Joanna.

"Is he one of your teachers?" Catherine asked.

"No. He's a professor in the drama department and the director of the play. I only met him last fall."

Seeing an inquisitive look in her mother's eyes, Joanna worried something had given them away. But it was too late to analyze the brief meeting. She knew Catherine would bring up the subject in her own time if she'd found anything to question.

~ * ~

By the time Joanna could break away from the hubbub of the after-curtain-call rowdiness, her parents had been waiting for several minutes in the lobby. Joe wandered down the hall to find the men's room, leaving Joanna alone with her mother.

Putting a hand on Joanna's arm, Catherine said, "Jo, we're going to need to talk, you and I. Something I saw, no, something I sensed, has me very concerned. Am I wrong?"

"About what?" Joanna asked, her heart racing, her face feeling warm.

"Dr. Fowler. He's not just a professor you worked with on the play, is he? There's something else there, something more serious. I saw how he looked at you today; I saw how you looked at him. I'm afraid for you. Please don't do anything foolish."

Joanna hugged her mother close, watching her father walk toward them down the hall. "Don't worry about me. When we can, we'll talk, not now. Please, don't worry."

~ * ~

Jared was the last to arrive at the party.

"Sorry I'm late, everyone," he said to the group who greeted him with a cheer as he came through the door. "I had to take the kids home and get them settled. They were still pretty keyed up from the excitement."

The food was abundant, the music loud. After about an hour, Jared took the microphone and introduced each member of the cast and crew to noisy approval from the crowd.

When he called out her name, Joanna went up and took his hand as he gave a flattering description of her work. He held her hand longer than he needed to, but nothing prepared her for what came next.

"Guys, gals, I need your attention for a few minutes," he said, looking at Joanna with regret in his eyes. "Some of you may have heard by now that this will be my last stage production at Manning."

A loud groan of protest spread through the crowd. Joanna stepped back into the shadows.

"In September, I'll be starting a new chapter in my life as assistant director of the Auditorium Theatre and professor of drama at Roosevelt University in Chicago."

More groans, a few boos, shocked faces at every table.

"Believe me, leaving Manning will be one of the hardest things I've ever had to do," he said, quieter now that he had everyone's attention. "The years I've spent here, especially this last one, have been among the most precious of my life and I'll never find in Chicago what I've found here."

Looking in vain for Joanna, hoping she was still there, he said, "I wrestled very hard with this decision. It wasn't something I sought and believe me, I didn't accept the new job without a lot of soul-searching and deep sadness. Thanks for everything you've done for me."

He was mobbed when he put down the microphone. Over the heads of the students, he looked for Joanna, finally spotting her at the edge of the crowd. Try as he might, he couldn't get to her for the insistence of the well-wishers. When he finally broke free, she was nowhere in sight.

He felt a hand on his arm.

"I saw her go out the back door," Beth said. "Give her some space, Dr. Fowler—this is very hard for her."

"You know?"

"I guessed. Joanna refused to talk about it for the longest time, but she needs a friend. She finally told me about the two of you, about your leaving. I'm sorry, but I feel a lot of loyalty to Jo and I want to help her if I can."

"Thank you. Please, just be there for her. These next months, this next year, will be very difficult and lonely, for both of us."

As soon as he could leave, Jared hurried back to Kenton. Joanna was sitting in his car, staring straight ahead, trembling slightly.

"Joanna? My darling, are you all right?" He slid in beside her and folded her in his arms. "I know it was awful. There was no way I could have prepared you, no way I could have escaped making the announcement. It was a no-win situation all around. I'm sorry the evening had to end like that."

She crawled deep into his jacket, burying her face against his chest.

"It was horrible. I heard what you said and I knew you were talking about this past year with me. So did everybody else. How do you think I felt? I couldn't wait to get out of that room. How could you, especially after what we've been through? Why not wait and tell your classes when I wasn't standing there?"

"Forgive me. I never thought of the implications, I guess. I didn't mean to make it so hurtful. You have every right to be angry. I'm so, so sorry, my darling."

"I know. It's just that times like tonight make it so real. You're really going away, and there's nothing I can do to change it."

# *Twenty*



*"Which wife is Dr. Fowler taking with him?"*

Jared pulled up to a small hotel on West 43ʳᵈ Street and 8th Avenue in midtown Manhattan. Leaning over to look up at it, he grimaced ruefully.

"It's certainly not the Statler, but at least we'll be together."

As soon as they opened the door to room 923, Joanna went to the window. "There's not much of a view, but we're in Manhattan, so who cares?"

Jared took off her light jacket, his hands working under her sweater, unfastening the hooks on her bra. Her full, bare breasts were warm and inviting. The April sun was shining in the windows, but they were oblivious to time of day, making up for the nights they'd been apart. After the false alarm they'd weathered, though, they'd become more cautious, making sure not to take such a risk again.

"I've missed you, Joanna. I hope I didn't cause a problem by calling, but I couldn't wait until today to hear your voice."

"No, no problem. The girls all know your voice and I'm sure it's no secret to anyone anymore that we're far more than friends.

I'm amazed, though, that no one has blown the whistle. With so many people knowing about us, I keep waiting for someone to call Vicki or Dr. Reade. Maybe they like us too much to make trouble. Maybe they think we're good for each other."

Jared stretched, turned to take her face in his hands.

"I know how good you are for me, my darling. But so many times I feel like I'm doing irreparable damage to your life. I saw a puzzled look on your mother's face Sunday. She suspects, doesn't she?"

"Uh-huh. She told me it was the way we looked at each other that tipped her off. When I see her at Easter, I know she'll want some answers. I haven't decided yet how much to tell her." She rose on her elbow to look at him. "Did I tell you what beautiful children you have? I'm so glad you brought them. Now, when I think of Michael and Marina, I'll be able to picture them. It did make me a little sad when I thought about what it would have been like having a child with you. But we both know everything worked out for the best."

"I know. I was thinking the very same thing but I hoped you wouldn't mind my bringing them in to meet you. So often, I fantasize about a future for the four of us, maybe even the five of us some day. I guess I want it so badly I let myself pretend for a second or two by putting us all together in the same place. It was foolish of me and really didn't help. Now I want it more than ever."

~ * ~

"Let's walk tomorrow," Joanna suggested as they went into their room after the play. "We didn't explore this part of the city when we were here before."

Jared sat and took off his shoes. "Sounds good. For now, though, I think we could both stand to be off our feet for the next ten hours or so."

Their lovemaking was leisurely, both of them content to take it slow. Joanna loved tracing his face, using just the very tip of the nail on her index finger, from forehead to each eyebrow, down the classic nose, around the lips and from one side of the jaw to the other. Her touch was feathery light, sensuous to the point of madness.

~ * ~

On Thursday and Friday, they walked the city, giddy as children on a school trip. Each day, they wound up at the Battery, taking the ferry ride over to Staten Island. Now, they could stand on the top deck without the weight of heavy coats, breathe the fresh air and listen to the sounds of seagulls and boat horns as they hung over the rail. Jared stood with his eyes closed, face raised to the breeze. Joanna touched his cheek, pulled his head down for a gentle kiss.

"*'Blindfolded, I could kiss a thousand mouths and know your lips,'*" she whispered.

"Walter Benton," Jared said, his eyes still closed. "*'I knew your eyes by heart after the very first reading.'* Benton must have known there would be a Joanna when he wrote his poems."

~ * ~

All too quickly it was Saturday. Another farewell, this one particularly poignant in its finality.

"Who knows if we'll ever come here together again," Joanna said sorrowfully. "There's so little time left."

Jared took her hands. "I promise, we'll come here again."

~ * ~

On the way back to Manning, they talked about the upcoming Easter holiday. The offices and dorms would be closed for a week for spring cleaning, and Joanna told Jared she'd already planned what she would do for the mini-vacation.

"I've already told my parents I'd be home for Easter Sunday but then back on Monday. They think I'm staying with Beth at her cousin's place in town ... at least I think my dad does. I'll find out about Mom on Sunday. Anyway, I'll be back on Monday with the whole week in front of me and nowhere to stay. Unless, of course, there's a certain cabin in the woods that could take in a boarder."

"That would be wonderful, my darling. Dan's place is marvelous in spring. Sitting on the front porch in the afternoon with a good book, hiking through the little trails that run on all sides of the house. It'll be a perfect place for a getaway."

"I thought you'd like my idea. Don't worry ... I know you'll be busy with the children so I'll have plenty of reading material and good music to listen to. But when you can, you'll come to me and we can be together."

~ * ~

Jared called Monday night.

"Joanna, can you talk?"

"Yes. What is it?"

His words tumbled over one another. "They're going back to Florida. I can't believe her parents are doing this, but Vicki's folks want to fly her and the kids down for Easter vacation. It seems like they just got back from the last trip."

"What about you? Did you say anything to Vicki about going along?"

"Not this time. Even though I'm sure she wouldn't want me there, I'm not risking it. Knowing you're planning on staying at Dan's, how could I take the chance she'd surprise me and agree to my going along? So I hugged the kids and told them I was jealous that they'd be swimming in the Gulf while I was home working. It's happening so often they accepted it without protest and they're excited about going."

"Oh, how wonderful! When do they leave?"

"Saturday at noon. I should be back from the airport by two or so. When are you going home?"

"I need to be out of here early on Friday when the dorm closes. Either I go home with Mark or I hitchhike Saturday. I'm sorry, but I'll be gone until Monday."

Jared's voice was wistful. "Well, I guess I'm on my own for a couple days, but that's okay. I'll go to Dan's, do some basic housekeeping and get ready for you. Call me sometime if you can."

~ * ~

Joanna's house was quiet when she let herself in on Friday afternoon. She wandered slowly from room to room, trying to remember what it had been like to live there, what *she* had been like before Jared. This was the place of her childhood, where she had dreamed about the kind of love she'd found with him. But in her dreams, she'd lived happily ever after.

Suddenly she had a thought. High on the top shelf of her closet were the yearbooks from her first two years at Manning. Sure enough, there in the faculty section was the photo of Jared in suit and tie, smiling slightly. She put her index finger on the page and gently and slowly traced his face. She could almost hear him moan. How would she live without him?

~ * ~

The talk with her mother came earlier than she'd anticipated. She was in her room reading Saturday afternoon when Catherine tapped on her door.

"Jo? May I come in?"

"Sure." Joanna put down the book as her mother sat on the edge of the bed.

"Your dad's out helping Uncle Fred with his boat. He'll be back in time for dinner, but I'm kind of glad he's out. I want to talk to you. I think you know what about."

Joanna sighed, her eyes on her hands. "Jared Fowler. I know … it's time we talked."

"It's none of my business, but I'm worried. Back at Christmas, you told me you were involved with someone, but the future wasn't certain. You said you didn't know where the relationship was going, if anywhere. Were you talking about this man then?"

"Yes, I was." Joanna shifted in her chair, tucked her legs beneath her, leaned forward and put her hand under her chin.

"We met in October. Doris introduced us one day in the snack bar. It started out as a friendship ... we found each other so easy to talk to, shared so many interests. We tried to keep it that way, but the longer we knew one another, the harder it was to keep from admitting how we really felt. But now I know I'm in love with him."

"He's much older than you, isn't he?"

"I guess you'd say so, although we don't feel the age difference at all. You've always said I got along better with people older than I anyway, and when I'm with Jared I feel like we're contemporaries. He's intelligent, sensitive and caring. He makes me very happy."

"I'm confused. Jared's son said he was moving to Chicago. How can his ex-wife take them and move that far away?"

Taking a deep breath, Joanna said, "Jared and his wife aren't divorced."

Catherine's expression froze. "He's married? He's still living with his wife?"

"I know, Mom, I know. That's why I couldn't tell you before. That's what makes it so hard to talk about now. I knew you'd be very upset and angry with me, but believe me, there was nothing I could have done to keep from falling in love with him."

Catherine leapt to her feet, clasping and unclasping her hands. "You could have called a halt to the whole thing before it got to that point," she said in a harsh, angry voice Joanna had never heard from her mother. "Obviously you knew he was married when you met him. How could you let this relationship grow? How could you continue seeing him, knowing how you were feeling?"

"I couldn't do anything else. Look, I know you're disappointed and angry; I don't expect you to understand. This goes against everything you taught me, everything I grew up thinking was moral. But I need Jared in my life. I've made him happy for the first time in years; he's made me feel like I only dreamed I could. After he's gone, I'll have to deal with what happens next. Until then, I need to be with him."

Catherine paced back and forth without replying. Finally, she stopped, her face grim.

"You said Doris introduced you. How could she let you put yourself in this position? Why didn't she talk to him, make him leave you alone?"

"Doris talked to *me*. She pointed out the pitfalls of becoming involved with him. But it's like I've already said ... none of it matters. We struggle every day with the complexities of our relationship, the consequences to his children, to him and to me. We were starting to deal with those questions when he was offered the new job in the Midwest. Now, we'll have to continue to work things out long distance."

Catherine sat again. Joanna had never heard her mother's voice so stern. "I can't believe my daughter is in this situation. After what your father did to us, leaving us for another woman, I cannot believe you're a party to breaking up someone else's family. How could you?"

Joanna looked down at her shoes. "I didn't break anything that wasn't already heavily damaged. But don't think I haven't given a lot of thought to the very point you're making. There is a difference here, though. Jared hasn't left his children; he may never leave them. There may not be a future for us, mainly because Jared is so committed to being a father who's there for the kids when they need him."

"And what about you? How can he say he loves you when he's got you in this limbo? What are you supposed to be doing while he makes up his mind? Oh, Jo, don't do this to yourself. Please, please cut him out of your life. Leave him now and try to get on with the plans you had before you met him. Don't do it for me; do it for yourself, for your own future. Promise you'll leave this man to his problems before he destroys your life."

"I can't promise that, as much as I know I should. We're bound together, Jared and I, in a way I don't understand. I do know it would be easier for me if he weren't in my life, but would it be better?" She answered her own question. "No, it wouldn't. Something like this comes along once in a lifetime. I think you had the same feelings for my father and you never forgave him for abandoning you, abandoning us. But you felt it once, didn't you? You know how strong it is, how unshakable. Don't ask me to cut Jared out of my life, because I can't."

Catherine nodded slowly and left the room.

Throughout the day Sunday, as family members came and went and the house was filled with a steady stream of holiday visitors, Catherine didn't look directly at Joanna. When everyone had gone, Joanna went to her room, packed her few things and sat on the bed to try to read. When she replied to a tap on her door, it was her stepfather whose head peered around.

"Got a minute, honey?"

"Sure, Dad, always for you. Come in. I was sort of expecting you."

He sat next to her and took her small hand in his, the carpenter's callouses rough but his touch very gentle.

"Your mother and I had a long talk about you last night. She told me about this man you've fallen for, the professor we met at the play. This has her real upset, you know. Honey, these past years all I ever wanted was for you to be happy. I hoped you were, living here with me, that I somehow helped you get over the loss of your dad. I know from what Katie told me this man isn't making you happy. It isn't right for you. I know you think you're in love ... you can't do without him and all that. But you have to put yourself first. You have to forget this guy and put your life back in order."

Joanna squeezed his hand. "I wish it were so easy, Daddy. I don't think it was ever an option, not from the first day I met Jared. We were heading toward one another the whole time we were fighting to stay apart." She sighed heavily. "I know you're upset with me, you and Mom, and I'm not surprised. But I can't do what you want me to. I can't behave the way you think I should this time."

Joe stood slowly and walked toward the door. He turned with his hand on the knob, sadness etched in his face. "We've tried our best. There's no sense in wasting any more of our breath. Your mind is made up and I see there's no changing it. I wish it was different."

When he had gone, Joanna turned out the light and closed her eyes, wishing she could be spirited out of the house and back to Dan's where Jared waited for her. Emotionally exhausted, she slept.

~ * ~

By the time Joanna got up Monday, her parents had gone. On the kitchen room table was a note.

> *I didn't want to wake you before I left for work this morning. As always, having you home for the holiday made it extra-special. Dad and I won't stop worrying about you until this man is out of your life, but we know you have to handle this yourself. Give us a call when you can. We love you very much.*
>
> *Mom*

It seemed to take forever for Jared to answer the phone.

"Hi! I'm sorry I couldn't call earlier, but I wanted to let you know I'm on my way. I'll be there before lunch. Is everything okay?"

"Sure. I missed hearing from you, that's all. Did everything go well at home with your mom and dad?"

"I'll tell you all about it when I see you. I talked with both of them and I know I wasn't able to set their minds at ease, but at least it's out in the open and they know. I'll give you details when I get there."

181

~ * ~

The days that followed were surreal. Joanna surrendered and allowed herself to live in her fantasy world. By day, she and Jared roamed the countryside, taking a picnic lunch to Bowman's Tower, driving far into the northern portions of the state to the Pocono Mountains, going into Philadelphia shopping for presents for Marina's birthday. In the evenings, they ate out or cooked in Dan's kitchen, often sitting on the porch to eat, listening to the symphony of sound performed by the creatures in the woods. Twice they went to the club to listen to Jim.

Nights were like magic. On Thursday, it was unseasonably warm, so they spread blankets on the lawn, their bodies illuminated by moonlight, the darkness broken only by the stars.

"'*A star breaks, arcs down the night—like God striking a match across the cathedral ceiling.*' Remember, my darling? I'll bet Walter and Lillian were outside like we are now, happy and filled with love."

"No, they weren't. Benton wrote that after he and Lillian parted. The next two lines, well, they're probably what I'm going to be doing once you're gone."

"What do you mean?"

She sighed. "'*Therefore I wish: see my lips move—making your name. It is so still, so still. I am sure that you must hear me.*'"

He drew her close and kissed her hair.

"I'm sorry, I didn't mean to make you sad. I'd forgotten the rest of the poem; the image of the match just came to me, looking up at the sky filled with stars. But you're right. Wherever you are or wherever I am, I'll hear you say my name and you'll hear me whisper yours."

~ * ~

On the seventeenth of May, the college newspaper carried the yearbook photo of Jared with the news of his coming departure. After citing his accomplishments at the college, the author wrote,

"Dr. Fowler will relocate to Chicago in late August. A wife and two children will accompany him."

"They meant *his* wife, Beth. I'm sure it was only a mistake," Joanna protested when Beth hinted the error was deliberate.

The following week, the paper ran a tongue-in-cheek question on the front page: "Which wife is Dr. Fowler taking with him?" Beth gave her an I-told-you-so smile. Joanna only shrugged.

On Tuesday, there was a letter.

*My darling Joanna,*

*I hope and pray the snide little comment in the* Target *doesn't cause you any problems. For my part, it doesn't matter what anyone's saying anymore. You, on the other hand, will be here a whole year with some of the same people who wrote that stuff. I know how highly everyone thinks of you so I'm trying to believe it was an honest-to-goodness attempt to poke fun at themselves for their earlier mistake. Whatever, it preys on my mind that once I'm gone, you'll have more to contend with than you deserve.*

*I never did thank you properly for everything you did to help make Marina's eighth birthday so wonderful for her and for me. She has no idea how much your thoughtfulness helped make her gifts perfect, and the way your love helped me put her first on a Saturday I wanted to be with you.*

*Every day, you do or say something that tugs at my heart and makes me sick with dread at the thought of leaving you. Forgive me if I seem morbid at times—I'm trying to keep things positive, but I'm not always good at it. I want to run off with you to a place where no one will ever find us. Childish, isn't it? Bear with me; I'm working hard at being ready to be alone again and I'm finding it more painful than I could have imagined.*

*I love you, my darling, and I always will.*

*Jared*

# Twenty-one

*"We're not over... I believe that."*

On official school letterhead, the message offered Joanna a place as a student teacher at Claybourne Junior High where she would work with seventh and eighth graders of all ability levels under the supervision of Gabriel O'Donnell, her cooperating teacher.

"I'm sure your call had something to do with my being accepted," Joanna told Doris when she gave her the news. "Thank you."

"It wouldn't have mattered what I said if your record hadn't spoken for itself," Doris countered. "I've never been to the school, but it's new and everyone says it's very progressive. This will be the real test of if you want to teach."

~ * ~

Commencement Day arrived on June 9th. Many of Joanna's friends were graduating; the seniors in the dorm were packed up, getting ready to leave Manning, armed with their new teaching certificates.

Jared called near lunchtime. "Hello, my darling, how are you?"

"Sorry, I can barely hear you. There's so much going on here today, so much noise, so many people ... where are you?"

"On campus. I have to walk in the Grand March today, remember? I came in early to pick up my robe and I thought we might go to lunch. Are you free?"

After a quick sandwich, they went back to his office where Jared opened a large box that held the black gown trimmed in gold, the mortarboard cap and satiny hood he would wear. He put on the robe and Joanna slipped the long hood over his head. She straightened it so it fell in a graceful fold at his back and fastened the fabric loop over the button of the gown to hold it in place. She stepped back and examined the finished product. "You look so serious. You really could pass for a creaking old academic. Come on, brighten up that stodgy outfit with a smile."

She stepped back and chuckled. "I *do* want to remember you like this, though, that's why I brought this." She took a small pocket camera out of her purse. "Let's go out front where the light's better so I can take a picture of Doctor Jared Fowler Ph.D. wearing his best professional attitude."

Outside, Joanna snapped a picture as Jared stood poker straight, wearing the slightest of smiles, holding the cap in his right hand, his left hanging stiffly at his side.

"Now, go on out there and knock 'em dead, Doc."

~ * ~

They went to the club after dinner. When Joanna came out of the ladies' room, she found Jared in earnest conversation with Jim, who was nodding and saying something quietly. They stopped talking as Joanna neared.

"Don't let me interrupt," she said.

"Not at all." Jared put his arm around her waist. "Jim and I were talking music. He's adding some new stuff to his repertoire and I mentioned a couple of songs we'd like to hear."

~ * ~

On the eleventh, Joanna moved into an apartment with Beth. Campus was closed except for summer school students and Joanna had long since decided not to be in Atlantic City for the final two months of her time with Jared. Without much explanation to her parents, she said she'd be staying in Manning.

"Beth's taken a summer work fellowship," she told Jared as they walked along the Delaware Canal in New Hope one warm early June evening. "She can use the help with rent on a decent place in town and I need to be here where you are. It's as simple as that. She'll be going home often, so we'll have another place besides Dan's to spend time."

~ * ~

Throughout June, Jared devoted his mornings to the children. Marina attended a half-day recreation program, so after he brought her home, he drove to Manning and spent every afternoon with Joanna. Cleaning out his office didn't take long. With Joanna's help, the contents of desk and closet were sorted, packed or discarded and soon the office walls were bare, a small stack of boxes by the door the only evidence someone had once spent hours working there.

~ * ~

After weeks of rewrite, Doris's paper was ready for final proofreading. Joanna sat in the quiet of a library carrel going over the document word for word, checking one last time for any misspellings or typographical errors. As she reviewed the work she and Doris had done in what seemed like another life, Joanna couldn't fail to be struck again by the findings of the research project.

"I guess I realize now," she told Jared that night, "that all those experiences of my childhood—being without my father, living in such fear in my uncle's house—are at the root of my connection with you. I believe I've been looking at us through glasses filtered by an unconscious need for a man, probably an older man, to make me feel safe and loved. It's unsettling to know my childhood may have made me neurotic enough to be hanging on to someone I can't have while the reality is I won't end up being safe at all."

~ * ~

On Sunday, with the paper properly bound and packed in her briefcase, Doris kissed Joanna goodbye.

"I'll be in Seattle for four days. I'll read the paper at the general session on Wednesday. I wish you could be there to hear it; you deserve the most credit for its being presented at all, you know. Thank you, honey."

"I wish I could be there, too. I'd be so proud I'd want to shout. You're going on to Florida after the conference?"

"Yes. I need some time there. I left a lot of very good friends when I moved north. I want to keep those connections alive. As long as I'm not needed here until school reopens, I want to spend as much time as possible where I *am* needed."

"You know I'll always need you, but I suppose there's such a thing as too much need, isn't there? My little drama will simply have to play out and then hopefully you'll be around to help me pick up the pieces."

~ * ~

"I need to see you." Jared's voice was hushed, almost a whisper.

"Of course. When and where?"

"May I come over? Will Beth mind?"

"Beth's at the library tonight working on her project. She'll be back about ten. Can you give me an idea what about? Is it the children?"

"No, it's Vicki. It's not earth shattering, my darling, but I do want to share it with you. I'll leave in a few minutes."

~ * ~

"She says she's only making the move to Chicago temporarily." Jared paced the small living room as he talked, running his hand through his hair.

"Start at the beginning, please. You and Vicki finally had a talk about the move?"

He sat next to Joanna, resting his arms on his knees.

"Finally. I had long ago stopped trying. I was tired of getting the back of her head every time I tried to ask for a time we could talk. She's just been going on as though nothing were going to change, although she's on the phone a lot with her mother and I suspect she's complaining to her. That's all well and good, but the time's getting very close now and nothing's been done to prepare. I didn't even know if she was coming with me."

Joanna touched his arm and he turned to look at her.

"There must be so much to do. What about the move?"

"I guess I'm going to do it, especially after the little chat we had earlier tonight."

"Tell me what happened."

"She's decided, she said, to move to Chicago and 'try it out.' Nothing permanent, mind you, on a trial basis. She said her parents had made her an open offer to come home to Florida any time she wanted, but she thought it might be hard on the kids now, so she figures she'll make the move and decide later whether to stay. I asked her what would influence her decision once we were there that hasn't already happened but she didn't answer directly. She said she couldn't be any unhappier in Chicago than she is now, but when I pressed her to talk to me about why she's unhappy, she wouldn't."

"Do you think she knows you're seeing me?"

"I don't know. I doubt it, because I was never home *before* I met you, so my pattern hasn't changed. Maybe she senses I'm somehow different, more *in*different than I was before this. No, even if she's considered that possibility, I don't think that's what's driving her. I wish I knew what was."

He stood and lit a cigarette.

"Now the amazing part. She's moving out. She's taking the children and whatever belongings she can manage and moving to

Florida with her parents. She plans to stay there and then come to Chicago after I've been there a few days."

"She's not going to pack up the house and go to Chicago with you?"

"No. Her mother will fly up there with her and the kids on the thirtieth and stay for a couple of days. Vicki says she wants her mother there when the kids start school."

Joanna was incredulous. "But that won't give the children any time to get used to the new neighborhood or anything."

"I know. I tried to reason with her, but she said the kids could get acquainted at school and they'd have plenty of time to adjust. Then she said something about not wanting them to get too used to being there, in case they don't stay."

"This doesn't make things any easier, I know, Jared. But you wanted her to open up a little, tell you what she was thinking. At least now you know this much. Doesn't that help?"

"Not much." He took her hand, put it to his lips and kissed it softly, lingering on each finger, his eyes staring vacantly ahead.

"I wish I had the courage to tell her not to come with me at all, to move to Florida, file for divorce and work out an agreeable visitation schedule for me. I think she might even jump at it, given her state of mind. But when I remember the looks on the kids' faces when they found out I wasn't going to be spending that week after Christmas with them, I haven't got the heart to risk hurting them again with something as painful as a separation. Am I wrong?"

Joanna didn't answer right away. She held his hand tightly.

"Don't hurt them. I know what you want to do, what *I* want you to do, but we don't matter now. What matters is the children are ready to move to a new city, a new neighborhood and a new school. There's too little time for them to absorb the news of a change in plans, a move to Florida *and* the loss of their daddy. As much as it pains me to say it, you should follow through on your plans, get ready for the move and be there when they arrive."

Jared had been studying her face. "This is the little girl in the dark bedroom talking, isn't it?"

"Possibly. No, probably. I feel their fright, their terror at losing their world as they know it. If it hadn't been for my own childhood nightmares, I'd be begging you to leave, to put me first, put *us* first. But those years of being without my father took their toll, as I've always known they did. I can't be the one who makes you do that to your children."

She leaned forward and rested her head on his shoulder.

"I love you more than I thought I could ever love anyone, but as I've told you once, I can't fight for a place in your life if it means your children lose out. If you and Vicki try to make a life for them in a different place and it doesn't work, I'll come to you. But you owe it to the children not to spring this kind of change on them now."

~ * ~

Vicki left on August 4th. She took clothes, toys and her personal belongings. Everything else was left on shelves, in closets and in drawers, in the basement, the attic and the garage.

"I hate to see you with all that work to do, Jared. Honestly, I wouldn't mind helping."

"This is hard enough on you. I won't have you packing up the remnants of my life with Vicki in that house where we've been so miserable. The movers will do the bulk of the packing; I'll handle the preliminary stuff so they can deal with what's left on the twenty-fifth."

~ * ~

Dan's cabin was ready for his return. After one last night spent in the quiet of the lush forest, Joanna and Jared put everything in order, left the door key under the mat and, one last time, locked the gate behind them as they drove out of the lane. Neither spoke as they fought back tears, a few splashing over Joanna's cheeks despite her efforts to contain them.

"I talked with Dan last night," Jared said "He'll be back the first Saturday in September. I told him about you, about how much we loved his house and that you would have the gate key for him. I also asked him to call you now and then to see you're okay."

They were inseparable during the days that followed, each tick of the clock bringing them closer to the parting. They had a picnic at Bowman's Tower and spent a long afternoon in New Jersey at Island Beach soaking up the summer sun. Sometimes they went to the club and came home to Joanna's room afterwards. Their lovemaking often ended with tears instead of the satisfied glow that once surrounded them.

~ * ~

On August 15th, Joanna turned 21. She and Jared spent the day in Bucks County, walking along the canal in New Hope, having a quiet lunch in the little café and stopping for manhattans at the Spread Eagle.

"Let's go to the club," Jared suggested as they made their way to the inn's parking lot. "I have a special reason for asking."

The bar was nearly deserted with only one couple sitting at a table in the back. Jim gave them a broad smile as they walked in. Jared put their drinks down and turned away.

"I'll be back. There's something I have to do."

To Joanna's surprise, he went behind the bar, spoke briefly to Jim and then sat on a stool next to the piano, a small microphone in his hand.

As Jim started to play "Autumn Leaves," Jared sang to her, his voice filled with emotion, nearly breaking at times. Then "Misty," then "Stranger on the Shore," then "Willow, Weep for Me" and finally, "Unchained Melody."

When the last note faded away, Jim leaned over, straightened up after a few moments and handed a reel of tape to Jared who put it in a box, shook Jim's hand and came back to Joanna.

"Happy birthday," he said, handing the box to her. "Jim and I cooked up this little surprise quite some time ago. I hope you'll like having it and it'll bring me close to you whenever you need me. I'll think of you listening to this music and know I'm there with you. In a way, knowing you have these songs will help me, too.”

“It’s beautiful and I’ll cherish it. I know there’ll be many times in the coming year when I’ll need to hear your voice, feel you near. When you sense I’m reaching out to you, it’ll be because I’m playing this tape.”

He leaned across the table, put his index finger under her chin, tilted her face and brushed his lips lightly over hers. “Remember, my darling, I love you and I always will.”

~ * ~

Joanna woke up that last Friday morning with a blinding headache, a sore throat and chills.

“You have a fever,” Jared said, his hand on her forehead. “Get dressed; I’ll take you to a doctor.”

“No, that’s not necessary. I’ll take some aspirin and it’ll go away.”

Before Beth left for home, she said her goodbyes to Jared, hugging him. She whispered in his ear.

“Be well, Dr. Fowler. I’ll keep an eye on Joanna for you. I only hope this isn’t the end for the two of you. It will break her heart.”

When he held her close that night, the heat of her body alarmed him.

“Joanna, why haven’t you said anything? You’ve been pretending all day, haven’t you? You’re no better than you were this morning ... you’re worse, aren’t you?”

Her throat was so sore she could only whisper. “I really don’t feel very well, but these hours are all we have left. Just tonight and then you’ll be gone. How could I ruin them? How could I not hold you, hang on to every last second? Oh, now that it’s here, I don’t think I can do it.” Her voice hoarse, Joanna began to cry.

Jared wrapped her in his arms and pulled the blanket over her. In spite of the August heat, she was shivering from the fever. Throughout the night, Jared lay awake next to her, getting up every few minutes to rinse out a soft cloth and put it on her forehead. He took her temperature in the middle of the night; it was nearly a hundred and two. Still she refused to let him take her to a doctor.

"I promise I'll go tomorrow," she whimpered, her arms around his neck, her bright eyes begging him not to force her to go.

By morning, she was no better, but she'd dropped off to a restless sleep. Looking at his watch, Jared realized he had only three hours before the moving van was to arrive at the house.

Quietly, he left the bedroom, picked up the telephone and dialed the information operator.

Catherine answered on the first ring.

"Mrs. Ransome, this is Jared Fowler. I'm calling about Joanna. She's very ill. She's running a fever that aspirin doesn't seem to touch. I've tried to get her to let me take her to a doctor, but she's refused. In a few hours the movers are coming and I have to be at the house to meet them. I'm sorry, Mrs. Ransome, but please come and take her home."

Catherine's voice was icy.

"How good of you to take such loving care of my daughter, Dr. Fowler. I wish I had the time now to tell you what I think of what you've done to her life, what I think of *you*, but I'm in a hurry to leave. I'll be there as soon as I can. Please tell Joanna her mother is on the way." She hung up with a sharp click.

He returned to the bedroom, lifted Joanna's head from the pillow and held her to his chest.

"How do you feel? Any better?"

She mumbled a few unintelligible words, then "Hold me. Please just hold me." She slept again.

After a while, Jared gently put her head down on the pillow. He found her suitcase in the closet, packed some clothing from the drawers and closet and checked to be sure everything she would need was out of the bathroom and in the bag. He quickly assessed the contents of her purse, making sure her wallet was inside, placed it on top of the suitcase near the front door and wrote a brief note to Beth explaining that Joanna was ill and had gone home.

*Take care of her when she gets back, please, Beth. And hold on to this, my special gift to her, until she returns.*

Putting the note on top of the tape box, Jared left it on Beth's nightstand next to her bed.

It was nearly time to leave. Jared tiptoed back into Joanna's bedroom and gingerly sat on the bed. She was sleeping fitfully, murmuring, her brow furrowed. He sat wiping the damp hair from her face, watching her, for a very long time. Finally, he slipped his arm under her neck and raised her head. He put his index finger under her chin, tilted her face up and covered her mouth with his very gently. He started to stand as she opened her eyes, smiled at him and parted her lips for another kiss, this time longer, deeper. Her lips were very warm.

"I have to go, my darling. This is breaking my heart, leaving you so ill. If only I could stay with you and take care of you." Her arms tightened around him. The tears came, her sobs wracked and hoarse.

"I've called your mother; she should be here soon. I've packed some of your things so she can take you home, have you looked at by a doctor. Oh God, I don't want to leave you."

Still she clung to him. Gently, he removed her arms from his neck, laid her back on the pillows. Her eyes tightly closed, Joanna's chest heaved with sobs, the tears running down both sides of her face.

"I'll call you as soon as I can and I'll write often. We're not over, I believe that. I'll carry you in my heart, no matter where I am."

He kissed her again, feeling the hot fever blazing in her face. Standing up, he backed toward the door, releasing her hand slowly as he went.

Jared stumbled toward the steps and down onto the sidewalk, tears in his eyes. A woman got out of the car at the curb and briefly blocked his path, her fists clenched at her sides. Then she said something to him, stepped aside and watched as he got into his car and drove away.

# *Twenty-two*

*"Something will have to give."*

Joanna alternately slept and cried. She woke once to the prick of a needle and looked around at the blue walls of her room in her parents' home. Dr. Frank Cinessi, her doctor since childhood, was bending over her, removing a syringe from her arm. She slept again.

When she awoke the next time, she looked up as her mother came in quietly. The soothing touch of Catherine's nurse's hand was cool on her face.

"What happened, Mom? How did I get home?"

"I picked you up at the apartment this morning, honey. Don't you remember anything about the ride home?"

"No. Oh, my throat is so sore."

Catherine bent to kiss her on the forehead and saw Joanna's eyes fill with tears, take on the look of a frightened animal.

"Oh, God, Jared. Jared's gone, isn't he?"

"Don't talk about that now. It only upsets you every time you think of it. You need to rest."

But the sobs came again, deep, gulping sobs that hurt her throat and made it hard to breathe. Catherine sat on the bed, took Joanna in her arms and rocked her as she had when her daughter was very small.

"Don't do this, honey. Don't make yourself sicker. You won't get well if you don't rest. We'll talk when you've had some more sleep and I promise I won't be angry. Rest now. It'll be all right."

For two days, Joanna slept and cried. Finally, the tears subsided. She ate sparingly and said little, lying in bed with her eyes closed, the ache in her spirit too painful to express.

During the long hours her parents were at work, she slept and wrote ... page after page of her first letter to Jared, pouring out her loneliness, her anguish at having been too ill to say goodbye. She didn't know where to send the letter, so it grew until it covered both sides of five sheets of paper.

By Thursday, Joanna was well enough to be out of bed and dressed. The illness had left her weak and tired, but classes were due to begin on the fourth and she was expected to report for her student teaching assignment the day after that. She didn't have much time to get ready.

Catherine came into Joanna's room after dinner and sat on the bed watching as Joanna sorted through the things in her suitcase, getting ready to repack.

"I'm glad you're feeling better. You had quite a siege, you know."

Joanna stopped what she was doing and sat next to her mother.

"Thanks for taking such good care of me. I know you missed work on Monday and I appreciate your staying with me. I felt like a little girl again, having my mommy soothe away the hurt."

"I couldn't nurse away all the hurt, could I? He left you in a lot of pain that had nothing to do with your throat."

"Jared. I think that's the first time I've said his name out loud in days. Pain? Like nothing I've never felt. I've known all along he was leaving; I tried to prepare for it. But nothing worked. I don't even know where he is now, how to contact him. Everything was so awful before he left and I was too sick to do anything about it. All I can do is wait."

She turned older, sadder eyes on her mother. "I wish I could forget him, wipe him out of my memory and be back where I was before. But I can't. We had almost a year together and, even if I never hear from him again, I'll have memories of Jared that will always stay with me. But I can't think like that. I won't. Jared will call; he'll write. I even believe he'll be back if he can. I have to hold on to that. Otherwise, I don't know what I'd do."

Catherine put her arms around her daughter.

"What you did certainly wasn't morally right, but even more important, it wasn't right for you. You're young and beautiful. You should be going out with a lot of boys, dancing, partying, and doing all the things college girls do. This man cost you a year of your life. Don't give him any more."

Joanna replied sadly. "I'd give him all of it if I could. I hope to heaven I get that chance."

"Are you planning to go to Chicago?"

"No. Jared needs time to get adjusted to his new job, to see what happens with his wife and children. She only went with him on what she called a trial basis. He doesn't know what will happen after she's been there a while. She needs counseling—even if he has to go with her, Jared intends to try to force the issue. It's not that he wants to reconcile—he can't see himself leaving the children, hurting them with the trauma of a separation or worse. I told him if things didn't work out, I would come to him. So don't worry, I'm not about to drop everything and follow Jared. I'll go through student teaching and finish my degree. By the end of this year, my direction should be pretty clear. Until then, I have to get through my days as best I can."

"I'm sorry, Jo. I'm so sorry you're going through this awful time. I don't condone this affair with a married man, you know that. But you're my daughter and I'll always love you, no matter what. Your dad and I brought you up to make your own decisions, live your own life. Naturally, we thought life would be the way we wanted it … you'd finish school, get a job close to home, meet the right guy, get married and give us grandchildren. We had it neatly packaged. What we didn't count on was you falling in love with someone like Jared. It breaks our hearts to see the pain you've gone through, but we know we can't fix it, so I want you to know I'm here. I may not like what's happened with you, but I'll never shut you out because of it."

~ * ~

Joanna was back in the dorm before ten on Monday morning. There wouldn't be any mail until Tuesday, thanks to the long Labor Day weekend, but as she turned toward the stairs with her suitcase, she looked over at her box anyway. Naturally, it was empty.

Beth was waiting for her at the top of the steps. "Jo, I'm so glad you're back. I've been worried about you, even though you sounded okay when I called. What happened?"

Joanna leaned over, giving her friend a kiss on the cheek.

"I'm okay, thanks. It was strep, the doctor said. I was pretty sick for a few days, but everything's fine now. Thanks for packing up what was left of my stuff. I hope it wasn't too much trouble for you."

Beth pointed to the box on the floor and the pile of clothes on the bed. "It's all here. You didn't leave all that much. Oh, there's one other thing. Just a sec."

When she returned, Beth handed Joanna the red, black and white box with Jared's note still on top of it.

"I've taken extra special care of this. Something tells me you're going to be spending a lot of time listening to it. Did he leave you a message?"

"No. Jared recorded our favorite songs and gave it to me for my birthday. When I can listen to it, I'll share it with you. Now, I'm not sure if I could handle it. I'm still missing him too much."

One by one, the seniors on the floor stopped in to say hello and welcome Joanna back. They were warm and kind, no one mentioning Jared, not knowing what to say. On her way down the hall from the bathroom, she passed the phone as it began to ring. She picked up the receiver. "Bentley, third floor."

"Joanna? Dear God, how I've wanted to talk to you! Tell me how you are, my darling."

Joanna's knees buckled. She slid to the floor, her eyes wide with astonishment and joy. "I'm fine, really I am. It's so wonderful to hear your voice. I've been so worried about you."

"You've been worried about me? Oh, Joanna, you have no idea. It's been pure torture ever since I left you … worrying about your health, your time at home with your parents, your state of mind. Believe me, if there had been any way for me to stay with you … oh, but you're healthy now. That's all that matters. Tell me about it. Please."

"I was sick, I got better and I'm back on campus. That's about it. The most important thing is I'm talking to you, you're on the other end of this phone line. Oh, and I've been writing to you. You'll laugh when you get the letter. It goes on and on for I don't know how many pages. But I wrote it all. All of it from the time I woke up and realized you were gone until the second before I finally seal it and send it wherever you can get it. Now tell me. How are you and how did the move go?"

She sat on the floor, letting his deep voice reverberate in her head, listening as he described what happened after he left her that awful Saturday.

"The movers were waiting for me when I got there, though I really wasn't in any shape to work with them. It took everything I had to keep from leaving them and running back to you. But I knew you'd be on your way home by then, so somehow the packing got done and the truck left about four. I just got in the car and headed out myself. I drove until I was too tired to drive anymore. I know I was probably somewhere in eastern Ohio when I stopped for the night. You have no idea how many times I reached for the phone to call your house, see how you were, but I figured your parents wouldn't want to hear from me, so I stifled the urge and wrote it instead. I've got a book I've written since then, like you. I'll mail it tonight now that we've talked. Anyway, the van and I arrived at almost the same time. It's a nice house, smaller than our other one, only three bedrooms, no basement, no garage, but it'll do. I spent all last week worrying about you and trying to keep my mind on the new job and all the new faces and names.

"The kids and Vicki finally got here with her mother in tow. The children were so happy to see me after so long. We took the grand tour of the house and the university and then I drove them around the city a bit. Tomorrow, I'll take them to school. Michael's a little reticent; everything is so new to them both. But the teachers are young and patient and I'm sure they'll work with him. He'll be fine. And Marina can't wait to get into her classroom. She never has any problem making new friends."

"What about Vicki? What's happening there?"

He sighed. "We haven't had two minutes to talk without her mother hovering about. I hope when Helen leaves, we can talk about what happens next. She should be out of here in a day or so. They've gone shopping so Vicki can begin to get her bearings in the city. It's really quite beautiful, even if it is tough to get through all the traffic."

"Not like little Manning?"

"No, it's not. There's no Kenton office, no tree, no table for two in the snack bar, no Jim, no anything that has any meaning. I'm terribly lonely and missing you more than I can say. But I am glad all is well. When do you start teaching?"

"Believe it or not, I'm at Claybourne tomorrow for introductions and in the classroom on Wednesday. I'm scared to death."

"You'll do wonderfully. Those kids will be so lucky to have a teacher like you. They'll love you ... everyone there will love you like I do."

"I wish I were as confident. I'll let you know all about it when I write. And where can I write to you?" She took the pencil off the shelf, tore off a piece of message paper and wrote down the address he gave her.

~ * ~

Her supervising teacher was pleasant enough, with blue eyes and fiery red hair. He seemed distracted and anxious to get away, insisting they skip some of the introductory meetings.

"These are the class rosters," he said, piling a stack of notebooks into Joanna's arms. "You'll find everyone's name in alphabetical order. I'm sure you have your lessons planned out for the whole marking period and we'll look them over in a minute. There's not a lot more to tell."

He waved his hand around. "This is your classroom. The bulletin boards need to be decorated, but you can do that after school. You have four sections of English ... two fairly average classes, one pretty gifted group and one that needs a lot of help. They're well-behaved, though. Oh, here's the number where you can reach me if you have questions. I'll be in and out a lot, but just keep trying until you catch me."

"Aren't you here every day, keeping an eye on me, making sure I'm doing what I'm supposed to?"

"Oh, some supervising teachers do, but I decided not to approach the job that way. You'll learn a lot faster if you're on your own. As long as you can find me for an occasional conference about your progress or to get answers to questions, you'll get the hang of it fast."

After a few more minutes of passing on some general information about lunch hours, grading, tests and where to find the faculty dining area, O'Donnell paged through her lesson plans, pronounced them fine and left.

Joanna was bewildered, confused and very frightened. So this was student teaching. Somehow, she'd have to survive, but she didn't think it was going to be easy.

~ * ~

On Thursday evening, she got in late, having stayed for two hours after school to put cutouts and decorative borders on the bulletin boards in her classroom. She was tired and scared. This was nothing like she'd planned. On top of it, she'd have to grab something to eat in the snack bar now that the cafeteria was closed. Joanna had been trying to avoid going there since her return, but tonight was unavoidable.

For the first time since Jared left, she sat at the table for two. Her sandwich kept getting stuck on the lump in her throat as she looked across at the empty chair, picturing Jared sitting there, almost hearing his voice.

"Excuse me, are you Joanna Ransome?"

She looked up at the sandy-haired man standing next to her. "Yes, I am. May I help you?"

"I'm Dan Kearney, Miss Ransome. One of the girls in your dorm told me I'd find you here. I'm sorry I didn't call first, but it's been a hectic day and I didn't want to wait any longer to see you. May I sit?"

"Of course. Jared spoke of you as a good friend, someone he knew I would like. It's good to finally meet you. Welcome back from Alaska."

"Thank you." His dark eyes were sympathetic and kind. "From what he told me, I'm sure leaving Manning must have been very difficult for Jared. He was so unhappy for so long and then he found you. I can only imagine what leaving you did to him ... and to you. How are you holding up?"

"So-so. He's on my mind all the time and I miss him more than I can say. This place..." she looked around the room, waved her hand at the window "...it's full of Jared. This is where we sat. I could see his car from my room, so I always knew when he was here waiting for me. All of this has been very, very hard. But you've had a terrible loss of your own, and compared to that, I have no right to complain. I have something for you, though."

Joanna reached into her purse, pulled out the gate key and handed it to Dan. "Jared asked me to hold onto this until I saw you. We didn't want to leave the gate unlocked the last time we left the cabin."

Dan pocketed the key and looked at Joanna earnestly. "I'm very glad you and Jared were able to use the house. I hope the two of you found a sense of safety and comfort there."

"We did. Toward the end, it was like our own home."

"Come visit me any time you want. You don't even have to call first. I'm there almost every evening. I'd love to have the company."

"Thanks, Dan, but I can't. Once Jared took his children to the house to spend a few hours alone with them. He told me he couldn't stay; it was too painful to be there without me. I know I'd feel the same way. It's best for me if I keep Jared in that lovely house in my memory."

~ * ~

Joanna struggled through each day in the classroom, never thinking she should seek help from one of the other teachers or, better yet, report O'Donnell's persistent absence. Gradually, the work became easier, the children more responsive, but still she was uneasy.

Jared's letters came twice a week, although he didn't call again. She read each one over and over, adding it to the growing stack in a box she kept on the shelf of her closet.

*October 6, 1962*

*My darling Joanna,*

*I'm so sorry to hear about student teaching. This man isn't doing the job a supervising teacher is expected to do. I believe you should go to the chairman of the education department and tell him what's going on. No practice teacher should be flung to the winds and let drift like that. Of course, if it had to happen to anyone, you're the one best equipped to handle it. You're so strong and capable. I'll bet the children can't wait to spend time with you.*

*All goes well here. Michael and Marina are flourishing in their school. Michael turns six on the 11th and already has enough friends for a birthday party at the house on the following Saturday. He seems to be growing out of the shyness somewhat, thanks to the efforts of his teachers.*

*Vicki has gotten a job. The first week here, she read about an opening for an associate at the Museum of Art and applied. They hired her last week, part time, of course, but it gets her out of the house and gives her something to do while the kids are in school. We still don't talk much, but the surliness seems to be abating. I haven't broached the subject of counseling, but I believe it's the only way get to the bottom of the problem.*

*I miss you terribly. I miss Fridays at the club with our manhattans, our visits to Dan's cabin (I'm so glad you finally got to meet him) and, most of all, I miss holding you in my arms, feeling your warm, wonderful body next to mine. I had a hard time sleeping the other night so I picked up Benton to help me feel closer to you. His June 11 entry said it all: "Darling, oh, I want to remember you always, everywhere—in a tavern or in church, asleep or taking bath. I must not ever forget the look in your eyes when you had drunk and wanted to hurry home and be loved to sleep."*

*Write when you can. I love you, my darling, and I always will.*

*Jared*

*October 28, 1962*

*My darling Joanna,*

*I've tried to time this so it will arrive on Halloween. Funny, but when I look back on all the times we've shared, that evening in the snack bar when we talked about your earliest memories of Halloween sticks out in my mind. I remember thinking what a marvelously strong person you are, how you survived those horrible years and grew into a warm, beautiful woman with so much to give. How lucky I am to have been the recipient of all that love. Ah, my darling, you are so easy to love and you bring me such joy. There is only emptiness where you should be, standing next to me, holding my hand, walking with me through life.*

*When I take the children around their new neighborhood for trick or treating in their costumes on Wednesday, I'll think of you reading these words, knowing I'm with you in thought and with every fiber of my soul.*

*I love you, my darling, and I always will.*

*Jared*

~ * ~

"Teaching isn't doing it for me," Joanna lamented to Doris as they sat in the snack bar one afternoon. "I don't feel comfortable in the classroom, and when I think of what I want to be doing ten years from now, being in front of twenty-four kids doesn't come into the picture. I certainly can't see myself teaching for the rest of my life. Maybe not ever. Wouldn't that be a waste of four years of energy and money?"

"Not at all. You'll have the certificate you can fall back on if you need it, you've had four years of some of the best instruction available from a batch of really fine professors and you've worked with me. Now how bad can that be?"

Joanna laughed, a sound not heard too often in past weeks, which Doris welcomed with a return chuckle.

"I don't mean to sound pompous, Joanna, but it's true. No amount of college education is ever wasted, even though it might not be put to the exact use intended at the onset. And the research project we did? Don't tell me you won't carry what you learned from that for the rest of your life. Every time you encounter behavior from someone that seems totally off the wall, remember the mirrors and glasses. Having that little piece of knowledge can help you size people up in a hurry. Perhaps you've already had a chance or two to use it."

Joanna took a sip of her Coke. "Oh, don't get me wrong. I know my years here haven't been wasted. Meeting you was the highlight, of course," she said with a grin, "but I have learned a lot that will help me, especially from the instructors I had in the English department. They've helped me polish my writing skills; they've been objective and fair critics and in general made me a better writer. And then, of course, there's Jared."

"Mmmm. Jared. What are you hearing from him these days?"

"Letters about twice a week. He's adjusting, like me. The kids are happy in their new school. Believe it or not, Vicki has a job in the art museum there and Jared sounds like he's enjoying his work in the theater. He misses me, he says. His letters are full of how much he misses me. Lord knows I miss him. Some nights I can't sleep for thinking of what it was like to be with him. I miss everything about him ... his voice, his touch, his fabulous sense of humor, just being with him. Something will have to give. I can't imagine going through my whole life like this. Either I'm with him or I'm not, but I've got to find some resolution."

"Agreed. Last year was tough, honey. This one won't be much better unless you make a plan and stick with it. Student teaching is finished the Wednesday before Thanksgiving, isn't it? Have you been observed yet?"

"Three times, always by Dr. Allbright. He's satisfied with what he's seen, but I know he's looking for a spark of excitement in my classroom that simply isn't there. I don't think I'll make a good teacher. So now I wonder where I would do well. Thankfully, I have some time before graduation to decide what's next. I'll have to begin earning a living one of these days."

# *Twenty-three*



*"I need more time..."*

*November 5, 1962*

*My darling Joanna,*
*The first really good thing has happened since I began this new job. The director called me to his office this morning to give me a special assignment. Hold on to your hat! I'm to attend a conference on dramatic arts from November 19th through the 21st. Guess where? How does the island of Manhattan sound? Honest, Joanna, Manhattan! I could hardly believe my ears as he sat there apologizing for shipping me to the conference so close to Thanksgiving. Inconvenient, he called it. Inconvenient? Heaven sent, I say.*

*I'm arranging it so I can be out there on the 16th. I'm not sure where I'll come in, probably Philly for sheer convenience, but my plan is to take an airport taxi to Manning, meet you and then we can take the train to New York. We'll have the whole weekend, my love. My conference starts at 8 a.m. on Monday and you'll have to be back anyway for teaching, so I'll put you on the train Sunday night. Then when my conference is over at noon on Wednesday, I'll take the train back and stay with you until Thanksgiving morning when I leave for Chicago. I'll be back in time for dinner with the kids and you can head on home to your family. What do you think of my ingenious planning?*

*Of course, it all hinges on your being able to work out the details on your end. We have to figure out where to meet on Friday and I'll make arrangements for where to stay in Manhattan. I already have an idea about that anyway.*

*Oh, Joanna, now that I know I'm coming, I can hardly stand the wait. It's only been a couple of months, but it seems like a lifetime since I've looked into your beautiful eyes. Please, please try to make this work. I can hardly wait to be with you again.*

*I love you, my darling, and I always will.*

*Jared*

Joanna's pulse raced, her heart pounding in her ears. Jared was coming back. Oh, it was two weeks away yet, but those days would fly now that the end of this terrible loneliness was in sight, no matter how temporarily. From Friday to Sunday and then again on Wednesday. It was almost too good to believe, but here it was, in his own handwriting. Jared was coming back.

~ * ~

Teaching on the sixteenth was agony. Never had a day passed so slowly, in spite of the festive spirit in the hallways as the kids got into high gear for the coming holiday. At the sound of the dismissal bell, Joanna bolted to the door, raced to her car and sped the short distance back to the college, so excited she hardly remembered to breathe. The senior permit limited her options for parking the car but she ignored them and left it in the circular driveway in front of

Bentley. Pausing only to try to gain some composure, Joanna walked into the dorm and into Jared's waiting arms.

She was enfolded in that familiar, comforting embrace, his arms wrapped around her waist, hers around his, those soft brown eyes drinking in the sight of her. He put his index finger under her chin and raised it to meet his lips. Everything else forgotten, she returned his kiss, feeling slightly dizzy as she clung to him, savoring the touch of his mouth on hers.

"Let me look at you, my darling." He pushed her hair from her forehead and gazed at her. "You are every bit as beautiful as I remember. Oh, how I've wanted this, hoped for it, prayed for it. I promised you we'd be together again soon, and here we are."

"I can't find the words, Jared. I can only hold you and love you. I'm so glad you're here."

They kissed again and again until they heard a discreet cough from the doorway.

"Please let me interrupt," Beth said with a gleeful smile. "I know my timing is terrible, but I'm on my way out and I simply had to stop by and say hello. Dr. Fowler, it's wonderful to see you again."

Jared gave her a hug. "It's good to see you, too. Thank you for everything you've done for Joanna and for being such a good friend to both of us."

"You're two of my favorite people and I'm always glad to help. Now, scoot! Get out of here and go have a happy reunion in New York. Maybe I'll get to see you on Wednesday when you come back. If not, take good care of yourself, Dr. Fowler … Jared. Everyone misses you."

~ * ~

"The Times Square Hotel. Don't tell me. The same room?"

"I promised you. Luckily, I called so far in advance I could request a specific number."

Despite the long separation, they came together slowly, exploring anew the bodies they shared so openly with each other.

"I honestly didn't know if we would ever be together like this again," Joanna whispered when they were lying quietly, coming back to earth. "I was so afraid I would never see you again."

"You're part of me," Jared said. "No matter how many miles separate us, you'll always be with me and I with you. I've stopped trying to analyze why it's so; I've just accepted that's the way it is. We've been connected since the first time we met. And I suspect we'll be connected for the rest of our lives. I wouldn't have it any other way."

"Do you want to talk to me about how things are going with Vicki?"

"Of course. I've always told you everything. Nothing's changed between Vicki and me. She seems to be quite different, though, in a lot of ways. She relates better to the children and she has more interest in the house. Lunches get packed, laundry gets done, that sort of thing. Before, she left all of that to Genna or me. She seems eager to get to the museum on the days she works and when I hear her talking to her mother on the phone, it sounds like she's satisfied with what she's doing. But Vicki and me? We haven't talked about where we're going. I haven't had the guts to bring it up. I guess I'm afraid of shattering the new peace in the household. She's civil to me; I'm polite to her. It's far better than the outright hostility we had before, but nothing's any closer to being decided."

"In a way, I'm glad to hear that. It must be easier for the children now, having at least that much of their mother back."

"Yes. She's more involved with them than she's been in a long time. Michael especially seems happier. He needed his mother so badly. It's almost like he's a different kid. Marina's pretty self-sufficient, but I know she's glad to have time with Vicki too. They go shopping together, take walks along the lake, things Vicki never would have done before."

Joanna sighed. "Well, sooner or later, you'll be confronted with her real feelings about you. I'm prejudiced, but I think she'll eventually remember why she married you and want to try a new start. That frightens me beyond words. In fact, let's forget I even brought it up. I don't want to talk about it any more."

She put her arms around his neck and pulled him close, fitting her body to his easily in the way of one long familiar, the missing part of the puzzle that makes the picture perfect when it's found.

"I'm afraid, too," Jared said softly. "If Vicki wants to try to fix our marriage, I don't know how I could ever be with her again, not after you. I would feel disloyal, like I was being unfaithful to you. I feel more committed to you than to the woman I've been married to for so many years. As I've often said, if it were a matter of a choice between being with you for the rest of my life or Vicki, there'd be no question how it would go. But throw in the children and the equation isn't so easily solved. I need more time."

"You have whatever you need, you know that. Your being here with me now is the most important thing in my world. The rest will take care of itself."

~ * ~

The two days flew by, filled with hours walking the Village, catching the last few colorful leaves that had managed to hang onto the trees of Central Park and riding back and forth across the harbor, the seagulls following overhead. The nights started early with dinner in their room then leisurely hours in bed, sleeping only after their energy was depleted and their eyes were forced to close with happy exhaustion.

Jared took the cab with her to Penn Station on Sunday night, where he stood on the platform as her train slowly moved out of the terminal toward Manning. As she watched him growing smaller and smaller, his hand still raised in a farewell wave, she leaned back in the seat, closed her eyes and slept, his face her last conscious thought, his voice in her mind lulling her to sleep.

~ * ~

The last three days of teaching were filled with after-school meetings, grading final exams and being evaluated by her supervisor. She didn't really care what the outcome was; her mind was already made up. Teaching was not for her. Only one question remained: what was?

~ * ~

After all the farewells on Wednesday, she got to the station as Jared stepped off the train. Taking his arm, she reached up to kiss him hello.

"I've missed you."

"Me too. The conference was dull, the speakers boring and the nights long and cold. I wish I had come back with you on Sunday so we could have had those days together."

"Ah, but what would have told your new boss? 'Sorry, sir, I couldn't stand being apart from Joanna, so I played hooky from the conference you paid me to attend?' Unlikely, my love."

"It was tempting, believe me."

"Do you still want to do everything we talked about? The club, a visit with Dan?"

"Let's talk about that in a minute. This suitcase is heavy and I'd like to sit while we make our plans."

Once in the car, Jared put his head back on the seat and closed his eyes. When he opened them, Joanna had the key in the ignition and was sitting, concentrating on his face.

"I've been thinking. Would you mind a change of plans?"

"Of course not. What do you want to do?"

"I'd still like to visit the club and listen to Jim if we're lucky enough to find him playing. But I have mixed feelings about the visit with Dan."

"Me, too. With him there, it's back to being his house, not ours."

"I knew you'd understand. If you still want to go, of course we will. I'm only concerned about the effect being at Dan's again might have on us."

"Agreed. Did I tell you Dan invited me to visit him whenever I wanted? Well, I never did. I'll never be able to, for the same reasons we can't tonight. When I close my eyes and remember Dan's cabin, I see us there in front of the fireplace, Johnny Mathis singing to us, our manhattans on the table. We pretended for a long time Dan's house was ours. I don't think I want to go there and give it back. Do you think he'll understand?"

"I'm sure he will. Dan's had his share of sorrow. There's no way he would insist on our doing something that might cause us pain."

"It's settled then. Let's find a place to stay, leave your suitcase and go to the club. Bet you could use a manhattan about now."

They drove a short distance on the main highway to a commercial area just outside the city. While Joanna parked the car, Jared registered at the front desk of the small motel.

"This isn't even the Times Square Hotel, let alone the Statler," Jared complained.

"It doesn't matter. I would be content to be in a cave in the forest if you were with me."

~ * ~

Jim saw them come in the door and stopped in the middle of the song he was playing to begin "Misty," nodding at them as they sat at their favorite table. Jared stopped on his way back from the bar with their drinks to say hello.

"Jim's very happy to see us again. He said he misses having us come in every week. I had to tell him I'd moved and we were only back for the night. He said to tell you to come in any time—the manhattans would be on him."

Joanna smiled in Jim's direction and mouthed a thank you.

"That's something else I won't be doing. Coming here without you would be out of the question. No, I'll remember the Downtown Club as our hideaway, the first place we found refuge when we were very new."

~ * ~

By the time they got back to the motel, Jared had a headache. It was excruciatingly painful, forcing him to keep his eyes closed to shut out even the tiny light next to the bed. For hours, Joanna sat quietly while he waited for the aspirin to relieve the agony. She kept cold cloths on his forehead, not saying anything so the sound wouldn't add to his discomfort. Finally, in the middle of the night the pain lessened, leaving him weak with exhaustion. Joanna helped him out of the chair into bed, lying down cautiously next to him, afraid to touch him, frightened at the sight of the pain he'd endured. Very quietly, she asked, "Does this happen often?"

"For a month or so now. The doctor calls them cluster headaches, whatever *they* are."

"Can you do anything to prevent them?"

"Nothing definite. The doctor seems to think I should stop drinking anything alcoholic, something I really don't want to do unless he can absolutely guarantee it'll stop the headaches. But he might have a point; I should probably at least give it a try. These things are terrible."

He turned and ran his fingers down Joanna's arm, across her chest, lightly caressing each breast, then dropping his hand back onto the blanket.

"I'm sorry. I'm so tired. Let me rest for a little bit. I promise I'll be okay in a few minutes."

"Close your eyes. I'll be here."

Joanna slept fitfully, waking often to reassure herself Jared was still resting.

The room was very dark when she awoke, the sound of the highway traffic quieted to the occasional rumble of a passing truck.

Jared was not in bed. In a few minutes, he came out of the bathroom, felt his way gingerly back and laid down, his face toward Joanna's. She took her index finger and slowly traced his face, from forehead to brows down the aquiline nose, around his mouth and across the chin. Before her finger could retrace its route, Jared groaned, pulled her to him and gently parted her legs, filling her with himself, repeating her name, climbing with her higher and higher until they reached the pinnacle and burst with light and heat.

~ * ~

There was no time for sleep. Jared's plane was leaving at ten; they'd loved until early morning and still had to drive to the airport.

"I worry about you, driving home with so little rest," Jared said, holding Joanna close before they left the room. "I can sleep on the plane; you don't have that luxury behind the wheel of a car."

"Don't you worry about me. I'll be okay. All the way home, I'll be remembering these wonderful days with you, reliving every moment, wondering if we'll ever see one another again. That will certainly keep me awake."

Jared's smile vanished. "Don't even suggest we won't see each other again. I don't know when or how, but I will be with you again, I promise. And by now, I think you should know I keep my promises. We will be together again, believe that."

When Jared's flight was called, Joanna walked with him to the door of the stairway and kissed him goodbye, clinging an extra moment in the circle of his arms. She kept her eyes locked on him as he walked down to the tarmac. He greeted the stewardess, turned to wave at Joanna and was gone.

Joanna stood close to the wide, massive windows overlooking the departure gate. She was very still, one hand on the window, lips moving soundlessly, while the big jet rolled backwards, slowly turned and taxied out of sight. It was a long time before she left, tears coursing down her cheeks.

# Twenty-four



*"It's my only New Year's resolution."*

"I've been giving my future a lot of thought, Doris," Joanna said. She crossed her legs and leaned her elbows on the desk. "Believe it or not, I paid attention when you said I needed a plan to get me though this year and beyond, so I've spent a lot of time mulling over what I want to do."

Doris leaned back in her chair. "And?"

"And I think I'm going to try to get into graduate school. I know my junior year grades weren't as good as they could have been and that's my fault. But my overall record is okay and I think I'd do well on the GRE. The remaining question, and it's a big one, is what would I take a master's in? I can tell you for sure education won't be my choice."

"Why not? Just because you had a bad experience with student teaching doesn't mean that's the only avenue in the field you can pursue. I'm sure you'd do well on the Graduate Record Exam. Why not think seriously about training to be a counselor?"

"Counselor? Me? I've spent my time *being* counseled! Aren't you afraid my neuroses would get in the way of being good at it? Of actually being able to help people?"

"Nowhere is it written a counselor has to be neurosis-free," Doris said. "If that were a criterion, there wouldn't be anyone qualified for the job. No, kiddo, you're a natural. You were born with a gift few people have: empathy. You relate to people based on the way you feel about the way *they* feel … does that make sense to you?"

"I'm not sure."

"Well, let me try to put it another way. You're able to get inside people's heads and feel their emotions, not simply feel sympathy for them. That can't be taught. It's not a skill, it's a gift and you have it. I think you'd make an outstanding counselor and I believe you should consider it as a career option."

~ * ~

*December 10, 1962*

*My darling Joanna,*

*I think Doris is absolutely right. You would make a perfect counselor. You have such a natural way of relating to people and a true understanding for their feelings. I really hope you're seriously considering her suggestion.*

*Never having lived in the Midwest, I have to admit this wind and cold weather is tough to get used to. We are very close to the lake and there are days when it's an effort to keep from being blown off one's feet with the force of the wind. The cold is different, too. We could never be atop Bowman's Tower this time of the year out here. It's a damp, bitter cold you feel all the way to your bones.*

*The children don't seem to mind the cold a bit. Their classmates have filled their heads with stories of sledding, ice skating and making angels in the huge snowdrifts they expect to get. They're doing so well. Marina is a Brownie in a local scout troop. She loves wearing her uniform and working on projects with her new friends. Michael stays close to home, but seems happy.*

*Now to Vicki. Same old Vicki, at least as far as settling anything with me is concerned. We've had a couple of tentative talks—I never know how far to take them for fear of sending her back into her shell—but nothing has been decided. She admits to being more content here than she expected, thanks to the museum job, I'm sure. But she's still unhappy with me, I know that, and I can't say I blame her. My mind isn't here. My heart isn't here. I'm not helping her with the shambles that is our marriage, because every time I think of being with someone for the rest of my life, it isn't Vicki I put in the picture.*

*I want to be with you. I want to share my life with you. I love you, my darling, and I always will.*

*Jared*

The Christmas card came before Joanna left for home. As she sat reading it, one of the girls called her to the phone.

"Merry Christmas, my darling. I couldn't let you go home without talking to you."

"Jared! It's so wonderful to hear your voice. You must be psychic. I was just reading your card. It's beautiful."

"So was yours, thank you. I was getting ready to go home when I started thinking about Christmas and how different it will be this year. No fireplace at Dan's and, worst of all, no Manhattan and no Joanna. I'll miss all of that more than I can tell you. Will you be all right?"

"I'll certainly try to be. We're off from tomorrow until January fourteenth, but I won't be staying at home the whole time. I need to be where I can get your letters and maybe even talk with you once in a while. That's here at Manning, so I'll probably come back the seventh. Will I hear from you after the holidays?"

"I'll call you at home; I still have the number. Will you be there New Year's Eve or are you partying?"

"Partying? Hardly. I'm going to be home in front of the fireplace with a good book and a manhattan. My folks will be with their friends as always. How about you? Partying?"

"Touché! As a matter of fact, I'm babysitting. Vicki will be with some of her museum associates at a party there. I didn't particularly want to go, not that I was invited, so I offered to stay with the children. I'll be alone, my darling, thinking of where I was last New Year's Eve and wanting you so much I could die. Can I call you?"

"I'd be disappointed if you didn't."

~ * ~

Before he and Catherine left for their New Year's Eve party, Joe built a fire and made a pitcher of manhattans for Joanna.

"Now, we don't have to go, you know. We'll gladly stay with you and ring in 1963 together. Are you sure you don't want us to?"

"Thanks, Dad. I have a new book, some quiet music and a fire to keep me warm. I'll be long asleep by the time you get home. Have a great time and don't worry about me."

Jared's face danced among the flames, the Andy Williams album playing softly in the background. The book forgotten in her lap, Joanna closed her eyes and relived the memories. They were so vivid she could almost feel Jared's touch and hear his voice. It was strangely comforting to be back there, bringing him closer if only in thought. The phone jangled her out of her reverie at midnight. It was Joe and Catherine, their voices shrill and loud over the din of background music and noisemakers.

"Happy New Year! We're thinking about you and we'll be home soon."

Joanna hung up without leaving the chair by the kitchen window. Outside, the Christmas decorations on the neighbors' homes danced in the night. It was cold but clear, the stars glittering in the winter sky. She searched for especially bright ones, wondering if the sky were this clear in Chicago, wishing she could be with Jared.

The ringing phone snapped her out of her contemplation.

"Happy New Year!"

"Oh, Jared, I wish it could be. It's been such a lonely night. I've spent it thinking about last year, about you. I miss you so much."

"Likewise. I was on the front porch, braving the cold for a few minutes to look up at the sky. It's crystal clear and the stars are spectacular. I was wishing on one particularly bright one, hoping it might bring you to me."

"I'm sitting here doing exactly the same thing."

"Joanna, I promise you something. This will be the last New Year's Eve we go through this uncertainty. I'm giving Vicki and me another few months to settle our situation and move on in whatever direction we're going. It's torture wanting to be with you and knowing Vicki and I have to be resolved one way or the other before I can make any plans. It's my only New Year's resolution and I intend to keep it."

"Don't issue any ultimatums. Don't make any decisions based on anger. Take your time; we have plenty of it. I've been doing a lot of thinking as well. I think I'm going to apply to graduate school in the Midwest. The counseling program at the University of Illinois is one of the best in the country, with a faculty that includes some of the very people who wrote the textbooks. Doris thinks I can get in; I intend to try. If I do, I'll be three hours away from you. We can see one another occasionally while you figure out what you have to do."

"That's a big step. I would love to have you that close and yes, we might be able to see each other occasionally. But please don't make this move just because this is where I am. I couldn't take the burden of the guilt I'd feel if you left your family, your corner of the world, to be near me when I can't promise you any definite future."

"I won't lie to you. I chose the U. of I. partly because it's nearer to you than some of the others. I looked into Northwestern, which would be even closer, but I can't afford the tuition and can't get any kind of financial help. At U. of I., I have a shot at an assistantship that would help pay the way, so I'm going to go for it. Besides, it won't hurt to have a master's degree from one of the best places around."

*April 3, 1963*

*Dearest Jared,*

*Now it's my turn with the good news. I'm coming to Illinois. I have an interview with the department of education at U. of I. on the 18th, so I plan to fly into Chicago on the 17th and take the bus to the university the next day. I'll only need a few hours there, maybe enough time for a tour of the campus and then I'll come back to Chicago and fly home on the 20th. I hope you'll be able to find some time for me in that fantastically busy schedule of yours. It sounds like you've been taking the theater scene by storm out there. It's wonderful to hear the excitement in your letters.*

*There isn't much time left until graduation. I thought senior year would go slowly without you here to share it with me, but it hasn't. It's flown by, thanks to your letters and phone calls and the wonderful memories that get me through the days.*

*Let me know when you can about your schedule. It won't be much, but we could at least have some time together.*

*I love you and miss you terribly.*

*Joanna*

*April 7, 1963*

*My darling Joanna,*

*I could hardly hold the stationery still enough to read what you wrote. Can I fit you into my schedule? Try to stop me! We're very busy now with the spring production, but I would stop the earth from revolving if I had to so we could be together.*

*As soon as you know, give me your flight number and tell me which airport so I can meet you. Try to fly into O'Hare ... it's new and utterly fantastic. I can stay with you until your bus leaves for Champaign-Urbana and then pick you up on Thursday when you come back. I'll find a place for you to stay and we can spend Friday together as much as possible. There's so much to show you.*

*I promise a longer letter later. I love you, my darling, and I always will.*

*Jared*

"I don't know about this, Jo honey." Catherine Ransome's eyebrows knit in a concerned frown. "I understand this university is the best place for you to get your master's, but is it wise to be so close to Jared again? It seems you've been doing so well, getting on with your life, putting him in the background. Why be so close that you'll be tempted to see him again, start things all over again?"

"I *will* see Jared again. That's part of the reason I decided on the U. of I. Doris and I agreed a while back that I need to have a plan for my life. I have to know where I'm going and with whom, or without whom as the case may be. Jared's promised a decision, probably by the end of the summer. If I'm closer to him, I hope he'll be less likely to forget what we had. In the end, his decision will be based on what he thinks is best for the children. At least I'll be somewhat nearer to him while he's weighing everything."

"You're still holding out hope? After all he's put you through?"

"I can't give up on us. Not until I have to and I hope that never happens. Jared is part of me in a way I never thought anyone could be."

~ * ~

He waited at the end of the airline stairway, his arms open for her embrace.

"Joanna, Joanna, Joanna. I can't believe you're really here. It's been such a long, long time. Let me look at you." His eyes searched her face, warming her with the love she saw there.

"There's so much I want to say, Jared. It's been pent up inside for what seems like forever, but now that I'm really here, I can't think of anything except I love you. Isn't that silly?"

"No, my darling, it isn't. All the way out here, I rehearsed what I would say when you stepped off the plane. I think it was pretty good stuff, a nice welcoming speech filled with everything I've been storing up for the past four and a half months. Now? You're here, I can touch you, look in your eyes ... what good are words? Just let me hold you."

They found the familiar blue and white car easily in the vast parking lot. Joanna slid across the front seat, unlocked the driver side door and settled in next to Jared.

"Now I really feel like I'm with you. It almost seems like we could drive out of this lot and into the one next to the Spread Eagle or the Downtown Club."

~ * ~

Joanna was too absorbed in Jared to pay much attention as they drove through downtown Chicago. He talked animatedly about the various buildings they passed, the hotels and shops along Michigan Avenue, the high-rise apartment buildings that fronted the lake. She grew more attentive as they neared Roosevelt University, passing Navy Pier and the Museum of Art.

"That's where Vicki works. Did I tell you she's gone full time? She's worked it out so she can be there when Michael and Marina get home and, if she's running late or has a special project, there are programs after school that can keep both of them occupied until she gets there. Or, if my schedule permits, I manage to meet them when they get home. I wish you could see them, Joanna. They've grown so fast. Marina is still my blonde bombshell and getting prettier every day. Michael wants to play baseball this spring. Imagine that—he's old enough for sports already. They're doing great."

He pointed at a square building with a clock tower atop the back portion. Slowing down and pulling over to the curb, Jared gestured out the window at the massive entryway doors.

"This is the Auditorium Theatre. The rest of the university is all around us, but now the focus is on this particular building. There's so much renovation going on. The plan is to restore it to the glory days when everyone who was anyone in Chicago attended productions here. My office is up there, on the fifth floor."

Joanna looked out the window. It was hard to imagine Jared spending his days there after the serenity and isolation of Kenton Hall.

"I'm extremely busy every day," he was saying as he pulled back into traffic. "I'm supervising four master's candidates and we're in the middle of last-minute preparations for the spring production. We're doing *The King and I* with the Roosevelt University Symphony Orchestra, and it's promising to be an extraordinary event. I wish you were staying long enough to see it."

Joanna listened to something new in Jared's voice. At first, she couldn't put her finger on the change, couldn't give what she heard a name. The longer she listened and the more he talked about his new life, the stronger the feeling there had been a radical change. Lightness, that was what she heard. Lack of pressure, lack of stress, almost a carefree tone. Back at Manning, Jared's voice had sounded like that only when they were together—at Dan's, at the club or at the Spread Eagle. The pressure of his worry about the children and Vicki always seemed to creep into his mood, erase the lightness, darken even the brightest of times.

Now, the strain seemed to be lifted. At least it was for Jared.

~ * ~

He checked Joanna into the Allerton Hotel, an ornate old building with Italian architecture and an elegant, formal lobby.

As they rode the elevator, Jared asked, "What time does your bus leave tomorrow?"

"I have to be at the terminal at nine. My interview is set for one and then I guess there will be a brief tour of the campus—if I'm accepted, that is. I plan on taking the three o'clock bus back."

"That will get you in at about six," Jared said with a frown. "I'll see what I can rearrange so I can meet you."

No sooner had the door closed on them than Jared took Joanna in his arms, raised her face to his and kissed her. Closing her eyes, she let the feeling sweep over her, blocking out the nagging concern she'd felt since landing at the airport. This was the Jared she'd missed so terribly. Of course, he was excited about his new career and it was only natural he would want to share it with her. But, feeling those sensuous lips on hers, listening to that deep, rich voice repeating her name, she knew ... Jared still loved her. That much had not changed. How could she have doubted him?

He released her slowly, then looked at his watch.

"You'll need some time to unpack, freshen up, maybe even rest awhile. It's nearly five, so I'll dash home, make sure the kids are okay and spend a few minutes with them. I'll be back to take you to dinner at about seven. Will that give you enough time?"

Joanna nodded, not trusting her voice. Enough time? How long would it take to open the suitcase, hang up the two dresses she'd brought, splash some water on her face and freshen her lipstick? Rest? She was brimming with energy, her spirits lifted to the heights they always reached when Jared was near.

He kissed her lightly, turned toward the door, car keys in his hand. "I'll be back shortly. See you then."

Joanna stood looking at the closed door. Sighing heavily, she turned toward the bed, opened the suitcase and began to unpack slowly.

At seven, Jared still wasn't back. It occurred to Joanna she didn't know his home phone number and she couldn't call it even if she did. Instead, she lifted the telephone and placed a call to her parents to let them know she'd arrived safely.

"Be careful out there, Jo," her mother warned. Joanna knew Catherine wasn't talking about watching how she crossed the street.

Jared was knocking on the door as she disconnected the call.

"Was everything okay at home?" she asked as they got on the elevator to go downstairs to the dining room.

"Yes. I'm sorry I'm late, but Vicki waited until now to tell me she has a meeting tonight and she expected me to be at home. It took me a while to find one of the neighborhood girls to stay with the children."

They sat in the elegantly appointed dining room and ordered manhattans.

"This isn't the Spread Eagle. It isn't the Statler either. But we're together again and I can't tell you how happy it makes me to look at you."

Upstairs, Jared reached for the light switch as they walked into the room arm in arm. He locked the door behind them, turned Joanna toward him, tilted her face and kissed her deeply, his tongue parting her waiting lips. A trail of clothes fell as they stumbled toward the bed. Their lovemaking was feverish, hurried, lustful. Jared kissed her softly when it was over, perspiration glistening on their faces.

"Nothing changes, does it?"

She wanted to believe him. "No, nothing. My love for you simply grows stronger. Time increases the strength of our bond."

~ * ~

The university offered Joanna an assistantship covering the cost of tuition, room and board, fees and books. She was also to be paid a small stipend, which would help with meals. The summer session would begin on June seventeenth, giving her very little time after graduation to make the move.

Jared met her at the bus terminal. He found a small restaurant not far from the hotel where they had dinner and Joanna told him about her experiences.

Back at the hotel that night, they loved more slowly, touching, caressing. All of the sensations they knew so well flooded them, drowned them, pulled them back to the surface and carried them on waves of feeling.

At eleven, Jared rose to dress. Joanna watched him, feeling a tired sadness that echoed from months past.

"I couldn't free up the entire day tomorrow," Jared said, leaning over Joanna to take a last-minute kiss from her tender lips. "But I'll get here as soon as I can. Sleep in; explore the neighborhood if you want. I'll try to be back by one."

Masking her disappointment, Joanna returned his kiss.

"Will you be able to spend the afternoon and evening with me or is your time limited?"

"I may not have been totally able to stop the earth from revolving, but I have put it on hold for the rest of the day after noon. You're going to like the place we'll go tomorrow tonight. It's not exactly the Downtown or the Spread Eagle, but it's a good substitute."

~ * ~

It was nearly two when Jared tapped on the door.

"I'm finally back. It wasn't as easy to get away from the office as I'd planned. Unfortunately, we're very close to the dates of the show and last-minute glitches keep coming up I have to take care of. Are you ready to see Chicago?"

Throughout the drive, it wasn't lost on Joanna that Jared made no mention of taking her on a tour of the university or showing her where he worked. Try as she might, Joanna couldn't ignore the hurt the omission caused. Once again, she felt left out, second best.

They had dinner in the hotel, drinking manhattans before and after, as though they could somehow bring back their old haunts and the times they shared in them. As they finished their last drinks, Jared lit a cigarette, inhaled deeply and sat back against the plush seat.

Joanna asked, "Will you be teaching all summer?"

"Mmm-hmm. I'll have summer school students and plans to make for the fall play. There's still a lot of work being done on the interior of the building that'll step up over the break, but I'll find a nook or cranny to work in while the construction crews pound away."

"What about Vicki? Will she work all summer, too?"

"We're still figuring that one out. Michael and Marina finish school on June first. The university school has a terrific summer program that could keep them busy at least half days, but one or the other of us would have to be home when the children are there. It's pretty much out of the question for me, but Vicki may be able to work something out so she can go back to half days while the kids are out of school. So far, she seems okay with it."

"You seem to be getting along better, or is it my imagination?"

"I don't know how to describe what's been happening between us. One minute she's distant and emotionally removed from me and the children and the next, she's attentive and affectionate to them and almost tolerant of me. Most of the time, she's good with the children and it's really been great for them. We still have a long way to go toward deciding what to do about us."

He stubbed out the cigarette and turned to Joanna, taking her hand.

"But I promised you. I promised this uncertainty wouldn't drag on and it won't. Once the children are out of school, I intend to get this relationship between Vicki and me resolved. Don't think for a minute I haven't dreamed of how perfect it would be to have you here, to come home to you at the end of each day, to walk along the lake with you in the evenings, to wake up with you at my side each morning. That's still my dream."

From the restaurant, they took the elevator up to the twenty-third floor to the Tip Top Tap, the cocktail lounge made famous as the site of the broadcast of Don McNeil's Breakfast Club. It was romantic, dimly lit and surrounded with windows that overlooked the dazzling downtown and shoreline that was Chicago.

As they finished their manhattans, Jared's forehead creased, his mouth twisted in an odd shape and tears formed in his right eye.

"Is it one of those cluster headaches?"

He nodded, pressing his thumb to his face just above the cheekbone to try easing the discomfort. It was obvious after a few minutes his attempt wasn't succeeding, as the pain got worse by the moment.

Joanna stood, motioned for the waiter and scrawled her name and room number on the check.

"I'm sorry, my darling. I probably won't walk very fast. Sometimes the pain is so severe my eyesight blurs and I can't really see to navigate very well. Be patient with me and let's go back to your room."

Once again, Joanna kept watch as Jared fought with the pain of the attack. This one was so severe he couldn't bear even the slight pressure of the cool cloth on his face, preferring instead to lie perfectly still in the dark, hoping for some relief from the onslaught of agony. After an hour or so, he opened his eyes.

"What time is it?"

Joanna looked at her watch, holding it up to the faint bathroom light. "It's nearly eleven. Rest a little longer."

"I can't." He tried to sit up but rolled back against the pillows a couple of times before he succeeded.

"I need to drive while the pain's let up some. Besides, I have medicine for this at home. I really should go while I can, before it flares up again."

Joanna helped him to his feet, walked with him to the elevator, across the front floor lobby and out onto the street where he had parked the car. She slid in next to him, leaned over and kissed him lightly.

"We'll have a little time in the morning, if you feel better."

"I know your flight leaves at two," he said in a hoarse voice. "There will be some time for us before I have to take you to the airport."

~ * ~

By eleven o'clock, Joanna was frantic. Jared hadn't called; she didn't know how he was. It was time to leave for O'Hare and she was paralyzed with indecision. Should she leave, take a cab to the airport?

As she was reaching for the phone to call the front desk, there was a tap on her door.

"Jared, thank God!"

He looked exhausted, his bright, perceptive eyes dulled with fatigue. Stepping into the room, he took Joanna in his arms.

"I'm so sorry! Our last chance to be together while you're here and I get another of these blasted headaches. I was up most of the night and finally fell asleep at dawn. Vicki slipped off with the children and didn't wake me. Imagine my distress when I opened my eyes and glanced at the clock. I've wasted our morning. I'm so sorry."

Joanna led him to the sofa and sat close by his side. She gently traced his face with her index finger, lingering over the area where the pain had seared his cheek the night before. When she reached his lips, she brushed them with her own, parting them with her tongue, sighing deeply as he returned her kiss with longing passion. When they parted, she looked at her watch.

"I suppose we have to leave. Even without a lot of traffic, we'll get to O'Hare barely in time for my flight."

Jared said sadly. "If only I'd gotten here a little earlier, we might have had time—"

"Don't dwell on it. In a few weeks, I'll be a short bus ride away. We can close the distance between us any time we want."

Traffic was a mess. They inched their way to O'Hare, arriving at the terminal minutes before her flight was to leave. The skycap at the entrance quickly tagged her bag.

"I'll call the gate and let them know you're on your way, miss," he said. "Better hurry."

There was no time for Jared to park the car. There was no time for anything except for a quick but fierce kiss goodbye before Joanna fled through the revolving doors into the cavernous airport.

# Twenty-five

*"I know I can't have it both ways."*

*April 20, 1963*

*My darling Joanna,*

*    I came back to the office so I could write to you while the disappointment of how we parted is still fresh. It wasn't a very memorable farewell, was it? I had planned a leisurely morning, loving you, having brunch in your room and spending your last minutes in Chicago holding you close as we waited for your flight to be called. That's how it was supposed to happen and I can't tell you how bad I feel it didn't. I should have remembered to set the clock so I wouldn't risk oversleeping. But by the time I got back to the house, took the medicine and waited for the pain to go away, I forgot about a safeguard. Usually, I'm up early (that's a change from the Manning days) and we should have had plenty of time. These blasted headaches are increasing in frequency, I'm afraid, so I'm*

*guessing the doctor may be on to something. I seem to have them only on the heels of a couple of manhattans. How I would hate to have to give up the cocktail that so reminds me of you.*

*I've been trying very hard to find a reason to fly to New York at the beginning of June so I can be there for your graduation. Mind you, I don't know yet whether I can manage it, but I wanted you to know I'm trying. I would be so proud to see you in your robe and mortarboard, looking like a creaking old academic.*

*I can't wait to talk with you. I want to hear about your flight home and any new plans you might be making now that you know you're accepted at U. of I.*

*Remember, I love you, my darling, and I always will.*

*Jared*

*May 10, 1963*

*My darling Joanna,*

*The house is quiet; everyone is asleep. It's Marina's 9ᵗʰ birthday and Friday night, both of which make me think of you with a longing so great I don't think I can take it anymore.*

*Marina had a wonderful birthday. Her classmates gave her a party at school and then we had about a dozen little girls at the house this evening for games, cake and ice cream. All in all, it was a happy time for her.*

*I know from reading your letters that, graduation notwithstanding, you're not happy any more than I. I feel the same sense of incompleteness and loss you talk about. It helps to stay busy, and Lord knows I do. But every time I have some quiet moments, spaces in time that aren't filled with work or something the children are doing, your face drifts into my consciousness, soft and sweet, warm and wonderful, and fills me with such need it's all I can do to keep from weeping.*

*I'm sorry to be so morose. It's been a depressing day, I guess, playing happy dad and loving family for the neighbors and Marina's friends to see. My heart wasn't in it at all. I promised you this wouldn't go on much longer and now I know it truly can't. Either I find a way to fashion a life for us together or I resign myself to losing you and forging a future with the children and Vicki. Something has to give and I promise it will.*

*Finally, and this is probably why I'm so depressed, I have to tell you I can't be there with you on the 8th. There wasn't anything I could invent that would take me away from work. My students are finishing up and will be taking finals and I simply have to be here. I'll be thinking of you, wishing you sunshine, a happy graduation and a quick return to me.*

*Remember...I love you, my darling, and I always will.*

*Jared*

~ * ~

When she awoke on the eighth, the rain beat against her window. The thick clouds hung low, rain coming down so heavily she could barely see the Student Center across the street. Unless something changed drastically, graduation would be moved indoors to the only auditorium big enough to handle it—Kenton Hall.

At ten, Joanna's parents arrived. After a rainy walk on the path to Kenton, they parted, Joanna going downstairs to join her classmates, her parents finding a seat near the front of the auditorium. As she walked the familiar hallways, her breath came in ragged gasps, her forehead felt like someone was tightening a vise around it and she fought back the urge to run. She hadn't been inside this building since Jared had locked his office door for the last time, and being there again brought back too many poignant memories.

At the sound of the first strains of "Pomp and Circumstance," the class moved up the stairs, through the polished hallways and into the lobby where they paused to wait for direction from inside the auditorium. Through a haze of tears, Joanna looked at the door to Jared's office, closed now, belonging to someone else, but where first they had kissed and crossed another line in their relationship. She remembered helping him pack his things to prepare for the move to Chicago. Closing her eyes, she could feel his skin under his robe, just a year ago.

The group began to move and her partner tugged at her sleeve, but Joanna lingered for a moment outside the door, silently wishing she could turn back the clock and have Jared walk out smiling, his hand reaching out for hers. Finally, knowing he was still very much in her future, she went past the door and into the auditorium.

~ * ~

A week later, Joanna walked into the graduate residence hall in Urbana. The trunk filled with her belongings had already arrived, shipped from home the prior week. She found her way to her new room on the second floor, a narrow space with concrete walls crowded with bed, desk, tiny closet and a door leading to the bathroom she would share with the woman next door. Bare and austere, the room was cold and uninviting. Dismayed, Joanna mentally compared it to her cozy nook in Bentley House, then shrugged off the negative thoughts and plunged into making her new quarters more homelike.

As she was stocking the medicine cabinet on her side of the bathroom, someone knocked tentatively on the adjoining door.

Joanna found herself looking at a puckish grin on a tiny heart-shaped face with a deep dimple in the chin and a head crowned with thick, wavy blond hair.

"Is there room for me in here?" she asked Joanna.

"Sure is. I think that cabinet there is yours. I'm Joanna Ransome, your suitemate, I guess they would say."

"Bonnie Holt. I'm glad to meet you. Where are you from?"

"Atlantic City, New Jersey. Here I'm in the college of education, beginning work on a master's in counseling and guidance. What about you?"

"Oooh, Atlantic City! I've heard that's one of the nicest vacation spots in the country. I've never seen an ocean, though. Lake Michigan is as good as it gets for me. I'm from Winnetka and I'm working on a master's in sociology. What brings you all the way to Illinois? Surely you could have found a good grad program somewhere closer to home."

Joanna gestured toward her room. "C'mon in if you have a few minutes." She sat on the bed, motioning Bonnie to the chair by the desk.

"Of course, there are fine grad programs nearer home, but this one attracted me for a couple of reasons. The first is the faculty ... some of the best names in the field teach here and the second is its proximity to Chicago."

"Do you have family there?"

"No, someone very important to me. I wanted to be close enough to see him once in a while."

"Him?" Bonnie looked around the room, settling on the photos of Joanna's parents and the enlarged one of Jared in his academic robe on her desk. "Is that him?"

"Yes, it is. He's been at Roosevelt University since September and I've only seen him a couple of times in the past year. What about you? Anyone special?"

"Nope. I'm not even looking. I don't have much time for men, for reasons I'm sure you'll wangle out of me sooner or later. I've enjoyed my freedom for too long to want to get hooked up with some guy who wants everything his way—what he wants when he wants it. Not for me. So, does this guy of yours have a name?"

"It's Jared. Jared Fowler. And he's not really my guy, yet. If everything goes my way, he may be my guy one of these days, but for now we're working things out."

"What's he studying at Roosevelt?"

"Oh, he's not a student. Jared's an associate professor of drama and assistant director of the Auditorium Theatre there. Have you heard of it?"

"Of course. No one can live as close to Chicago as I have all my life without knowing about Roosevelt. Wow! Assistant director at the Auditorium. Wait a sec … how old is this guy?"

"He's got a few years on me, but that doesn't matter. Since the day we met, there was a connection between us that got stronger as we got to know each other better. When he took the job out here and I decided to go for the master's, it was only logical I'd pick a school close to him."

"Well, I know where you'll be on weekends. Greyhound will have a faithful customer, no doubt. And if I'm ever going home, you'll be more than welcome to tag along. Roosevelt is a hop, skip and jump from Winnetka."

"I've been there. When I came out for my interview in April, Jared took me for a ride up the North Shore. It's so beautiful."

"In spring and summer, yes. In winter, that's another story. I've never liked the cold weather, so it's a heck of a place to be from. Now Atlantic City—beaches, nightclubs, ocean, sunshine—that definitely sounds more like my cup of tea. Anyway, I think you and I are going to get along great as suitemates. I was about to go for lunch. Are you hungry?"

"Always. It'll be fun having someone to explore with. I don't have any idea where the dining hall is."

~ * ~

"Hello, Jared. I'm here!"

"When did you get in?"

"About mid-morning. I took a very early flight and I'm utterly exhausted, but it's very exciting being here and I've already made a new friend, so my time's been well spent."

"When do you start classes?"

"On Monday. Bonnie—she's my new friend and suitemate, actually—and I are going out this afternoon to walk around and get our bearings. She's from Winnetka, but she's new to this campus like me, so we'll learn where everything is at the same time."

"There's so much I want to ask you and talk to you about. Graduation for instance. You didn't say much about it in your last letter. I was surprised. How did everything go?"

"It was okay. It rained and forced us all inside. I ended up standing outside the door to your office waiting to walk into the auditorium. You can imagine what that did to my state of mind. Otherwise, it was fine. Everyone was suitably proud of their creaking old academic. I missed you terribly."

"I know, my darling; I loved the pictures you sent. I wanted so badly to be there. Maybe if I had, Kenton wouldn't have been so painful for you. But we're so busy here, even now the semester is over and everyone's gone. There are summer students and the blasted construction—that never-ending construction—it keeps making life noisy and miserable. You were on my mind from early morning on the eighth until I finally fell asleep thinking of you, wondering how your day had gone."

~ * ~

Joanna and Bonnie decided to go to the get-acquainted party Sunday evening.

"We might as well meet our neighbors," Bonnie decided. "I'm not much of a joiner, but it won't hurt to see who else lives here."

Not many people had made the same decision. Of the dozen or so in the room, most were clustered around the coffee pot, sampling sandwiches and cakes, conversation sparse and quiet.

One of the women walked over to Bonnie and Joanna. "Hi, I'm Denise. You two look like ideal candidates to volunteer to help on the grad residence council. What do you say?"

Joanna held out her hand. "Joanna Ransome, nice to meet you. Sorry, but not I; not yet at least. I've been on campus exactly one day, have no idea what kind of course load I'm expected to carry, where my assistantship is and how demanding it will be. Somewhere down the line I might want to be on the council, but for now I have to say no."

When Denise turned to Bonnie she said, "Bonnie Holt. Ditto for me."

"Well, you can't blame me for trying. I always check with the newcomers to the hall to see if I can snag anyone to help out. Don't think you're off the hook completely, though. I'll try again in a few weeks."

She looked behind them. "Oh, hi guys. You're a little late. I could have used your help to recruit Joanna and Bonnie to our council. Got turned down flat, but they managed to be pretty nice about it. Joanna, Bonnie, these are the rest of the council members ... Rosemarie Corrigno, Patrick McKernan and Philip Webber. We need at least one more person, so if either of you changes your mind, please let one of us know."

Joanna and Bonnie shook hands all around. Unlike Patrick, who turned out to be the life of the party, Philip was very quiet. Joanna knew she'd like Rosemarie, whose dark eyes danced with good humor. She was especially pleased to learn the petite brunette was also in the college of education and lived across the hall. The two women quickly made plans to walk together for the first day of classes the following morning. She couldn't wait to tell Jared about all the new people she had met, about her feeling she was going to enjoy being there.

*June 21, 1963*

*My darling Joanna,*

*I'm thrilled for you that everything is going so well. The assistantship sounds interesting, even though I know you're certainly capable of something far more sophisticated. Seems a shame to waste your talent for research by putting you in a data entry job. Perhaps as time goes on, you can move away from that and get involved in a more challenging part of the project. The folks at U. of I. need to know about Doris's mirrors and glasses and how you almost single-handedly pulled that together.*

*I loved your idea about coming up for my birthday. The children want to celebrate on the 29th, but if you came to Chicago on Saturday, we could spend Sunday together. I hate the thought of your having to take that bus ride in this heat, though, so you might want to consider the short commuter flight into O'Hare. I could meet you at the airport and we could stay around there for our time together so you could be close by for the flight back. It would be wonderful to see you and be with you for whatever time we could steal. Think about it and let me know.*

*Marina and Michael are both involved in summer programs. Michael's been playing baseball with the neighborhood Little League and Marina has begun taking ballet lessons. She looks absolutely smashing in her white tutu with that shining, fair hair of hers. Her class is practicing for a recital in September.*

*Vicki is enjoying the museum job and she seems to be gaining a new sense of confidence. I see some very obvious changes in the way she's relating to people she meets and especially to the children. I intend to broach the subject of counseling very soon and, more particularly, the unsatisfactory status of our marriage. Doris's advice to you also applies to me. I need to have a plan for my life— reaching for you and building a future for us with whatever time we can devote to the children or resigning myself to a life with Vicki that would give the children a permanence I know they need. The latter terrifies me because, although I know it would be best for the kids, it would mean I would be losing you. There would be no way we could keep hanging onto what we had with the hope that it would survive and grow. It would mean I would have to go through some kind of counseling with Vicki and try to resurrect the marriage so we could give the children two parents who were together in more ways than just sharing a house.*

*You know I want a life with you. Since that rainy day in October so long ago, I've known we had something special. Every moment I spent with you intensified my desire to face each day of our future joyously, hand in hand, because we were meant for one another. But I know I can't have it both ways. You deserve an answer; you deserve to build a life of your own if I can't share mine with you. I promise you … I will discuss things with Vicki and put an end to this uncertainty.*

*Call me as soon as you know when you'll be arriving. Each time I write to you like this, I want to touch your face and know the wonder of your kiss. It's wonderful to know I won't have to wait too long.*

*Remember, my darling, I love you and I always will.*

*Jared*

Joanna read the letter with a cold knot forming in her stomach. Despite Jared's pretty words about seeing her again, she heard something he probably didn't intend to come through. A warning perhaps? A whisper of what might be in store?

Then there was the matter of the visit. She checked with the airline and found a commuter flight to Chicago at three on Saturday afternoon, arriving at four-fifteen. That would probably work for Jared, who shouldn't be working and could meet her at

O'Hare. But then what? What would she do alone in a hotel room Saturday night? And Sunday morning, while he took the children to church and sang in the new choir he'd joined?

Joanna struggled with the stubborn voice that jeered in her head, taunting her with the reality that she fit into Jared's life only when it was convenient. And those times were becoming less and less frequent. His newfound happiness, the newfound happiness of the children, didn't seem to make him need her as much as he had in the darkness of his old life. And where did that leave her?

Joanna shook off the bleak sense of foreboding. After all, she was very much in love with Jared and he with her. All of this worry would be for naught, of that she was certain.

# Twenty-six



*"It was always her decision."*

By Wednesday, Joanna had finalized all the details of her overnight trip to Chicago. Only a call to the airport to hold the tickets remained before she'd be ready to make the flight.

"Jared, hi, I have news."

"I'm so glad you called. I'm afraid I have news, too. And if yours is what I think it is, I'd better go first."

"Why? What's happening?"

"I hope you haven't made plans yet to come up on Saturday. As badly as I want to see you, there's been a glitch on this end. Michael's been sick for the past few days and he's still running a fever and having a lot of difficulty breathing. The doctor thinks it's a bad bronchial infection, but it's taken a lot longer than we thought for it to clear up. The birthday celebration for me has been cancelled and I'm afraid I'll need to stay close to home until he's out of the woods and feeling a lot better. I'm sorry, but I don't see how I could be out of touch with home even for a few hours."

Joanna tried to sound calm. "Of course. Don't worry; I haven't made any plans that can't be cancelled."

She heard her own voice and realized it was stiff and flat.

"You're disappointed; I hear it. So am I, believe me. Ever since you said you might be able to come up, I've been dreaming about being with you again. I'm terribly upset it can't happen now. Will you come up next weekend instead? There won't be anything in our way then and we could have all of Saturday afternoon and Sunday, if you can spare that much time."

~ * ~

The week flew by. Almost every day, Joanna and Bonnie met one of their friends for lunch or dinner or for a quick Coke before calling it a night. Joanna didn't share much about her own life and said nothing about Jared. She wasn't anxious to get into an explanation of the relationship. The little group was fast gelling into a tightly knit sextet and when she called Jared Wednesday to tell him she'd be flying in on Saturday, she described them, eager for him to share, even from a distance, her new friends.

Philip was the exception to the outgoing nature of the crowd with which she now spent most of her time. While he faithfully joined everyone at the daily get-togethers, he didn't join in the fun, remaining on the outside of the circle, content to watch the goings-on without getting involved. At first, Joanna thought he was probably only shy, but she often caught a glimmer of frustration in his eyes, like he very much wanted to be a part of their intimacy but didn't know how.

As it turned out, it was Philip who drove Joanna to the airport. He was the only one in the crowd with a car and he quickly volunteered to take her as soon as he heard she was planning to take a cab.

"You don't have to do that; it's pretty expensive. I can drive you out there. What time do you have to go?"

"My flight's at eleven, so I should be there by ten-thirty. Is that too early?"

~ * ~

As they pulled away from the curb in front of the grad hall, Philip looked shyly at Joanna. "Are you visiting someone special?"

"Yes. There's someone at Roosevelt University who's very important in my life. It's been over three months since I've seen him."

Philip nodded solemnly. He answered Joanna's questions about the town with one or two words, but seemed uneasy with a lot of conversation, so she relaxed and watched the flat Midwestern scenery go past as they neared the airport.

~ * ~

Jared was waiting at the gate when the little plane touched down and Joanna joined the few people on board as they walked down the stairs and across the tarmac to the terminal. His welcoming hug was unusually tight. When Joanna looked in his eyes, she saw something that caused her heart to flutter in her chest.

The usual love was burning there, but there was something else— he looked for all the world like someone who would rather be any place else. She rested her head for another lingering moment on his chest, hearing his heart beat, her arms wound around his waist, feeling his face in her hair.

When she stepped back, he tilted her chin with his index finger and kissed her, his eyes tightly closed, his lips brushing hers gently at first, then with a fierceness that held a sense of desperation in it.

"Are you all right, Jared?"

"Let's get out to the car and over to the hotel and we'll talk," he replied, busying himself with her overnight case, leading her down the hallway toward the revolving doors. "You look wonderful, my darling. Graduate school agrees with you. How is the coursework going?"

Joanna took his cue reluctantly, preferring to delve into whatever was on his mind, but knowing he would open up when he was ready. As they crossed to the parking garage, she filled him in on the progress she'd been making, being careful to keep her tone light, to conceal her apprehension.

"Oh, you still have the old faithful station wagon. It's so good to sit in it again. I was afraid you might have replaced it by now, especially after your news about the renewal of your contract. There's nothing like a little job security to take the pressure off the bank account, is there?"

Jared didn't respond with his usual good-humored chuckle.

"Not yet. I'm delighted, of course, that the university is pleased with my work and wants me to stay on, but I'm not ready yet for a major expense like a new car."

"Tell me about the children. How is their summer going?"

"It's been very good so far. Michael's been playing baseball nearly every day. I've gone to almost all of his games and he really seems to have a talent for it. He started at first base and then went behind the plate as a catcher. He looks very imposing in that mask. Marina's looking forward to the start of school. She's spent most of her free time practicing ballet with her friends. The recital is set for September fourteenth and she's quite serious about it."

It didn't take long to get to the hotel, register Joanna and take the elevator to her room. Jared put the key in the lock and opened the door. She went in ahead of him and waited while he closed the door and put her case on the bed. Taking his hand, she led him to the chairs next to a large round table by the window.

"Sit down. It's time. Look at me and tell me what's on your mind. There's no point in putting it off any longer. I know you're holding something very serious inside and I need to hear what it is."

Jared looked intently at Joanna, his eyes searching her face, then dropping. He sat silently for a moment, then stood and began pacing back and forth in front of the big picture window. Finally, he sat again, reached across and took both of her hands.

"I was hoping to stave off talking about this until after we'd had time together alone for a while. It's been a long time since I've held you. But that damned connection of ours is still working, isn't it? I can't hide from you. You read me too well."

He sighed heavily, reached into his pocket and pulled out his cigarettes. He lit one deftly with his left hand, inhaled deeply and raised Joanna's hand to his lips for a gentle kiss.

"It's happened finally. Vicki and I have had the talk that was so long overdue."

Joanna held her breath, her heart seeming to grow still in her chest, a sudden chill settling over the room. Releasing Jared's hand, she hugged both arms to her body and leaned forward. "Tell me."

"Michael and Marina were staying overnight with friends on Thursday night, and for once, both Vicki and I were home at the same time. I was reading in the living room when she came in and told me she'd like some time to talk. I knew what she wanted to say ... she'd given it a good try, but it wasn't working and she was ready to make the move to Florida. I figured she'd been talking it over with her mother and was ready to drop the news on me."

He put out the cigarette, stood and began pacing again. Stopping in front of Joanna, he said "But that wasn't the way the conversation went at all. Just the opposite. She wants us to find a counselor and work on making our marriage succeed."

He exhaled slowly, as if relieving himself of a heavy pressure deep in his chest. Joanna's eyes widened with shock and dismay.

"What did *you* say? Did you agree? Is this what you've decided to do?"

"What did I say? I was so surprised that at first I didn't say anything. Then I told her I wasn't sure if that was the right decision for us, that so much had happened in the past few years I wasn't sure if I could do an about-face and pick up where we'd left off, just like that. She asked me if there was someone else. She said she wouldn't have blamed me if I'd found someone, but she hoped our still being together meant I might consider trying over again. She knows now. I told her and she knows there's a Joanna. But she asked me to think about it, to consider the impact a divorce would have on the children and asked if we could talk about it again tomorrow. She wanted to talk today, but—"

"But I was coming today and you wanted to tell me about this first."

"I needed to see you. I needed to hold you and talk to you about this, not make a decision that's so final without knowing how you felt, what you wanted to happen."

Joanna's gaze froze on Jared's face. She fought to suppress the urge to scream at him, to pick up something heavy and hurl it against the wall, beat her fists on his chest and sob. Managing to maintain control, she said, "So I came here to get the bad news in person, is that it? To your credit, it couldn't be on the phone or in a letter. It's much more humane this way."

Jared started to speak but Joanna interrupted. Her voice rose, heat flooded her face and tears pooled in her eyes.

"What do *I* want to happen? How can you ask me that after all we've been through in the past year? What do *I* want to happen? I want what I've always wanted. I want a place in your life. That hasn't changed since the last time you asked me, sitting in Dan's living room. But something else has changed. Vicki. She's done what I was afraid she'd do ... she's realized why she married you in the first place and she wants you back. Now, after all the pain and heartache, she wants to do whatever's necessary to make your marriage work, give the children a stable home. Isn't that noble of her," she spat out in a derisive tone.

"This decision was never really about you and me at all, was it? Or even about the kids. It was always up to Vicki; it was always *her* decision. Here I was, thinking you might actually be able to find a way to keep us together when all the time it didn't matter what you wanted or what I wanted—it was what Vicki wanted. Well, now she's decided and you come to me for what? For my blessing?"

Regaining her composure, she raised her eyes, lifted her chin and spoke in a tightly controlled voice.

"Well, I won't give it, but I've already told you what to do if this happened, haven't I? I've already given you permission to stay with Vicki and work it out, haven't I? 'Don't hurt the children,' I've said over and over again. So how can I change my tune now? How can I take all that back and tell you not to stay? What else do you want? What do you expect from me?"

Jared didn't meet her eyes, didn't see the tears splashing down her face.

"You've already made your decision, haven't you? You love what's been happening since you got to Chicago … your wonderful job, Vicki's new attitude and the fun the kids are having. You haven't got it in you to turn their world upside down, to deal with the guilt you'd feel if you left them. So tell me why you have to ask me what I want to happen. It doesn't really matter."

"My God, Joanna, it matters. You matter. Your love is what's sustained me through this past year. Finding you, loving you, has been a miracle in my life, and I never want to be without you."

It was quiet, no sound in the room save Joanna's ragged breathing, an audible effort to hold back sobs.

Jared's voice was pleading. "But I can't have it both ways, my love. I can't give the children the home they deserve, work with Vicki to make things better and still continue to see you, write to you, talk to you, want you. Don't you see, Joanna, it won't work. I would never be able to make a real effort to fix my family if my heart were still yearning for you. And you? How could you ever free yourself of me and get on with a life of your own? Find someone else, marry and be happy?"

Joanna swiped at her cheeks with the backs of her hands, fumbled in her purse for a package of tissues and dried her eyes.

When she looked up at Jared, fresh tears were already glistening there.

"Find someone else, marry and be happy. Of course, maybe I'll do that someday. Maybe I'll stop thinking your name when my eyes open in the morning and before they close at night. Maybe I'll stop hearing your voice inside my head. I have a long life ahead of me with lots of time to work on doing that. I guess I'd better get started this minute."

Joanna walked to the telephone, called the front desk, asked for the time of the next shuttle back to the airport.

"Joanna, don't do this. Don't leave now. We have time ... time to talk, to—"

"To what? Drag out the farewells? Make some more memories for our old age? No, I can't stay here any longer. It's over. I suppose in some dark corner of my heart I knew this day would come. But now that it's here, I don't know how to handle it. I only know I can't keep pretending anymore. My dream is over and I don't want you here when the reality of it sinks in."

Jared stepped closer, reached out to pull Joanna into his arms, but she moved away, holding one hand in front of her.

"Let's not prolong this, please. We've been luckier than most, almost two years of a kind of closeness few people ever dream of. I know I'll go through my entire life wanting you, wishing it had turned out differently. But I understand your choice. Maybe some day I'll even be able to accept it."

She held open the door. "Please don't say anything more. Just go."

His eyes filled, Jared moved toward the door, turned and put his hand on Joanna's cheek. She gently took it away, kissed its palm and turned her back.

# Twenty-seven


*"You were smart to forget that guy."*

From somewhere far off, she didn't know how much later, Joanna heard the muted sound of a telephone. Staring vacantly at the closed door in front of her, she tried to shut out the incessant ringing. Finally, there was silence. Still she stood, hugging herself protectively, numb with grief. She stood and waited, listening for a footstep outside the door, waiting for Jared to come back, tell her it was all a mistake, take her in his arms and make her forget the awful emptiness he'd left in his wake.

Feeling lightheaded, Joanna dazedly sank to the floor, her back against the door. What had happened here? How could the visit she'd so anticipated turn into a ten-minute cataclysm that brought her whole world clattering down around her in ruins? How could Jared have done this? He and Vicki had talked the night before ... why didn't he call and warn her away? Why go through the motions of meeting her at the airport, booking a hotel room, acting as if he could hide this calamitous news for long and, worse yet, that she could stay once it was told?

Her mind went blank, refusing to allow her to process what he'd said. She sat still, staring straight ahead, disregarding the passing of the day, until the phone again began to ring.

Rising on wobbly legs, Joanna walked slowly to the table. As if she'd never done so, she gingerly lifted the receiver.

"Joanna? Please let me talk to you. There's so much I still need to tell you, so many things I need you to hear…"

Jared's wonderful voice, hoarse, choked. Jared. What more could he say that wouldn't wound even deeper?

Joanna put the receiver back on the cradle. The ringing began anew but she made no move to answer.

It was impossible to admit any coherent thought into her consciousness. Half-sentences, bits of phrases, parts of questions, nonsensical clutter floated around in her head. Didn't she say…? Wasn't he supposed to…? Why didn't they…? Nothing was complete, like someone had short-circuited her brain, leaving her unable to reason.

She sat in mindless silence as the hours passed, the room growing dim in the late afternoon. When the phone rang again, she focused slowly, realizing she couldn't see it because darkness had descended all around her, like the black cavern into which her spirit had retreated.

The phone rang and rang. Slowly, Joanna got up, walked over to the window and closed the drapes. In deep and total darkness, she felt her way back to the chair and sat, surrendering again to the comfort of witless solitude.

Jared would never hold her again. She would never feel the warmth of his body, the tenderness of his lips. Never again would she trace the outline of that marvelous face. And nowhere except in her mind would she ever again hear his wonderful deep voice speaking her name, whispering endearments after love. Love? That, too, was gone.

She shivered, hugged herself even closer and gradually admitted her surroundings back into awareness. Then reality slammed into her chest like a dull knife. She doubled over, staggered to the bed and fell face down on the mattress, abandoning herself to heavy, deep sobs. Twice more the phone jangled repeatedly, its demanding bell unheeded.

Sobs giving way to whimpers of pain, Joanna gradually quieted. Curled against the pillows, knees drawn toward her chest, she huddled in the darkness, allowing herself the quiet blessing of thoughtlessness once again.

"Miss Ransome … Miss Ransome … are you in?"

A knock on the door, at first tentative, then more authoritative, roused Joanna, bringing her back to awareness.

She forced herself to answer. "Who is it?"

"Bud, Miss Ransome. I'm the night manager. Someone's been calling your room and not getting an answer, but I didn't see where you'd checked out and no one saw you leave. Is everything okay?"

Raising her voice, trying to make it sound normal, Joanna replied. "I'm fine, thanks. No need to worry."

"Well, *somebody* sure is worried. This guy keeps callin' and callin'."

"If he calls again, tell him I've checked out."

"Okay, miss, if you say so. You have a good night."

Joanna never heard the parting comment. She'd buried her face in the pillows and once again tried to shut out the pain.

Exhaustion must have won out, for the next time she opened her eyes, there was light leaking around the corners of the drapes and she could make out the vague sounds of traffic on the roadway below. It took a few seconds for her to orient herself to the dark and strange surroundings and then the enormity of the previous afternoon's events struck anew.

Nauseous and lightheaded, she stumbled to the bathroom and retched dryly, again and again. When the waves of nausea passed, she opened her overnight bag and took out the cosmetic case, her toothbrush and fresh underwear. Standing under the steaming shower, she closed her eyes, swayed slightly and opened them before she totally lost her balance. Towel-dried, she stood in front of the cloudy bathroom mirror, aware only of the dull, expressionless face that peered through the mist, feeling that her brain was as foggy as the glass.

At the bottom of her overnighter was the slender volume of poetry she'd hoped Jared would read from after they had loved. Lifting it carefully, as if it were a precious piece of fragile parchment, she leafed through the pages, stopping at the lines that had somehow found their way into her mind.

*"I stood long where you left me. Night was all around me and the stars pecked at it with fierce acetylene silver beaks. A little thin moon scarred the sky. Then I walked ... my arm around the emptiness of you beside me."*

She closed the book, put it back in the bag and repacked the rest of her things. Without looking back, she left the room, rode to the first floor and went to the front desk. A sunny-faced clerk cheerfully checked her out, directed her to the airport limousine waiting area.

At the airport, she managed to change her flight. It cost a little more to leave earlier, but Joanna was beyond caring about money ... or much else. She sat close to the window in the near-empty plane, staring at the billowy clouds, wishing she could simply vanish into them, leaving everything behind.

An hour later, her plane touched down in Champaign. The little airport was virtually deserted, a lone cab sitting in front of the terminal. Numb, she gave the grad hall address and lapsed into silence.

Then, without knowing how she got there, she was in her room, looking around at the now-familiar bed, desk, chair, pictures of her parents and the one of Jared. Putting down her bag, she crossed the room, lifted the photo and put it, face down, on the desk. Her phone rang. Fearing it might be her parents, she picked up the receiver.

"Joanna, please my darling, please don't hang up. Let me talk to you."

Her voice was barely a whisper. "No, I can't. Please don't do this."

She hung up, hand over her mouth, eyes squeezed shut against the bright sunlight coming through her window. It was done; she'd closed the door at last. It was truly over. But what would she do? How would she keep on going without Jared in her life?

The tears began anew as she sank to the chair by the desk and put her head on her arms.

"Jo, my God, what's happened?"

Bonnie put her cheek against Joanna's, held her close. Looking over Joanna's shoulder, she saw the photo frame on the desk.

"What happened? Did something happen with Jared? Please tell me."

But the tears wouldn't stop, the sobs belching up from deep inside. Bonnie held on, crooning in Joanna's ear, "It's okay; it'll be okay."

Her head still in her arms, Joanna slowly stopped crying. Without rising up, she muttered "It's over. I've lost him. I'll never see him or hear from him again."

Bonnie tightened her grip on Joanna's shoulders but kept silent, hoping Joanna would talk, let out more of the grief.

"What am I going to do? How am I going to go on, day after day, with the memory of Jared clamoring in my head? He said he wants me to find someone else, get married and be happy. As if I could snap my fingers and it would happen. He's part of me. How can he expect me to simply cut him out, like amputating a limb and expecting a new one to grow in its place? For almost two years, I've centered my life on Jared. He's been the focus of my universe and now I feel like everything is dark and dead. I wish I were, too."

Bonnie took her shoulders and guided her out of the chair onto the bed so she could sit beside her.

"I'm sure it feels like that now. God knows how badly you're hurting. But there isn't a person on the planet worth dying for, worth giving up for. He said he loved you and I'm sure you believed him. Okay, he wants someone or something else. It really doesn't matter. You think your life is over because of it. The point I'm trying, probably pretty badly, to make is that Jared is going on. His world hasn't stopped turning and neither should yours. I know you'll mourn and there'll be many times when you'll need to cry it out. But you have to keep moving ahead through all of that. And you need to rely on your friends. We all love you and we'll be here for you. You won't be alone unless you want to be. And we'll all respect those times, I promise."

Joanna looked up, her eyes red-rimmed and swollen, her porcelain skin blotched, her long eyelashes stuck together, still shimmering with the last of her tears.

"I know all that," she said in a small, still voice. "I'm grateful I've found all of you. But now I can't think. It's like my mind's frozen and I can't thaw it out enough to get the synapses sparking again. I feel like all I want to do is stay still, keep my eyes closed and stop functioning for as long as it takes to make the pain go away."

Bonnie stood. "I'll be next door if you need anything, if you want to talk some more. Sometimes that helps and I'm always ready to listen. Have you eaten anything today?"

"No. Nor yesterday, I don't think; I really don't remember. It doesn't matter anyway. I'm not hungry."

When Bonnie left, Joanna stayed on the edge of the bed staring into space. When she let herself think, all she could find pounding in her mind was the image of Jared.

*"Don't you see, Joanna, it won't work. I would never be able to make a real effort to fix my family if my heart were still*

*yearning for you. And you? How could you ever free yourself of me and get on with a life of your own? Find someone else, marry and be happy?"*

"Free yourself of me," she muttered. Again the words of Walter Benton echoed in her mind…*"I shall never forget you…nor will your memory be free of me. For your arms are my home—and my arms the circle you cannot leave, however far you go."*

Bonnie's head poked around the corner of the bathroom door.

"Here. Patrick brought this from the kitchen. He's been storing extra snacks and goodies for a rainy day, I guess, but when you said you hadn't eaten in a while, I asked him to pick out something you might enjoy."

Bonnie put down a tray carrying a sandwich, a small red apple, a little bag of potato chips and a Coke.

"Everyone's very worried about you. How much can I tell them to put their minds at ease?"

"I don't care. It's no big secret. I suppose I need them to know so no one will ask me about Jared, wonder when they're going to meet him, when I'm going to Chicago the next time. Yes, tell them for me, will you? I don't think I could go through the telling again."

~ * ~

The next month passed in a blur. With the understanding compassion of her friends, Joanna gradually rejoined them for their daily get-togethers. Seeing a faraway look in her eyes every now and then, one of them, usually Rosemarie, gently patted her hand, smiled her understanding. As always, only Philip said nothing, though Joanna thought he often looked puzzled, his fair eyebrows knit over aloof blue eyes.

By the middle of August, Joanna and Bonnie began making plans to find an apartment and leave the grad hall. Luckily, one of the men in Bonnie's department owned property on campus, not far from the education building. There were four apartment units in the large house, one of which he occupied and the others he rented out. They were pleased with the apartment he showed them. It was furnished, with two bedrooms and a large living room, a tiny galley kitchen and even smaller bathroom. But the apartment had its own entrance and gave them the privacy they wanted, so on August eleventh, the women signed a contract to rent from September first through June thirtieth, delighted at the location, the reasonable cost and the spaciousness of the apartment.

In her mail on the fifteenth, Joanna found a square envelope addressed with a familiar scrawl and the return address of Roosevelt University in the corner. She let it sit unopened on her desk for most of the day. Her friends took her to dinner to celebrate her birthday, gathering around her in a warm circle of support and love. Even Philip got into the conversation and seemed to want to let her know he, too, cared.

Finally, when everyone had returned to their rooms and the hall was dark and quiet, Joanna sat at her desk and slit open the envelope. She'd thought about it all day, wanting to read it so badly she fought the urge several times to run back to her room and rip it open. But being afraid to reopen the wound that had begun to scar over, she put it off. And still there was a choice. It was open but she didn't have to read it. She could throw it in the wastebasket or take it downstairs to the office and shred it.

But even as she was thinking of her options, her hands were acting on their own, opening the envelope to reveal a pale pink card with a red rosebud on it and the words, "Happy birthday to the one I love." There was no verse inside, just Jared's message.


*August 13th, 1963*


*My darling Joanna,*
*My days are empty, my heart shrunken and hollow. I*
*go through the motions, but everywhere I turn, your face,*

*your eyes wide with hurt, appears in front of me. I'll take that image with me to my grave, knowing the immeasurable pain I've caused you.*

*My counselor is helping. He's given me an outlet for the grief leaving you has caused, but he can't erase your face from my memory, nor can he help me forget. Remember what Benton said about forgetting?*

*'Each season of each year I will be forgetting you all over. Each season, every year. I will need to forget you each summer, spring...autumn and winter. I will be forgetting you each day and every hour. Each night and day, each hour something wonderful and dear of you will ring in my heart and knock upon my mind. When a star falls, I shall wish for you. When the moon is new, I shall wish for you. When a bird looks into my window, when a leaf falls before me, when I find a fern in flower —I shall wish for you.'*

*You are a part of my soul, Joanna. Nothing will ever change that. I love you and I always will.*

*Jared*

She read it again and again. Funny, there were no tears this time, only a vacant feeling in her heart, an emptiness where once his words had stirred warmth and comfort. He was truly gone and somehow, she must move on.

Forget him? She knew that would never happen. They were connected on a soul-deep level, part of each other, destined to own pieces of each other's hearts for as long as they lived. They had spent winter nights curled tightly together in the big bed at Dan's, spring wandering the streets of New Hope, summer kissing behind the dunes at Island Beach and autumn on the ferry in New York harbor.

*"Each season of the year, I will be forgetting..."* How could she ever forget? Did Benton ever forget his Lillian? Could Jared ever forget her? How could he go back to his marriage after what

they had, make a life there? He'd have to reconnect with Vicki, and Joanna's mind clamped shut when she tried to think of the two of them together. Never having seen Vicki, Joanna didn't have a face to put to that someone, but she knew Jared's face so well she could see his closed eyes, feel the warm lips, smell the fragrance of his skin ... try to imagine him with someone else. Shuddering, Joanna pulled back to reality. She put the card in her desk drawer. Finally, lying in the darkness, wanting him so badly she felt physical pain, Joanna cried herself to sleep once again.

~ * ~

On August thirtieth, Bonnie and Joanna moved into the apartment. Joanna left a forwarding address at the post office, but the phone was listed in Bonnie's name and, though she'd given the number to her parents and friends, no one else would know how to find it.

Her classes were fascinating as she listened for hours on end to people who had spent their careers studying human behavior, learning about why people act in certain ways, what forces drive everyone from deep inside the subconscious. She looked forward especially to the two afternoons each week her therapy group met. No one could earn a master's degree from this program without having gone through therapy. At this point, Joanna eagerly participated in her group, listening to the innermost thoughts of the others and sharing her own. Jared had said his counselor was helping him; Joanna's group had become her salvation as well. They talked a lot about intimacy, without which no relationship can survive. But there was another kind of intimacy that arose out of their discussions ... a deep sense of sharing that bound the members together with the glue of empathy for one another. How Joanna welcomed that intimacy!

"Sometimes I lie in bed at night and try to imagine what it was like to be with someone I loved. I close my eyes and try to feel his arms around me and hear his voice, but I can't. I'm so lonely," she said once, when it was her time to share.

~ * ~

By mid-October, classes were in full swing and it was beginning to get colder. Every day, she checked the mailbox on their porch, but the letter from Jared was never there. Her mother wrote faithfully, not saying it directly but in many subtle ways letting Joanna know how relieved she was that Jared was gone for good. Joanna's letters were filled with news of her new friends, her coursework and her apartment. Never once did she let on that her life had little meaning without the hope of sharing it with Jared. Her mother wouldn't want to hear that anyway. They had decided Joanna would stay on campus for Thanksgiving but would fly home for Christmas and stay until winter break ended in the middle of January.

~ * ~

Bonnie had gone home to Winnetka to get a head start on the weekend, so the gang was one short when they went out on Friday night. They found a big table in the café on University Avenue and for once, Joanna ordered a beer. She wanted to make it a manhattan, but no one drank cocktails and she knew she couldn't have one without wanting to cry. They talked and drank for several hours until Denise looked at her watch and announced it was time for her to leave. It took them a long time to find coats, make their way to the front of the café and get ready to walk into the brisk night air.

"I'll walk you guys to the hall," Patrick said to Denise and Rosemarie, putting an arm around each of them. "Philip, you make sure Joanna gets home, okay?"

Joanna was more than a little shaky, the effect of the unfamiliar beers finally taking hold. She looked at Philip questioningly. "Do you mind?"

"Nah, I'll be glad to walk you. Good night, everybody. It was fun."

Joanna and Philip turned toward Armory Avenue and walked slowly up the street. The wind was picking up and Joanna huddled into her coat, feeling her own warm breath against her scarf, weaving and very unsteady on her feet.

"Are you cold?"

"No, thanks, Philip, I'm fine." She giggled lightly. "It's only a block or so anyway."

Inside, Philip helped her with her coat and put his on a nearby chair.

"I like the decorating you and Bonnie have done to the apartment," he said, looking around the spacious living room. "It really looks like you've made a home here."

"It is nice, isn't it," Joanna said, her speech slurred. She was still feeling woozy and sat to stop the room from spinning.

"Do you like it here in the Midwest?" Philip asked. "It must be a lot different than being near the ocean."

"Uh-huh. I miss the beach a lot."

"I grew up in Ohio. My folks have a farm not far from Columbus, but it's a really small town they live in and I'm pretty used to country living."

Joanna had never heard Philip say so much in one breath. She watched him ... a shy, good-looking young man with blond hair and a round face, his hands with their thick fingers resting on his knees.

Trying to organize her thoughts and make coherent conversation, she asked, "Did you always want to be an engineer?"

"No, not always. When I was a kid, I wanted to stay and work the farm with my dad, but farming's getting really hard. Big business is starting to edge out the family farmer, and my dad wanted me to have more of a future than he thought I'd get if I studied agriculture and came back to be with the family. I've always been fascinated with anything that flies, so I decided to try my hand at aeronautical engineering. It's sure different from anything I ever studied, but I seem to have an ability for it."

Joanna realized he'd inched over on the sofa until they were almost touching.

"I'm sorry you had such a bad time when you first got here," he said. "I've never loved anybody, so I can't imagine what it was like for you, but you were smart to forget that guy and get on with your life. You deserve someone who can really care for you."

*He hasn't an iota of understanding about how I feel.*

He stood and walked toward the door.

"Well, I better get going."

Joanna took his coat from the chair and held it out to him. Instead of taking it, Philip leaned over and quickly kissed her mouth. He stepped close, put his arms around her and kissed her again.

It was a different kiss. Tentative. There wasn't any passion, any feeling of soul-deep need, just a nice warmth that seemed to radiate from her lips through the rest of her body.

It had been so long. So long since she felt wanted, since someone had told her this way she was desirable, loveable.

Philip's kisses became stronger and bolder. They stumbled backward toward the sofa where they lay side by side on the narrow cushions. Though he continued to kiss her, Philip didn't say anything. No words of endearment, no husky repetitions of her name. But still it felt so good to have someone's hands on her skin, lips on hers. She closed her eyes as her head swam and gave herself over to the sensation, vaguely aware she was letting Philip's hand touch her where only Jared had ever touched and his body fit where only Jared's had ever gone and that she didn't really care. Jared didn't want her anyway.

~ * ~

"I'm sorry, Joanna, my God, I'm sorry. I don't know what got into me. I never meant to go this far."

Suddenly sober, Joanna sat up, straightened her sweater and looked on the floor for her slacks and underwear.

"Don't apologize, Philip; it takes two to tango. We've both had more to drink than we should have. I'm still feeling hazy. We got carried away."

"I'm not the kind of guy who sleeps with a girl the first chance he gets," Philip said frowning. "I don't know what happened…"

"I know we're both going to regret this in the morning," Joanna said. "I don't know what came over me either. This isn't my way of saying thanks for an escort home."

Philip got up and retrieved his coat. "Really, I'm sorry."

"Nothing damaged. We'll forget this ever happened. No one need ever know."

But Joanna told Bonnie anyway.

"I don't know how I could have done it. Sure, I like Philip; he's very nice, but he's definitely not the kind of guy I would choose for a long-term relationship. With Jared, I felt total commitment, a connection that went far beyond the physical. He was wide open to me, emotionally as well as sexually. Philip's the polar opposite. He's locked up inside, uncommunicative, unemotional. Maybe someday he'll find someone who'll settle for that, but he's not what I want. What could have gotten into me? How could I have done it?"

"You probably got caught up in the moment. You said you had a lot to drink. I certainly don't see the two of you together either and I'm frankly surprised it happened. Since when do you drink beer? I thought you didn't drink at all."

"I don't, at least not since Jared. We always had a couple of manhattans whenever we went out or when we spent time at his friend's cabin, but I don't remember ever getting so drunk I didn't keep my wits about me. Not that I would have with Jared anyway. It didn't take alcohol to make me want to make love to him."

Bonnie shrugged. "Well, it happened. I'm sure Philip will be embarrassed when you see him again, as will you. The good thing is it'll never happen again. You've both learned that much."

# Twenty-eight

*"Things could be worse."*

Joanna and Philip were both uneasy when the group met in the café Monday after dinner. As they were leaving, Philip took Joanna's arm.

"I want to say how sorry I am just one more time. I didn't mean any disrespect ... it happened. I really like you a lot and would never do anything to hurt you. Are you okay?"

"Thanks, I'm sorry too. We both know it was a mistake. Let's forget about it and be friends, okay?"

But by the second week in December, Joanna's constant longing for Jared was replaced with an icy fear that dominated her days and kept sleep at bay.

Every morning there were attacks of one wave of nausea after another. The very thought of food was repulsive and she often felt lightheaded, on the verge of fainting. Thinking back, she realized she'd skipped her November period. Thoughts of the only other time she'd missed kept hammering in her head, but this time the added symptoms were chillingly alarming.

Without telling anyone, Joanna hastily made an appointment at the university clinic. The doctor was kind and gentle as he examined her and took the specimen she provided to send to the lab.

"From what I can see, Miss Ransome, I would be pretty willing to guess you're pregnant. It's very early and I could be wrong, so let's wait until the results come back before we jump to any conclusions."

For two days, Joanna went about her studies with a deep sense of dread. On the third day, she called the clinic.

"The test was positive," the doctor said with no emotion in his voice. "You're definitely pregnant. I want you to schedule an appointment so we can begin your prenatal care. Can you set up a time now?"

Joanna couldn't answer. Her mind had shut down at the word "positive," and she hadn't registered the rest of the doctor's comments.

Feeling faint, fighting nausea, Joanna hung up. She sat in the chair by the phone, lowered her head between her knees and breathed deeply until the dizziness passed.

Pregnant? It had only been one time. How, after all those wonderful nights with Jared, how could it happen now? Why, if she had to be pregnant, why couldn't it be with Jared's child? Why? Pregnant! It must be a mistake. The test was wrong— someone else's results got mixed up with hers—that's it, that's what happened. But while she fought to deny it, she knew it was true. She'd read enough to know the signs ... this wasn't a mistake. She was going to have Philip Webber's baby. What was she going to do?

Joanna was still sitting by the phone when Bonnie came in from class.

"Hey, Jo, what are you doing home? Don't you have a group meeting? Jo? Jo, what's going on?"

"I'm pregnant," Joanna said in a voice half-filled with surprise. "I'm pregnant." This time, her voice was tinny, harsh, bitter. "What do you think of that?"

Bonnie sank to the sofa, her hand reaching for Joanna's.

"What? Oh my God. Are you sure?"

"As sure as the doctor at the university clinic can be. There's no mistake. Except the whole thing is one huge mistake. What am I going to do?"

"Have you told Philip?"

"No. I just found out myself. Oh, God, this is terrible! I can't tell him until I know what to do. I can't tell anyone, especially my mom and dad. They're beginning to breathe easier about me now that Jared's gone. I can't drop this on them now." Her fists clenched tightly, Joanna dissolved in tears.

"I don't agree, Jo. This is as much Philip's problem as it is yours. It's not fair that you shoulder the whole thing yourself. I think you should tell him as soon as possible. Like now."

"Oh, I don't know. I don't know what to do. Never in my wildest imagination did I think I'd be in this situation. I know I'm going to have to tell Philip, but then what?"

~ * ~

Philip sat next to her on the sofa. "What's up?"

"I don't know any easy way to say this, so I'm just going to spit it out. I'm pregnant."

"You're sure? Of course you are. You wouldn't tell me this without being sure."

He paused, looked down at his hands and then took a deep breath.

"I don't know you well enough to know without asking. Do you want an abortion? Are you thinking about that?"

"I'm not thinking about anything. I don't know what to think. Now that you ask, no, I guess not. I'd be scared to death of it. Where would I go ... it's illegal. But I also don't think I could do it ... after all, it's a baby we're talking about. No, I don't think I could go through with anything like that."

"Me either. It's probably the easy way out, but I think it's the wrong thing to do. What about adoption?"

"I don't know. Oh, Philip, I don't know about anything. I feel like the whole world is crashing down around me."

She put her face in her hands and cried, tears seeping through her fingers.

"This isn't helping," Philip said tersely. "I understand you're upset, but we won't get anywhere dealing with this emotionally. We have to decide, reasonably and carefully, what to do. We need to make a plan."

The detachment in his voice made Joanna stop crying and gaze at him in disbelief. His expression hadn't changed. It was like she'd told him a snowstorm was predicted for tomorrow. He was planning which sidewalk to clear first and mentally putting the snow shovel on the front porch to be ready. There was no support, no enfolding into warm, comforting arms, no words of caring.

"Look, Joanna, I guess I have to be blunt as well. I don't love you and I don't know if I ever will. Maybe I could learn to over time. You're just getting over somebody and you don't love me either, but we are friends. That's not the greatest combination for a successful partnership, let alone a marriage. But both of us would have a hard time walking away from this life we've created, so I believe that's our best option. What do you think?"

Joanna gasped. "Married? Us? What kind of parents would we be, what kind of examples would we set if there was nothing to our relationship but necessity? How could we commit to each other when there's no emotion, no love?"

"We'd be giving it a home and a mother and a father—"

"It? It's a baby, Philip, a baby, a he or a she. And I don't know if that's our best option."

"Okay, I'm sorry. If you think there's a better way, tell me. I don't see where we have a lot of choice. It's not like we don't get along; we've been friends for a few months now. A lot of people get married with far less going for them."

"But most don't. Most people marry because they're in love."

"Well, I think we could make a go of it. I'm willing to try. I get my degree in January and I already have a job offer in Chicago. We could move and you could finish your master's at one of the schools there. I'll be making enough to support us if we're careful about our spending."

Joanna looked for something in his eyes, something besides guarded caution, careful calculation. She thought about what it would be like, day in and day out, living with Philip, raising a child in a loveless marriage. Then she thought about the alternatives and she knew she'd fallen into a trap of her own making.

"I suppose you're right. We should get married as soon as we can. I'll have to tell my parents; so should you. This is going to be a real blow for them."

"Well, there's no time like the present. First, we ought to decide when we're going to do it so we can tell them our plans. How about next Saturday?"

Joanna shrugged. "Why not. We can go down to the courthouse and get a license and find a judge. It's not the way I always imagined getting married, but it suits the occasion," she said sarcastically.

"We can start looking for a place to live in Chicago after Christmas," Philip declared.

"Oh, Christmas. I haven't given that a thought. My parents expect me to fly home on the twenty-third and stay until winter break is over. Did you have plans?"

"The same as yours. I planned on driving home the same day. Well, we may have to postpone our family visits. First things first, agreed?"

"I don't know if I can simply call my parents, tell them I'm getting married and then, in the same breath, tell them I'm not coming home. This is going to be very hard, especially for my mother. You don't know my family, Philip; we're very close and I need to reassure them in person I'm okay … that we're okay. I need to go home."

"Let's not plan that far ahead now. We can talk about it after we take care of our immediate problem. I can skip a class or two if you can and we'll go down for the license. For all we know, there might a waiting period or some kind of blood test we have to have before they'll give us one. Let's get through the marriage and then we'll figure out how to see both of our parents and deal with their reactions."

He looked at his watch and stood. Reaching down, he patted her hand.

"I've got to get to class. Don't worry. In time, we'll probably be looking forward to having a little one around. Things could be worse."

Joanna was at a loss for words in the face of his implacable logic.

When he'd gone, she lay back on the couch and closed her eyes, trying to find some comfort, some solace from the fear that gripped her like a vise.

When the tears began anew, she wrapped her arms around her body and imagined Jared's warm embrace, his soothing voice, his own tears mingling with her own. *There's no baby,* he'd said then, grief in his voice. She wondered how he would have handled the reality of a child. Surely he would have found some joy, some emotion to express. For a while she lingered in her fantasy until it didn't work any longer and she knew Jared would be of no help to her then or ever.

~ * ~

Catherine held out her arms as Joanna came out of the stairway door. Next to her, Joe waited patiently.

"We're so glad you're home, honey. It seems like such a long time since we've seen you. Did you have a good flight? We're very worried about you, Jo. Your surprise news was like a lightning bolt, you know. When we get home, we want you to tell us all about this marriage.”

Not much was said on the long ride from Philadelphia. Joanna sat in the back seat, resting her head against the cushion, watching the familiar landscape along the Black Horse Pike pass her window. The last time she'd been on this highway, she'd been on her way to the airport, anxious to board a flight that would take her to Chicago and Jared, to her new life she believed would somehow include him. And now this ... a baby she hadn't planned and a husband she didn't want. What had she done?

~ * ~

“We're puzzled about why you got married so quickly,” Catherine said as the three of them sat at the kitchen table later that night. “Isn't it too soon for you, too soon after that terrible experience you had in July? How could you know Philip well enough to decide to marry him? Why couldn't you bring him home to us first, have a church wedding here at St. Anthony's?”

“This is going to be very hard for you to hear, Mom and Dad,” Joanna said, looking from one expectant face to the other. “We did it the way we did because we're going to have a baby. There didn't seem to be any other options. I'm sorry. I know how disappointed you must be with me. I'm unbearably disappointed with myself. It was a one-time mistake we intended to forget. Philip and I should never have been together. But we talked about what to do—neither of us could even consider abortion or adoption. We agree we're not marrying for love, but we're the ones who made the mistake. We thought we owed it to this child to at least try to make a home for him or her. I'm not asking for your forgiveness or any happiness, but I do need your support, now probably more than I ever have. Mom? Dad?”

Catherine's voice was unsteady.

“Jo, you have no idea how much your dad and I hoped you'd one day marry and have children for us to spoil. We always thought about how we would react to being grandparents and how much we would love any child of yours. So this should be very happy news."

She reached for her husband's hand. Joe's face registered his dismay. Catherine continued, "But you're our daughter first. Our concern is for you and your happiness. I admire you and Philip for the decision you've made, don't get me wrong. Of course, it wouldn't have been necessary if … but that's not important now. What matters is you two have decided to take the most important step in a couple's lives for the wrong reasons. Honey, listen. Where there's no love, there won't be a happy home. Dad and I want you to think long and hard about this. You said you were married by a judge, so it isn't valid in the eyes of the Church. You can have it annulled and find another way to deal with the baby's birth. Let us help you. Stay here at home; be anywhere you want. Keep the baby and we'll help you raise him. Don't tie yourself to someone you don't even know, let alone love, for as long as it takes before you find out how wrong you were, and you, Philip and the baby all suffer for it. Do you agree, Joe?"

"Positively. Listen to your mother. Look at what happened to you and her when you were so little. There was no love left in her marriage to your dad and you felt it even then. You lived with what that can do to a child; why set out on purpose to do it to your own child now?"

Joanna stared out the window, her eyes focused far into space. Looking back at them, she sighed.

"I hear you both and I love you for your concern and your advice. You've made a lot of sense, but I also know this child is Philip's as well as mine and I have no right to make decisions that deprive him of a say. I know he'd object to having the marriage annulled and my moving back home. He's a decent man. He's loyal and hard working and he has all the strengths a father should have, at least I think he does. The biggest problem I see is we don't know one another hardly at all and we don't seem to be on the same wavelength. Probably if we had dated a while, we'd have been better prepared to decide if we wanted to keep seeing each other or if we were better off going our separate ways. But we didn't. We had too much to drink and a momentary lapse of judgment and this is the result. I think we're doing what's best for the baby. I hope we are. Anyway, we intend to try to make it work."

"Okay, your dad and I understand. But I know I speak for both of us when I say this. If at any time, for any reason, you decide marrying Philip was the wrong way to go, bring our grandchild and come home. There won't be any questions asked or any judgments made. Just come home."

~ * ~

"My mother wants to come out when the baby's born," Joanna told Philip as they drove to the apartment from the airport. "My parents weren't happy about our getting married. They said it was for the wrong reason and won't work out in the long run. How did yours react?"

"About the same, I guess. My mother in particular was pretty angry. She said she thought you'd come out here from the big city looking for a husband and trapped yourself one. I told her she'd change her mind when she met you, but she says she doesn't ever want to do that. Don't worry. She was just upset. I'm sure she'll come around."

~ * ~

They found their new apartment easily, a two-bedroom in a newly constructed development about thirty minutes from Philip's office. Everything each of them owned fit in his car in one trip; they bought the living room and bedroom furniture and moved in about a week before Philip began his new job. With the check from Joanna's parents, they bought dishes and linens.

Joanna was indescribably lonely. At home in the apartment all day with no neighbors around, no car to use to explore her new surroundings, she spent her time reading and watching television, trying out a new recipe every night, learning the homemaking skills she'd never bothered to master.

The baby was growing daily, letting Joanna know by his powerful motions that he was gathering his strength for his entrance into the world. She didn't know why she thought of him as a boy ... it seemed easier to speak of him that way. She and Philip didn't talk about much else. They'd already picked a few names they liked. Philip came home from work each day with stories of fatherhood he'd heard on the job ... men much older than he, with several children apiece it seemed, all willing to share tales of raising kids.

Philip wasn't a reader, nor did he enjoy music as Joanna did. He was content to sit in the living room after dinner and watch television. On Sundays, he followed whatever sport was in season, often switching from one to another. When she'd had enough of watching with him, Joanna went to the bedroom to read or write to her parents, to Bonnie or in her journal.

One Sunday in April, Philip suggested an outing. He needed to stop by his office for a minute and then they could drive up the shore along the lake and have dinner somewhere. Money was always a consideration, but he didn't seem concerned about it this time and Joanna eagerly jumped at the chance to get into the city and out of the apartment.

"All done," Philip said, when he'd finished at his office. "Now, where shall we go? I kinda thought we might drive up the shore toward Evanston, maybe stop along the lake for lunch. Sound good?"

They'd driven about five blocks toward the lake when a red traffic light stopped them. As they waited for it to change, a small group of pedestrians crossed in front of their car. Joanna's heart stilled in her chest. She stopped breathing as her eyes followed the handsome man walking with a child on each hand, a beautiful blonde girl of about ten and a skipping, happy little boy with his father's fine features. She watched them reach the sidewalk and continue on, turning her head to follow them as the car pulled away. How happy they looked; how wonderfully relaxed Jared appeared. What a beautiful family they made.

"The lake sure is pretty," Philip was saying when she focused her attention back on him. "Any place in particular you want to go?"

Joanna didn't respond; she kept her head turned until she was sure there was no sign of Jared in her eyes. It should have occurred to her that Philip wouldn't have noticed anyway.

# *Twenty-nine*



Joanna's son Steven was born on July seventeenth. The few wisps of hair on his head were almost white in their blondness; feathery light eyebrows arched delicately above startling blue eyes and his tiny fingers, long and slender like his mother's, grasped Joanna's with surprising strength.

Philip was entranced by the baby, always eager to get up in the middle of the night to share the feeding, never seeming to tire of caring for him, lavishing his silent affections on the infant in ways that were helpful to Joanna, who took longer than she'd expected to recover from the difficult labor.

"You were right, Joanna," her mother said one morning as she held the infant, sated after his morning bottle and resting in his grandmother's arms. His azure eyes watched her face with solemn concentration, closing every now and then as he surrendered to sleep.

"Philip seems like a good person. He's certainly been considerate of you, anxious to make a nice home. And it's obvious he loves Steven. Who wouldn't?" she said, as she bent and gently kissed the tiny forehead. "I can't wait for you to come home for a visit. Your dad and everyone in the family are anxious to meet this little charmer of yours. He's asleep. I'll put him down."

When Catherine returned, she settled back in the rocking chair Joanna's grandparents had sent.

"When do you expect Philip's parents?"

Joanna shrugged. "I don't know. He doesn't want to press them about visiting. I know his mother's never really accepted the marriage. She says she isn't interested in meeting me or seeing the baby. Philip doesn't talk about it much, but he thinks she'll come around."

Catherine sighed.

"I don't understand at all, and I certainly don't know how a woman can stay away from her first grandchild. But that's her problem. And you? Are you happy? Do you love your son? Are you coming to love his father?"

Joanna met her mother's eyes with her own round, sad ones.

"Of course I love my son. He's beautiful and I want to give him the best of everything, including what basic mothering skills I've learned since you've been here. I'd never changed a diaper or filled a bottle, but after only a week, I feel like an old pro. I don't know what I would have done if you hadn't come."

"How could I not have come? Now that you're a mother yourself, you'll understand one's children always come first."

Joanna's eyes dropped as a sigh that seemed to come from her soul escaped her lips.

"Oh, honey, I'm sorry. That was such a thoughtless remark. Of course you know about children coming first. For a minute, I'd forgotten about Jared. Does it still hurt so much?"

"It will always hurt. Maybe not as badly as it did that awful day a year ago, but only because I'm using every ounce of mental strength I have to put him out of my mind, to expend my energy being a good mother."

"What about Philip? Are the two of you any closer?"

"I think we're as close as we're going to get. He doesn't get close. Not to me, not to his parents, not to the friends we barely see anymore. The only time I've looked into his eyes and seen love there was when he took the baby from my arms after he was born. And the love I saw was for Steven, not for me."

~ * ~

Steven was crawling all over the apartment by the time he was six months old. She'd just put him in his playpen when she heard the clang of the lid on the mailbox outside the front door. She greeted the retreating postman and went back inside, grateful for the warmth against a windy and bitterly cold mid-January day.

The usual pile of circulars was discarded without a second glance. As she sorted through the rest of the stack, one envelope made her heart flutter, her eyes widen in surprise. It bore familiar handwriting, but was addressed to her as Joanna Ransome at the graduate residence hall. Several forwards later, here it was—nearly two years since she'd last seen him—a letter from Jared. Somehow, it had found its way to her despite the new name and new location.

She stood at the door holding the mail, staring at the envelope with its assorted stampings and handwritten crossouts. It was postmarked Chicago but the return address was puzzling, not the address of his house or his office at the university.

Retrieving the toy Steven had tossed out of the playpen and handing it to the baby, she sat down on the floor next to him and carefully opened the letter.

*January 4, 1965*

*Dear Joanna,*

*I don't know if this letter will ever reach you, but I hope it does. It seems like a very long time since we've been in touch and I wanted to check and be sure you were okay.*

*My life has taken a few new twists in recent months. I still thoroughly enjoy my work and look forward to the time I spend with my students and at the Theatre.*

*The children are growing up. They live with their mother in the house near campus. Since Vicki and I separated, I have taken a small apartment nearby so I can be with the kids as much as possible. I miss being with them all the time, but they still play a very large part in my life.*

*You might be interested in news of a mutual friend. Do you remember Dan Kearney? He had the small cabin not far from Manning State. Not long ago, I got a call from him telling me he was selling the house and moving, of all places, to the University of Chicago to work in the biological sciences department. Although he lives on the other side of the city, we've gotten together several times. It's been comforting to have him here, sort of like a connection to a former life.*

*I hope you are well and happy. It would be nice to hear from you if you have time. Take care of yourself.*

*As ever,*

*Jared*

Joanna read it again and again, her sense of disbelief growing. Separated. He was separated. Separated. *A small apartment near the children.* Separated. The word echoed like a ring of mocking laughter. He'd left Vicki after all.

Steven began clamoring for release, his face screwed into a frown that was only seconds from erupting into a full-blown yell. Putting the letter on the table, Joanna rescued the baby, noted his need for a change and took care of him, settling him in his crib for a much-needed nap.

The letter stared up at her as she walked back into the kitchen. Again, she read those few stunning words: *Since Vicki and I separated, I've taken a small apartment.* Separated. Oh no, oh no, oh no. Separated. Something had happened to the plan to work on the marriage, and here he was, reaching out to her in a letter so casual and friendly it might have been read by anyone who happened to open it.

She had to hand it to Jared. He was cautious and circumspect, not revealing by the tone of his letter the depth of his previous connection to her, none of the emotions she wondered if he still felt. But of course he still felt them. Why else would he have written? What would he have hoped to gain unless it was a reunion, the resurrection of their relationship, picking up where they left off?

The enormity of it hit Joanna hard. She sat heavily in the chair, sadness overwhelming her, her fingers absently twirling the gold ring. Why couldn't she have waited? Why did she have to be so weak, so needy, so careless? If only she could turn back the clock, take back that stupid loss of self-control. She should have been free when this letter finally found her, free to run to Jared and build the life they'd dreamed about.

Making up her mind in a split second and acting on it before she could falter, she called the number at the top of the stationery.

His voice. The rich melodic tone warmed the telephone wires, touched Joanna's soul.

"Hello? Joanna ... is it really you?"

"Hello, Jared. Your letter came today and I wanted to talk with you instead of writing a reply. I hope you don't mind."

"Mind? Oh, of course I don't mind. Just hearing your voice— how can I tell you what it means to me? I tried so hard to reach you after that awful day at the airport, but then I decided I owed it to you to leave you alone. There was no way of telling which way my struggle with my problems would go and I couldn't ask you to put your life on hold while I tried to figure mine out. So many times, I've reached for the telephone but then lost my nerve. Finally, the wanting to reconnect was so great I took the leap and wrote. I'm so happy my letter reached you. Where are you?"

"In Chicago, not too far from you. I've been here a year now ... ever since Philip and I married."

She couldn't hear his breathing at the other end of the line.

"Are you still there?"

"Uh, yes, yes, I'm still here. You said married. When?"

"In December of '63. I met Philip in grad school and it all happened very fast. He's an engineer with a company here in Chicago and I'm back in school working toward the degree I never finished."

Steven began to wail in his crib. "Can you hold on a minute? I'll be right back."

Joanna rescued the sleepy infant, put him on her shoulder and picked the telephone up again.

"I'm sorry. Are you still there?"

Steven began playing with the telephone cord, making gleeful sounds of pleasure as he tried to force it into his mouth.

"Joanna? It looks like I'm in for more than one surprise. Do I hear a baby? Do you have a child?"

"Yes. Steven's six months old ... you can do the math. It should tell you all you need to know, more than you want to know, probably. I had given up on you, on us. It was a lonely life and a very sad one. No excuses, but just once I let down my guard and had too much to drink and *voilà!* ... life changed forever."

Her voice grew harsh, her tone resentful.

"And now I get the delightful news that you're free. Isn't that absolutely wonderful?" she said bitterly. "Tell me, how long have you been separated?"

"Since October. We tried to work it out, but there were so many problems, so many differences between us, it didn't happen. God, what have we done to one another? What have I done to the life we might have had?"

His voice broke. "I really don't think I can keep talking now," he said hoarsely. "Do you mind if I call you or write to you again?"

Joanna shifted Steven to her other shoulder and changed the phone to her other ear.

"No, I don't mind. I still want to hear from you."

*January 13<sup>th</sup>, 1965*

*My darling Joanna,*

*How easily that phrase leaves my pen. I can feel my fingers caressing your face as I write your name. We gave each other some heavy surprises today … mine in the mail and yours on the phone.*

*I was glad your little one was there making happy talk. Hearing him kept jarring me back to reality, making me deal with what is, not what I wanted it to be.*

*I hope you're happy. I hope this man you married has given you the same measure of contentment I could not. I know I have no right to ask, but when has that ever stopped me? Do you love him, Joanna? Does he make you feel as loved and beautiful as I know you need to be?*

*Foolishly, I had hoped you were still free. To be honest, your news was a real blow to the fantasy I'd been nurturing since I finally got up the courage to write. Presumptuous of me, wasn't it? After all, I told you to find someone, marry and be happy, didn't I? Ironic … you always told me to put my children first and I did, losing you in the process. I told you to find someone else and you did, while I was building a life with you in my imagination that won't ever be. What have we done, Joanna? What have we cost ourselves?*

*I should not have come back into your life, and I won't stay if it will bring you more pain. You need never hear from me again. But if that is your decision, please know I regret the loss of a life with you more than I can say.*

*Be happy and remember … I love you, my darling, and I always will.*

*Jared*

Joanna put down the sheet of paper, rested her head against the back of the sofa and closed her eyes, tears running down the sides of her cheeks, the house quiet as Steven napped. She could hear Jared's voice ... he was still always so close.

She wanted to tell him ... no, I don't love Philip. I still love you. I'll always love you. He's nothing you are and everything you're not. She opened her eyes and looked around the room, this room in her home where she and Philip were raising their son. How could she stay here, scant miles from Jared, without needing to go to him, simply leave Philip and go? How could she turn her back on this chance?

Steven woke and whimpered in his crib. Joanna folded the letter, put it back in its envelope and carried it to the bedroom she shared with Philip. At the back of the shelf of her closet was the box she'd brought with her and cached away like a secret treasure. She untied the red ribbon that had once hung on the stem of a single crimson rose and added this newest letter to the stack, retying the bow. She sat for a few minutes as Steven's cries grew more demanding, fingering the soft blue blouse, remembering.

Then, she closed the box, put it back on the shelf and went to tend to her child.

*January 20, 1965*

*My darling Joanna,*
*Selfishly, I'm overwhelmed with gladness that you wrote back. My sudden reappearance, with the news it brought, must have been very difficult for you. I'm sorry, my darling, sorrier than I can say and for more than just having written.*

*All too well I know about the soul-searching you're doing. As I hear you describe it, it's like reliving the agonizing I did before I decided to stay with Vicki and try to work things out for the sake of the children. My heart was torn between wanting to give them what I believed they deserved and what I wanted for myself. Now, you're suffering the same way.*

*I can't ask you to leave Philip for me any more than you ever asked me to leave Vicki. I can't ask you to take your son away from his father, although I would love him as if he were my own. I spend a lot of my time with the children, trying to keep the continuity of my presence in their lives. It can be exhausting sometimes, both emotionally and financially, and I find myself wondering what good I would be to you and Steven with the strain of caring for two families instead of one. You would have to work, I fear, since my salary is stretched to the limit with keeping two residences and meeting all the needs of the kids. Vicki's income has grown slightly and will continue to do so as she takes on more and more responsibility at the museum, but she still can't meet household expenses, so we agreed I would continue to provide that support for as long as necessary. I'm happy to do it, but it does cause some pretty lean times on my end.*

*And then there's Philip. You still haven't told me if you love him. That should be my answer. If you did, you wouldn't be writing to me; you wouldn't be reaching out, even considering leaving him. Another sadness I can add to the pile of emotions I've created. You married someone for whom there's no fire, didn't you? I did the math as you suggested. I drove you to another man's arms, someone you didn't even know, let alone love, and now we're both caught in this insidious trap.*

*Of course, I won't make any attempt to see you. You didn't have to ask. I know how hard it would be—no, how unbearable it would be—for us to see one another now. I want nothing more than to hold you and love away the hurt I've caused you, but we're both too vulnerable.*

*Write to me; call me if you want to. I won't do anything more than answer your letters and be here when you want to talk. Do what you have to do for your own peace of mind. I'll try to help you by staying out of your way.*

*Remember I love you, my darling, and I always will.*

*Jared*

Joanna was unable to rest at night. She went through the days in a sleep-deprived, dazed state, tending to Steven, cooking, cleaning, shopping, reading her assignments and trying to concentrate in class. All the while, though, she juggled the possibilities and searched for options.

It was a short distance from here to Jared's. Philip could see Steven whenever he wanted. It hadn't been a valid marriage; the Church would annul it. But where would she and Steven live while she was going through the legal process to make it all happen? How would she pay for the lawyer she would need to represent her? What if Philip refused to let her take Steven and she ended up having to fight for him? So many scenarios presented themselves as she sat in the dark night after night pondering her options. Finally, she bitterly concluded there were none.

Philip was unaware of Joanna's inner struggles. She knew he accepted her presence as he might a housekeeper's or a nanny's. He ate what she cooked, played with the baby while she read, took over Steven's care while she went to class. It never occurred to him she wasn't content with the arrangement and it never occurred to her to tell him otherwise.

Joanna longed for someone to help her decide what to do. She couldn't turn to her mother whose joy in her grandson would be dampened by worry over this new development. She was afraid to confide in Doris who'd recently left Manning and returned to work in Florida and who would greet her news of a resurrected Jared with intense dismay.

She knew she was simply grasping for someone to tell her something other than what she already knew, help her find a way to get what she and Jared wanted. Disprove Doris. Wanting *could* be having.

The reality was otherwise, and she knew it. Sometimes as the night wrapped wrapping around her, she wept silently with the heaviness of the wanting. It weighed on her body, leaving her tired and drained, the pain of the jaws of the trap she'd set for herself clamped unmercifully on her soul.

*February 15, 1965*

*My darling Joanna,*

*I'm sorry it's taken so long for me to reply to your letter. I didn't know how and I guess I wanted to believe by not answering you I wouldn't have to accept your decision. It's not that I was surprised by what you told me. I've been expecting it. It's just that I was feeding a vain hope it would go the other way.*

*I understand you have to try. I hear all your reasons and I'm listening to an echo, a disturbing remembrance of myself on those long summer nights spent sitting on the porch staring at the stars, trying to convince myself my children would be fine without me, that I deserved a life with you, knowing I was trying to find a way of wanting and having. It didn't work. It didn't work for you either.*

*Do whatever you must to bring yourself some contentment. You won't be much good to Steven if you're miserable and unhappy. And you and Philip will never have even the slightest chance if you're bitterly regretting this decision. Find peace for yourself, my darling. I'll be here whenever you need me.*

*Remember I love you and I always will.*

Jared

~ * ~

Supper was over and darkness had fallen outside in the cool March air. Philip dozed in the chair with a sleeping Steven's head on his chest while Joanna struggled with a complex chapter in a textbook when the telephone rang.

*March 8, 1965*

*My darling Joanna,*

*I was heartsick by your call, my joy at hearing your voice immediately doused by the seriousness of your tone, the news of your mother's illness.*

*I only saw her once after the day of the play. Maybe she told you, probably she didn't. It was that awful day in August when I left. Your mother was arriving as I walked out the door, nearly out of my mind with grief. I wanted to say so much to her and to tell her how much I loved you, but I saw only a momentary flicker of something remotely resembling understanding in her eyes before she told me how much she hated me for what I'd done to you, and I left without answering her. It was obvious she loves you very much.*

*Of course you'll go to her. I only hope you'll find time to let me know how her surgery went, whether they were able to remove the cancer, what the prognosis is and how she's faring. I'll need to know about you, most of all. Take some time once in a while to remember I'm thinking of you and wishing I could be there to cushion your fear, ease your worry.*

*Be safe, my darling, and remember I love you and I always will.*

*Jared*

Philip drove her and the baby to the airport, his silence conveying his unhappiness that she'd insisted on going east. Catherine had plenty of people around her to help, he had argued. Having a small child around would only add to the chaos and, besides, it wouldn't be good for Steven to be in a home filled with sadness and fear.

Joanna knew better than to appeal to Philip's emotions. Her decision to be with her mother had little or nothing to do with practicality or wanting to be available to help out. He was right about that ... there were enough nieces and nephews who loved her to see Catherine didn't want for anything. But she knew how much her mother needed the solace of her presence. There was no way she would stay so far away and deprive both of them of that comfort.

Tight-lipped, Philip waited for them to board the plane. Once settled in her aisle seat with Steven on her lap, Joanna rested her head on the back of the seat, moved the sleepy infant to her shoulder and closed her eyes. She said a silent prayer that everything would go well for her mother and thought about Jared.

# Thirty

*"It seems we missed so many chances."*

*March 22, 1965*

*Dearest Jared,*

*It's everything I was afraid it would be and more. Mom's surgery went as well as it could. It was a radical mastectomy, so she'll have a long, painful recovery. As always, though, her spirits are high and her unfailing optimism has taken over.*

*Did I ever tell you she and Dad were opposed to my marrying Philip? They said it was too soon after losing you. They wanted me to find another way to deal with impending parenthood other than tying myself to Steven's father. How wise they were and how bitterly I regret not having listened.*

*Philip wasn't happy with my coming east with the baby. He never talks about his own parents and I've never met them, so I don't know what he would do if the shoe were on the other foot. My guess is he'd check in to be sure his mother was okay and then go back to work. We see things so differently.*

*It's comforting to be home. I didn't realize how much I've been missing it until now. Yesterday I took a long walk on the beach while Dad stayed with Steven and Mom. I always do my best thinking with the breaking waves as background and it helped me decide I can't stay in the Midwest now. They took lymph nodes from under Mom's arm and there was evidence the cancer has probably spread, even though they can't predict where or when it might crop up again.*

*As much as I'd hate being so far from you, I'm going to talk to Philip about moving back here. There's a place nearby that would be excellent for his type of work and I don't think he'd have a problem getting in, thanks to contacts Dad has there. I only know I need to spend time closer to my mother.*

*We'll be leaving for Chicago in a couple of weeks. I'll call you to say hello when we get back. Take good care of yourself.*

*Love always,*
*Joanna*

Philip met them at the airport, swooping his son into his arms, smiling broadly at the giggle the baby gave in return.

"Golly, it seems he's grown a few inches in this short time. It's so good to have him back."

*April 15, 1965*

*My darling Joanna,*
*My heart aches for the upheaval in your life. I was particularly upset when you told me about Philip's reaction*

to your return. It's understandable, of course, that he was happy to see Steven after so long, but it's too bad he can't see beyond the baby to the rest of the gold he possesses.

Good luck with the attempt to make the move. I'm glad Philip's at least willing to consider it, for your sake if not for mine.

Having you halfway across the country might make it a bit easier to adjust to the reality we've created. Now, knowing you're only a few miles away, I continually fantasize about dashing up to your front door, throwing it open and declaring my intention to sweep you and the baby away, Philip be damned! Ah, fantasy! See? I'm still wanting and dreaming of having.

The children are doing great. I spent the evening with them last night and even stayed long enough to put them to bed.

Vicki has found a counselor she likes a lot and has started therapy on her own. I'm glad she's going. Maybe she can dig a little deeper and hunt out some of her personal demons. I faced many of mine early on in my own therapy and still deal with the aftermath of having found them as I continue to work with my counselor.

Keep me posted on the possibility of a move. I know it's out of the question, but I would love to see you once before you go. Again, the old wanting and having.

Take good care of yourself. Remember I love you and I always will.

Jared

*October 1, 1965*

*Dearest Jared,*
*I've spent a lot of time since we last talked wrestling with my conscience, that still small voice that warns me to be aware of the potential folly of something I'm contemplating, the one I've too often ignored.*

*With the move back east looming ever closer, I find myself struggling with wanting to see you before I put a thousand miles between us once again.*

*What could it hurt? We'd only be together for a few hours at most. We'd be in public, where we could look across the table at each other ... maybe accidentally touch hands. I could drink in the face I still see simply by closing my eyes and imagining you.*

*But the more I think about seeing you again, the more clearly I understand why it can't happen. Listen to what I wrote in the last paragraph. You can hear my longing for you in the words, stark and impotent in black and white. Imagine what might happen if we were to be together again under any circumstances and with the best of intentions. How could I not lean into your comforting embrace, breathe in your breath, sink into the warmth that is you? Impossible. I don't trust that I could keep the resolution I made to stay with Philip. Seeing you, for no matter how short a time, would unravel my resolve and make me question how I could throw away the chance for the life we dreamed about.*

*My degree? The closest place that will accept my credits and offer the master's I need to go into private practice is Temple University in Philly. As soon as we're settled, I'm going to get my transcripts sent and knuckle under to finish the coursework.*

*And you? You don't talk much about what's going on in your life. I read the reviews of your play in the* Tribune *and am so proud of everything you've been able to accomplish. I know you love your work but I hope there's more for you than that.*

*Take good care of yourself.*

*Love always,*

*Joanna*

*October 29, 1965*

*My darling Joanna,*

*I've been doing fine. I was very pleased with the rave reviews for the fall production (yes, I knew you'd probably read them, thank you) and now I'm devoting my time to my students who are nearing the end of their journeys toward advanced degrees.*

*Work continues to be very satisfying for me, but you've said it … it's not enough. I read the unasked question in one of your letters from a few weeks ago, and the answer is no. There is no one in my life. I've seen a couple of women I met at the university, but nothing came of it. There was only one woman I thought I would marry and she married someone else, so I'm alone and not at all happy that way. I want to have someone with whom I can share, especially after discovering the wonder of sharing with you, but I'm afraid you've spoiled me for anyone else.*

*My heart aches at the thought you'll soon be gone. I think about that wonderful Halloween four years ago when we looked into each other's souls and found ourselves. What I wouldn't give to be able to turn back the clock to that precious time.*

*I've long accepted your decision not to see me before you go. I know we couldn't just sit there and talk. My arms would ache to hold you and I would feel your need responding to mine. I respect you too much to try to persuade you to change your mind. Perhaps someday we can meet again. I know if that time ever comes, I'll jump at the chance and hope you'll feel the same.*

*Write to me when you can. I miss you every day. I love you and I always will.*

*Jared*

*January 1, 1967*

*My darling Joanna,*

*It seems like a long time since I've written, or you either for that matter. New Year's Day, five whole years since we were together to celebrate a new year, seemed like a good time to sit down and dash off a few lines to be sure you're okay. Are you?*

*My life goes on as always, with a few ups and many, many downs, although the down times are becoming fewer and further apart. It's taken some adjustment to living at home with Vicki and the children again, but I think the decision to try once more was the best one. I'm delighted being with the kids on a full-time basis.*

*Michael is beginning to gain some height and his face is losing its babyish good looks in favor of a more serious, mature appearance. He's still pretty quiet, but has kept his athletic ability and his unusual grace. Wonder where he got that? He's asked to take dance lessons, of all things, but he seems very serious about it so we've enrolled him in a course at the university that's geared toward kids his age.*

*Vicki and I are making good progress. We've been in counseling now for nearly six months, learning what made things go wrong and what to do to be sure we don't travel that road again. A lot of what you and I had together helps me articulate my needs and, although she will never be you, Vicki is trying as hard as I am to make things better. I believe I'm getting the most out of it now that I can be under the same roof as the children again, sharing their lives and their interests as they grow.*

*Congratulations on getting your master's degree. It must be a relief not to have to take that grueling drive into the city so many times a week. When do you begin accepting clients or do you already have some?*

*Happy New Year, my darling. I hope you are happy. I admit not hearing from you for so many months has me worried. Are you going through something you don't want to share with me? Or are you simply very busy? I hope it's the latter, since I couldn't bear to think of you in any more pain than you've already had. Please write when you can so I know everything's all right.*

*I love you, my darling, and I always will.*
*Jared*


*January 25, 1967*


*Dearest Jared,*
*I've been a terrible correspondent, I know. As always, you've looked beyond my letter-writing lapses and touched the real reason you haven't heard from me.*

*Things aren't going well here. Oh, professionally everything couldn't be better. I have five full-time clients and some of the local doctors are beginning to mention me to their patients who might benefit from therapy, so I guess I'll have a full slate soon. It's a good feeling to be able to help people deal with their problems as my counselors, starting with dear Doris, have done for me.*

*Doris isn't well. She had a bad fall about a year ago and went on painkillers to ease the discomfort she felt just by moving around. I'm worried about her to the point I'm going to fly down there next month to be sure she's okay. I want to help in any way I can. Lord knows she's helped me enough in the years we've been friends.*

*And then there's Philip. You knew that, didn't you? You know there are problems, but you're too sensitive and caring to ask.*

*He's grown more and more resentful of the loss of the relationship with his parents. They never call, never write. He initiates whatever contact there is and long ago stopped asking when they were going to see Steven and meet me and my family. It's like they've cut him out of their lives and, though he says otherwise, I think he blames me, though I can't imagine why. I've offered to fly to Ohio with him and Steven, but whenever he mentions it to them, there's no interest on that end. They've disapproved of our marriage since the first and seem determined to keep their distance.*

*Anyway, it's wearing on Philip. My folks have made him part of the family. He appreciates it and things have been somewhat better between us. But I think he feels terribly guilty about his own parents' reaction to him. Naturally, he won't talk about it. I've suggested he see one of the other therapists in the area, but he's angrily refused. And that's the other thing. He's angry a lot. It's a quiet anger mostly, but once in a while he's abrupt with Steven, who doesn't understand at all. It isn't healthy, and I can't let it go on like this. Philip needs to face whatever is going on inside of him and take steps to deal with it.*

*Enough of my problems. I'm sorry to waste our precious time together complaining about my life. For the most part, it's good, especially my work and being so close to my mother. She's doing great and enjoys being back at work.*

*I think about you often. More than often ... constantly. I wonder how you are, what you and Vicki are doing, whether you're happy in your re-created marriage. The good thing is Vicki loves you and you once loved her. That's a lot to use to rebuild a marriage. As always, darling, I wish it had turned out otherwise. But I'm happy for you that you're finding contentment with your family. Sometimes—no, most of the time—I think Philip and I will never work out. My mother knew what she was talking about when she said a marriage without love couldn't succeed. Philip doesn't love me; he said so before we married and nothing's changed. I don't love him either. I don't know where we'll go from here, but I'm afraid we're heading for a showdown. Now that I've told you all of this, I'll keep you posted on where it goes, but please don't worry. I'll be fine.*

*Thank you for prodding me to write. I felt I'd be inflicting too much of my troubled life on you while you were busy resurrecting your good one. I should have known you always have room for me in your heart and God only knows I need to curl up in there once in a while and feel safe and loved. Be well, dear heart. Write when you can.*

*Love always,*
*Joanna*

*June 27, 1967*

*Dearest Jared,*

*Happy 43rd birthday! How I wish I could see you to give you my love in person, but as always, long distance will have to do.*

*There has been a major development here. Philip has received his draft notice and will soon report for basic training prior to being sent to Vietnam. His skills with aircraft will be much in demand and we are hoping he won't be involved in combat. For now, he's gone to Ohio to see his parents. The last time he called, his mother said something about his father being ill but she was pretty vague about what was wrong, so Philip felt he needed to go, find out for himself and break the news about being drafted. I know he really wants to see them and be home for a while. He's very unhappy here and talks often and bitterly about how wonderfully different life is in the Midwest. He's never said it in so many words, but I know he wants to go back. We'll have that discussion when he comes back from the service, but it will definitely be a problem. I can't live there. My work is here; my family is here; this is where I want Steven to grow up, among family and friends who love him and are there for both of us whenever we need them. Living in Ohio or Illinois or anywhere so far from here would deprive us both of the support system we have and I'm not willing to give that up. Fortunately, that decision doesn't have to be faced right away.*

*I guess things would be different if there were a deep love between Philip and me, but we've both known for a long time there isn't.*

*Steven will go into nursery school for half days in September and I'm back in school working on my Ph.D.*

*Even with Philip gone it won't be much of a problem, since my parents are delighted to grab Steven whenever they can and keep him as long as I'll let them.*

*There are some tough times ahead, I know. But being able to share with you will help me do what I think is right when the time comes. It's not as good as having you with me, but it helps. God, I miss you so! Take good care of yourself for me. I love you very much.*

*Always,*
*Joanna*

*October 31, 1967*

*My darling Joanna,*
*I'd be lying if I didn't say how devastated I was at your news of the crash of Philip's helicopter. I wish I could be with you to ease the pain. Oh, for sure, you and Philip had your difficulties and there was even more trouble ahead when he returned, but I know facing all those decisions would have been far preferable to this. My heart aches for the turmoil you and Steven are experiencing.*

*There are no guarantees for tomorrow, are there? Thinking about what you have gone through reminds me that what really matters is living for the moment. So I fight to shake off the occasional melancholy and find some happy thing to do with the children or Vicki to yank me back to reality once again. And reality is my family, where I've chosen to make my life.*

*To that end, Vicki and I have decided to build a house, the first one we've owned. There's a piece of property on the lake further up the north shore we want to buy. Both of us love living near the water and it's only a 20-minute commute to either Roosevelt or the museum, so it's just about ideal.*

*Dan came by last weekend. He's met a wonderful woman and they've set a wedding date. I couldn't be any happier. He asked about you and, when he heard the sad news, asked to be remembered to you.*

*After Philip's untimely tragedy, there is something that needs to be considered. I've asked Dan to let you know if anything ever happens to me and I'd like it if you would find someone on your end who will do the same for me.*

*Oh, my darling, it seems so unfair. My life is in order and there's even real happiness in it. But what of you? Yours is turned upside down and I worry about how you'll be able to mother and take care of Joanna as well. Promise me you'll find time for yourself. Even if it's only a quiet few minutes spent listening to those Beethoven symphonies you love or writing to me, I'll always be here to listen.*

*Remember, my darling, I love you and I always will.*

*Jared*

~ * ~

It had been a long day and Joanna sagged a bit as she closed the door on her last client for this hectic Thursday. What a way to celebrate a birthday. As she reached for the light switch, the phone rang. For a minute, she considered letting it ring. Then, thinking it might be a client, she picked up the receiver.

"Happy birthday, my darling!"

"Oh, Jared! How wonderful of you to call."

"How does it feel to be twenty-seven, you old person you? What special plans do you have for the celebration?"

"Celebration? Absolutely nothing. My parents are having Steven and me over for dinner tomorrow night and I know they'll want to make a big deal out of it."

"How is Steven taking Philip's absence?"

"He's doing okay. It's been very hard for him to grasp the concept of death, but I tell him his daddy is with God and he'll see him again some day. As he gets older, I know the questions will be more specific, but I try to keep my answers at his level now. It's been pretty tough."

"I'm sure it has. But you'll find your way through this, I know, as strong as you are. I only wish you could have found happiness instead of all this grief."

"Thank you. I guess we're only given what we can handle. Steven and I will be fine."

"Joanna, did you destroy the tape I gave you for your birthday that last August?"

"Destroy it? Oh my, no, I couldn't destroy it. I don't have the tape recorder any longer so I can't listen to it, but it's safely tucked away and one day I'll find a way to hear it again. Why do you ask?"

"No special reason. I thought about it today when I was remembering that special night at the club and wondered if you still have it. I'm glad you do, and I hope you can hear it one day."

"I hope so, too. It seems like only yesterday you and Jim hatched the plan to put those songs on tape for me. Where did the years go?"

"We're hanging onto them. We each need those memories, for whatever reason, so we're hanging on. I, for one, love every second of mine. The only thing I'd rather do than talk with you like this is see you again. Do you think we'll ever get that chance?"

"I don't know. If we do, I'd go anywhere, anytime. It would be a glorious gift I'd grab in a heartbeat."

# **Thirty-one**

*"Just say you'll come to New York ..."*

> June 27, 1970

> Dearest Jared,
> It hardly seems possible it's time for me to wish you another happy birthday. And yet, when I think about how old we both are (you more than I, of course) and the fact that I will soon have a first grader, I realize how fast time is passing.
> Thanks for your calls and the caring concern you're heaping on me. I confess to needing it.
> Mom made it through her surgery but hasn't bounced back like she did from the first one. She's still in a good deal of pain, very uncomfortable and depressed. I can't imagine how devastating it must be to think you're out of the woods, the magical five-year survival period has passed and then, wham! it's back. I find her questioning everything now, not

*the least of which is her faith in God. That's especially distressing because it's what she's held on to all these years to help her through the other tough times she's faced. Anyway, she's not working yet and seems at odds with herself.*

*Steven is the bright light in her life. He 'helps' with her chores, dries dishes and draws pictures that make her smile. He has quite an artistic bent, one of the good traits he inherited from his dad.*

*That reminds me. Remember a while back, you asked me where Michael's grace came from? I guess it never occurred to you to watch yourself in the mirror when you move. You're very much like a dancer yourself, graceful and sure. I can still see you striding into the snack bar with that purposeful, confident step, your eyes sweeping the room until they rested on me. What I wouldn't give to relive just one of those days.*

*Whenever I face adversity, I wish for your strength and your love and I feel the comfort of your arms around me.*

*Write to me when you can. Your letters are the tonic I need to get me through. I love you very much.*

*Always,*
*Joanna*

~ * ~

Catherine's condition didn't improve. She was in constant pain, barely able to move an inch of her body without crying out in agony. Joanna spent every moment with her mother ... reading to her, talking for hours about anything she could think of that would take Catherine's mind away from the relentless fire in her body.

The icy winter seemed to arrive early and intensify as first Halloween, then Thanksgiving came and went. There was no big family dinner this year, although the cousins, aunts and uncles came by to tiptoe into Catherine's room, touch her hand gently and leave with tears unchecked. On December third, death brought a merciful end to the suffering.

*December 5, 1970*

*My darling Joanna,*

*The sadness in your voice broke my heart. Losing your mother has been an overwhelming burden and I wish with all my heart you didn't have to carry it alone.*

*You need to express the sorrow. You need to give it sway, let it out and allow yourself to mourn. I know this is far from perfect, but do this for me, please. Close your eyes; rest your head on my shoulder and cry. Cry for your mother, for the loss to that little girl who held on for so many years to the love she got from her. Then, when at last the tears won't come anymore, let me dry your eyes. Feel my hands on your face and rest on my shoulder. I'm there if only in your mind.*

*Find time for yourself. Don't be too hasty to help your stepfather with the house and all the things that will reopen the wounds. Put yourself first for a change and call me if you need me to nag you from time to time.*

*I love you, my darling, and I always will.*

*Jared*

~ * ~

Throughout the following months, Joanna threw herself into her studies, seeing clients during the day and poring over textbooks and research documents at night. Her contact with Jared suffered a bit, but she knew he understood how important it was to her to get the degree that would cap the years of work.

*March 3, 1971*

*Dearest Jared,*

*My dissertation is finally finished. My committee meets in a few weeks to review it, I'll sit for the orals and, with a lot of luck, I'll be able to put Ph.D. after my name. Doctor Webber! Has an interesting ring to it, doesn't it? Who would have thought one day I'd also be a creaking old academic with a funny hood to wear over my academic robe? How I wish you could be at Temple's commencement in May to help me put it on.*

*I wish my mother were here to share the joy. Dad is still wandering around like a lost puppy, poor thing. He spends a lot of time at our house playing with Steven and I know he visits his sister and her husband often, but there's a huge empty spot in his heart that will hurt for a very long time.*

*I'm keeping busy with my clients. Sometimes, I'm absolutely drained at the end of the day. I know fighting one's way back to emotional health is hard work, but I sometimes think the therapist is working just as hard, if not more so.*

*I'm anxious to hear about your potential promotion. Write when you have time. I love you very much.*

*Always,*
*Joanna*

*October 31, 1971*

*My darling Joanna,*

*Another Halloween with all its memories, and this one especially rewarding on my end. The board of trustees has granted me a full professorship and named me director of the Center Theatre. It doesn't mean much in any way other than professional satisfaction, but I'm delighted to have been given the honor. It means my work continues to be appreciated.*

*Marina is getting ready to apply to colleges. Her choice of career still stumps me ... I never saw it coming. Granted, she was a good student in the sciences and I know she likes children, but a pediatrician? A doctor? I didn't think they let pretty blondes into medical school, but I guess I'm showing my chauvinist tendencies as well as my age.*

*Michael will enjoy having us to himself for a couple of years once Marina's gone. He likes hanging around the theater, watching the performers, even trying his hand at a dance routine or two. Now, if he were to choose a career in the performing arts, I wouldn't be surprised one bit.*

*Whatever my children do with their lives, I hope they find happiness and are wise (and lucky) enough to hold onto it. It seems we missed so many chances.*

*Remember, I love you and I always will.*

*Jared*

*June 27, 1973*

*Dearest Jared,*

*Thanks for the newsy letter. I know we try to keep up with one another and our letters are often notes, but occasionally it's nice to get a long one from you, filled with updates on your family. Like you, I try to stay very busy. Besides being a fully scheduled therapist, I'm a fourth grade room mother and an assistant scout troop leader as well. And in the middle of it all, I'm seriously considering moving back to Atlantic City. It's been nice living in the country like this, but I miss the ocean. It's not that far a drive for my clients, some of whom will welcome the change since they live there anyway, and I can escape to the beach whenever I need some comfort or some quiet time. It will do Steven good to be close to the shore as well. He loves it as much as I and for the same reasons. When we visit Dad, he often asks if he can go to the beach, no matter what the weather. Guess that's something good he's gotten from me.*

*Atlantic City is rapidly losing its luster as a resort and I think it's sad to see the town deteriorating as fast as it is. But housing is readily available and at bargain basement prices, so I'll find something that can suit our needs and move as soon as I can sell the house we're in now.*

*Well, Dad, how does it feel to have a daughter that's almost as old as I was when we met? What would you do if she came home, as I did, hugging the secret of her affair with a married professor close to her heart? It looks different now, doesn't it?*

*At the time, we thought nothing of the anxieties we were inflicting on those around us, so intent were we on what we had found. Now, from the perspective of years, it takes on a different luster. That said, I know I would relive it without hesitation, just to spend those golden days falling in love with you, living for each meeting, each kiss, each song that bound us closer together. I do hope, though, that Marina is enjoying college life, sans illicit love affair.*

*You asked about my visit with Doris. It was stressful. She's getting progressively more disconnected from everyone around her. I left her in the care of her housekeeper. You know how you worry about people sometimes without reason, just a gut feeling something isn't on track? I've felt that where Doris is concerned so many times in recent years and been on the money every time. Now I have a sense of foreboding about her, a fear she won't be with me much longer. I hope I'm wrong.*

*When you see Dan and his wife again—did you say her name was Pamela?—give them my best. Tell Dan I don't want that call from him for many, many more years. Beth and I try to get together once a month or so, depending on our schedules. She was such a help to me after you left Manning and she was pleased I asked her to be the one to call you if anything ever happens to me.*

*I don't believe it, but I've actually written this whole letter without referring to the fact that it's your birthday! You're one year shy of the big five-o. I hope it was a happy day.*

*Stay well and write when you can. I think about you far more than is healthy, but it makes me feel warm and loved to remember how it was to be in your arms.*

*Always,*
*Joanna*

*September 20, 1975*

*My darling Joanna,*
*I've had a wonderful few days of rest, fishing and enjoying being so close to the water, like you. Admittedly, your pond is bigger than my pond, but I can't see anything but lake all the way to the horizon, so I guess it's not really too different.*

*Marina has decided to enroll in the University of Massachusetts for medical school. She debated coming back closer to home, but the lure of the prestige of a big school near those outstanding hospitals is too strong. I was kinda hoping she'd be closer to us, but that's not meant to be. We'll see her on holidays, but she's determined to be on her own.*

*Michael loves life at Roosevelt. For him, there was never any question about where to go to college. He's been at home here since he was a very little boy and is in his element as a dance major. He's living in campus housing, his concession to his parents' insistence that he experience college life to its fullest. Michael has never been a joiner or a party guy, so we don't worry about dorm life corrupting him. He's into his art and is totally focused on being the best he can be.*

*I'm glad your stepfather remarried. Life is too short to travel alone. And I guess I'm not just talking about him, am I? It's been a while since Philip died ... isn't it time you put yourself back into the social swing, met someone ... oh, listen to me ... I hear an echo. Forget I said anything. It's not my place to tell you how to live. It's just that I'd feel better if I knew you had someone who was there to give you the love you deserve.*

*I'll try to do a little better in the letter-writing department, if you promise to do the same. Remember I love you, my darling, and I always will.*

*Jared*

*May 10, 1976*

*My darling Joanna,*
*Sometimes, wanting is having. I've gotten an invitation to the opening of a play being produced by a friend from Chicago who left the city a few years ago to pursue his career elsewhere. Vicki is busy preparing for a major exhibit, so I'll make the trip alone.*

*Oh, did I think to mention my destination? How does Manhattan sound? Just a quick ride up the highway, or an even faster train trip. You could even fly. Say you'll come to New York. Please say you'll come, any way you can get there. Write back to me and tell me you'll meet me. Better yet, call. The wait for a letter would be agony.*

*I have five days in the city, June 10th through the 15th, and Sylvester only has my Friday night scheduled unless I want it otherwise. Please say you'll come. It would be a dream come true to see you again. I can hardly stand the wait for your answer. Remember, I love you and I always will.*

*Jared*

Joanna put the letter down on her desk, her mind racing. After thirteen years. To see Jared, once again experience Manhattan with him … how she'd hoped for the chance.

Instantly, the doubts flooded in. How could she be content with a simple reunion, a drink or two at the hotel bar, some reminiscences of the old days? He was finally happy in his marriage, only in New York alone because Vicki couldn't come along, not because he didn't want her there. Obviously, this would be nothing more than a meeting of two old friends. Would she be able to settle for that?

She walked over to the mirror on the wall, looking at herself critically for the first time in months. There were some worry lines around the eyes; the shorter, honey brown hair had lost some of its sheen. Her stomach wasn't as flat as it had been before Steven, but the slender figure Jared had so loved was still pretty good. She tried to see herself through his eyes … would he see the woman he'd loved or be disappointed by the obvious changes that had come from more than a decade of stress, sorrow and missing him?

It never occurred to her to wonder how he had changed. She knew she would always see him as he had been, slim, straight, tall and confident, his eyes burning with love for her, his lips perfectly formed to fit her own.

She thought again about coming face to face with him. She was thirty-five, he fifty-two. Who could say if this chance would ever come again? Even if he politely shook her hand and they made small talk for an hour—that was an hour she could store carefully in her heart and take out again and again to savor and remember.

He answered the phone immediately.

"I'll make my plans and let you know as soon as they're final. Steven can stay with his grandfather. We have a huge gap in time to bridge, and I have to warn you—Manhattan is still our Oz, no matter how many years have passed. I'll understand if you change your mind and decide we shouldn't meet."

Jared's voice was very deep. "Don't even think of it. Every time I think of being with you again, my heart races and I can barely breathe."

# Thirty-two



Already, at eight in the morning, the sun was shining and it was getting hot as Joanna put her small suitcase on the back seat of her new red Camaro and slid behind the wheel, reaching quickly for the air conditioning controls. She was sure her temperature was already well above normal, just from the excitement of what lay ahead, but the near eighty degrees outside didn't help make her any more comfortable.

The shuttle at the Park 'n Ride in Secaucus was standing by, Joanna the last passenger to board before it pulled away, bound for the Lincoln Tunnel. She closed her eyes and tried to imagine what it would be like to see Jared again.

When she opened them, the bus had pulled into its berth in the Port Authority garage. Lifting her suitcase from the empty seat next to her, she went out into the bright sunlight and hailed a cab for the short hop to the Statler.

Then she was on the elevator, walking down the heavily carpeted hallway of the fourteenth floor. At the door to Jared's room, Joanna raised her hand to knock, then lowered it, suddenly afraid. Of what, she couldn't say. Perhaps it had been safer all these years putting her feelings on paper. Now? Now she was here and so was he. What would they say? How would she open a conversation?

As her mind raced through the questions, the door opened and he was there. Jared. Tall, slightly heavier perhaps, streaks of silver in his hair, but Jared as she had pictured him through the lonely nights, the haunted days.

Taking her case, he reached for her hand and guided her through the door, closing and locking it behind her.

His eyes never left her face as he put the bag on the floor and took her other hand with his. For what seemed like an eternity, he stood silently, a slight smile on his face.

"You are as beautiful as I remembered," he said, still holding both her hands. "The years and all your troubles haven't dimmed the light in your eyes and the softness of your mouth. Joanna..."

She was falling into him as his lips searched for hers and found them. He met them gently at first, tentatively, then bolder and more certain, then fiercely, passionately and possessively. It went on and on, the kisses, his wonderful voice murmuring her name, the musky sweetness of his skin under her hands, the way her senses, so long dormant, roused to his touch.

Leaving her mouth, Jared stepped back, regarded her pensively, his eyes half-closed, a slight flush on his cheeks.

"I was so worried that when you came through that door, we'd be at a loss to find a beginning. I worried you'd hold out your hand, give me a friendly, long-lost-buddy look and suggest we go downstairs for a drink and reminisce about old times. How foolish of me."

"Me too. All the way up, I tried to imagine what would happen when we finally came face to face. Your letters have been so wonderful, the phone calls so supportive, and even though I've heard the love in both of them, I wasn't sure how you'd react to me. But the minute you took my hand, I felt the connection closing back in, like there'd never been a span of time without you near enough to touch. The years haven't passed, have they? We're still the way we used to be."

His mouth stopped her, his breath inhaling hers, his arms tightening around her, one hand grasping her head, his body fitting to hers.

With pieces of clothing trailing behind, some part of them always touching, they stumbled backward coming to rest at the edge of the bed.

Jared held her face gently, his eyes bright with need.

"Am I taking you for granted? Is this what you want, too?"

In a hoarse whisper, she said, "I've wanted this every day, every night, for the past thirteen years, dreamt about how it would be to hold you again."

It was a comfortable homecoming—familiar and synchronized.

As they rested, Jared shifted so he was facing Joanna, his hair tousled, his mouth curved in a happy smile. With one finger, he traced a line from her neck to her thighs and back again.

"You're still so beautiful, my darling."

"I've missed hearing you call me that. No one else ever has, nor ever will, I suppose. Sometimes, I'd close my eyes and try to remember how your voice sounded saying those two words ... my darling. It wasn't easy after a while as the years went by. But when I needed to hear them the most, when things were at their worst, there they were, those comforting words."

"My darling, my darling, my darling. Those are words only for you. When I think them, it's your face I see, your touch I feel. Then I put them away, reserved for the next time I need to take them out on paper in a letter."

"Am I very different?"

"No. Your face is more serious, but still beautiful as ever. And your touch? Your touch is still very dear. Ah, and what do you think of the mature, aging man I've become?"

"I think you're as perfect as ever. Time hasn't dimmed the caring in your eyes, the feathery gentleness in your fingers when you touch me, or the wonder of your voice. I certainly don't see the father of a medical student and a college junior."

Jared chuckled, his face lowering to meet hers. In an almost-whisper, he said "There's a good reason for that. Here, now, there's no one but you. No one in my world but my darling Joanna, and you are all anyone will see in my eyes for as long as we're together."

~ * ~

Downstairs later, they had a light lunch, barely aware of what they ate. The conversation flowed seamlessly, Jared picking up the threads of Joanna's thoughts, finishing her sentences, echoing her feelings. Years bridged in minutes, little left to discover after the steady flow of letters.

"What do you want to do, Joanna? Take a walk in our Emerald City? See the world from the eighty-sixth floor? Ride a ferry to Staten Island?"

"Perhaps tomorrow. But now? I want to be alone with you with no world to intrude. I think that's what you want too, and for now, wanting is having."

As soon as the door to their room was closed, she was back in his arms, hers wound loosely around his neck.

"You said on the phone you had a surprise for me. What is it?"

"Manhattans. I can drink them again. Tonight, I can allow myself a luxury I've waited to be with you to enjoy."

"Oh, the headaches. You said in one of your letters they were still bothering you but not as badly."

"Nor as frequently either. My doctor says I can have an occasional cocktail without bringing one on. And the new medicine seems to have far fewer side effects than anything else we've tried. So after dinner, when we're settled back in, we can order up our manhattans. It's been a long time since I've had one, and anyway I couldn't hold a glass without seeing your face reflected in it."

They sat on the small sofa near the windows, touching.

"Tell me what's new since your last letter. For obvious reasons, you haven't mentioned Vicki. I'm grateful for that, but it's really okay to talk about her. Things keep getting better, don't they?"

"Still my amazing Joanna. Yes, things are better. We still work very hard to improve our marriage. With both children gone, it's pretty much the two of us, but it's still okay."

"Have you ever thought now might be the time to leave, to start a life with me? No children to fret about, Vicki finally self-sufficient, no professional worries..." she let the thought hang in the silence.

Jared looked down at his hands. It was a long time before he answered. Finally looking up, he exhaled slowly.

"I couldn't do that to her. I still couldn't do it to the children. Forgive me, but it's taken too long to get to this point, so much trust that had to be built, so many walls demolished. I guess I'm trapped in my traditionalist ways of thinking, my guilt if you will. Sounds strange, doesn't it, coming from the one who could hardly wait to make love to you again. But that's all part of the dilemma. I don't feel any qualms about being with you, loving you, needing to keep you in my life, but the thought of dropping a bombshell on Vicki and the children by leaving them? Impossible to imagine. They would be devastated, Vicki especially, knowing I'd kept the connection with you this whole time without her knowing it. It doesn't mean I love you or want to be with you any less; it means I'm not strong enough to yank the rug out from under my family and see the shock and disappointment on their faces. I wish there were some way I could explain it better."

"As much as it hurts, I understand. If Philip and I ever had any chance at a relationship that might have worked, I couldn't have left either. But there's always been one difference between us. My parents knew about you; Philip knew about you and Steven knows there is a very important person in my life who writes often and occasionally calls. I can't imagine not being able to say your name out loud to someone who knows what you are to me. No one in your world knows I exist. But then, I'm not trying to hold a marriage together like you. You don't believe Vicki could stand knowing that we write, that we talk once in a while?"

"Good Lord, no! Vicki has made a lot of changes, come a very long way, but to find out you're still in the picture would be devastating to her, and everything we've built would be destroyed in an instant. As long as I can sit in my office and write to you, you're still in my world, even though no one but Dan knows it. I can keep you in my heart without hurting my relationship with Vicki and the children."

"I think you're leaving something out ... I don't think you're being totally honest. You care for her more than you're telling me ... why else would you stay? Why would it matter if she knew about me?"

Jared pulled his cigarettes from his pocket.

"Still smoking, I see," Joanna teased gently. "When are you going to listen to all the research about how harmful it is?"

"Probably never. I have cut back a lot, in case you haven't noticed. But smoking relaxes me and lets me think. Your last question kind of threw me. Why else would I stay? I guess you're more in touch with my feelings than I am.

"She's a good person, smart and competent, Joanna. She's had some very difficult times, but the strength of her own desire to make a good home for the children helped her overcome a lot. She's gained a reputation as a valued member of the museum staff and she's become a supportive mother and an attentive wife. Yes, I suppose I do care for her more than I admit, even love her, I suppose. I know I can't hurt her, and leaving her now would be more than she could take." He took a long drag on his cigarette, letting the smoke drift toward the ceiling.

"It occurs to me, though, that in trying so hard to preserve my so-called image with my family, I'm asking you for a lot. More than I have a right to."

"It doesn't matter anymore. I couldn't stop wanting to connect with you even if I tried. So let's change the subject; let's not talk about this anymore. I know you, Jared Fowler, probably better than you know yourself. If we could have found a way to stay together in the Manning days, we would have made it. That was our chance. At Manning and then twelve years ago when you were alone and came looking for me. I guess we don't get any more chances. Your loyalty to Vicki, in spite of this interlude of ours, the importance you place on being a positive, loving role model for your children ... they'll never let you consider a life with me now."

"Please don't be sad, Joanna. If it could be any other way, I'd want it to be."

"I'm not sad. At least not the way I was when I was younger. I often remember Doris's glasses and mirrors and I know we all act in ways that are consistent with how we see ourselves. I know you well enough to believe you still love me as much as ever, but you can't leave your family now any more than you could then. I'm simply very grateful we're together."

*June 15, 1976*

*My darling Joanna,*

*You've only been gone a few minutes and I miss you terribly already. I wish we could have spent more time together. Now it's time to say it again ... wanting is not having.*

*What we did have was wonderful. After you left, I sat for a long time in the chair next to the window and heard your laughter, felt your touch, the sense of completeness I've always known when you're near. How I wish we never had to say goodbye.*

*I will see you again. I don't know when or where, but we'll meet again. How could we not after this?*

*Rediscovering our deep, familiar connection, sliding back into one another's hearts as easily as sinking into a soft, familiar featherbed and feeling as comfortable. It will always be like that, won't it?*

*Thank you, my darling. I love the memories we made. Remember, I love you and I always will.*

*Jared*

June 15, 1976

*Dearest Jared,*

*I've missed you since I rode away from the hotel. Hope your flight back to Chicago was good. I'll bet Vicki was glad to have you back. Lucky woman. It would be helpful if I could resent her more. But through you, I've come to feel an almost affection for her, so I can just wistfully say how lucky she is and let it go at that.*

*Steven was almost sorry to have me pick him up at his grandfather's. They had a high old time while I was gone. He leaves tomorrow for Ohio to visit his grandparents. Since we took Philip home to be buried there, Steven's come to know the Webbers and he enjoys visiting. I'm glad they opened their hearts to him.*

*But back to us. It was wonderful. I knew it would be, but I admit to having had doubts, doubts that vanished the moment you opened the door. Did I tell you how age becomes you? Age and, of course, success, both professionally and personally. You've managed to build a wonderful life in spite of the rocky points along the way.*

*I need to apologize for cutting off the discussion of my life. It wasn't that I didn't want to share anything with you; it's just that there isn't anything you or anyone else can tell me I haven't already told myself. I don't want to be alone. I want to have someone in my life, someone*

*to care for like you care for Vicki. But I'm not looking ...
no one else has your eyes, your hands and your voice.
Our time together will warm me on many cold, gray
winter nights. I love you very much.*

*Always,*

*Joanna*

~ * ~

Professional recognition and success were in abundance during the next years. Joanna had a large circle of good friends, offers of dinners and parties and even an occasional date with someone a friend decided was "perfect" for her. She enjoyed going out, especially to the revues offered at the new casino that had been built on the shoreline, filling the city with buses, and the boardwalk with tourists who flocked to the gambling house in search of the big payoff. She was much in demand, no doubt because of her sparkling sense of humor and easy conversation style, but she rarely saw the same man twice and ignored questions about when she would finally settle down and get serious about a relationship.

The youth center occupied much of her time when she wasn't in her office. There were so many boys and girls needing support and esteem building. One child in particular, a lovely blonde of about eight, tugged at Joanna's heartstrings every time she talked with the insecure, frightened product of an imminent divorce. She could, Joanna mused, be Marina at the age she'd first met her. It was this very psychological upheaval Joanna had urged Jared to avoid at all costs. Well, she'd certainly gotten her wish. Marina was a healthy, well-adjusted woman now, but what a price she had paid for the mental health of Jared's children.

*October 31, 1980*

*My darling Joanna,*
  *I wonder how many couples mark anniversaries of
finding one another on a day dedicated to witches and
goblins. I only know the day never comes without my*

*thinking of the way you looked when you spoke about your memories of an awful Halloween when you were six. I think I fell in love with you that night. You touched my heart with emotions I'd thought long suppressed, and my life has not been my own since.*

*So you've decided not to take the job at Resorts. It sounds like you had to do a lot of hard thinking to make that decision, but I'm sure you did what was best. I still think you would have been an excellent human resources director. Anyone with your obvious natural compassion for people and background as a business professional would be ideal in that spot. But I understand your loyalty to your clients and your love of what you do. Imagine how many people are living fuller, happier lives because of the time spent with you.*

*Michael has finished most of the requirements for his master's of fine arts. His dance troupe will be touring Europe next summer ... he's very proud of them. Some of his former students have successfully auditioned for work in New York theater. His apartment downtown is the unofficial home to many of them. They sit for hours talking theater stuff. I envy their youth and exuberant outlook on the future.*

*Marina has found a small private practice on the south side that needs another pediatrician. For the time being, she'll hang her stethoscope up there and pitch in with the kind of work that's crying to be done in the inner city. I think I told you she's dating someone seriously. I wouldn't be surprised to find a ring on her finger at Christmas. Vicki and I both like Andy very much and will be happy to welcome him to the family.*

*I've begun working with my new assistant to groom him for his ascendancy into my job. Oh, don't even think I'm going to retire yet, but I do see it on the horizon. I've worked a long time and it might be nice to stay home, read the books that have sat on the shelf, do some fishing and wait for a grandchild or two to spoil. Now, though, we're well into the last-minute details of the fall production—did I tell you we were doing* Who's Afraid of Virginia Woolf?*— so any thought of stepping down has to take a firm back seat.*

*I wasn't surprised at your news that Steven has decided to major in architecture when he goes to college. He's always had that disciplined artist's bent he got from Philip. It's hard to believe he's 16. Are you teaching him to drive? I can almost picture him behind the wheel of that red Camaro you're so fond of.*

*Write when you can and remember I love you and I always will.*

*Jared*

*May 12, 1981*

*Dearest Jared,*
*Once again, I feel as though my world has fallen apart. Two days ago, I was notified that Doris is hospitalized in a coma and fighting for her life. I feel so responsible. She hasn't got anyone else to look after her, no family and no friends left after the changes in her personality over the past years. I was the one she turned to and I feel I should have tried harder to make certain she was following doctor's orders and taking care of herself. I want to go to her now, but something else has happened that's keeping me close to home.*

*My dad has had a serious heart attack. He's in the intensive care unit here at Atlantic City Medical Center, and the prognosis is guarded. Naturally, he's very frightened and reaches out to his wife, Steven and me constantly, needing one or the other of us to be there whenever we can. I'm torn between wanting to go to Doris and needing to be with him. If he shows any improvement in the next few days, I may try to take a quick trip down to Florida to reassure myself she's recovering. Now would be a good time to be twins.*

*Oh, Jared, how does anyone ever prepare to lose people they love? All these years I've thought we would all go along as always, that they would simply be there. Now everything may be about to change and I don't know if I can handle it.*

*I'm so grateful you're still on the other end of this connection of ours. Knowing you understand and share my sadness as well as my joy makes life bearable, even when things go horribly wrong. Thank you for everything you are and have always been. I'll call you if there are any developments.*

*Love always,*

*Joanna*

*June 22, 1981*

*My darling Joanna,*

*Two terrible losses in so short a time! I was saddened at your news about your stepfather and Doris. It's almost too much for one person to absorb. I hope you're coping as well as it sounded on the phone. No, I never mind your calling me when you feel the need. I would have been upset if I thought you'd held back when you really needed to talk.*

*The death of his grandfather must be very difficult for Steven, too. They were so close. I'm sure memories of their happy times together will get him through this, but it's still a hard thing for a young person to endure. Lucky he has you for a mother.*

*You must be very glad you made the last trip to Florida when you did. At least you were there while you could still bring her the comfort of your love.*

*It was typically unselfish of you to ask about me. How am I? How is anyone at 57 who still works too hard and smokes too much? Seriously, darling, I'm fine. Spring's upon us already, the time of year when I remember you with particular longing.*

*Wonder how my little tree is faring. Occasionally, I think about the first time I introduced you to him. You got right into the spirit of it. I loved you for your sensitivity.*

*When you have some difficult times in the days ahead, remember I'm here. Keep writing, and sharing your thoughts and feelings with me. Remember I love you and I always will.*

*Jared*

# Thirty-three

*"I'll have a memory, please ..."*

*October 31, 1982*

*My darling Joanna,*

*Has it really been twenty years? My heart tells me no, but the calendar doesn't lie. Nor does the fact that I have adult children to remind me of the swift passage of time.*

*Marina's wedding was beautiful. I was so honored they asked me to sing. Mrs. Andrew Buckman. Nah, she'll always be my beautiful, blonde bombshell, a happy, outgoing girl with boundless energy. Now she's directing that energy to the children who need her skill so badly.*

*Michael's life continues to revolve around dance. He talks a lot about one of his co-workers, a girl named Ellen, and since it's the first time he's mentioned a woman more than once or twice, we think he might have found someone who's more than a casual friend.*

*I think of our days together with a mixture of regret and joy. Some of the details have dimmed, I know, but some are as vivid as the moment they occurred. I'll never stop being sorry for the hurt I put in your eyes more than once, and I'll always be immensely grateful that nothing I did stopped you from loving me.*

*Try not to miss Steven too much. I know North Carolina must seem like the end of the earth to you, but he'll be home for visits and you can be down there in a matter of what, seven hours or so? Again, his leaving home makes me wish there were someone there to watch over you, care for you. Yes, I know ... get off my soapbox. You keep telling me you're happy with your life as it is but I can't stop wishing you had someone to share it.*

*Stay in touch. I watch for your letters as I have for ... my goodness, did I say twenty years? Remember I love you and I always will.*

*Jared*

*November 25, 1982*

*Dearest Jared,*

*It may have been Halloween for you, but it's always been Thanksgiving for me. I knew I loved you (though not yet how much) when we went to Dan's and came ever so close to making love for the first time. You and your sense of ambience, or as you insist on calling it, romantic instinct. Whatever, I knew then that I would love you for the rest of my life, no matter how long we lasted or how far apart we were. Of course, in those days I hung on like a lovesick schoolgirl to my own romantic notion, the idea we would live happily ever after in a world unmarred by a wife and children. I'm afraid I clung to that fantasy far longer than I should have, certainly far longer than you ever encouraged. Anyway, not a Thanksgiving passes that I don't think back, remember the way I felt then, the wonder of falling in love with you, and wish with all my heart I could go there again. The schoolgirl is still alive, I guess, despite my best efforts to appear mature and beyond believing in fairy tales.*

*Steven loves Chapel Hill. He lives in a huge dorm, quite unlike anything we had at Manning, and is already talking about the "guys" he's met and the plans they have for spring break. When I'm tempted to pull in his reins, I remember how grown up I thought I was at his age and how my parents gave me some slack and let me make my own mistakes, so I back off. Somewhere along the line, I'm sure he'll probably experience his share of hurt and disappointment, but we parents can't shield our kids from that part of life, can we?*

*Now that I have a grown child, I understand more than ever how much my relationship with you must have pained my parents. They stood by and watched me walk defiantly over the cliff, helpless to save me from myself as I fell. The best we can do, I know now, is to be there to pick up the pieces and gently push them back on the road where they'll try again and again until they find their way. It's a tough lesson, isn't it, but one that good parents learn early on and always practice.*

*I've decided to sell this house and move. Not very far away, just to another island and even closer to the water. Atlantic City is never again going to be a place people can call home. The developers have their eyes on our little island and all they see are dollar signs ... more casinos, more tour buses and far less of the things people need for comfortable lives. So, I've been looking around and last weekend I found it. I wish you could see this place. It's a first-floor condominium on the beach on the* island of Brigantine, across the bay bridge from here. The entire front of the house is glass, so I'll have a breathtaking vista out of every square inch ... the skyline of the city with all its neon and flashiness, the sparkling lights of the northern end of the island and the sea with all its moods. I fell in love instantly and put a down payment on it before someone else snapped it up. One day I'd love to show it to you, but until then, I'll take pictures and send them. Now I have to pray we don't have any major hurricanes.

Speaking of pictures, I still have that photo of the creaking old academic in his ceremonial getup with a silly grin on his face. For a long time, it was hidden away in the box with your letters, but only the letters are in the box now. The photo is on my desk, the Benton book in the drawer of my nightstand and the blue silk blouse hanging way in the back of my closet, too small to fit but too dear to discard. Do you realize that picture is the only one I have of you, except for the ones in the yearbooks, but they weren't taken by an expert who knew the model so intimately.

I hope your Thanksgiving was good, but how could it have been otherwise with the announcement of a new engagement in the family? Have Michael and Ellen set a date?

Steven will be coming home for Christmas. It seemed very strange not to have him here for Thanksgiving, but I couldn't argue with him ... it's a long drive to make for a day or so. I missed him nonetheless. Not having Mom and Dad, and now Steven, well, suffice it to say there was little to brighten the holiday.

Listen to me, feeling sorry for Joanna. Ignore that, please. It doesn't happen often and with the bounty of good *things in my life it shouldn't happen at all. Whenever I want to feel warmth, I settle back in my favorite living room chair, close my eyes and remember. It's oddly comforting. Don't ask me why.*

*Take good care of yourself. I love you very much.*

*Always,*

*Joanna*

~ * ~

It seemed like Jared's letters came in spurts during the next few years. One day, there would be two in the mail and then months would go by before another arrived. Joanna was busy, too, although she wrote more often, still sharing her thoughts and activities with him. Moving in to her new home had been a delight—shopping for new furniture, finding new niches for her treasures. And best of all, sitting for hours each day either on the beach or in front of the windows in the living room watching the ever-changing moods of the ocean in front of her.

*October 31, 1985*

*My darling Joanna,*
*What a terrible correspondent I've been! I'm sorry it's been so long since I've had a chance to write. Your birthday was the first chance I'd had to breathe since I don't know when and here it is our special time of the year already. Where does time go?*

*I appreciated the darling card you sent. Being a first-time grandfather is quite an experience. Just wait, Steven will find someone before you know it and it will be your turn.*

*Marina and Andy are thrilled, but no less than I, having a new grandson to spoil. Jason is absolutely beautiful and a very good baby.*

*I was glad to hear Steven decided to go for his master's. Of course, it will mean he'll be away another couple of years, but he won't get very far as an architect these days without it. You must be very proud of him.*

*Work is getting stressful. I think I'm looking forward to retirement more than I admit. It will be good to push the director's chair into a corner and watch the shows from the audience. On a happy note, the university is recognizing my contributions in a very special way on my birthday this summer. The students, along with several of my graduates who have long gone on to bigger and better things, will stage a special performance of Les Miz in my honor. Actually, it's a whole day dedicated to little ol' me—a luncheon reception for the cast, a series of workshops presented by many of my current students and then the performance followed by a cocktail party in the grand ballroom. It will be almost more than I can imagine, but I'm honored that everyone's going to such lengths to say thanks.*

*The only sour note in all of it is you won't be here to share it with me. I'd like you to see this gorgeous place where I work and meet the people who've surrounded me all these years. I feel like you already know most of them anyway.*

*Every time I need to bring you closer to me, I take the photos of your house out of my desk drawer at the office and imagine you living there. I can sit with you by the front windows of your living room and look out at the sea as it rages in a storm or shimmers in the sunshine. How thoughtful of you to send me pictures of each. It's a magnificent place to live, my darling, and I'm so glad you've found such a haven.*

*I promise to write again sooner this time. You do the same. Remember I love you and I always will.*

*Jared*

*August 27, 1986*

*My darling Joanna,*

*I'm so glad you enjoyed all the mementos of my day. I couldn't resist sending you the mock playbill the university had printed for the special performance. I still can't believe all of those accolades were particularly well deserved, but it is nice to think your co-workers and students think so highly of you.*

*As the day draws imminently near, I'm even more convinced that my early retirement was a good idea. As I watch my colleagues go about the business of beginning a new semester, preparing syllabi, revising reading lists and getting ready to meet new classes for the first time, there is admittedly a slight pang of regret, but it's instantly smothered by an intense feeling of relief. And as the day draws near, I find myself looking forward to and even planning retirement activities. I have lots of projects lined up, not the least of which is serving as a consultant to some budding playwrights who are anxious to have their scripts read by someone with a director's eye. So please don't worry I will simply stagnate in retirement. I plan to stay very busy, but doing what I want to do.*

*Write when you can. I know how hard it can be to find time, especially with your clients and your volunteer work at the youth center, but I do love hearing from you. Remember I love you and I always will.*

*Jared*

~ * ~

Jared's retirement talk was beginning to make Joanna think. Oh, she was far from ready to fold up her therapist's couch, but she knew the time would come when it would be an option. What would she do to fill her days? At times like these, she wished she'd found someone special, someone to face old age with her.

But she tossed aside the occasional lapses into self-pity and worked, spent time at the youth center with the children, read or wrote in her journal or to Jared, knowing his responses would be erratic but somehow always popping in when she needed to hear from him.

*March 20, 1992*

*My darling Joanna,*

*Okay, it has been quite a while this time. It isn't that I think about you any less often. Indeed, I seem to think about you very often. How could I not, with all the reminders there are, from the broad to the very specific.*

*Springtime is Joanna. When I enjoy a Manhattan, it's Joanna. Have I told you the headaches are entirely gone? So much so that now I can have a before-dinner cocktail or a beer after outdoor work. The cocktail is always a Manhattan, and I drink it with warm memories. In fact, sometimes I think I'm going to slip some day when I order one and instead of saying "I'll have a Manhattan, please," I'll say "I'll have a memory, please."*

*Life goes on for me on a very even keel. I stay very busy with Jason, golf, fishing, reading and working outdoors.*

*Marina and Andy are enjoying their freedom, thanks to my grandson's preference for spending time with me. I must admit I enjoy him in a way I wasn't able to enjoy the early years with Michael. This grandparenting is all it's cracked up to be. At seven, Jason is turning into an avid fisherman. I'm really closer to him than I was to my own children. I guess it's having more time and being so much more relaxed.*

*So you see I'm well and doing well, except at letter writing. Write to me soon, my darling, and I promise I'll do better. You are very often in my thoughts. I love you and I always will.*

*Jared*

*August 15, 1992*

*My darling Joanna,*
*'You are ever in my heart … nor time nor distance nor silence can ever dim the wondrous memories of what we had or take away from what we have…'*

*Life goes on. I'm not sure what one is supposed to feel like at 68, so I don't concern myself too much with it. I feel great; my health continues good except for some arthritis in, of all places, my left hand, making writing something of a task. I may have to go to the typewriter, word processor or, horror of horrors, the computer. I've already had to take one break in writing this. My handwriting never was very good (okay, so it was virtually unreadable) and now it has deteriorated very rapidly into something I only hope you can read.*

*I have a major news item! Ellen is pregnant. She and Michael are ecstatic, as are we all. So far, everything is fine and all indications are we can expect the new grandchild in early February.*

*Happy birthday, my darling. You are constantly in my thoughts, even though I don't write as often. There are so many, many reminders and so many memories to relive. You will always be a part of me. Write when you can and remember I love you and I always will.*

*Jared*

*February 27, 1993*

*My darling Joanna,*

*I've been doing better lately, no? Admittedly, it's just finding a place to write to you that's becoming so difficult. My old office at the university is still available any time I want to use it, but I find it harder and harder to fight the traffic and go into the city to get there. Life on the lake has spoiled me.*

*Vicki got what she wished for. Michael and Ellen have presented us with a beautiful little granddaughter, all soft and sweet. I think Vicki has bought about everything frilly and pink she can find. Personally, I'm hoping little Sarah grows into a blonde bombshell like her Aunt Marina. It'll be fun having a little doll around to show off. Jason is already feeling like an uncle; he loves to hold the baby and feed her.*

*Steven's job sounds exciting. I know Atlanta is certainly the area for anyone interested in new construction and the young firm he's joined sounds like it's really going places. Just think ... when you retire you can visit him in the winter and spend your summers in your marvelous home.*

*So now you, too, are an in-law. Abigail sounds exactly like a person you might have handpicked and I'm sure Steven is very happy.*

*I think about you much. So many, many things remind me of you. Just a couple of days ago, someone I didn't even know twisted her mouth into that quizzical expression you used to use. Not as attractively as you did it, but enough to give the heart strings quite a tug. Take care of yourself, my darling, and remember I love you and I always will.*

*Jared*

*May 24, 1993*

*My darling Joanna,*

*See how much better I'm becoming. Only a few months this time, instead of the usual long wait. Please forgive the typewritten letter. The arthritis in my hand is too painful to allow me to complete one without a lot of breaks and the handwriting is so bad I doubt you could decipher it.*

*Jason and I have spent the early part of this spring together a lot. As soon as he's out of school, I pick him up and we go out on the lake. I love being with him.*

*Vicki has decided to retire. She wants to spend more time with Sarah and is even taking a shift when Ellen needs to be at the theater with Michael. I'm glad. It means I can spend my free time with Jason without feeling I'm neglecting anyone.*

*While he and I were out on the boat the other day, I began wondering why spring reminds me so strongly of you, but as I thought about it, I realized there is something in each season that brings you close. The fall is a vivid recollection of Manhattan. Remember my having to borrow a tie to get into the restaurant? The winter brings warm memories of walking across the campus to the student center for coffee. I used to wonder what people were saying as we sat there together. Wonder, not worry. The spring and summer are trips to Ye Olde Spread Eagle Inn (was that the name? I'm not very sure of that, but I'm very clear on the bar and the jukebox) and especially trips through the country to the little lane in the woods. Those days seem almost like a wonderful dream; I'm so grateful they were real. Keep writing, and remember, I love you, my darling, and I always will.*

*Jared*

*August 2, 1993*

*Dearest Jared,*

*Now that I'm finally able to think clearly, I wanted to write and share my experiences of the past couple of days.*

*On Saturday, I finally bought that little book Oprah and everyone's been talking about,* Bridges of Madison County. *I wanted to read something light and romantic while I sunbathed on the beach. Well, it was quite an experience. Overwhelming describes it best.*

*I set up my chair after lunch, intending to read for a little while and then move indoors away from the hot afternoon sun. By four o'clock, I had finished the book with a nasty sunburn to show for it and a heavy, heavy heart. It was a romantic story, all right, but there was nothing light about it. Thank goodness the seagulls can't tell tales. They circled around squawking while I sat and sobbed out loud, reading this incredible story that brought back so many emotions I'd thought—okay, hoped—I'd stored deep inside somewhere too far to resurface. You must read it when you can and let me know how you react.*

*By Sunday morning, I was still thinking about it ... and you. I needed to reconnect. I needed to be some place where I could feel you. So I drove up to Manning for the first time since I graduated thirty years ago. It was virtually deserted. I had the place to myself, and that was a good thing, since I could hardly find my way around. It's so big! Our little campus is dwarfed by the sheer expansion of the complex. The Student Center is gone, with a new huge building in its place. I sat on the Kenton steps for a while, walked down by the lake (Doris's house is gone, too) and walked through the woods from the library. Your little tree is now a towering pine, straight and proud. He didn't seem to recognize me, but I suppose even trees forget.*

*From there, I went on to the road to Dan's. Again, what changes! Houses everywhere. Anyhow, I drove past the lane twice before I realized I'd passed it and finally found it, only to discover the mailbox was rusted and looked unused and the gate was covered with overgrown weeds. Guess no one has lived at the cabin for a long time, if indeed it's still there. I didn't want to brave the thicket to find out.*

*Bowman's Tower was the next stop. Progress has really done in my memories. I paid my $3.50 (yes, there's someone who mans a little souvenir booth at the entrance and they charge admission), walked toward the tower prepared for my ascent and found myself facing—are you ready for this?—an elevator door, of all things. The newly passed Americans with Disabilities Act required the park authorities to install an elevator. And in doing so, they removed most of the spiral stairs. I rode up to the top with a sharp sense of loss. The view from the top is still marvelous, but the charm is lost forever. Thank goodness the memories remain.*

*I didn't go to New Hope. Instead, I went to look for the Old Spread Eagle Inn. It's where it always was, but now it's surrounded by strip shopping centers, gas stations and a major roadway that encroaches to the front door. It was closed and frankly didn't look too inviting. If it hadn't been for the distinctive roof, I probably wouldn't have recognized it. Another treasure lost. I wonder whatever happened to the jukebox and the checkered tablecloths.*

*I read a magazine article about Jim Brodborough not long ago (he opened his own place further north on the river) and it mentioned the Club had been torn down, so there was nothing there to revisit.*

*It should have been a very sad day. Driving the route we traveled so often, sitting on the steps at Kenton, looking out over the countryside from the tower ... I should have felt overwhelming sorrow. Instead, I was comforted by the memories we made in all those places. I felt close to you, reliving those times, reassuring myself, I guess, that it all really happened. Sometimes it seems like a dream, but being in our special places made it real again, and very, very sweet.*

*For now, I thought you'd like to hear how I found things. My only regret about the day is I spent it without you. How I wish you had been there.*

*Love always,*

*Joanna*

*August 15, 1993*

*My darling Joanna,*

*Happy whatever birthday. I don't dare mention your age, do I, although I'll bet you still look exactly as I remember.*

*So you finally got back to Manning. I'm not surprised it took so long for you to do it, but to say I was shaken by your letter would be an understatement. The marvelous sweep of warm, incredible, vivid and bittersweet memories was simply overwhelming. I know that "bittersweet" is an oxymoron, but I must have looked like an ox-eyed moron, sitting there with tears streaming down a smiling face. I read it through again and again, with many pauses, "seeing" us in the places you recalled and almost feeling your presence. Such memories, my darling, such memories.*

*Life continues to treat me reasonably well. A couple of trips to the hospital this summer, but no big deal. The doctors are watching my lungs ... I had a tiny bout of pneumonia in July and some difficulty breathing. I'm on some new medication while they watch, but I've been fine since then so no reason for concern.*

*I've been wanting to read the book everyone's talking about, the one about the covered bridges. You mentioned you read it and were deeply affected by it. Hope to get to it soon. I'll let you know my reaction.*

*Write me when you can. I rather enjoy looking like an ox-eyed moron. Remember I love you and I always will.*

*Jared*

~ * ~

Joanna came off the beach early that Friday morning. It was getting cloudy and too breezy to keep her book open without a struggle. Better to finish it indoors where she could still see the ocean as it gathered itself for the storm to come.

Pausing at the mailbox as she went in the front door, Joanna shuffled through the handful of envelopes as she headed for the sofa. Another letter from Jared, two in the same month. *He must be feeling nostalgic,* she thought, as she sank into the cushions and slit open the envelope with her nail.

*August 31, 1993*

*My darling Joanna,*
*This will be a brief note, since I'm pushed for time. I wanted to let you know I'll be in New York in September.*
*I'll arrive on the afternoon of the 22nd at the Hotel Pennsylvania (that's what they renamed our Statler in recent years, I understand). The next day I'll be attending a conference and I'll leave afterward.*

*As I write this, I'm holding what I have left of my breath, hoping you'll agree to meet me. I know it's been a long time since I promised that we'd see one another in Manhattan again and you probably forgot all about it. But when the chance came to make the trip, I couldn't help myself from seizing it on the prayer it would bring you to me. I'll call in a few days, when I'm sure you've gotten this. It would be so wonderful to see you again.*

*Remember I love you and I always will.*

*Jared*

~ * ~

The stationery dropped to Joanna's lap. She stared out the window at the blowing dune grass, hearing the surf as it pounded further and further up with the tide and the wind.

Jared was coming back. It was like someone had heard her wish and benevolently granted it, perhaps a gesture to reward whatever good she'd been able to do in her life.

She stood to go to the phone and stopped, remembering Jared wasn't in the office at the university any longer. She only wanted to tell him she'd be there, anywhere he was. She realized she was smiling through a haze of tears. Now, she wondered, who was the ox-eyed moron this time?

# *Thirty-four*

*"What I'm doing is ending a deception…"*

It was almost noon by the time Joanna drove through Absecon and picked up the northbound Garden State Parkway. The trip seemed to drag, heavy shore traffic clogging the lanes, causing interminable delays at the toll plazas. Occasionally, she glanced down at the small package on the seat next to her, smiling as she pictured Jared's reaction to it.

Finally, she rolled up to the hotel, leaving her keys for the valet. She checked her face in the mirror before walking up the familiar steps of the old hotel.

She took the elevator to the fourteenth floor and walked two doors to the left. This time, she didn't hesitate. Ignoring the doorbell, she rapped quietly, her hand still in midair for another tap when the door opened and Jared was there, his hair nearly white, wearing glasses and a surprisingly shy smile.

They walked into the room, Jared treading backward so as not to let go of her hand or take his eyes from her face.

She was in his arms, resting against the comforting shoulder, feeling his kiss on the top of her head. His lips were warm and tender when they met hers. Soft, familiar, like coming home.

"It doesn't matter that we have only a few hours. You knew I'd come; you knew I'd need to see you again."

And still he hadn't spoken. Joanna watched him, studied his face and noticed the short, uneven breathing but kept her concern to herself.

"Joanna, my darling Joanna. Just as I thought. You never change. The same beautiful face and those eyes that reach into my soul. I'm so glad you're here."

They sat on the small sofa by the window, still holding hands. Jared's trembled slightly.

"It's been how many years? Seventeen? And look at us, my darling, in the same hotel, like dewy-eyed kids discovering one another."

"This is like the room where we came together the first time so long ago and where we last met. How like you to choose this place again."

"I suppose I was feeling nostalgic, too. Ever since I got your letter about your visit to Manning, I've had one bout of longing after another, wanting those days to come back, wanting to be young again with you. I loved hearing about it. Maybe one of these days we can go back together. If I'd planned better, we might have been able to do it this trip, but my conference starts at seven in the morning, is over at noon and then I'm on a plane home. Jason's band is giving a concert and I promised him I'd be in the front row. I know this doesn't leave us much time. But I promise to make the next visit last much longer."

Joanna looked at him carefully. With each sentence, he seemed to need a brief pause before going on. His eyes looked tired, his movements slower, more deliberate.

"Will there be another visit? Will we ever see one another again?"

He touched her hand gently. "I promise we will. I don't know how or when, but we will meet again. Now, what would you like to do?"

"I'd like to stay here in the hotel and be with you, and then I have something I want to share with you after dinner. Let's take a ride around the city a bit so you can enjoy the surprise."

That wonderful eyebrow raised, a question mark on his face.

"Okay. I made an early reservation so we could spend the rest of our time together alone."

~ * ~

Out in the lobby, the desk clerk took Joanna's valet stub and they walked to the door to wait.

"Give me a hint, darling. What's my surprise?"

Joanna hugged her purse close and took Jared's arm.

Settling behind the wheel, she pulled away from the curb and headed downtown, deftly guiding the car through the thinning evening traffic. At Battery Park, she pulled into a parking space facing the ferry terminal and shut off the engine, leaving the auxiliary power on. She reached into her purse and handed Jared a small flat package wrapped in tissue paper. "Open it."

Inside was a cassette tape. Joanna took it from him and inserted it into the player, leaning back on the seat. Taking his hand, she watched his face.

The first strains of Jim's piano came from the stereo, the sounds of "Unchained Melody" filling the car, Jared's voice strong and deep.

"Oh, Joanna! How did you do this?"

"The wonders of modern technology, my love. I simply took that old reel of tape to the studio of some friends of mine who do audio work for the casino nightclubs and had it converted to a cassette. There are only six songs on the original, so I asked them to keep recording them over and over again until the whole tape was full. I never get tired of listening to it. Only sometimes, as I know you'll understand, I can't listen to it at all."

He leaned over and kissed her. His voice was raspy.

"Thank you. I'd forgotten how I sounded. It's been so long since I've been able to sing."

They sat for almost an hour, eyes closed, listening. He held her hand so tightly it hurt. When it was over, Joanna rewound and then removed the tape from the player and put it back in the case.

"I love you for sharing it with me. It was wonderful to hear it. Thank you for bringing it with you."

"It's yours. This is my gift to you for all the comfort and love I've felt every time I've listened to it. I hoped it would bring you joy too. I have my own copy here," she patted the storage console between them, "and I listen to it whenever I need to have you near."

His eyes glistened with tears. Putting the tape in his coat pocket, he whispered, "You've always known how to please me. But this ... this is a very special gift that brings back the me that's been lost for so long. How can I tell you how much I'll treasure it?"

*October 12, 1993*

*My darling Joanna,*

*I am still basking in the wonderful joy of seeing you again. That special glow is still there, and you are as beautiful as ever. Now that I look back on it, it's amazing how immediately the years fell away and disappeared and how being with you seemed the most natural thing in the world. After you left, I went back up to my room and sat there for a long time, still hearing your voice, feeling your presence. There was some sadness in having to say goodbye again, but mostly a wondrous and warm joy in having those four hours with you.*

*We can't really go home again. The places we loved have moved along with the rest of time's ravages and changed as we have. What never changes is the way we feel about each other, the bond that has never failed to keep us connected. Know I am thinking about you and that I love you and always will.*

*Jared*

*February 17, 1994*

*My darling Joanna,*

*I know it's been quite awhile this time, but things have been rather hectic for me lately. First of all, I've had to relinquish my office at the theater, at least for a while. They're doing another major renovation and several staff members have lost their offices, at least temporarily. The new director (my successor) asked me if they could borrow mine. My only inconvenience is that my office has been my place for getting together with you.*

*I'm writing this at a table in the food court of a shopping mall. The only problem with it is the entire mall is a "no smoking" area. Nothing makes me want a cigarette as much as a "Thank you for not smoking" sign. No lectures, please. Old habits die hard.*

*I finally read* Bridges. *I think I was halfway afraid to read it after you told me of your reaction. Now I know why I was afraid. I had a very difficult time finishing it. It's very hard to read anything with your eyes full of tears, your breath coming only in gasps and your heart about to explode out of your chest. What a beautiful, beautiful story.*

*Don't let time go by without writing. Agnes is still at the office and holds your letters for my visits into the city and I'll answer as soon as I can. Remember I love you and I always will.*

*Jared*

~ * ~

Suddenly, the letters stopped coming. Each day, Joanna rapidly sorted through her mail, looking only at return addresses, becoming more anxious each time there was nothing from Jared.

Finally, she called his office at Roosevelt. Agnes hadn't seen him in months, she told Joanna.

"Don't worry about him, Dr. Webber," she said. "If anything were really wrong, I'd know about it. I'll tell him you called when he finally checks in."

*January 15, 1996*

*My darling Joanna,*

*First of all, let me reassure you there is nothing wrong. I'm okay, you're okay. Of course the world's a mess, but we're okay. It has been a long time, I know, and I'm sorry about that. Time seems to shoot by faster and faster. I still don't have my office space back and my handwriting has gotten more and more difficult and essentially illegible. I've had a few minor health problems lately, but nothing of consequence.*

*I felt guilty when Agnes told me you'd called. The last thing I want to do is worry you, but it appears that's exactly what I've done. I'm sorry, my darling.*

*I think I told you Marina and Andy have moved closer to us. Jason's school bus drops him here and he stays until one of them picks him up after work. Every day when he comes in, we sit and have a good long talk. Jason loves to "chat."*

*Enjoy your new grandson. I have had so much pleasure watching Jason grow and being able to be a positive force in his life. Your stories of life as a grandparent prove what I told you a long time ago. It's a wonderful stage of life, and I know Steven and Abby are lucky to have you sharing their little Brian.*

*I'd love to make this letter longer and spend more time with you, but I seem to tire more easily these days and need to rest more than I'd like.*

*Write when you can and remember I love you and I always will.*

Jared

August 15, 1996

*My darling Joanna,*

*Wow! Not one, not two, but three letters from you! Fantastic!!! It was good to hear from you and to hear things are going well. Retirement isn't bad, is it? Look at all the time you can spend with your grandson and the extra hours you can give at the youth center.*

*This hasn't been a good year healthwise for me. I've spent a few days in the hospital a couple of times, but I'm doing fine now. I feel very good and am able to do all the things I did before all of this started.*

*Because of all the problems, we haven't done any traveling this year. With things going so well now, we probably will take that trip we've promised ourselves and go to Florida.*

*I'm sorry to burden you with news of the health thing, but I decided it was better to tell you. Please don't get all upset and worried about me. As I said, I am now feeling fine.*

*Write me when you can and I'll try to do a little better next time. Remember I love you and I always will.*

Jared

*March 10, 1997*

*My darling Joanna,*

*I didn't do any better, did I? It's been a difficult few months, with what seems like one visit to the emergency room after another.*

*I haven't wanted to alarm you, so I guess I haven't been as forthcoming as I should. The diagnosis quite a while ago was emphysema. I think you probably guessed it when we were last together. Naturally, with a progressive disease like that, it would be helpful to quit smoking and follow a strict regimen of limited exercise and medication. Have I quit? I'm working on that part.*

*Marina keeps after me constantly, urging me to take vitamins, get outside and walk and kick the smoking thing. Vicki knows me too well to nag. I'm grateful beyond words for the care they've given me, and the support they lavish on me whenever I need it.*

*So that's it in a nutshell. I wish I could be more cheerful. The news from your end does lighten my heart, though. It's good that Steven's new job is in Philadelphia and they will be closer to you. Now at least I won't have the worry about who will care for you should you need someone nearby. Take good care of yourself and I'll try to do the same.*

*I love you and I always will.*

*Jared*

*April 10, 1997*

*My darling Joanna,*
*In your last letter, you said I sounded different, almost preoccupied. You're right. I am different and I suppose*

*preoccupied is as good a term as any. In telling you something of my medical problems, I have tried to keep it as light and non-specific as possible while being honest with you to keep you from worrying too much. I guess if my concerns are showing through, I should level with you completely.*

*My illness is getting worse and I've had some other complications not directly related to it that have been of concern to my doctors and to me. They may or may not be correctable but surgery is the only answer and I'm not a good risk for that. It's a double-edged sword and I often feeling like simply falling on it and giving up.*

*I have had to face the fact that I am old and many of my parts are wearing out. The prospects of getting any better are very slim, whereas the prospects of further problems from aging are fairly great. So yes, I am different and preoccupied, or whatever we may choose to call it. I'm trying very hard to continue my lifestyle, but it's difficult. Vicki and Marina have been terrific in caring for me and trying to keep my spirits up, and I simply don't know what I would do without them.*

*Added to my difficulties, I have experienced a growing sense of guilt and concern. Vicki, the children, and now the grandchildren, have always regarded me as an eminently open, completely honest and straightforward person. They have often spoken of this as my most outstanding virtues. Yet, for all these years I have been dishonest and deceitful about my relationship with you.*

*Perhaps now would be a good time for us to finally say our goodbyes and discontinue our contact, nebulous as it is. Better, perhaps, for us to remember each other as we are now, with all the wonderful memories of what we've had.*

*You'll be hearing from Dan tomorrow or next week or next year, or perhaps not for several more years if I'm lucky, but inevitably you will hear. Better to learn it then all at once rather than to watch me deteriorate in my letters to that point.*

*I love you. I love you very much, but I would rather not have you see me as I am now, knowing it will only get worse.*

*Jared*

~ * ~

Joanna sat staring vacantly out the window, letting the letter drop to the floor.

Say our goodbyes? Our goodbyes? No. Goodbyes were mutual things. People decided together to say them; they weren't dropped like a ton of steel on someone without warning. No, he couldn't mean that. How could he take it upon himself to make this dreadful decision for her?

Outside, the daffodils that lined the wooden walkway to the beach swayed slightly in time with the marsh grass. Another spring had come almost unnoticed. For the first time, she felt the utter silence around her. She shifted in her seat, her eyes darting around the room like a frightened child. *What if he means it? What if I never hear from him again? How will I cope? What will I do with my end of the connection?*

*April 13, 1997*

*Dearest Jared,*

*Your letter was like a bolt out of the blue, throwing me to the ground with such force I could barely breathe. Surely you can't be doing this, ending what's been a lifeline for so many years for both of us at times, but for me far more often than you. Only a few short weeks ago, you were exulting over having received three letters at a time from me, telling me to keep writing, how much hearing from me meant to you.*

*What happened, my love? Has your illness frightened you so badly you needed to pull yourself into a black hole and shut me out?*

*I can't just stop. I can't let it end like this. Please let me keep writing to you, let me keep the connection alive. I can send my letters to Dan and when you get together, he can give them to you. I can send them to the university where Agnes can hold them. If you can't respond, I'll accept that, just let me keep talking to you, sharing my life, knowing you're there listening.*

*I love you so very much.*

*Joanna*

*May 19, 1997*

*Dear Joanna,*

*I had not intended to write again, but now I find that I must. I need to tell you Dan has moved to Champaign and will not be able to get your letters to me. If anything happens to me and you are sending letters to the university, Agnes will, of course, send my mail to Vicki. She will, very naturally, open any letters in case a response is needed. So please, please, no more letters.*

*I know this is traumatic and hurtful for you. It hurts me, too. Try as I might, however, I can't come up with any solution to what has become a very serious problem that does not hurt someone. In the final analysis, I believe you and I can take the hurt better than Vicki would be able to.*

*I don't really feel I am ending our relationship. It can never end. What I am doing is finally ending a deception that has become unbearable. Our letters have essentially become reminders of what we once had and there are many, many reminders without them.*

*I guess it is finally time to agree with what Doris always said, "wanting is not having."*

*Love!*

*Jared*

~ * ~

In the days that followed, Joanna sank into a deep, black depression, avoiding everyone. Everywhere she looked, she found darkness, emptiness. Her journal was filling up with her grief, her heart pouring out the things she wanted to say to Jared.

Finally, unable to handle it alone any longer, she made an appointment with a colleague whose counseling skills and gentle ways had always drawn Joanna to her.

Talking about it helped a bit. Sheila suggested Joanna put her feelings on paper, write to Jared as often and as frankly as she needed in order to get all the feelings out, whether or not she chose to mail the letters. Beyond that, there was nothing to be done except to bear the crushing sadness and try to hold her life together.

By day, she occupied the hours with her grandson or at the center. At night, she often sat either at the edge of the gently lapping ocean or by the window, wishing for anger, wanting to feel vengeful, needing some emotion other than the sorrow that ruled her heart.

*June 27, 1998*

*Dearest Jared,*

*This is another in a string of letters I've written but never sent since that awful day last year when I got the last I'll ever receive from you. You'll never know how savagely your words bruised my soul, the coldness, the lack of the love I always read in your words. And my first thought was to defy your wishes and write anyway. There is so much I need to say.*

*I can't accept that there is no other way for us to keep in touch, so I'm assuming you simply want to end the contact but don't want to say so. You say you can't hurt Vicki, but that's not really it, is it? It's the fear of being found out, having to face her with the truth after all these years, tarnishing the image you've so carefully protected.*

*What pains me the most is that you made this decision for both of us, telling me I could handle the hurt of your loss better than Vicki could deal with finding out about our relationship. How dare you? How dare you even presume I would respect your decision? You're counting on me to fade away, not to betray you by writing to you or calling you at home. Do you take my love for granted so completely? Yes, I believe you do. I believe you're confident you've put me away in a dark closet and you trust me not to rattle the doorknob and alert your world that I exist. How could you? How could you say you love me and do this? What do you think I'm doing with this insidious rejection? How am I coping? Or is it that you simply don't care? I'd sooner die than believe that.*

*For almost four decades, you've been one of the most important people in my world. I've gotten through the most stressful times of my life with your help, knowing I could reach out in a letter or a phone call, pour out my heart and trust you to respond with the right words to help me see them through.*

*Now all that is over. I've made it through the past year, I don't know how. I go through the motions, run for the mail and hope you've changed your mind and decided you still need to connect. I sit in my house, watch the ocean roll in and out as rhythmically as if the world were still okay, but it isn't. My heart is broken and I feel utterly abandoned. How could you?*

She read it over again and again, finally folding the sheets of paper carefully, taking them to her office and pausing for a second before sliding them through the shredder atop the wastebasket.

Turning to her computer, she dialed up the internet and searched for a directory of University of Illinois faculty members until she found Dan's name. No e-mail was listed, but there was a campus address. She switched over to her word processing program and began to write.

~ * ~

Four days later, his reply was in her e-mail. He didn't know, he said, that Jared had been ill. He didn't understand how Jared could have cut off contact with her. It was time for him to call anyway, since they still kept in touch. He would be glad to keep Joanna advised about Jared's health and would even volunteer to act as a go-between so she and Jared could still maintain contact.

Her heart soared. She quickly responded.

*Dan, for now just tell me how he is. I have to think about whether I want him to know you and I are in touch.*

*Thanks so much for setting my mind at ease. Joanna*

The next day, another e-mail:

*Joanna, he's doing great. He's had some serious health problems but has managed to overcome them. Your name never came up in our conversation, but I'm not surprised, since he was at home when I called. Have you decided? Shall I tell him? Dan*

Joanna didn't have to think about her answer.

*Dan, yes, please tell him. We didn't have e-mail when he said he couldn't find another way. Now that's changed. Let me know what he says. Better yet, I'll hope for a message from him. Again, thanks. Joanna*

There was nothing on her computer screen the next day in the account she used only for Dan. It was the same the next day and the day after that.

At the end of the month, she wrote to Dan again, asking what had happened when he spoke to Jared, begging him for some news. There was no response.

Again, she e-mailed him, her desperation heavy in every sentence:

*Dan, where are you? Not a day has gone by that I have not regretted my decision to allow you to tell Jared we were in touch. What could he have said to you that kept you from even so much as replying? Obviously, no one has taken into account the toll this silence is taking on me. I am more and more at a loss to explain this senseless cruelty. Perhaps he misguidedly believes cutting off contact so completely will somehow cause me to forget him and stop being concerned about him, wondering how he's doing, caring if he's healthy or ill. He must know me better than that. I wake up thinking of him and a thousand times a day I say his name in my mind where it echoes hollowly like I'm shouting into a bottomless canyon, growing hoarse and weary with the effort of trying to make him hear me. I want to hurt back, call him at home, let him explain to Vicki who I am, but I still love him too much to do that. Instead of making me angry, as I wish it would, Jared's silence has made me unbearably sad. It is a cruel and unusual punishment where none is deserved. Joanna*

There was no response.

A week later, she tried again. *Dan, tell me if he's okay.* This time, her e-mail came back undelivered. Dan had changed his address. The connection was finally and totally broken.

~ * ~

Often in the ensuing months, Joanna mentally composed the kind of letter she wanted to write to Jared—accusatory, bitter and bitingly sarcastic. Once she even got so far as to stamp one and walk up to the mailbox ready to drop it in before she lost her nerve.

Occasionally, she sat with Sheila and talked about steps she was taking to regain hold of her life, deal with what had been such a crushing blow.

Sheila concentrated on the most obvious question—why did it matter any more? Couldn't Joanna get it? Jared had controlled their relationship from the very first, pulling her strings, being there for her only when it was convenient for him. Hadn't he chosen her, a young woman, naïve and trusting, knowing she needed to be loved? Didn't he know about her painful childhood? Hadn't he recognized her empathic nature? Didn't he know all those qualities would keep her from opposing him when he decided to stay with his wife and children? Didn't he count on her blind adoration to keep her from blowing his cover? And most of all, hadn't it always been about him and never about her?

Painful questions, even more painful answers, but Joanna kept going back to Sheila for more. She desperately needed to reclaim her life, but she wanted to do so while still holding onto her dreams of Jared. Again, wanting was not having.

~ * ~

As the days and months went by, Joanna spent more and more time with Steven, Abby and Brian, often staying overnight at their center city townhouse. She walked South Street with Brian, watched him skate on the outdoor rink at Penns Landing, explored the Franklin Institute and Art Museum with him. She loved taking him to the Academy of Music for concerts, trying to avoid stray thoughts of Jared even when the Philadelphia Orchestra played Debussy and Ravel and she was once again in his arms, their passion mounting with the rising crescendo of the music.

Back home, in the quiet of her beachfront refuge, Joanna still looked hurriedly through each day's mail. She was unable to comprehend that Jared had simply vanished. She wondered with each advent of spring what he did with the remembrances.

Did he ever wonder about her health? Her family? Her mental well being? As the seasons came and went, had he forgotten what they had? Did he ever think about her at all?

She knew Sheila was right. She needed to feel anger. It would have been such a relief and, she suspected, far healthier than the sadness and the constant conjecturing about what Jared might be thinking. And once in a while, a glimmer of anger did creep into her heart.

How could he? Hadn't he meant any of those professions of devotion? Had he lied all those years? And if so, was she so needy she couldn't let him go, leave him to his precious family and his ego?

Gradually, Joanna badgered herself into shooing away thoughts of Jared that intruded on her contentment at the strangest times. She adopted a mantra she schooled herself to use: "Forget him, Joanna, you're stronger than this. Forget him—he's forgotten you."

It worked most of the time, often giving her a string of days without the ghost of Jared haunting her heart.

But in spite of her resolve, she couldn't erase him completely. Each day before she turned off her computer after surfing the net or sending e-mails to her friends, she opened the other account, typed in the password and waited.

Sometimes she played a little game, closing her eyes and imagining what she'd find when she opened them.

Like a child, she chanted silently: *Please, please let him be there.*

# Epilogue

*August 15, 2001*

*"So many chances lost, so much pain."*

The computer waited on a small desk in the corner.

He shuffled toward it, a soft shock of white hair falling on his forehead, his breathing labored and harsh.

So often he'd done it, a message written and then deleted without being sent.

Exhausted, he slumped into the chair, rested until his breathing was eased. Summoning his strength, he slowly struck the keys. Here he was, once again intruding into her life, but now he had something very important to say.

*My darling Joanna,*

*It's been a long time and I wouldn't blame you if you deleted this message without even reading it. But each day brings some wonderful memory of you, of those magical times we had together forty years ago, and I had to connect with you one more time.*

*Through our letters, we've shared our lives. In these last years, I've had a lot of time to think and I've recognized something about myself that has caused me even more guilt than I felt over the deception with Vicki and the children. I see my role in our relationship in a different light, and I'm not very proud of what I've discovered.*

*Doris tried to explain it to me once, although I never told you. You came into the snack bar just as we were finishing our conversation and we quickly changed the subject. She warned me I would keep pursuing you, to your detriment, until I got what I needed more than anything, your unconditional love. I think she used the word 'adoration.' I don't need to tell you I ignored what she said, brushed it off as so much psychobabble and then did exactly what she said I would.*

*You gave me that unconditional love. And I always felt adored when we were together.*

*But now, as I look back on the past years, I realize that, while I went about living my own life, realizing my own professional and personal successes, I wasn't willing to let you do the same. It would have taken courage I didn't have for me to step out of your life permanently a long time ago, to give you the freedom you gave me.*

*So instead, I selfishly came back time and time again, making sure you were still there to fill the emotional gaps in my life while I knew the connection with me was keeping you from living yours to the fullest. The health thing was honest, but not completely. I was more afraid of having Vicki find out what I'd been hiding all those years than I was of finally breaking your heart. How could I have done that to you? What does that say about me?*

*Not a day has passed that I haven't wished I were a stronger person, willing to lift the veil and reveal myself as I am. Not a day has passed, too, that I haven't wanted to break the silence and tell you how much I've missed your letters, having you to talk to, sharing your thoughts and remembrances of our shining days together.*

*They were shining, my darling. I could not rest if I thought you believed for even one moment that everything we shared had been a sham, or my feelings for you were anything but deep and very, very real.*

*I can close my eyes and feel your fingertips on my face. I can hear Jim playing our favorite songs and see the flames dancing in your eyes. I can see Manhattan from atop our Emerald Palace and feel the spray from the wake of one of our ferries. I still see you in every season, in every kind of weather and always with love and longing. Please, please believe me.*

*Perhaps by now, after the way I've abandoned what we had, you feel anything but love for me. I couldn't blame you for anger, even hatred, but I pray it hasn't come to that. I still need your love and want you to know you still have mine.*

*In spite of the sadness, the tears and the lonely years, think of me gently and with compassion.*

*Remember, my darling, I love you and I always will.*

*Jared*

Scrolling slowly to the top of the screen, he read the words. He closed his eyes, remembering the way she looked the first time he sat with her and felt himself losing his heart to her. So long ago, so many chances lost, so much pain. He pointed the cursor to the "Send" button and hesitated.

~ * ~

Halfway across the continent, Joanna exhaled slowly and opened her eyes. On the computer screen, yielding only disappointment for so long, was a single sentence.

*You have one new message.*

# *Meet Jeanne Howard*

Poet, essayist and now novelist, Jeanne Howard's work has expanded over the years to include women's fiction.

Jeanne holds a bachelor's degree in English and a master's in counseling psychology. In 1973, she was co-founder of a successful group of weekly newspapers, which she continued to operate until 1994.

A resident of southern New Jersey, Jeanne retired as director of communications for a large school district. She is the mother of two daughters and the grandmother of a grandson and granddaughter. Jeanne and her husband, Howard, reside in central Burlington County with their beloved cat, Selma.

# *Dear reader,*

I hope you've enjoyed reading this story of forbidden love and
loss as much as I enjoyed writing it.

Your opinion is valuable to other readers like you,
who may be looking for books like mine.

Please consider taking a few minutes to post a review, however
brief,
on the site where you purchased this book
or on the Wings ePress web page.

You may also want to visit my author page
at the Wings' website, where you can find
the other book I've written.

Thank you!

Jeanne Howard

# Visit Our Website

For The Full Inventory
Of Quality Books:

## Wings ePress, Inc

Quality trade paperbacks and downloads

in multiple formats,

in genres ranging from light romantic comedy to general

fiction and horror.

Wings has something for every reader's taste.

Visit the website, then bookmark it.

**We add new titles each month!**

Wings ePress, Inc.
3000 N. Rock Road
Newton, KS 67114